D1103833

MOSCOW X

Also by David McCloskey

Damascus Station

MOSCOW
X

A Novel

David McCloskey

W. W. NORTON & COMPANY
Celebrating a Century of Independent Publishing

Copyright © 2023 by David McCloskey

All rights reserved
Printed in the United States of America
First Edition

For information about permission to reproduce selections
from this book, write to Permissions, W. W. Norton & Company, Inc.,
500 Fifth Avenue, New York, NY 10110

For information about special discounts for bulk purchases,
please contact W. W. Norton Special Sales at
specialsales@wwnorton.com or 800-233-4830

Manufacturing by Lake Book
Book design by Daniel Lagin
Production manager: Louise Mattarelliano

ISBN 978-1-324-05075-9

W. W. Norton & Company, Inc.
500 Fifth Avenue, New York, N.Y. 10110
www.wwnorton.com

W. W. Norton & Company Ltd.
15 Carlisle Street, London W1D 3BS

1 2 3 4 5 6 7 8 9 0

For Abby, yet again co-conspirator and muse

She loves, loves blood
This Russian earth.

—*Anna Akhmatova, from* Anno Domini MCMXXI

Part I

ZAGOVOR /
CONSPIRACY

Dushanbe, Tajikistan
Present day

THAT DAY ARTEMIS APHRODITE PROCTER WOUND UP IN THE PENALTY Box.

She awoke to darkness and the air clouded with a strange musk, teeth chattering like a clockwork toy. Her eyelids were heavy, reluctant to open. Hardwood chilled her skin. Procter blinked through a spray of her curly black hair across the floor of a room she did not know.

Then footfalls and a hairy-knuckled hand gently lifted forelocks of hair from her face. A man knelt and waved.

"Good morning, Artemis," he said in cheerful Russian.

Her mind swam and churned, thoughts lost in the murk. She took in the room. A table. Two chairs by a window. Her pineapple-print panties rumpled on the floor. A drained bottle of vodka tipped on its side, halo of someone else's purple lipstick along the rim.

She sat up against a couch, stark-naked and cold. The Russian went to an armchair by the window. He lit a cigarette. She bent her knees into her chest and shut her eyes because the room was spinning.

"Quite the night," said the Russian. "I have seen things no man should ever see." Click of the tongue. "You monstrous little woman."

"Who are you?" Procter said, also in Russian. Her eyes were still shut—light brought rotation, tilting.

"Anton," he said.

After a minute she hobbled to her feet and looked around for her clothes. Other than the panties, she saw only her leather jacket and muddy Reeboks. And it struck her that there was a hole blown clean through her memory, pure black since ordering drinks last night. She'd been with a Russian developmental, a Moscow party boy with access to heavier hitters: the Kremlin, the security services. And he was either dead or in on this. Probably both.

As her vision steadied, Procter could make out the morning bustle on Rudaki through the window. A light rain pattered on the glass. The table in front of Anton was spread with platters of food, cups, and glasses for the morning hundred grams, the *sto gramm*, of vodka.

Procter struggled into the Reeboks and panties, twice nearly losing her balance, and then paused for a breath before starting on the jacket. She felt along the front and discovered the pockets emptied of her phone, keys, and switchblade. Then she flopped into the chair across from the Russian.

Anton chuckled. "Artemis Aphrodite Procter. CIA Chief of Station. Underpaid civil servant. And, according to my sources, yet again bypassed for promotion to the Senior Intelligence Service. Quite the fall from Amman to a backwater like Dushanbe. And all due to unspecified discretions."

"My discretions," Procter said, "were quite specific."

Anton clapped his hairy hands and laughed with the cigarette pinned in his teeth. "Yes, the good Procter. Sexual wanderlust. A deviant with certain . . ." He fixed her with a grave stare. "Appetites."

"And hands wet with Russian blood," she said.

A shadow fell over his eyes. He stubbed his cigarette into a brass ashtray and began to pick at his plate of *selyodka*, pickled herring with potatoes and onions.

A liter of yeasty horse milk sweated in a glass bottle. Russkies had done their research. Though more of a Kazakh or Kyrgyz delicacy, when granted the rare privilege in Tajik Dushanbe, Procter partook of the horse milk. But when Anton poured her a cup, she dumped it on the floor.

The Russian snickered and stepped over the slithering white stream to collect a buff-colored folder from the sofa. He handed it to Procter and returned to his food. "We have many more photos, of course. This is merely a teaser. There were a few of you facedown, for example, but I don't think you'll see them in there. I must say, though, I am curious about the tattoos. And why nine of them? I am sure the stories are riveting. Anyhow, go on, have a look." He took a bite of fish.

Procter flipped through a stack of nude photos snapped while she'd been drugged. Some were quite imaginative. Artistic, even. Two or three were nearly perfect: the lighting, the energy, the intimate angles, these appropriately captured what Procter considered to be the animal spirits of her sexual id. Others were banal and garish: unworthy of trade in even the seediest flesh market. Procter, stranger to shame, found not a one embarrassing. Her tits, she thought, looked pretty good across the board. She tossed the folder into the puddle of horse milk. "Go fuck yourself."

Anton lit another cigarette. "Artemis, please. If you don't cooperate, well, then these unfortunate pictures will be posted online. And we will out you as CIA."

"You're going to do that anyway, Anton. Aren't you? Now, where are my damn pants?" The world had stopped gyrating. Slowly, she got up and began wandering around the room.

"You'll be sent home, Artemis. Another black stain on your career."

"Your pitch sucks. Whole point of this is to send me home. You're after me because I like working Russians. You want me gone. In any case, you should invest in a better photographer, because some of those"—she jabbed a finger at the milk-sopped folder—"are terrible. My answer is this: Fuck you. I'm leaving now to report this to Langley and the ambassador. Say, better idea. How about instead of writing up a cable that makes you look like a dumbass, why don't you spy for me? What do you say to that?"

Anton cast a jet of smoke across the food. "Screw off, Artemis."

Procter was smiling. "I guess we understand each other. Now, where are my pants?"

She tossed a few couch cushions to the floor in a vain search. Pretty worked up about the missing jeans. A breach of the rules, she thought. Unprofessional. Nasty. She turned the place upside down for a few minutes while Anton smoked. Had they actually tossed out her pants?

"Come on, Anton. It's cold and I'm a decent woman. Can't roll out of here in pineapple panties and a leather jacket." She stood over him, arms akimbo, while he burned down his cigarette. His chuckle at the word *decent* sent dark fantasies cartwheeling through her mind.

"Artemis, think of your Station. If you go home, they will have no Chief. And I hear a colleague of yours recently departed. Unfortunate medical situation."

Two months earlier, Procter's Deputy Chief of Station and his family had awoken in their apartment with vertigo and headaches. Wife went blind in one eye. Russian directed-energy attack, Procter suspected. Microwaves that fried your fucking brain.

Anton was smiling and examining her bare legs.

Procter was scowling and examining Anton's pants. A siren was ringing through her skull.

Then Procter had her hand down on the drained vodka bottle and she'd shattered it against the table for a nice length of jagged neck, and before Anton could duck she'd slashed him across the cheek and packed the glass into the meat of his left shoulder and it just stuck there, purple-glossed rim pointing square at the ceiling.

Anton howled, tried to stand and pull out the glass, but she kicked him in the chest and he fell back into the chair. A run of blood washed down his cheek. She punched his nose, again, a third time, until she heard a sweet wet crunch and a ragged moan escaped his lips. Then she snatched the milk bottle from the table and broke it over his skull. His head slumped, the milk and blood mingling into pink braids.

Procter overturned the table and smashed it into the wall and harvested a splintered leg to churn Anton's left kneecap into mush. After a batch of strikes, light filtered through her rage blackout and she tossed the table leg aside and smacked his cheek to wake him up. He did not.

"Anton," she said, "wake up. I got a skosh carried away. Anton, can you hear me?" A few finger-snaps in front of his face. "Anton?"

Two fingers to his neck. She felt a pulse.

Never thought she'd be happy for a live Russian intel officer, but praise god.

Then she looked around the wrecked room and out the window and wondered if he had partners or a team watching on cameras. She shimmied off his pants and slipped them on herself and told the unconscious Russian, "Serves you right for ditching my jeans."

He was much taller and wider, so she rolled up the pant legs about a foot and cinched the belt tight as it would go. The folder of nude photos disappeared into her jacket. Then she pulled it back out, rifling through until she found the one: A nice shot showcasing her flexibility and rugged femininity. Her quiet fucking strength. Crumpling the photo into a ball, she shoved it into Anton's underpants. Then she was out the door.

———

THE DAY CONTINUED ITS UNRAVELING. AT THE EMBASSY THERE WAS A struggle session with the prick ambassador. She sent a cable recounting the ordeal and received a nasty gram response from the Director and the Langley mandarins. Then a clipped conversation with Deputy Director Bradley, words and tone evoking the reassurances whispered to a beloved dog moments before it is euthanized.

Dinnertime: The pictures appeared on several burner websites, the links amplified by Russian bot accounts across social media platforms. They also outed Procter as COS Dushanbe.

The formal cable recalling her to Langley arrived later that evening. End of tour: Get on the first flight out in the morning. Support officers would shutter her apartment and ship her belongings to Virginia. The assault had violated a bevy of Tajik laws and, more importantly, raised the specter of Russian kinetic retaliation for hospitalizing what CIA had since learned was a senior intelligence officer dispatched from Moscow. Doctors expected the Russian to recover, said a memo from a Tajik liaison officer who overshared with CIA for cash. But Anton would have residuals: namely a patchwork of scars, a permanent limp from Procter's knee work, and, courtesy of a bottle of horse milk, the ever-present specter of diminished mental capacity. A few intrepid Station officers organized a hasty send-off for the Chief, complete with an improperly stenciled cake. (*We will miss you, Chef.*)

When the Station had cleared out for the evening, Procter shut down her computer and put the hard drive in the safe. There was little to pack: her sterile office boasted no family photos, no Me Wall of gifts and trinkets, no art. No decorations of any kind. Her one indulgence was a baseball bat autographed by every member of the 1997 Cleveland Indians World Series team: Procter's secret managerial recipe for boosting Station productivity. In Damascus she'd kept a shotgun in her office, but in Amman there'd been complaints, and now she had the bat. She carried it around; she glanced longingly in its direction during morning ops meetings; it leaned against the wall in a corner, visible during video calls with headquarters.

Procter swung the bat in a lazy arc through her office's recycled air. She couldn't stay in Dushanbe, she knew that, but she despised the headquarters hive, humming with crawlies hungrier for doughnuts than the fruits of espionage. What a pig of a day.

She brought the bat down on the particle board table in her office. A seam appeared. Then again, and it cracked, and she kept at it until the table was kindling and she was good and sweaty. She flicked off her office lights. Bat on her shoulder, she began locking up the Station.

Headquarters, lord almighty. But what else could be done with Procter, an impulsive reprobate and also a well-respected Chief and operator with years of experience in the foreign field?

She was in the Penalty Box. A two-year headquarters stint under close supervision. Once that was completed to satisfaction, she might one day run a Station again. Because she was competent, not a fuckup who couldn't run ops, Deputy Director Bradley had hinted he would find something important for her. Procter checked to be sure there was no paper on the desks. She confirmed the safes were shut. Then she spun the lock on Dushanbe Station's thick metal door for the last time.

2

Langley

JET-LAGGED THE MORNING AFTER HER ARRIVAL STATESIDE, EARS ringing with exhaustion, Procter waited to meet with Ed Bradley, the CIA Deputy Director. Procter sat on one of the couches outside his office on the Seventh Floor. The waiting room had been decorated by a government procurement catalogue: all the furniture in dark faux-wood, slightly chipped or peeling or torn. A lightly stained coffee table was littered with magazines. As in all waiting rooms everywhere, for all time, the reading material, like the furniture, had long expired.

When she was finally permitted entry, Bradley was at his desk hunched over the MLP, a printer-sized secure phone linking the fourteen national security principals. A button for the Director, the National Security Adviser, Secretary of State, of Defense, and on and on. His office had large windows overlooking the trees shouldering the Potomac: now bright with gold, red, and orange. Bradley was six-foot-two, a former linebacker at the University of Texas and a legendary case officer who had retired after serving as Chief of the old Near East Division. A new Director had asked him to return as Deputy. He and Procter went back decades.

The Me Wall behind Bradley's desk was mostly bare, just as she remembered. But on the credenza sat pictures of his wife and daughters, along with a few gifts from special friends. Procter recognized a twisted metal scrap from when she'd helped blow off the door of a Mitsubishi Pajero in downtown Damascus a hundred years ago. And affixed to the wall were Bradley's favorites—a neutralized missile system gifted for leading the Stinger program against the Soviets in Afghanistan, and, more recently, a Javelin for covert action work in Ukraine against the Russians.

Procter shuffled toward a chair downrange of the launchers while Bradley reviewed the three-by-five index card that held his daily calendar. A disgusted gaze shifted between the card and the MLP, as if he could not stomach his next task. The card disappeared into his pocket when he looked up and saw her. He gave her a thin smile.

"Another century," she said wistfully, staring at the launchers. "Another bailout for the Russian zinc coffin industry. That which is done shall be done, and all that. Amen."

Bradley said amen and gave her a big hug. "Artemis, how are you holding up?"

"Peachy, Ed."

He made a face. "I'm sorry. Goddamn Russians."

"We should put that on a T-shirt around here."

"Are you getting what you need? Docs and psychologists are saying—"

She put up a hand. "I'm in the Penalty Box, I get it. But don't bench me. I'm fine, I just need a job. Something to do."

"You really should rest."

"And do what, exactly?"

"I'd say make sure you're actually fine. Get your head straight."

"Ed, come on. We've known each other for more than twenty years. That ship has sailed."

"I'm concerned about you, Artemis."

A flicker of sadness traced Bradley's stoic mask, but it washed away when Procter made a wet noise.

"You're getting mushy in your golden years, Ed. Good grief. I told you, I'm fine. If you want me to not be fine, then go right ahead and put old Artemis on four months of administrative leave so I can drink myself to death in the Reston Town Center. That what you want? Cops calling you at home because I'm ripping tequila shots and screaming about CIA in the parking lot?"

"The Director wanted to fire you. Said he would have if this were a normal organization."

"A normal organization would never employ me. Now, have the Russkies lodged a protest?"

"Not a peep yet."

"And what are we thinking on the response?"

Bradley looked away. Pumped his fist into a ball.

"Jeez, Ed. Really? Nothing? Russians drugged me. Took a bunch of nudie pictures. They hit my Deputy with a directed-energy attack."

"That investigation is still ongoing, Artemis."

"We did an analysis proving wet-work teams arrived in Dushanbe three days before it happened."

"And I agree with that analysis. I am merely saying that the investigation is ongoing. And that the White House has so far been reluctant to back aggressive retaliatory options."

Procter groaned. "If we do nothing, Russians keep poking. They are barbarians without limits or morals, Ed. It's how they operate. And this is not about me. For the past ten years or so we've all watched Putin poke and prod and generally fuck with CIA and the United States with complete impunity. He crosses lines, we do nothing. He invades Georgia. He carves up Ukraine, stirs up a low-grade insurgency, then properly invades and commits a fuck-ton of war crimes. He shuts down power grids. He's noodling around inside our grid, planning for god knows what . . ."

Bradley put up a gentle hand, which Procter barreled through. "He's lit us up by waves of cyber and ransomware attacks. His ghouls have poisoned and murdered people all over the world: in the UK, Bulgaria, hell, even here in Washington. They tried to orchestrate a coup in Montenegro. Fucking Montenegro, Ed! The Russians physically attacked our officers in Moscow. The fucking Director of the FSB punched one of them in the head! In the head, Ed, after his arrest! Their militias shot down a Malaysian airliner over Ukraine. Russkies paid bounties to the Taliban to kill U.S. soldiers. They have fucked with our heads on social media here at home. They have scrambled the brains of dozens of CIA officers with directed-energy weapons. And, yes, they drugged me and took pictures of my knobs. And none of it"—she cleared her throat—"has resulted in more than a hand-slap. We've got to start drawing bright fucking lines that the cockroach in the Kremlin will not cross."

"I agree with you, Artemis, one hundred percent," Bradley said. "I'm on your team."

"I want to be in the game," Procter said. "And I hear there is a vacancy, the new backroom shop running all the spooky Russia ops. Moscow X."

"The Moscow X job? Artemis, the Director is not a fan of yours, not after—"

"The unpleasantness in Amman. And now Dushanbe."

"Right. The unpleasantness makes you a hard sell."

"Where else do you want to put me, then?"

Bradley looked up at the launchers. "I do want you working Russia."

"Well, then sell it."

———

THE FALL MORNING WAS UNUSUALLY HOT AND WET WHEN PROCTER crossed the parking lot of the Original Headquarters Building. The Langley clock-punching crowd coursed around her like water. A two-year sentence in this prison camp, she thought, unbelievable. The upside was that if Bradley could convince the Director to give her the Moscow X job, she'd have a better shot at wrecking Russkies from Langley than just about anywhere. And she had so many beautiful ideas for how to fuck the Russians. She motored her Prius out of the compound toward the Vienna Inn, the dive bar that had hosted countless happy hours, ops celebrations, promotions, and even an Irish wake or two following funerals for Agency comrades. Procter planned to bed down there for a two-, maybe three-day bender.

Procter sped through northern Virginia, titillated by a lurid vision of chaos in Moscow set to the rich melody of *Swan Lake*. Had she been a religious woman, Procter might have believed the hand of God had painted it on her mind. She didn't really know what to think about God, but she figured that by this point any reasonable deity would have a bone to pick with the Kremlin. After all they'd done, God wasn't going to stop her from running a solid op sticking it to the Russkies.

3

Saint Petersburg

IN THE FIRST HOURS OF A WET SAINT PETERSBURG EVENING, A MAN in a well-cut suit exited a black government Mercedes and entered the lobby of a bank. Though his business that evening was robbery, he carried neither knife nor gun. His weapon was instead a stack of official documents, which permitted him to move a large quantity of gold bullion from the bank's reserves, held in a vault four stories below the street and minded at that hour by a well-armed team of guards and several clerks, only a few of whom were presently asleep.

The papers authorized the suited man, Lieutenant Colonel Konstantin Konstantinovich Chernov of the Federal'naya sluzhba bezopasnosti, the FSB, Russia's Federal Security Service, to transfer two hundred and twenty-one bars of gold from the bank to a strategic reserve in the east.

Chernov's black Ferragamos clacked over the lobby marble, their spotless heels trailed by a large crew of regular policemen pulling carts and crates. The police had been unhappily conscripted by the FSB for an evening of manual labor. The bullion, after all, was heavy: each bar weighed just over twelve kilos. Bank Rossiya's head of security greeted Chernov in the lobby. The man had been a colonel in the army; he knew the game. The FSB had dozens of spies inside the bank. The FSB made the rules. Chernov would do whatever he wanted.

They exchanged icy greetings. Chernov was dead-eyed and firm but polite, the paperwork was drearily official, and though the mood was tense there was neither argument nor bickering, not a voice raised in anger. Chernov had once been soldier and priest, so he knew there was no law but God's and that God spoke this law through Russia alone. His orders that night would have been considered arbitrary, even illegal, in many societies, but to Chernov they might well have been God-breathed, no different from Holy Scripture or a Kremlin decree.

Chernov's features were unremarkable except for his considerable height. He was pale, bald, and rosy-cheeked. His eyes were still and contemplative. The black suit was Savile Row via the dip pouch and well-tailored to his massive frame. His words were often the first hints of madness, and that evening few had yet crossed his lips.

From the lobby Chernov trailed the head of security to a spacious office overlooking the square. There they rolled through the evening's first protest: whether Andrei Agapov, the bank's principal shareholder, should be phoned at that hour to learn of the state's requisition of a pile of gold bullion valued at nearly two hundred million dollars. "He should at least know what is happening," the head of security said to Chernov, desk phone clenched in his white hands. He was set to dial Agapov but hung there, awaiting permission. Chernov nodded.

The head of security spoke to Agapov for a few minutes. He read high points from the papers. He gave Chernov's name and rank and department. He asked Agapov for instructions. Then he hung up.

"Are you to refuse us?" Chernov asked, eyes lit with curiosity.

"No," the head of security said, "but I'm to make it a challenge."

"Do you feel that is wise?" Chernov asked.

They agreed that it was not. That the head of security would do exactly nothing to delay or complicate the transfer, but if pressed Chernov would insist resistance had been irritating, even formidable. Then they descended into the vault, where Chernov walked the rows, fingers gliding along the cages holding the gold bars, one of the police officers trailing behind to check the serial numbers against the papers they carried to make this robbery legal. Once Chernov was satisfied, his men began packing.

They filled the bottom of each crate, spreading a thick cloth over the gold. They added two more layers until they feared that the gold might buckle the crates. Then they sealed on the tops with wood screws, affixing premade labels to note the run of serial numbers each crate contained. The bank's security men did not draw their guns; no one touched radios or phones. They stood dumbly at attention. What is to be done when the police are robbing you?

The head of security watched the crates scud by with the forlorn expression of a man watching the burglary of his own home.

And then, unable to help himself, he muttered about Chernov stealing Andrei Agapov's gold.

Chernov turned to him. "You say this is Agapov's gold?" His voice was measured, though he could now feel his blood twisting and sloshing through him like mercury. A hint of salt and metal flickered on the tip of his tongue.

The head of security examined his reflection in his shoes, his hands on his hips in anger, but he held his tongue.

"I asked," Chernov said, "if it is your position that this gold belongs to Andrei Agapov."

The man raised his head but did not meet Chernov's eyes. "The paperwork admits as much."

"Then I ask you this," Chernov said. "Who owns Andrei Agapov?"

The head of security fiddled with his tie. He was sniffling, Adam's apple bobbing away.

Chernov sighed. Few understood. "The lawless power of Russia redeems God," Chernov said. "A failed God becomes one with Russia through this redemptive work. So it is God, ultimately, who owns this gold. Do you see?"

The man was swallowing harder now, fingers tugging at his tie knot. He did not reply. He did not meet Chernov's gaze.

Crates slid past.

Chernov led the man by the shoulder toward an empty crate. A policeman was stapling a label onto the wood. Chernov told him to stop, give us a moment. The taste was thick now—had he bitten his tongue? He swabbed his mouth with a finger, but it glistened clean and clear.

"Ideas," Chernov said, "are the only weapons capable of obliterating history, fact, and truth. As good Russians, you and I understand their power. In the last century millions of our compatriots nobly suffered under the banner of once-obscure ideas. I pray that many more will follow in the one to come."

Still clutching the man's shoulder, Chernov motioned to the empty crate. "Get inside."

"What?"

Chernov's grip tightened. He peered into the crate and down through the bottom into the dark hole in the Syrian countryside where they'd stuffed him for months. And he knew that the black vine stretching through his body was what this banker must feel now.

Chernov emerged from Syria to watch another crate slide toward the vault's freight elevators. "Get in."

A thin line of sweat dappled the man's hairline. Chernov's massive hand softly brushed the man's earlobe and slid gently onto his neck.

"Please," the man said. "Please."

"Get in."

Chernov's thumb moved just inside the man's ear. They looked at each other for a moment.

The man stepped inside the crate.

"Sit down."

He folded up his quivering legs and sat.

Chernov stooped over him. "My idea of Russia is that of a body. A perfect, God-born, virginal body. Made of cells, just like our own. And these cells have roles. Each its proper function. If a cell does not function, then it must be cut from the body."

"Please," the man said. "Don't."

"Lie down," Chernov said, "so you are snug."

The man did. Then he shut his eyes.

Chernov picked up the top and stood casting a shadow over the crate. He chewed on his cheek until blood at last spurted into his mouth. "I have a message for Agapov from my master: We are worried that your cell no longer functions. That it seeks sinful freedom. That the stubborn former KGB general, the scrappy industrialist, the proud landholder, has become convinced that his own person, family, and money are separable from the Russian state. That Agapov, as an individual with rights and protections under the law ... well, the old fool imagines now that he can do what he likes. But the loss of this gold tonight should demonstrate that the law is nothing but ritual, it is a glorious gesture of subjugation to our leader. Power and violence trump the law, and violence is what will come if Agapov continues to put his interests above those of Russia. Evil begins where the person begins. There is only the Russian nation, there are no people. There is no Agapov."

Then Chernov slid on the top. He took a drill and brought it to full rev and drove the first screw into the wood.

"Oh God," the man screamed, "oh God."

4

RusFarm, outside Saint Petersburg

ANNA ANDREEVNA AGAPOVA HEARD THE WHINE OF THE BRAKES AND felt the mansion pressing down from above. She looked out the car window: Nearly every room was dark. They were always dark. Four of the staff shuffled cautiously down the wet marble steps under the glow of the lanterns and the brutal horsehead gargoyles. It always cheered her to see the consequences of her husband's awful design sensibilities, but unfortunately none of the staff slipped on the slick stone. A squat woman opened the door and Anna put her blood-red Louboutin boots onto the gravel and stuffed her hands in her pockets.

She looked up at the house again, but now the sight of it made her angry, so she turned to squint at the lights illuminating the racecourse and the roofs of the stables beyond. How many horses out there now? Probably more than one hundred. Sleet was picking up, slivers in the quickening wind. And it was only October. God, she detested the Saint Petersburg winter. Wet and frigid and gunmetal-gray. The inspiration for a litany of suicidal Russian literature. Anna, like everyone else, simply called the city Piter. Eyes still on the stables, she asked the woman, "Where is he?"

"The office," the woman said, "but he's—"

"My dear," her father's voice broke in. She turned to see Andrei Agapov emerge from the foyer. The staff stood silent and stock-still in his presence. His white hair was neatly combed. He was well dressed in trim slacks and a cashmere sweater. But his eyes looked exhausted.

His face had the pallor of an ashtray. Anna did not have details, but the urgency of this meeting and his relocation to RusFarm hinted at a man in the crosshairs of conspiracy.

"How was the trip?" he asked.

"Fine. Easy." She stopped at the top of the steps, just before the threshold.

"I'd like to speak with you now," he said. He motioned for the staff to collect Anna's bags. The squat woman opened the trunk and stared. It was empty.

"I'm not spending the night here," Anna said.

He waved Anna into the foyer with a scowl. She shook her head.

He tilted his to the side. "Just for a moment," he said. "It's cold. Come in, I'll get my coat. Then we can talk outside in this snow"—he waved up at the sleet—"otherwise we might end up cleaning the damn stuff in endless Siberia." Again he waved, and it said: *Come on inside, little girl.*

Anna smiled and blew frosty breath into the sky at the euphemism for jail time. She jerked her head away from the house. "I'll wait out here while you get your coat. Maybe we talk at the racecourse or in the stable?"

Then Anna heard a faint buzz. She turned to listen and it grew louder. Blades beating the air. She knew this one's sound. "The CIA?" she asked.

He laughed, shook his head, and went inside for his coat.

———

PAPA'S FAVORITE HELICOPTER HAD ONCE BEEN OWNED BY THE CIA. IT was a Soviet-made, twin-engine Mil Mi-17 that Langley had flown in the opening days of the war against the Taliban in 2001. When the mullahs retook Kabul, they had captured this one and sent it to Moscow as a gift. Her father said he'd won it in a bet with the Minister of Defense. She'd never asked what he'd wagered.

In the helo they shared a flask of Papa's favorite Dagestani cognac. There were several gun cases and sheaths—some quite large. A crate groaning with ammunition. What looked to be a rocket-propelled grenade launcher spread on the floor. Two silent pilots. The two Agapovs, father and daughter.

This cargo hovered upward, bound for the shooting range on Rus-Farm's southern edge. A tattered moon peeked through the clouds. They did not even try to speak over the rotors. The helicopter paused for a moment before it swung into a descent. Anna steadied herself on a handle.

They stepped down through the wash of rotors and onto a gravel drive that led to the shooting range. The pilots unloaded the weapons. Her father sipped at his cognac while he watched. The sleet had grown into swollen snowflakes. "It's been a while since we did some shooting together, Anya," he said, hand on her shoulder. "I thought it might be nice."

Papa clicked a switch and floodlights drenched the range. The pilots left the weapons on a wooden table behind the firing line and went to warm themselves in the helicopter.

Anna examined the armory. There was an MP-443 semiautomatic pistol, known as the PYa, or *pistolet yarygina*, the Russian military's standard sidearm. Too boring for Papa's collection—what was it doing here? There was an RPK-74 machine gun with the bipod and a Kalashnikov grenade launcher. Where was her favorite? Had he forgotten? She saw an ADS amphibious assault rifle. Then an ancient AK-47 fabricated for the initial Soviet military trials in 1947. It still worked.

Finally she found it: a velvety black case the length of a pen. She clicked it open and smiled at the tube. A lipstick gun. The Kiss of Death. The original design dated to the KGB days: single-shot, 4.5-millimeter, wildly inaccurate, not once used in the field. The techs had updated Papa's model in the nineties. The sole operational purpose had been his amusement. The tube now fired a single nine-millimeter round. To make the guns easier to smuggle, the firing device had been designed so actual lipstick could snuggle over its top, underneath the cap. But Papa's dusty model had long since lost its waxy pink hat.

He watched her turn it over in her hands. "You and that damn thing," he said.

She clicked it shut and returned the case to the box.

Papa chose the AK-47. Steel targets hung downrange in front of an earthen berm the height of a two-story building. He fired, adjusting his aim until there came the sustained and satisfying clink of rounds meeting steel. Then the click of an empty magazine.

"Why are you at the farm?" she asked.

"I've got men doing a sweep up in Repino," he said. "I'm worried it's all wired up. Needed a place to work in the meantime. Here." He handed her the AK-47.

Anna clicked in a fresh magazine. Flicked the safety off. She pinned the stock into her shoulder and reached under the gun with her left hand, fingers outstretched so she wouldn't scrape her knuckles on the receiver. She quickly slid back the charger with her thumb. Anna looked downrange. She bent her knees, squared her shoulders, and leaned in a bit. She rolled her shoulder into the stock until it was snuggled near her collarbone. Gripped the magazine. Looked down the sight at the dangling steel plate. Squeezed the trigger. Her small frame swallowed the jarring recoil. Clink.

Twenty more rounds, eighteen clinks. Not bad, though Papa wouldn't say a kind word about it. They went shooting when they were getting along well. And it had been a while. She flicked on the safety and set down the gun. He joined her at the table, handed her the flask, and produced a folder from the pocket inside his sheepskin greatcoat. He set it on her lap.

"You brought your Repino office in your coat, I see," she said between sips. "What is this?"

"Something I should not have. But first I will tell you why I have it." He took the cognac. "Yesterday evening, an FSB officer from Internal Security, a Lieutenant Colonel called Chernov, arrived at the bank with papers authorizing him to transfer my gold to a strategic reserve, supposedly a military bunker out east. Lies, of course. It was a robbery, pure and simple. They made off with over two hundred bars of my gold. Packed my head of security into a damn crate and shipped him to me with a psychotic message that I'm to bend the fucking knee. Poor bastard worked his fingers down to bloody nubs clawing at the walls of the box. Took almost three hours to get his wits about him so he could pass the message."

Papa's eyes were wolfish, fists balled so tightly that when he uncoiled them a spot of blood blossomed on his palm where he'd sunk in a fingernail. He sucked at the cut.

Anna sipped cognac until Papa could speak again.

Then he whispered, "This Chernov works for Goose, Anya. The message is from Goose."

The name seemed to open her coat to the looming Piter winter. Vassily Platonovich Gusev. Goose. Former Director of the FSB, current Secretary of the Security Council, one of Putin's closest advisers. Across three decades, her father and Goose had waged a proper Russian power struggle—long on blood, short on victory. The captains still stood, though, warily eyeing each other across the field.

"They said they would stop after they took my shipyard," her father continued. "But now this? A bank robbery? There is less of everything, and yet they tax us this way. Do they want a war?"

"Can you talk to the *khozyain*?" Anna asked. The Master. President Putin.

"The *khozyain* did nothing after the shipyard shakedown. I will try again. But in the meantime, we have a lead. We fight them." Her father smacked his palm on the folder.

Anna opened it, scanning the first pages for official seals or the blue stripes of an operational report. She saw nothing, and shut the folder.

"Where did you get this?" she asked.

"Just read it," her father said. He took the flask and a slug of cognac. "We have someone listening for us and he's heard something quite interesting. *Neofitsialnye mery.*"

Non-official measures. No paper warrant authorizing the wiretap. No assurances that this originated even in the realm of telephone law, the shadowy calls from the Kremlin bearing hushed directives. This came from her father alone. A quiet voice inside told her to stand up and leave, but he had never summoned her in this way. Come to the farm, he had said. Come right now, Anya. She had not visited RusFarm in more than a year. And she was curious about the intelligence, a child feathering fingers over a gift-wrapped box. What could be inside?

She opened the folder and leafed through the papers. Transcripts. A thick stack.

"Here are the highlights," her father said. "We've been paying attention to a few of Goose's moneymen in Europe. London. Greece. Switzerland. And in one of the London transcripts there is a gem of a slipup, because two of them are talking about the shares and how they should have the lawyers organize things so everyone is square on their cut. They go through the usual names, and they say the *khozyain* isn't in on this one. This is for a separate, strategic fund."

"Shit," Anna muttered.

Her father put a hand on her shoulder. "Goose stole my money and he is hiding it from the President."

Anna took the flask. She watched it curiously, as if she didn't own the fingers attached. She listened to her heartbeat, mind sewing together the strands. Maybe Papa made it all up. She told him that.

"You are serious, Anya? My God." He laughed.

"Do you have the audio?"

"Yes."

She held out her hand, palm upturned to the sky.

"Not with me."

A snowflake fluttered into her open palm.

He rolled his eyes and fished a USB stick from his pocket and slapped it into her hand. "Don't plug that into a computer that's connected to the internet."

Anna slipped it into her coat pocket and stood to collect the lipstick gun from the box. She smiled as she clicked it open to load a round into the tube. Walking downrange, Anna was careful to keep the tube pointed away from her. A lipstick gun did not have a safety. She wanted to think, so she strolled until she came to a plywood target near the berm. You had to get in close with these guns. They were accurate only to a few meters—if that.

She stopped two or so meters from the target. She aimed, and thought it a bit far. One big step closer. She pointed the tube at the target and twisted until it clicked and fired. A miss. This damn thing. Anna returned to the wooden table and slid the tube in its case.

"How does Vadim feel about the race in Dubai?" she asked. "Is the horse ready?"

"Ask him yourself. He's your husband."

"Which one is running?"

"Judo Master."

Anna made a face. "Hopeless."

"Maybe," her father said, wiping a dribble of cognac from his chin. "We should discuss the bombshell report I just handed you, instead of the horse business you gracelessly abandoned. Or some other distraction."

She turned from him, chastened. Last thing she needed was a summons to this awful farm.

He spoke more softly now. "Anya, do you know what Goose might do to us?"

She had ideas. She'd watched powerful men squabble all her life. When she was a little girl there had been a bloody struggle in Piter in the shadow of the Soviet collapse. Amid the gangland violence, Papa had packed her and her mother away to this farm, then a run-down Soviet collective. She could still picture her father's men scanning the car undercarriages with mirrors tied to long poles, searching for bombs underneath.

When she'd been a teenager her father left the Service to rise through the ranks of former security men who snatched Russia back from the chaos. He was now chairman of Rossiya Industrial, a conglomerate swollen with some of the state's most strategic assets: weapons manufacture and export, one of the oil champions, the country's second-largest pension fund, a chain of bakeries, of all things.

The price for her father's rise had been steep, though. He'd purchased loyalty through an alliance with the Kovalchuk family: bankers, they managed much of Putin's money.

He'd paid with Anna.

Anna touched her bare ring finger. "I know what will happen, Papa."

"Goose will squeeze us to sell off more assets," her father said, "maybe try to exile us with all the damn artists and ballerinas and professors who packed up when the war got rough. Maybe chop up a few of these horses, for god's sake."

He spoke calmly into the darkness, prophesying with the certainty of a man who had done all of it to others.

"You," she corrected. "He comes to gut you, not me."

"There is no me," he said. "There is only us. And if you don't see that, Anya, well, then god help us all."

She shivered and pulled tight on her coat, not certain who was correct. "What do you want, Papa?"

"We need more evidence before we go to the *khozyain*. I want you to find where they've hidden the damn money." He tapped the folder. "There are clues in here. A London law firm, Hynes Dawson, is involved. I'd start there—they will be the ones establishing the accounts. The lawyers will understand the full structure. They will probably have power of attorney on some accounts. Could help us steal the money right back. You'll dig through this, come up with an ops proposal. Time for us to fight back. Show him we won't fucking grovel."

"I see," Anna said, her lips curling into a sardonic smile.

His cheeks reddened. "What is so funny?"

"For six years you've complained about my work. Told me I should quit and have babies."

"And?"

"And now you want me to put it to use. That's why I'm smiling, Papa."

"Well, stop it, Anya."

"I am running other cases. One in Geneva, for instance. What should I do about those?"

He did not acknowledge this. "Are you going to help me, or are you going to sit by and watch?"

She knocked her knee into his and he handed her the flask. She drank. "You have someone who can help with resources?"

"You can speak with Maximov in Moscow."

The silent birch forest prickled suddenly with the whump of rotors in the distance.

She looked up. "Vadim's helicopter?"

Her father nodded. "Your husband probably wants to check with the trainers before they put the horse on the plane to Dubai."

And then she was moving, saying she would return to Moscow tonight.

"Why not just stay the night, Anya?" Papa bellowed, still seated. "Fly back first thing tomorrow. I'll arrange another helicopter."

The *whump-whump* grew louder. She looked to the sky, fresh sleet stinging her face. Vadim's chopper crossed over them toward the helipad near the mansion. She nudged her head at Papa's helicopter in the clearing ahead. "I'm going to have them take me back to Moscow now. Is that a problem?"

"Anya, just stay the night."

"Do you want my help or not?"

Papa smiled, sighed to the ground, and waved her along.

– 5 –

London

A S WITH ALL THE BEST STORIES, SIA FOX FIRST HEARD THE ONE
about Goose's gold from a drunk with a fabulous accent. The drunk
was Mickey Lyadov, the accent a charming blend of the English of Eton
mixed with the Russian of a Siberian concrete plant. They were in the
wood-paneled private room at the Berkeley, where her law firm, Hynes
Dawson, entertained top-shelf Russians. Mickey was deep into his
champagne, asking Sia about her own accent.

"Well, love, what is it?" Mickey was saying. "Been meaning to ask
since we started working together. The roll of the *r*'s. Fabulous. A bit
delicious, if you can take a compliment."

"Afrikaans," Sia said. "Cape Town."

"Perfect," Mickey said. "It's perfection."

The evening was winding down and Sia had long since shut off her
own champagne spigot. But she'd sidled up to Mickey, pretending to drink
with him to poke around about the money. The Hynes Dawson partners
had been fed the usual lines during the exhausting formal dinner: about
Mickey's clients having decided, spur of the moment—naturally—to
move a vast sum of money—provenance unknown—into a new
matryoshka-doll-like structure of accounts controlled by shell companies nested inside yet more shells. In the British Virgin Islands. Nevis.
Switzerland. The Isle of Man. Locales with upstanding reputations for
secrecy and discretion.

Sia knew Mickey moved money for Goose. All the Hynes Dawson senior partners knew this, though no one spoke of it. What Sia wanted to know was where this tranche had come from. And Mickey, she thought, wanted to tell her. There was a story, and his eyes said it was a good one. She refilled his champagne.

"It's quite a lot, Micks," she said, "even for you and your clients. One hundred fifty million dollars on short notice? Quite substantial. Any juicy bits, or is it all terribly secretive and Russian?"

"Well, it is terribly important to my people," Mickey said. "Terribly, terribly important." Then he said, "*Zayebeese.*" Sia's brow crinkled, and Mickey laughed.

"I'm sorry," he said, "I'm saying my work is so bloody important the boss will fuck me if I screw it up." He laughed again, then drank more champagne and beckoned her closer when, perhaps too excited or too drunk, Mikhail Lyadov said that the money had once been gold.

"Gold?" Sia asked, face brightening. "Wow, Micks, that's damn incredible. And I say you're full of it."

He laughed, then became serious. "No, I swear," he said. "Gold. From a Russian bank." He'd heard rumors some of it was stolen, but that was probably too good to be true. Too bloody sexy. The truth is probably boring, he offered glumly. It's gold my clients need out of the country, smuggled through Europe, turned to clean cash by a few friendly Swiss dealers, and stashed properly on humid isles by Hynes Dawson and the bankers. The usual business, the grind for hard currency and all that. He took a swig of champagne. But it began as gold, he insisted, hand to his heart, from a bank vault in Saint Petersburg.

"Micks, how in the hell did they get all the bars out?" Sia asked. They were hunched over the long table, whispering conspiratorially.

"Heard that they packed them into crates from the Hermitage," he said with a wink. "Sent them to Florence, a museum partnership, naturally, and then by lorry to God knows where. Probably Switzerland." His smile buckled in disappointment. "Though I fear that bit is also too bloody good to be true."

She wanted to ask what the hell Goose planned to do with the money, but Micks wouldn't know. The question would make him fidget and ramble in that posh accent.

"New subject," she said, leaning into the table, intending nothing of the sort. "I hear that your friends in Russia are having trouble with one of the businessmen. Is *oligarch* the right word? He doesn't own football clubs or yachts, I'm told, but he's positively glittering with cash. What's his name? Ago-something . . ."

"Agapov," Mickey said, "General Andrei Borisovich Agapov. Though he's retired, love." He was sliding his champagne flute around by the stem.

"Agapov recently sold his shipyard at a savage discount," Mickey continued. "And now this business with the bank." Knowing shake of the head, more champagne.

"The bank is Agapov's, too?" Sia asked.

"Agapov is the bank's principal shareholder," Mickey said. "The man, of course, has certain enemies. Rather clever ones, in fact. The sort that spin webs deep inside the Kremlin's keep."

Grinning, he twirled the empty flute. They (Mickey) had drained the champagne. Sia snatched a bottle of brandy from the serving cart to top him off.

"No snifter? My god, Sia, you are a barbarian," he said. "Visigoths pour brandy in champagne flutes, dear. Visigoths and Vandals."

"On to the gates of Rome, Micks." She poured herself a flute and snatched an insignificant sip. A waiter entered the room; she waved him off, folded her hands on the table, leaned in for another whisper: "You were talking about enemies, Micks. Andrei Agapov's enemies."

"Indeed, indeed. Well, we've all got them, don't we, Sia?" Mickey said. "Look at your old Micks. At present: deep in his cups with a Visigoth. Totally surrounded." He chuckled and then examined his watch as if he had places to be.

He needs a nudge, Sia thought. A little help.

"I only pick up the rumors that make it from Moscow to dreary London," she offered, "but I've heard that Goose is putting the hurt on Agapov. In the bad old days Goose was head honcho at FSB, I think. Now he has an office down the hall from Putin. Hell, Micks, I read an article saying Goose was behind the shakedown of Agapov's shipyard. What gives? Something nasty slithering under the Kremlin sheets?"

Mickey zippered his mouth, threw the imaginary key into the cognac, and downed his flute.

Sia refilled it. "Well, now, Micks, the key's back in your glass. You drink it, we might just unlock those lips."

He shrugged and gave a thin smile after a long, slow sip. Drummed the tablecloth. Then, as had become Mickey's preferred method of sharing secrets, he spoke in a selective, passive tense. The active would have required him to assign Goose responsibility for things he should not.

"Agapov's gold was purloined, one might say. For strategic purposes that are of course a mystery to your lowly old Micks. But his gold was snatched right up, his shipyard, too, and a few of my little birdies back in the Rodina are singing that old Andrei is being punished because he doesn't play by the rules. He's got to pay his tribute, see, and he is being bloody stubborn about it. You mentioned Goose. And I won't comment on the articles. You know the papers here kick up all manner of slander and libel against patriotic Russians. But I do hear from my birds that Goose and Agapov despise each other. Both are legacy Leningrad KGB. Seed of their mutual hatred a timeless one: a girl. What bloody else? There's Helen of Troy, there's Galina of Saint Petersburg, God rest her soul. Galina was with Goose before she married Agapov. Now Goose is ascendant, he's got his goslings to feed, and he's doing what any reasonable man should, isn't that right, Sia?"

"And what's that, Micks? Rob an old rival blind?"

Mickey shook his head. "It's that, but more. Agapov built a powerful alliance with the Kovalchuk family. Thick as thieves, Agapov and Kovalchuk were. Hell, it was Agapov who took the controlling stake in the bank when Kovalchuk senior passed a few years ago. Agapov has even married his daughter, Anna, off to the son, Vadim Kovalchuk. One might wonder if the game here is both sweet revenge and good politics. Shake down an old rival, smash a powerful political alliance. Two birds and all."

"Fascinating stuff, Micks," Sia said. "Your clients are positively brimming with Stalinist intrigue."

"They have bloody hands," he said, wiping his palms with a cheerful smile. "Just like yours."

———

TWO PECKS ON THE CHEEKS FOR MICKS, A SHORT STROLL THROUGH moonlit Mayfair, and Sia was back at Hynes Dawson, where a pile of haggard associates careened into the seventeenth hour of their workday. She marched up the winding, creaky staircase and into her office, where she closed the door and stood staring out the dirty window onto the unkempt bushes lining the gravel courtyard below.

The fountain was dry; she had never seen it work. Benny Hynes, the firm's sole surviving founder and its emeritus managing partner, had insisted on the office's eclectic combination of premium real estate and tumbledown décor. Many of the big City firms boasted sleek, ultra-modern offices awash in amenities to compensate staff for their corporate slavery.

Not Hynes Dawson. The Mayfair town house might well have been the home of an eccentric family. Bookshelves lined the hallways and offices. The walls were clotted with oil paintings unrelated to the partnership, the clients, or the practice of law: the Battle of Trafalgar, a Cornish pastoral, a duck painted by Benny Hynes himself. Space was at a premium: Sia's office had once been a child's bedroom.

The firm's draw was simple: compensation was five times that of other London law firms. On a good year, the firm's profit-sharing plan might make that seven. The money compensated for the shambolic workspace. It also sought to make amends for a client list running the spectrum from the reluctantly shady to the unrepentantly corrupt. Client hands were jammed in dirty money pots all around the globe. And many of those hands tilted a shade murderous: Assad, Putin, Al Saud, Khamenei. Their names did not appear on the documents, but it was understood by the firm's Oxbridge senior partners that their representatives were Hynes Dawson's most valuable clients.

There was a knock on the door.

"Come in," Sia said.

Benny Hynes sauntered into her office. He was seventy-four, gaunt, with a shock of white hair and a three-piece charcoal suit. His pocket watch had once belonged to Churchill. He was awake and working at 1:03 a.m. They sat on the green leather sofa and for a moment watched a passerby through the window on the street below.

"You spent time with Mickey Lyadov?" he asked, still looking out the window.

"He likes to talk."

"Kremlin gossip?"

"Isn't it always? The money belonged to Andrei Agapov. Goose took it. Trouble brewing in Moscow, warring factions and all. Typical Russian business."

He grunted, fussed with his tie. "That explains the bullshit they fed us at dinner. Any risk for us if we help them wash the money? Does Mickey think we're in the crosshairs?"

"No more than usual."

"What the bloody hell are they going to do with it?"

"Mickey doesn't know."

"He never knows the important things."

"He's a bagman."

Benny stood and stretched. "They've just now sent the contract for us to start on the work. You get it set up for them, eh, Sia? Whatever they want, and they'll want the usual: shells on shells on shells until it's all vanished. Unless we think Agapov or some other Kremlin nasty is going to burn down this office, we help Goose stash his money. Because who cares? It's our job. It's why we exist, fuck all." A kindly pat on her knee, and Benny was up and headed for the door.

And it's why I've wriggled into your little mercenary outfit, she did not say. Instead, she beat Benny to the door and opened it to see him out, pat on the shoulder and a solemn promise that she'd assign a crack team first thing, have a tranche of Agapov's stolen money squirreled into an innocuous Caribbean account by lunch, afternoon tea at the very latest.

MICKEY HAD IT MOSTLY RIGHT. THE CRATES ARRIVED IN FLORENCE IN the hold of a Russian military transport plane on loan to the Culture Ministry. Museum exchanges had continued apace, even with the war. Chernov, whose official documents described him as a conservator attached to the Hermitage Museum in Saint Petersburg, accompanied a cluster of the boxes. The true conservators, traveling to oversee a loan of paintings and sculptures once owned by Catherine the Great, wisely kept their distance.

Chernov's crates were royal blue and unmarked apart from a serial number and a yellow sign reading OPEN THIS SIDE stenciled in Italian, Russian, and English. Chernov, supervising the unloading on the apron in Florence, exchanged greetings with a man he knew only by his unimaginative FSB nickname: Michelangelo. The man owned and operated a trucking company that specialized in moving paintings, sculptures, and other valuables throughout Europe. Two daughters had studied economics in London thanks to payments from the Russian FSB.

From Florence, Michelangelo's trucks ferried the crates overland to a gold-refining operation outside Dresden, where the bullion would be melted down and remolded with new insignias to disguise its provenance. Anti-money-laundering measures in the gold-refining business are thinly enforced—even more so when the owner and chief executive officer are on the FSB payroll.

The gold's path forked from the refinery, where it was sold to Swiss branches of two German gold wholesalers, both of which claimed executives similarly indebted to Lubyanka paymasters. Greed doubtless encouraged conspirators to overlook the fog shrouding the gold's birthplace, but those with lingering questions, or perhaps a fear of retribution—legal or otherwise—could also take comfort in the simple fact that Bank Rossiya had not reported the theft. For, as Chernov had insisted, it was not robbery because the gold was Russia's and therefore God's and all belonged to God. To any interested international organization or government, the bullion remained safely entombed inside the Rodina.

Once the gold had been sold off in fragments into the currency markets, Goose's moneymen, Mikhail Lyadov chief among them, arranged for the proceeds to flow into a byzantine structure of offshore accounts held by shell corporations: Sandalwood Ltd., Brockton Development, QRE Solutions, etc. By design the names were hollow. The corporations existed on paper alone.

It was the London lawyer, Sia Fox, who was destined to be the creator of the dizzying structure of Goose's offshore financial holdings, the architect and builder of a far-flung financial outpost well clear of the Rodina's borders. To most observers, her creation would be mind-numbingly dreary, tedious, and complex. But from above, and in just the right light, one could make out its true form: This was the scarred battlefield of a vicious Russian power struggle. And it was also quite possibly the largest theft of gold bullion since the Nazis looted Europe during the Second World War.

Sia knew which accounts belonged inside Goose's borders, though none bore his name. Sia knew how to move the money.

This was so because powerful men inside the Kremlin trusted Hynes Dawson. And though they did not know her name, by virtue they trusted Sia Fox.

And that, she thought, was a terrible mistake.

6

Moscow

A NNA PULLED OFF THE MKAD RING ROAD AT AN EXIT IN THE YASE-
nevo District marked with the words NO ENTRY in Cyrillic and English. She nosed her Range Rover down a narrow road and past another
sign that read SCIENCE RESEARCH CENTER, winding deeper into the woods
until she came to an unassuming gatehouse drenched in sodium light. A
single guard emerged. Anna did not have one of the maroon badges, so
the guard just stared, probably wondering if the tiny blonde had veered
off at the wrong exit. He glanced toward the bollards and the flat metal
plates set into the pavement, which he would raise if a car tried to dodge
the ID check. Anna had heard of that happening once, when a drunk
clipped through the gates only to pancake his Lada into a steel barrier
that had sprung up from the road. She handed him her driver's license
with a pleasant smile and explained that he was to call the Third Deputy
Director's office immediately; she would not be on the lists.

She pulled to the side while the guard made his call. After a few
minutes he hustled from the gatehouse with her ID, the boom swung
skyward, and she clopped over the plates into the compound.

In the vast parking lot Anna powered off her cell phone and shoved
it into the glove box. It was still early, but she could see that many offices
were already illuminated, including the third-floor executive suite that
her father had once occupied. Beyond the main seven-story building rose
a twenty-two-story high-rise, the hive for the worker bees. Directly west

of the endless—and increasingly jammed—parking lot was a swooping building that boasted a heavily discounted department store, two saunas, an Olympic-sized swimming pool, three gymnasiums, and a crop of tennis courts. Private dachas, once belonging to leaders of the KGB's First Chief Directorate, dotted the woods inside the security fence.

When the Soviet regime collapsed, the organization occupying the Yasenevo compound had been renamed the SVR, Sluzhba Vneshney Razvedki, the Foreign Intelligence Service. Her father, like everyone else, had not minded the rebranding because no one ever used its proper name. Closing her eyes, Anna listened to the hum of the electricity substation and the pines bristling in the chilly morning wind. SVR headquarters. She, like her father, knew it only as the Forest.

———

THIRD DEPUTY DIRECTOR MAXIMOV BOASTED A WIDE OFFICE IN THE third-floor executive suites. Picture windows overlooked trees parting the fog like ghosts in the morning haze. Maximov, like all of them, had a wall of pictures and memorabilia in a glass case atop the credenza behind his desk (baseball signed by Fidel Castro, handshake photo with a near-death Kim Philby, commemorative AK-47 gifted by the Syrian Minister of Defense).

Head in a pile of papers, he mumbled for her to sit at the lacquered table running the length of the room, fashioned from pine planking that had once graced a ship of the line commissioned by Peter the Great in the wars against Sweden. At the end of the office, another table groaned under the weight of an ornate silver samovar, looted from Terem Palace in Moscow during the Revolution. The faded outline of the Romanov imperial double eagle was visible from across the room even through Anna's drowsy eyes.

Maximov was heavy, with thick white hair on the sides of his head but none on the top. He often bellowed—the problem of volume had been raised during personnel reviews as recently as the late 2000s—and yet despite the bluster he was considered operationally conservative. He was a status quo man, almost certainly wary of her father's desire to position them as chess pieces in his match with Goose: to put her and Maximov—SVR, really—to work finding his stolen money. But thankfully, unlike many other creatures on the third floor, Maximov did not care about Anna's missing penis. He kissed her cheeks and joined her at the table.

"I have an office in one of the outbuildings you can use for a few days," he began, "and a few Line OT"—Operational Support—"techs to help with the analysis. No paper. No operational accounting. Use your judgment."

"Of course."

"When you have a target, I don't want to know. I need some distance from this one. You agree on those details with your father."

"Understood."

"But inside SVR, you report only to me, Anya. You keep your other cases going through the normal chain, but not this one."

She looked at him like he was an old fool for having to say that aloud.

"That was for my conscience," he grunted.

"Of course." Anna shrugged, patted the tabletop, and looked over the treetops. "I may need surveillance resources," she said.

"When the time comes."

At the door he brought her close and whispered into her ear, "Your father would be proud, Anya. Is proud."

She knew the old operations officer inside Maximov was working little Anya, bucking her up, sewing her into this whole sordid enterprise so she would keep at it even when the going got tough, as things would if they were going to fight Goose. "That's a kind lie," she said. He smiled and opened the door and kissed her cheek to see her off.

———

SHE LOCKED HERSELF INSIDE THE FOREST OUTBUILDING FOR THREE days, sustained on an endless drip of tea. The planning team, trusted techies selected by Maximov, squatted in a dilapidated conference room with grimy windows that shoved onto the edge of the woods. Here she walked into the fog surrounding Hynes Dawson.

On the first day they found a London address in the UK company register, a Mayfair town house on a quiet street a few blocks from Hyde Park. The Google Street View revealed a shabby property with rusted fencing, peeling paint, and mineral-stained stone. It did not look like an enterprise wealthy people would use to hide money. Which, perhaps, was the point.

Combing through unofficially borrowed UK customs and tax databases, the techies built a list of Hynes Dawson employees. Anna wanted the people working on Goose's accounts. Ideally not the senior partners—visible to Goose's people, less vulnerable to financial blandishments—nor the lower-level staff lacking direct access. She wanted an overworked employee in the middle of the pyramid with access to the information, but well off Goose's radar. Anna also required a target that would fit with her SVR commercial cover as a Russian banker.

And it was here that the team stumbled across a Hynes Dawson associate partner named Hortensia Rose Fox. A *Guardian* article detailing the impact of sanctions on the City and white-shoe London quoted her as a "lawyer with a focus on Russia and Eastern Europe."

They went deeper on Hortensia. The most recent picture Anna could find, dated eighteen months earlier, showed a tall woman with black hair, hazy gray eyes, and an aquiline nose. She was a South African–UK dual citizen. On her social media accounts, largely dormant since she joined Hynes Dawson, she called herself Sia.

That made sense.

Hortensia, Anna had said to Grigory, one of the techies, what the hell kind of terrible name is that? It wasn't Afrikaans. He'd shrugged. No one had ever heard it before.

The team built an incomplete biography. Raised in Cape Town. Cambridge for university, where she studied law. Then an odd pivot. She had moved to San Francisco to join Lyric, a tech company. They found pictures of Sia with the Lyric founder and CEO, Harry Hamilton. Lots of them. Smiling, laughing, hugging. She had quit Lyric for Hynes Dawson five years earlier. Anna liked the Lyric angle—if any of her other masters inside SVR asked what she was up to, she could dangle the intelligence value of a large U.S. tech company with a multibillion-dollar portfolio of defense contracts.

They scraped her cell phone number from the unofficially borrowed tax records. Then through an SVR front—a Turkey-based accounting firm with a branch in Geneva—the team purchased reams of publicly available information from companies that aggregated and sold data from common apps. A data scientist constructed heat maps showing Sia's movements around London and the British countryside. They learned how she traveled to the office, the doctors she visited, where she bought groceries.

What do you think? Anna had asked Grigory as they pored over the maps. Boring lawyer, he said, running his finger over the short walking route from her Mayfair flat to the Hynes Dawson offices. "She works fifteen, sixteen hours every day," he said. "She eats takeout, she treats clients to fancy dinners, she runs on the weekends." He made the point with a yawn.

Late on the third evening, Anna sat alone in the conference room considering the case. She started, as always, with her favorites: the rougher options. Sia might receive threatening phone calls and Anna might appear with a way to make them stop. Pets could be killed, but Sia did not seem to own one. (The geolocational data suggested she did not take nightly walks; she did not visit pet stores to buy food.) The aggressive approaches, though, were premature. She didn't yet know Sia's pressure points, her vulnerabilities, her addictions. And the woman was not a Russian, nor was she inside Russia. Yet.

Anna rolled her fingers along the rim of her Styrofoam teacup and considered the problem of access. She could dangle bait that Sia would find interesting. A lucrative client, perhaps? A pliable, wealthy Russian whose money might be enticing. Not a bad start. Though it might raise Goose's interest if discovered, she could explain it innocently enough: *We are hiding money, just like you.*

She put on her coat and gloves and trudged through the parking lot to the Range Rover. She fished the phone from the glove box and called her father. She told him what she needed. He told her what he wanted her to do.

"Oh, come, now, Papa," she said. "I cannot. There are other ways."

"Maybe, Anya, maybe. But your husband's already in. I told him. So go talk to him. See if you two can work something out."

She put her head on the wheel. Her husband. *Blyad.* Bloody hell.

That night she topped off a middling bottle of Georgian wine with a few cognacs and mindlessly watched the talking heads on *Time Will Tell* in the shadows of her Ostozhenka apartment in Moscow, acquired in the first unhappy years of their marriage, and yet another place she did not like. Whenever her mind rolled toward the conversation with Papa, she drank more cognac. On the TV, a debate was raging over the bloodthirsty methods the Americans might employ to solve the "Russian question," and the corresponding need for national self-purification, when Anna, at last, passed out.

Next morning Anna woke twisted in her robe atop churned bed-sheets. She did not remember walking into the bedroom. She lay soaking in her headache, fighting to merely open her eyes much less string thoughts together. Anna went to the club downstairs to swim. Two slow laps and she was spent. She took a steam to sweat out the alcohol. She was nearer to forty than thirty, but with a flat stomach and muscular legs courtesy of her mother's side. The thought made her sad. In the locker room she showered and lightly curled her blond hair and did her makeup. Ignoring the puffy bags below her eyes, Anna smacked bright red lips together and smiled to confirm she had not dredged lipstick over her teeth.

It was time.

———

ANNA HAD NOT SPOKEN TO VADIM IN FOUR WEEKS, SHE HAD NOT SEEN him in six. She was grinding her teeth just looking at the name in her contact list. She stretched and cracked her jaw and rode the usual emotional jumble that her husband conjured. Anna gripped the marble countertop, and when she let go she watched the damp outline of her fingers slowly evaporate. Then she dialed his number.

"Hi," he said, picking up just before it went to voice mail. Like her, she knew, Vadim would sometimes stare at the phone, contemplating whether to answer. Anna said she needed to see him. Could she come to Piter, if he was in town?

"I am in Piter," he said sadly. "Should we have dinner?"

"Yes, we have business to discuss." She imagined him scowling at that.

"I'll have my assistant make a reservation. What night is best?"

"How about tonight?"

"Fine," he said. "Will you stay at the apartment?"

"Where else would I stay?"

He coughed.

"Where else would I stay?" she repeated.

"With your father."

"I am not a child, Vadim. Is one of them living with you now?"

"Anya, please. There is no one here. Of course you can stay in the apartment. It is fine. I was just asking."

But why, why are you asking? she screamed silently. *Why are you asking, Vadim?* They circled in silence, listening to each other breathe. She clamped her teeth.

"I'll see you tonight," she finally said.

As always, he hung up first.

7

Saint Petersburg

T HE APARTMENT WAS IN ONE OF THE FEW RESIDENTIAL BUILDINGS on the Kutuzov Embankment of the Neva, occupying three floors of a mansion that had been the French Embassy when Piter was the Romanov imperial capital. She'd taken the Sapsan high-speed train, a comfortable four-hour trip from Moscow. Anna stood outside in a clump of Chinese tourists gawking at the fortress of Peter and Paul across the river. But she was gazing the opposite direction, up toward the ornate stone facades of their building, glowing pink in the draining midafternoon light. Beautiful prose had been written about this place, historians mulled the implications of a Fabergé-studded imperial capital springing forth, in incredible violence, from swampy frontier marshes. But Anna had never escaped the simple truths that the poetic language could not capture: here she had been born, raised, loved, sold (married, technically), ignored, and, here, in Piter, here she must endure. She lowered her head and went inside.

The smell of disinfectant and bleach crashed into her when she opened the apartment door. Walking toward the bedroom, she saw carpet groomed by a vacuum, shiny glass tables, and freshly made beds, the tacky zebra-print sheets primly tucked and folded, pillows tastefully fluffed. What a happy wife would have interpreted as a thoughtful marital gesture was instead logged as evidence that Vadim had hastily hired cleaners to eliminate evidence of the fuck-parade that regularly marched through this place.

She slipped on a belted red satin dress and four-inch Louboutin heels she'd packed for the trip. Picking through her jewelry, she selected a Tiffany pearl necklace and matching earrings. In the mirror she looked at her clothes and smoothed the dress. Thinking of Vadim's unwashed women, Anna called her doctor in Moscow to schedule blood work and her pharmacy to refill her medication.

During the Soviet years, birth control had largely meant abortions. The pill had been unavailable, and the Soviet condoms were talc-dusted and thick as rainboots, the second of two products made at the Bakovsky rubber factory, the first being gas masks. Now the pill was available to all. The problem was that many husbands wanted children. Anna disguised her stash in an aspirin bottle when Vadim was around. She swallowed her evening dose. Then Anna went to the wet bar in the living room to rummage around for one of his expensive cognacs. Correction. One of *our* expensive cognacs.

She filled the bottom of a snifter and took a long drink. It was still early; she should cut the alcohol with food. But this was one of those evenings to be endured, and she had just filled her second when she heard Vadim open the door. She turned and forced a smile toward her husband, who was on the phone. He motioned a silent apology for the call and wordlessly strode past her into the bedroom. Darkness was settling over the Neva. She was alone with her thoughts and her drink.

———

VADIM'S DRIVER FERRIED THEM TO THE RESTAURANT, PALKIN, IN THE armored Maybach. They started with martinis on leather oxblood chairs in the honey glow of the bar. Conversation was halting. Vadim asked about work, she offered little, then reciprocated. He was handsome, tall, and broad-shouldered, with soft brown eyes that she had liked for a season when they'd been young. During one of the many lulls in conversation Anna found herself wishing she could at least tolerate the strange confines of this pseudo-arranged marriage. They mostly lived apart, which made things easier. To fill the silence she asked about preparations for Dubai.

"Trainers can't fucking get their act together," Vadim said, tongue sliding along the bottom teeth, face darkening. She raised her eyebrows. The end. Good talk.

Vadim signaled for another martini as they moved to their table. The Art Deco dining room's glossy parquet floor clacked pleasantly under her Louboutins. The table sat in a quiet alcove next to a window overlooking the bustle on Nevsky Prospekt. The silky green drapes were sashed open, the blaze of the streetlights glittered on the silver and glassware. A slim brunette marketing her cleavage from a bar seat eyed Vadim when they shuffled by. Anna fidgeted with her pearls.

Her Piter was the second city of the new Russkiy mir, a Russian world battened down against a hostile and degenerate West. But the trenches, the bloodletting, the air raid sirens, well, to Anna that night they were faint thunderclouds on a faraway horizon. The special military operation in Ukraine, the war, had twisted deep into the Russian soul, but it had been slower to disfigure the body. Apple and Nike stores were gone, McDonald's had been renamed "Tasty and That's It," parts for Western-made cars now had to be purchased through online dealers, there were occasional, and limited, shortages at the grocery and department stores. But, as Anna had heard whispers of the Soviet days and experienced herself as a young girl in the dead empire of the wild nineties, the Russian capacity for suffering was limitless, unfathomable. And the present was nothing, a light graze on a body furrowed by deep scars. Tonight they would eat well, and expensively. They would just keep on going. Anna signaled for her own martini.

Vadim ordered beluga caviar without asking her what she wanted. They spread dollops onto quail eggs lathered with sour cream, clinked glasses without making eye contact, and then drank in silence while Vadim scrolled on his phone.

"So," he said finally, pushing the phone aside. "Your father spoke to me about this . . . business."

The waiter's arrival hushed the conversation. Vadim picked a French wine, a Petrus bottled in Anna's birth year, priced at about six months of an average Russian's wages. Vadim ordered Wagyu steak and Anna a stroganoff, simple by the outrageous standards of Palkin.

"I have a target, but we need bait," she said when the waiter had gone. "Something to dangle."

Speech hovered over Vadim's lips, but the waiter was approaching with the wine. Vadim permitted Anna to complete the wine service. After she had nodded, he told the waiter to give them a few moments of privacy.

But then Goose walked straight into Anna's sights, past a maître d' begging for time to finish readying the table. His security detail fanned out through the room.

Anna cursed softly into the table and muttered to Vadim.

A young blonde walked a step behind Goose in the polite manner of a daughter out for a special dinner with Papa. Daughter, though, was not this one's role. Goose spotted them on the way to his table, and now it was Vadim's turn, cursing under his breath as he stood to say hello.

"No choice, Anya, I'm sorry," he whispered as they painted on giant smiles to greet him. Goose shook Vadim's hand and introduced them to the doe-eyed Irina. Anna remembered that Irina had also been the name of his second wife. Anna shook Irina's hand and, accustomed to being shoved toward wives, girlfriends, mistresses, and hookers so the men might speak, simply turned from Irina back to the men.

Goose arched an eyebrow at her, then said to Vadim: "We are looking forward to watching what happens in Dubai. We've spent so much on that farm. When do you expect to start winning races?"

Vadim did that thing with the tongue sliding across his teeth, and he was starting to explain how it took time, but Goose was looking at her instead. She'd met him several times and always sensed that her presence agitated him. She was a walking reminder he'd not had a child with Galina. That she was Andrei's. Anna smiled at him as Vadim spoke. It will be nice to gut you, she thought. I might enjoy this.

They were arguing stupidly now, Vadim losing his temper, Goose smirking at the ease of the boat-rocking. Anna stopped listening. She gazed at Irina's perfect face, then painted a pleasant smile on her own before zoning out entirely, waiting for the argument to expire. To entertain herself she looked at one of the plants. Vadim walked off, Irina smiled icily, and they returned to their table. The food had arrived.

"This is why I do not like Palkin," she said, rearranging the napkin on her lap. "It is a scene."

Vadim downed the rest of his wine and glared at her. "This is life, Anya," he said. "A bunch of fights."

Not mine, she did not say. Their physical separation meant that she did not have to be worn on his arm at clubs and restaurants across Piter and Moscow for those fights. They had tried that for a season.

"The bait," Anna said quietly, "I think it should be you."

Vadim, technically a VP, ran the Private Wealth Division inside Bank Rossiya. Vadim's now-deceased father had snapped up the bank in the early 1990s. In the Putin years Rossiya became one of Russia's largest banks, eventually sprawling into a state-backed conglomerate ruled by an alliance between the Agapovs and Kovalchuks.

The booze usually made Vadim tired, but sometimes it surfaced anger, and there was a glimmer in his eyes as he contemplated her starring role in this operation. Vadim hated the SVR job, her independence. *You get to play spy games, I count the money*, he'd yelled at her once in the black days before she'd finally packed up for Moscow.

He waved his hand in an angry flourish: *Continue*.

"The profile is straightforward," Anna said. She held up three fingers. "Loyal to us. Wealthy. Able to travel with me for a few days. That's it. You're a perfect fit."

Vadim glared at Goose across the dining room. The crowd was thinning out, but instead of the relief that should accompany the evening wind-down, the staff were twitchy. They were trapped until Goose and Irina finished. "Fine," Vadim said. "Fine. But in exchange I get to ask you one question."

She looked down at the stroganoff, worried what he might ask. "Of course."

Vadim snapped to the waiter for an ice cream doused in cognac.

He ate his and Anna watched hers melt and sipped the hot chocolate served alongside. Vadim called for more cognac, and when the waiter had gone, he raised his snifter in mock deference to Goose and Irina, then to Anna. He stared at her red dress and Anna recognized that little spark in his otherwise lovely eyes, the angry glint that flashed when they circled each other in this cruel ritual. She sometimes wondered if her face twisted like that. If Vadim's feelings mirrored her own. She'd never asked.

Vadim leaned back in his chair and checked the rose-gold Breguet watch her father had given him on their wedding day. He was drunk, he had questions she would not answer, he was interested in her tonight, for reasons that she wished she did not understand. She did not want to go back to the apartment with him.

"How much money will we need to put at risk?" Vadim said at last, pushing aside the ice-cream dish.

"It is possible we will need to invest a little into the operation. Nothing material. And nothing would be at risk."

Vadim's tongue was cleaning his teeth again. "Okay. You tell me what you need from me."

"Thank you, Vadim, I will. Now, your question?"

He did not answer. Instead, he tossed his napkin on the table and stood drunkenly to leave. Anna followed, wordlessly brushing past Goose's table.

———

THEY RODE HOME IN SILENCE, EACH WATCHING DOWNTOWN PITER ROLL by through their own windows in the Maybach's backseat. In the building Vadim lolled into the lift's cherry-paneled walls. When they got upstairs, she said she was tired and not in the mood and she stupidly kissed his neck and promised that tomorrow night she would be less exhausted. He did not like that. He snatched her wrist, marching her into the bedroom, where he fell onto the bed and began to unzip his pants. He fumbled with his underwear, eventually wriggling them off onto the floor. He left the socks. Vadim was unbuttoning his shirt when he looked up at her, standing beside him in the moonlight. She was fully clothed and hopeful that he might yet pass out. For a beat they both hung there.

"I didn't ask my question," he slurred.

"Then ask."

"Not tonight," he said. "Later."

He stood and shoved her down onto the bed. Anna thought about fighting back. This had happened a few times, and in the morning he would not remember. But something deep down, in the part of her that wanted the marriage to smolder without consuming them in a blazing fire, this voice urged Anna to be a Good Wife. Other parts called for a fight, but the Good Wife smothered the cries. Morning would come. So, when he grabbed a handful of hair, she did not smash her forehead into his nose. When he pushed her face into the sheets, she did not break his knee. When he asked if she was still taking the pills, she lied and said no so that he might finish quickly, God grant her the mercy.

When he was done, he fell asleep crumpled into the sheets, snoring into a pillow smeared with her lipstick. One of her Tiffany earrings lay beside his neck. She felt for the other on her ear. Still there. In the kitchen Anna rummaged through drawers until she found where the maids kept the garbage bags. She took one. She padded past her sleeping husband and snatched up the Louboutins from the floor. In the bathroom she turned away from the mirror, toward the window. She slid off the dress. She removed the straggler Tiffany earring and the necklace. She slipped out of her bra. She tossed everything into the garbage bag and stuffed that into her suitcase so Vadim would not notice. She would throw it all away in the morning, after he went to work.

Anna took a hot shower. As the water coursed over her hair and back and shuttered eyelids, she imagined herself at a full gallop, warm sun on her face, golden hair flapping in the wind. They were riding fast. Anna was encouraging the horse, and she promised that everything would be fine if they just rode on.

8

Repino / Saint Petersburg / London

A NNA STOPPED THE CAR OUTSIDE THE HIGH IRON GATES OF HER father's villa and honked because the guard was sometimes asleep. Nestled outside the seaside resort town of Repino, her father called the place a dacha, but it bore no resemblance to the farmhouse on the old collective he had purchased in the nineties. The land that had become RusFarm. That farmhouse had been small, scarcely one hundred square meters. This villa was more than one thousand. From his hut on the far side of the gate, the guard pressed a button and the gates swung slowly inward. Nosing the car up the long birch-lined driveway, she parked and collected her purse, which held the document bag. Her hand stuck on the door handle for a moment; she listened to the fountain spit and gurgle. She took a breath. Then she went inside.

She found her father lounging in the living room, a leopard reclined on a suede chair watching a Premier League football match. She announced her presence with a cough. The old dacha would have nestled comfortably inside this two-story room alone. The vaulted cavern made her feel like a supplicant in some vast cathedral reminding all who entered that they were but specks of dust in the face of a mighty and gigantic God. The cough's echo lingered, bouncing along the walls and stone floors.

"Papa," she said as he approached the foyer. They embraced and she followed him up the floating stone staircase into the second-floor office. He took up behind a large mahogany desk in front of two sparkling trapezoidal windows that met to form a peak. Beyond him was a large balcony that jutted into the birch and pine.

"How is Vadim?" her father asked, hands folding into an arch.

Anna crossed her legs and flicked dirt from the side of her black leather boot. Her jaw clicked. "He is fine," she said.

Her father grunted. Good.

She plopped a folder from the document bag onto her father's desk. "We have a target," she said.

She briefed him on Hynes Dawson and Hortensia Fox.

Her father, enjoying the ops talk, bobbed his head as she spoke. Sometimes he got up to look out the window. He cut her off after ten minutes. "I'm convinced," he said. "Tell me how you play it."

"It's all in there," Anna said, jabbing a finger on the folder.

"I know, goddammit, Anya," he grunted. "Just give me the basics. The high points."

She did, stopping when he again grunted and waved to signal his agreement. "What if Goose's people are indeed watching her, or have her comms flagged? Or, hell, if she reports everything back to one of their worms? What's the cover?"

"Why in the hell would I need cover, Papa?"

He sat back in his chair. Beginnings of a smile creasing his face.

She continued, "They are using Hynes Dawson to hide money, and so are we. If they squeeze anyone, it will be the lawyer, for showing bad judgment by taking on other Russian clients." She shrugged, reached down to wipe flakes of dried mud from the other boot. She'd chosen a dark red nail polish to match her Chanel eyeglasses, which she now twirled in her fingers. They were nonprescription, but she sometimes wore them to look more serious for crusty men like Papa.

Her father quickly flipped through the rest of the folder. She rearranged her skirt and slipped the glasses back on her face.

"Good," her father said. "When do you make the call?"

"Tomorrow."

He nodded. Approved. She slipped the folder back into the bag, turned the key to lock it, and placed it in her purse. The papers would be fed to the shredder in the apartment. Papa stood. She remained seated, lowering palms to the floor. He hesitated, then complied and sat.

"Have you been able to get time with the *khozyain?*" she asked.

"I am working on it," her father said. The mention of Putin set his fingers rapping on the desk. "Goose controls access. He controls the gatekeepers."

"Right, Papa," Anna said, puckish grin unveiling teeth. "How could I forget?"

Her father bit his lip.

She knew he wanted her to stop, but she kept going. "We need the face time, Papa. Once we bag the lawyer, we will need to bring the evidence to the President. How can we get around Goose to—"

"Enough!" Her father smacked his fist into the mahogany. "I am working on it. You can be such a goddamn pest, Anya. You do your part. I'll do mine." He pointed toward the door.

Damn these old men, keeping her in the dark and milking her all the same. Still, why fight when you could not win? She perched her glasses atop her head and slipped her purse over her shoulder. "I will debrief you immediately after London." A prim smile, and she was out the door.

———

ANNA'S ROLE AS AN *APPARAT PRIKOMANDIROVANNYH SOTRUDNIKOV*, AN APS, OR member of one of the SVR's group of "attached employees" inside the bank, meant she had an office at Rossiya headquarters on Rastrelli Square. Though her work for the SVR was a state secret, most of the employees inside the Private Wealth Division knew it. Their fear of Anna, which she enjoyed and cultivated, meant they left her alone. Anna swung open her office door and turned on the lights.

Anna looked around, then double-checked the nameplate. It read: A. KOVALCHUK, MANAGING DIRECTOR. *Blyad.* Not my last name. Gaudy baroque furniture—all new—crammed the floor. Anna sank into a chair with gilded bronze legs, running her fingers over the bacchanalia engraved on the armrests. Vadim, the division's VP, had apparently redecorated. And he had a particular taste. Purple tassels dangled from the chair's seat. Anna was playing with one of them when teacups clattered in the hallway.

Anna's secretary, Katerina, a virginal waif with an unpredictable stammer, appeared with a tray, clanging it onto a table. "When did this happen?" Anna blew on her tea and motioned around the room.

"T-t-t-wo weeks ago."

"My husband brought all of this here?"

A nod.

Anna stood and set down the teacup. "I am going downstairs to collect a guest for my next meeting. When I return I want this garbage furniture stacked in the hallway. Do you understand?"

"Y-y-yes." Three bobbing nods.

On her way out, Anna ripped the nameplate from the door and slammed it in the trash. "Fix it," she called to Katerina.

———

TWENTY MINUTES LATER, ANNA AND GRIGORY, THE LINE OT TECHIE, reappeared outside her office. Tables and chairs were piled in the hall. An overall-clad crew of facilities workers huffed about, lugging the furniture off toward the freight elevator. A flimsy wooden table and two folding chairs had supplanted the gypsy rococo nightmare. Grigory and his other techies did a bug run to search for listening devices, then wired up the phone to record the conversation. Anna, fighting a wave of fatigue, finished her cool tea.

"What do you think of her, Grigory?"

"Who?" He was fiddling with a bank of cords on the phone, plugging them into his computer.

"Sia."

"She is a boring lawyer," Grigory said.

Anna looked at one of the pictures from Sia's file. Probably right.

"Do you think she is attractive?" Anna asked.

"Yes."

"Though she might be too tall for you." In the videos pulled from unofficially borrowed London CCTV coverage, Anna had seen that Sia's movements were more swagger than walk or strut. That was interesting.

"What do you make of the walk?" Anna asked. "Odd, no?"

Grigory sat down across from her. "She grew up outside Cape Town. On a farm."

"So?"

"So, we have a farm girl who is now a fancy London lawyer. She dresses like a woman accustomed to the upper rung but walks like one who is at home down on the violent end of the ladder, the segment that supports the elite in any Western society."

Anna laughed. "You are insane, Grigory."

The techie shrugged.

Anna sipped her tea and reviewed the script. She was Anna Agapova, a managing director at Bank Rossiya, exploring whether Hynes Dawson could provide the services that she and her husband, wealthy and thus vulnerable individuals, so desperately required. She fiddled with the red leather strap on her Piaget. Nearing four p.m. in London. The lawyers at Hynes Dawson were doubtless hard at work. Anna looked to Grigory, who nodded. "Ready."

Anna dialed Sia's office line. To keep things tight, there were several pages of scripted answers on the table. Thanks to her father's tour in London, Anna spoke English fluently, but she felt a little rusty and had spent the night before practicing the speech. Anna pulled the papers close to her as the phone rang.

[Recording begins 7:00 p.m. MSK]

Hortensia Fox: Hello?

Anna Andreevna Agapova: Hello. Is this Hortensia Fox at Hynes Dawson?

Hortensia Fox: It is. Please call me Sia. May I ask to whom am I speaking?

Anna Andreevna Agapova: Certainly, Sia. My name is Anna Agapova, I am a managing director in Bank Rossiya's Private Wealth Division, calling on behalf of a few of my clients.

Hortensia Fox: I see. [Three-second pause] May I ask how you stumbled across Hynes Dawson? We typically operate on a referral basis.

Anna Andreevna Agapova: [Reading from notes] I represent several clients in Russia, though it is probably best if I do not mention them on the phone. Hynes Dawson has come up recently in my discussions with them. And you, Sia, specifically. Glowing reviews. [Chuckles]

Hortensia Fox: [Reciprocates chuckling] I am always happy for positive reviews.

Anna Andreevna Agapova: Well, the reason for my call is that my husband—also a banker here—and I will be passing through London next week and I was wondering if we might have dinner? We are keen to understand a bit more about Hynes Dawson and whether it might offer opportunities for several of our clients.

Hortensia Fox: [Tapping sounds . . . Line OT comment: likely a keyboard] Very interesting, Anna. Well, face-to-face is certainly ideal for these initial discussions. I find those awful video calls to be terribly impersonal.

Anna Andreevna Agapova: I could not agree more, Sia. What do you say to dinner? Perhaps on Wednesday or Thursday.

Hortensia Fox: [Pause . . . Line OT comment: likely reviewing calendar] Well, I say lovely. Why don't we have the assistants coordinate? My email is hfox@hynesdawson.com. [Spells out]

Anna Andreevna Agapova: Perfect, Sia. I look forward to our dinner.

Hortensia Fox: Likewise, Anna. Cheers.

Anna Andreevna Agapova: Cheers.

[Hortensia Fox terminates call. Recording ends 7:04 p.m. MSK]

———

SIA PUT THE PHONE IN THE RECEIVER, ENERGY RIPPLING FROM A HAM-
mering heart to serene hands. Goose steals from Agapov and I am
charged with hiding the money, she thought. Then an Agapov calls me.
I am in the shadows. She'd scaffolded her life around the addiction of
this feeling. She could focus on nothing else. And she could not sit still.

Cinching the belt of her cashmere coat, Sia creaked down the circular staircase and outside into a dreary fall afternoon, charting a
winding route to her flat so she could think. Pale sun was filtering
through the clouds. Sia screened phone calls from three harried associates as she strolled past the rows of stucco town houses, glittering
jewelry boutiques, and an art gallery hawking a Balmoral watercolor
painted by the King. That caught her wandering eye until a sales associate with a barcode tattoo on her wrist appeared and Sia begged off.
She bought a chicken dinner from a high-end grocery in Belgravia
and went home.

In her flat Sia opened a bottle of white wine and, as she took
most meals, ate alone on her couch. She topped off the wine and
padded to the leather chair in the corner of her bedroom, glowing
under a reading lamp. Sia did not know precisely how, but the chair
had found its way into the shipping container that had ferried her
earthly belongings to London when she'd left Lyric in San Francisco
for Hynes Dawson.

She removed the cushion and used her left thumb to find the right spot on the frame. Applying pressure, she then found a second spot under the armrest and worked her right thumb around until she heard a soft pop and the concealment device, the CD, inside the seat opened. In the CD Sia stored forty-five thousand dollars in cash— evenly split between dollars, euros, and pounds—three clean alias passports, a prosthetic nose and jawpiece, disguise eyeglasses, a laptop, and a .38 Special handgun and a box of ammunition for which she had no paperwork.

She removed the laptop and shut the CD. The laptop had been issued by Hynes Dawson but had spent a few days with a technical team during one of Sia's first business trips back to the States. Sia typed out a long sequence—numbers, letters, symbols, compressing multiple keys simultaneously—until a blue screen flashed to indicate she had successfully accessed the laptop's second partition, which was staged online.

A generous sip of wine, and she logged in to the cable-writing software. Communicating with Langley was a bitch as a NOC, an officer under non-official cover. She operated alone, which she liked, but the comms isolation was miserable. She would lob a message to Langley, they'd lob back, and around and around it went.

Sia topped off her wine and felt a rush of adrenaline as she considered the case. She was swimming in a pool of Russian fish, targets of clear and immediate interest to Moscow X. These were the varietal of Russian scalp—moneyed, corrupt, connected—that might pave the way for her promotion to GS-14, finally put in the rearview some of the lackluster Performance Appraisal Reviews from her prior inside officer, who had accused her, rightly, of filtering information from her cables that would give Langley pause about approving her operations.

She finished writing up the Agapova phone call and submitted trace requests to Langley. She noted the wonkiness of her surface area with two rival groups of filthy-rich Russians but spun it as an opportunity. Which it was.

Sia hit the same keyboard sequence and saw her normal laptop screen appear. The Wi-Fi was connected, clandestinely pumping encrypted blobs from the partition back to Langley. She tossed back the rest of the wine. Pleasantly drunk, she shut the laptop in the CD and fell onto the bed. She was asleep in seconds, her last waking thought that she should probably take off her blouse. Or at least wriggle under the comforter.

9

San Cristobal, Mexico

MAXIMILIANO CASTILLO COULD FEEL THE THUNDERSTORM ROLL-ing down off the mountains. The pressure, the change in the air, set a dull pain knocking inside his skull. And the coming rain was nothing you'd want an Emirati royal to suffer through, even if His Highness Prince Saeed bin Maktoum bin Hasher al Maktoum was a minor player, a vagabond third cousin of the Sheikh of Dubai. The Emirati wanted to ride, though. So be it. Max wanted to break the Emirati and the rain might help, if it came to it.

The good Prince had been around horses all his life; he said so anyhow. He'd been dispatched to San Cristobal to consider the horseflesh, but Max didn't think he knew much about horses and probably didn't know much about rain, and Max was tired; two days with the Prince, and the smile was difficult to hold, the jokes impossible to summon. It felt like booting a mare to gallop that's got nothing left. *Pinche Arabe.*

Fucking Emirati.

He stood from his bed and went to the window and looked out across the western reaches of the hacienda.

The room had been his mother and father's, and his father's mother and father before that. And it went back five more generations until you got to a villa outside Toledo he'd visited once, with Papa, when he was ten. You could trace the Castillo name from there, and the last living one was here watching a roan mare canter through his western pasture. The mare was Valeria. A four-year-old broodmare out of his senior sire

Rex and a mare, La Duena Elena. The air was dampening and the horses could feel the storm, so he could feel it. He wanted to walk the barns alone, shoot pool and drink, and then talk to Roberto about horses. But the damn Emirati.

His eyes skipped quickly over the stucco capilla that was now Papa's living tomb, and drew up to the western horizon. The sun was filtering out.

Max got into his pants and a white shirt, hanging in the bathroom and still warm from Martina's iron. He splashed mescal into a glass and finished it. He picked up a pair of dark alligator leather boots given to him by Alejandra Garza Sada on their last night together before her wedding. He sat and got half his right foot in there and stopped. He still could not believe she'd gone through with it. He'd had to attend, of course, a Castillo could not miss a Garza Sada wedding, even if the Castillo in question had spent much of his adult life in love with the bride, often in secret. The sheets he'd churned in his nap, alone, brought soured joyful memories of Alejandra, and so he cracked his jaw around and put the boots back in his closet and stood at the window looking at his land. Sky was bad: Gray-green rim, open like a vault, the disturbance trickling nearer, turning to wind brushing the long grass and the juniper and piñon and the maguey. You didn't know this sky, and you wouldn't know what was coming, though. You'd think a clear bright sunset would be announcing the night.

He slid on the anteater-leather boots and belt that had been Grandpa's and the gold chain with the cross that had come across the Atlantic in 1782, from Toledo to Sevilla to Veracruz and up to Monterrey. No one who'd worn that chain had lived past fifty until Max's grandfather. Killed by all manner of accident and murderous violence but only recently by old age. Looking down at that old converted capilla, and he thought old age maybe wasn't so kind a murderer. He'd have preferred Papa knifed in a Sevilla whorehouse to what was killing him now.

Downstairs Max sat with Roberto in the salon. Hall clock ticking. His great-great-grandmother stared down at him through a painting on the wall above. An untouched bottle of champagne sweated on crunching ice. In the privacy of San Cristobal the Prince had taken to drinking without limit. Like a priest in a whorehouse. Tick tick tick. He looked to Roberto. "We ride the pass, after the business?"

"*Patrón?* It will be very wet. And that will take us well past dark."

"The Prince said he wanted an experience. And he's late."

With a snap, Max sent one of Roberto's men into the hall for a look. When he returned, he whispered to Max, "The Prince's bodyman sends his apologies and asks for fifteen minutes."

"Did he actually send his apologies?" Max asked.

The man's nose wrinkled; he coughed, slowly shook his head.

Max went outside. On the veranda he drank another mescal and smoked a cigar. He handed the one intended for the Emirati to Roberto's man and he didn't have to say anything for it to vanish back to the humidor. He tapped a short message to a strange number in his phone. He sensed Roberto behind him.

"There have been cougars up on the pass since June," Roberto said. "And the Emirati is—"

"Make sure there are jackets," Max said.

"The rain will be unpleasant, *patrón.* The good prince is not accustomed to this, I believe."

"Yes, our friend is a man of the desert. But we cannot be blamed for the weather, can we?"

———

MAX INSTALLED HIMSELF AT THE DESK IN THE LIBRARY LIKE A FEUDAL lord. He made notes in the stud book and reviewed again the papers for the twelve horses the Emirati's bloodstock consultants and trainer had selected. Max knew the bloodlines back four or more generations for each animal, and though this was his business he did not relish parting with the horses. But the Emirati operation was solid. The dandy Prince played a minor operational role; he was an emissary sent to handle a simple transaction. A troubled man in need of a task.

They'd been in the Emirati's room, of course, and knew about the Prince's pills, for focus and his wilting sex drive. The cameras were not installed for the purposes of improving San Cristobal's negotiation strategy, but they did not hurt: Max knew his price and he would extract more because the Emirati could afford it and he could not return without horses. Very few visitors came and left without horses. From a drawer of the walnut desk Max slid out a thick business card—gold-embossed with the raised farm logo of San Cristobal and a QR code. He snuggled it into the pocket of his sport coat.

In longhand he made notes for Roberto—on the renovation of the breeding shed, then the arrival of a mare from a Brazilian operation on a breeding contract with Smokey Joe, a prized San Cristobal stallion who'd run his last. The office clock ticked, and though Max preferred this work to his guest, after an hour it seemed to him it was part of the Emirati's negotiating strategy, and that set his pencil tapping the stud book's leather covering. He called Roberto.

"*Sí, patrón?*"

"Put the races on."

Max shrugged on the sport coat and left for the study, his boots knocking pleasantly on the fading red tiles.

———

THE THEATER HAD BEEN A PRIVATE CHAPEL UNTIL 1949. THE SMELL WAS musty and stale and an iron chandelier hung on a chain from the cupola above. The walls still bore faded frescoes, but the pews had been turned to credenzas running along the sides of the room and during races usually groaned with food and drink. "*Patrón*, shall I have Manuela bring out a few things?" Roberto asked. His eyes cast about the empty room.

Max nodded and sat on one of the sofas in front of the television. "Tell the Prince to come here when he's ready."

The pre-race coverage rolled on the television above. Max fetched another cigar from the humidor, and when he'd returned the Prince was sitting on the sofa scrolling on his phone. "Your Highness," Max said. He took a seat next to the Prince and puffed smoke upward. Manuela wheeled in a cart of bottles and mixers and glasses. She set a tray of nuts and popcorn and tortilla chips and salsas alongside and left.

"Business at home?" Max asked.

The Emirati hungrily eyed his cigar, awaiting an offer that did not come. Then he said, "A few pressing matters."

"Well, I trust you've settled them. Our business now needs a bit of settling. Your numbers do not work. Too low." He leaned the cigar on the lip of a brass ashtray shaped like a galloping stallion and stood to fix a drink.

A scratchy noise registered in the Prince's throat.

"What would you like?" Max asked, turning bottles here and there, brandishing labels.

"Johnnie Blue. Neat."

Max poured three fat fingers for the Prince and filled his own with a smoky mescal. Max returned to his seat and drew on his cigar and slid the card with the QR code from his pocket and put it on the Prince's knee, careful to touch his pants with his fingers and to press the card down harder than he should, indenting the fabric for a fluttering moment. The Prince's eyes flared, but the violation was too shadowy, too circumstantial to merit protest. He held his tongue, looked at the card.

"San Cristobal's entire inventory of horseflesh and recent global sales comps," Max said. "Have a look. You'll see that you're low, Your Highness."

The Prince's extended family ran Dubai, and someone had doubtless explained to him the folly of what he was now considering. But His Highness was an empty-handed emissary in a heathen land, agitated at the calculated disrespect and prone to foolishness. So he took the iPhone from his pocket and framed it over the card and pressed the little flickering blue button and Max counted slowly and silently one two three four five and the Prince was reviewing a report on twelve horses but something, deep and unseen, was burrowing into his phone, a gift from Max's more unconventional friends. He was treated to a familiar tingly jolt running clean through his balls.

On the television, Max watched a jockey wearing white, blue, and red racing silks trot a colt toward the starting gates. "RusFarm?" Max asked, pointing the cigar at the screen.

The Prince looked up from his phone. "My cousin felt the Russians should be invited. Horses are above international squabbles. Why should the Russians not race, just because of the war? And RusFarm is a private stable, after all. I've actually been there once," he said in his English accent. "Dark bloody woodsy place, but the facilities are top-notch, the talent they've acquired is excellent, and from a pedigree standpoint they were making progress before they stopped buying in the U.S. and the U.K." The Prince wrinkled his nose. "Bloody sanctions."

"I hear Putin owns it." Max let the comment hang in the air.

"Now, now, now. Nasty rumors. And who bloody cares about the owner? It's about the horses, in the end."

Max raised his glass; the Prince clinked his. They drank.

The starting gates flung open, and Max watched the RusFarm horse move. The chestnut Thoroughbred Judo Master banged into the metal, quickly slipping into the ninth position. The horse remained well off the fence and galloped with what Max could see were strides far too short for his height. Rattled from smacking into the gate. By the first turn he'd fallen into twelfth, fifteen lengths off the leader, a horse owned by the racing stables of Sheikh Mohammed bin Rashid Al Maktoum, ruler of Dubai and the host of the race. A third cousin to Max's current guest, as the Prince pointedly reminded him.

Through the television, Max tried to look the horse in the eye. You could see a horse's heart through its eyes and he wanted to see what kind this one had. Judo Master was an impressive physical specimen— well muscled, tall, with long legs and nice conformation—but heart was what won races, and by the second turn Max knew that the horse did not have it. With the leader halfway down the backstretch, Judo Master had slipped into the thirteenth slot and the jockey was uselessly working the whip to avoid an embarrassing last-place finish. Max didn't count, but he was pretty sure that by the time they rounded the far turn onto the homestretch, the jockey had reached or exceeded his twelve-strike limit. In Dubai you could only smack the horse twelve times during a race.

With Putin's horse now trailing by more than twenty lengths, Max turned his attention to the showdown between Sheikh Mohammed's horse and one owned by a Japanese billionaire. With fifty meters left, the Sheikh's horse tapped an extra reserve and began to pull in front, crossing the finish three lengths ahead. Judo Master straggled in dead last, nearly thirty lengths back.

"Nine million even for the whole lot of twelve," the Prince said, "and not a dollar more." There was a ring of hesitation in his voice, and they had the room wired anyhow and knew the Prince could go higher.

Max crushed his cigar in the ashtray and tossed back the mescal. "I find that I want to get on a horse after watching a race. Let's take a ride, continue this discussion in the fresh air, what do you say? A trail runs from the pastures up into the mountains. Beautiful country. Back by dark."

"I'm out of time, I'm afraid. So no, thank you. Next time. This is the final offer, Castillo. They are fueling the plane and I am expected in Dubai tomorrow." The Prince stood and stretched and feigned a yawn and met Max's eyes, but he could not hold them.

"Anything to say?" the Prince said. His tone had stiffened.

Another man might have relented. Might have wondered if he'd overplayed his hand negotiating against one of the world's premier Thoroughbred stables. But another man would not have access to intercepted communications that revealed the Prince's bluff. It was true that he was expected in Dubai tomorrow. With horses.

"No," Max said. "No, I don't suppose there is."

———

MAX LEANED ONTO THE PICKUP'S HOOD ON THE RUNWAY APRON, watching Roberto's men load bags into the Emirati's G800. The Prince had said goodbye and disappeared into the cabin, and the flight attendants, two slender Slavic blondes in too-tall heels and too-tight uniforms, were chatting with each other and reviewing Max with undisguised interest. When he met their eyes and smiled, they smiled back and giggled and turned away and shared a secret. Someone called from inside the aircraft and they climbed the steps and disappeared into the plane with a flirty wave. The door shut. The engines rushed. Lights blinkered to life. Max spat on the concrete. The plane crawled forward. Stopped. Engines died. For a moment it sat there. Then the door cracked open, stairs descended, and the Prince's bodyman emerged, trotting down to meet him.

———

LATER THAT EVENING, WITH THE PRINCE IN THE SKIES BOUND FOR THE Gulf, Max unsaddled his favorite mare, Penelope, brushed her, and saw to her evening feed. He took a long hot shower and retrieved an iPad from the safe in his closet. He took a mescal to the chair in the bedroom where he'd been read to as a boy and now sat alone as a man.

On the iPad, instead of his standard six-digit passcode or fingerprint, he entered a twenty-six-count alphanumeric sequence to unlock a partitioned hard drive hidden on the device. He opened an app, identical to the Notes app pre-loaded on every Apple product. He saw a short note from Artemis explaining that they'd successfully accessed the Prince's phone. There was a clipped reference to the bonus that would be wired through the usual maze to arrive at an account held by a shell corporation owned by a San Cristobal subsidiary. Papa had explained how it all worked, but the amounts were so meager he'd not checked the balances in well on two years. The Castillos didn't do this for the money, not now at least, not since the first years back in the sixties, well before his birth, and though he understood why the money was necessary for everybody to feel good, he didn't want to look it in the face and think about that. He deleted the message.

He punched out a sparse note summarizing the Prince's visit. Then he put down another glass of mescal and, relishing the white-hot fire flooding his throat, he held a specific combination of buttons until the message vanished. He locked the iPad, then entered his usual six-digit passcode to check that everything was normal.

He found Roberto eating a steak on the veranda to the whine of crickets and the piddling watercourse of the pool fountains. Max sat. Manuela brought *arrachera*, blackened flank steak, sliced over a bed of charred green poblano and onions, a stone bowl of her red salsa, and a warm plate with tortillas shrouded by cloth. She squeezed the juice of half a lime over the meat and uncapped a bottle of Tecate and Max kissed her cheek and held the veiny pallor of her hand for a brief moment. She left them. When he'd taken his first bites, Roberto slid an envelope across the table. Max had known the Emirati's handwriting since reviewing the footage of his room, and he'd known that slight curl in Roberto's lips since he'd helped the man break horses, once, when he'd been much too young.

10

Langley

ARTEMIS PROCTER HAD ONCE INVOLUNTARILY PARTICIPATED IN A consultant-led focus group on the topic of CIA "Modernization." The consultant explained the concept to Procter, describing the wholesale reorganization of CIA using terms such as "organizational health," "business process improvement," and "enterprise agility." He chattered of openness and information sharing, which rang to Procter's ears of outsiders inviting her to loosen up, get her agents killed and dragged through the streets with their ears and whatnots hacked off. She had found the focus group experience on par with that of a recreational episiotomy, and she wrote that on the feedback form.

Procter had decided she would stop Modernization's march at the gates of Moscow X. Her reign as Chief would be characterized by decidedly pre-Enlightenment rules. On her first day, she'd taped above her office door a poster of Putin's head on a spike with the words BACK TO THE DARK AGES emblazoned on top. Modernization be damned.

Part of the deal with Bradley had been that she would not be required to situate Moscow X in the main Russia House spaces. She found them cluttered and distracting, clotted with discarded furniture and posters and flags and bookshelves that made her feel like she was working in a bombed-out Home Depot. Procter instead set up the Moscow X shop in a room that had belonged to a now-shuttered entity called the Russia House NOC Advisory Support Team, or the RH/NAST. But because uncleared tourists and foreigners traipsed through Langley on the daily, the silver plate on the door dropped the RUSSIA HOUSE and NOC and simply read ADVISORY SUPPORT TEAM. Everyone had called it the NASTy. Members were known as Nasties. For the most part, people had steered clear. Procter liked it that way.

Moscow X, like most Langley components, occupied a drab cubicle farm, though the vault did boast two luxurious windows overlooking a gravel-covered rooftop of the Original Headquarters Building. Most vaults boasted flags, memorabilia, and photos. Across the hall, in Russia House proper, Soviet flags fluttered in recycled air and a brass bust of Gorbachev sat near the door. People rubbed his wine-stain birthmark as they came and went. The Russia House walls were flocked with photos of Putin acting like a weirdo: falling during a hockey match, smiling at a topless protester, kissing a young boy on the stomach, pointing a crossbow at a gray whale. But not the Moscow X vault. Procter frowned on such cheerful sentimentality.

And though Moscow X is among the most insular, secretive CIA components, within its walls rumor and gossip flow like water. Soon whispers of the sordid affair surrounding the new Chief's departure from Dushanbe tickled the ears of even its lowliest officers. The stabbing elevated Procter's legend, while the online availability of hundreds of nude pictures fueled, for a few days, a tug-of-war, a dilemma pitting curiosity against the punishments that would surely be meted out to those known, or suspected, of having imbibed.

One week into Procter's rule, a GS-9 analyst mentioned the photos in an instant-messaging conversation and the next day vanished from Moscow X. He turned up weeks later, exiled on a two-year rotation to the Langley printing shop, arm in a sling, slight hitch in his stride. I fell down the stairs, he stuttered to a colleague over lunch in the cafeteria, slunk into a darkened table thick with the chemical-bread smell of the nearby Subway. A nasty fall. Clumsy me. The matter was settled in favor of punishment, and the photos, though not forgotten, would never again be mentioned.

Procter's new office sat at one end of the vault. A single light shone down on her desk and a metal chair faced the wall, presumably for special guests, though visitors would be rare. A QVC segment hawking wide leg crop pants blared from a wall-mounted television. The old Cleveland baseball bat was propped against the wall. In this comforting glow, Procter opened a bag of Twizzlers and began sorting through shots from the Moscow X NOC stable.

She opened the cable from Sia Fox. By the time she had finished, the licorice rope had fallen from her mouth onto the keyboard.

Not only was Anna Agapova a well-connected daughter of Russia, but she was also the wife of Vadim Kovalchuk, a Putin moneyman. A gift from the gods of espionage, Procter mumbled to herself. CIA Christmas come early. So much potential.

She had a butterball analyst for odd jobs. Ripping open her door, she yelled for Debman to get in here, pronto. Procter, who had been told in several gobbledygook upward-feedback reports that she possessed the leadership instincts of a tiger centipede, instructed Debman that he would not leave the building until he'd finished the report. He disappeared to his cubicle to conduct traces and run early research.

Returning to her office late that evening, Debman placed the results in front of Procter as if it were a burnt offering and took the extravagant liberty of sitting in her guest chair while she read. Procter cracked back open the Twizzler bag and got to it.

1. CI TRACES ON ANNA ANDREEVNA AGAPOVA REVEAL THAT SUBJ IS 36-YEAR-OLD RUSSIAN NATIONAL AND CURRENT EMPLOYEE AT BANK ROSSIYA. BORN IN LENINGRAD/PETERSBURG IN 1987 TO RETIRED KGB/SVR MAJOR GENERAL AND CURRENT CHAIRMAN OF ROSSIYA INDUSTRIAL, ANDREI AGAPOV, AND GALINA TIMOFAYEVNA PETROVA (DECEASED—1998).

2. SUBJ IS GRADUATE OF LOMONOSOV MOSCOW STATE UNIVERSITY (2009). REF A COLLATERAL INDICATES SUBJ WORKED AT BANK ROSSIYA IN GENEVA (2010–2014) BEFORE RETURNING TO RUSSIA.

3. SUBJ MARRIED VADIM YURIVICH KOVALCHUK, SON OF FORMER BANK ROSSIYA CHAIRMAN AND CEO YURI KOVALCHUK (DECEASED—2017), IN SAINT PETERSBURG CIVIL CEREMONY IN 2011.

4. VADIM KOVALCHUK IS THE PRINCIPAL OWNER AND OPERA-
TOR OF RUSFARM, A THOROUGHBRED HORSE OPERATION. REF
B COLLATERAL INDICATES FARM IS BACKED BY A CONSORTIUM
INCLUDING ANDREI AGAPOV AND THE RUSSIAN PRESIDENT.

Leaning back in her chair, Procter realized Debman was still there. "Holy hell, man," she gasped. "You scared the shit out of me."

Shooing Debman from the office, Procter ate a few more licorice ropes and extinguished the lone desk lamp.

She lay down on the floor.

To any observer it would have appeared as though Procter had entered a liminal space in which her body remained prone in the office, her mind long evaporated. Her eyes were shut, her palms faced the ceiling, her chest rose and fell slowly as if she were in a coma. Her adductor muscles were scorched from afternoon thigh work in the gym.

An hour later, the idea first tickled. Two hours after that, Procter thought she had enough to get to work.

She sat up and wiped the corners of her mouth. Somewhere along the journey she'd fallen asleep for a bit. She ate more licorice and wondered if she should get Bradley involved. Nope. We're still tits-deep in the operational soup, Procter thought, no need to worry the boss man.

She opened a database and entered a cryptonym, TX/MANCUB, into the search engine.

Nearly all CIA assets are foreign citizens. The TX digraph denoted the oddity that MANCUB, true name Harry Hamilton, was an American, the founder and CEO of the technology company Lyric. Harry allowed the CIA to use Lyric to build cover for some of its NOCs, and he typically played ball when Procter asked for help.

But this time, Procter expected, would be different. Alone in her office, she scanned a database of auction prices for Thoroughbred racehorses and chuckled aloud. Harry had zero interest in horses. He did not own a horse. He did not attend horse races. He may have never sat on a horse. Harry was not going to like this.

11

Palo Alto

M AX WALKED ACROSS A STRETCH OF APRON AT PALO ALTO AIRPORT, moving past the CIA Air Branch loadmaster as he reached the top of the stairs to enter the Gulfstream G550. The interior's prodigious use of faux-wood and its cud-colored carpeting indicated that this aircraft was owned not by a celebrity or a billionaire, or even his ranch, but instead by a government bureaucracy whose procurement machinery, despite the benefit of a corporate cutout, had failed to update the upholstery to anything more contemporary than "Hawaiian avocado." Across the tarmac sat his own jet, San Cristobal's G650ER. He understood from the cables that Procter had a proposal for him, and that a NOC lawyer Hortensia Fox was somehow involved. He also understood the request to be unconventional. Artemis had included so few details in her message that there could be no other explanation.

Max shuffled over the stained carpet toward Procter, who stood to shake his hand. Hortensia Fox trailed into the plane. Her walk was assured, even aggressive, and in her slipstream hung a scent of floral and citrus that transported him to San Cristobal's gardens. The rough pads on her offered hand ran pleasantly against his own.

"Max Castillo," he said. "Pleasure to meet you, Hortensia."

"Sia Fox," she said, withdrawing her hand. "Not Hortensia. Never Hortensia."

For her part, Procter was sporting mobster vibes: a red velour tracksuit and blue tennis shoes. Six cans of Coors Light chilled in an ice bucket on the table, a bottle of mescal alongside. Sia sat across from him, next to Procter, who cracked open a beer. Max examined the mescal, deciding to risk it though he did not recognize the label—in his experience with Procter labels were typically unrecognizable.

"Mescal?" he said to Sia, lifting the bottle. "Though I can't vouch for it."

She shook her head, almost impolitely, and instead removed a bottle of water from her purse.

"It is good to see you, Artemis," Max said. "You look well." In truth she looked older, weathered. Her black hair, though, as usual, gave the impression she had been plugged into an electrical socket. He'd met Procter once, a few years before, when he'd helped CIA gain access to a Jordanian businessman's computer. Then, Procter served in CIA's Amman Station. He was not sure of the role. They did not offer that information unless he asked. And Max never asked.

"Well, that's kind of you," Procter said. "And you're not looking so bad yourself. Horses treating you just fine."

"They tend to."

"And kudos on the op against the Emirati. The intel's been helpful to the analysts working on Russia's sanctions-busting networks in the Gulf." Procter saluted with her beer and a long thirsty pull. Max reciprocated with a quick sip of his mescal.

"And Sia," Procter said, "you look swell, too. Nice to see you, hon. Thanks for popping across the pond for this."

"Of course, Artemis. Dying to know what you've cooked up."

Max stole a glance at Sia. Long dark hair, hazy gray eyes, sun-colored skin. Afrikaans lilt to her speech that he found interesting. And she was tall, almost as tall as he was, and fashionably assembled, dress and heels custom from somewhere in London or Milan, he'd wager. He'd seen these women come and go at San Cristobal, usually on the arm of a wealthy and older man. Most of them seemed accessible, overly so. So open and flirty and casual that you knew there would be no challenge, no dance, and that if they didn't make you work they hadn't made other men, either. But her back was straight, upright, whatever engine inside her the type that does not stop ticking even when it should. Or could. Her eyes bore through him now and they were assessing, searching for danger, threats, weakness, he sensed. They'd not known each other five minutes and she was already thinking of breaking him. He normally enjoyed that look, but it hadn't happened to him on an op before. He sipped at the mediocre mescal. He wasn't sure what to think of this Hortensia Fox.

"The cables were vague," Procter started in, "and I'm sorry about that. I get antsy putting ideas this terrific in formal channels. Gives me hives." From a folder in her purse Procter produced photos and spread them on the table. "Vadim Kovalchuk," she said, "is the son of the now-deceased Yuri Kovalchuk, one of Putin's childhood friends. Vadim runs a piece of Putin's private office out of Bank Rossiya in Saint Petersburg. Insofar as we can separate Putin's finances from the state, this is where it happens. He knows where a lot of Putin's personal stash is spread and buried. High-priority target. And it turns out Vadim here also operates Russia's premier Thoroughbred operation. Putin is involved. Little Russkie version of San Cristobal. You know it, Max?" Care to give us the scoop?

"Of course. Though they just got flattened in Dubai, RusFarm has been on the move as of late. Unprecedented investment in top bloodlines out of the Gulf and, if the rumors are true, the U.S. and U.K. when they can find the right sanctions work-arounds. Some nasty whispers about doping the horses, but I understand they've not been confirmed. I've never met Kovalchuk, though. And I've never visited the farm."

"Wait, are you an FNO or a NOC?" Sia asked him. A NOC was an American citizen, sometimes with a foreign passport. Max, a foreign national officer, was a trusted non-American who did sensitive contract work for CIA. NOCs had to play by the bureaucracy—expense reports, the GS pay scale, sending a cable before you scratched yourself. Max did not. Sia's was a fair question, but NOCs tended to be edgy about the distinction, and her voice seemed flavored by a bitter undertone at her presumed second-class status.

"Family's been doing business with CIA since the sixties," Max said. He did not acknowledge the FNO title. CIA could log him in their databases as whatever they wanted. The acronym had no claim on him.

Sia's body stiffened, and Procter, taking no notice, rolled on. "But this is where we got lucky," she said. "Because our little friend Vadim is married to this woman, a prospective client of Sia's, Anna Andreevna Agapova." Max accepted the photo, which appeared to be scraped from Bank Rossiya's website. She had flaxen hair and chilly blue eyes and high cheekbones. Her face told the camera to screw off. He liked her already.

Max turned the photo to Procter. "Different surnames?"

Procter grunted. "They could be estranged. Who knows?"

"I've got a meeting with Anna in London set for next week," Sia said, turning to him. "And she's bringing Vadim."

"But here's the problem," Procter said. "Sia's got the access to the Russian couple through her law firm. Max has the farm—a place we can operate, dangle some horse bait, see if we get a bite. Vadim, Anna, Max, and Sia." Procter counted them off until she held up four fingers, which she wiggled at each of them. "There is one missing connection in this joyful little foursome," she said. "The one between you two. So that got this girl thinking. What's the best way to ensnare Vadim Kovalchuk?" Procter shoved aside the beer and spread a page of chicken-scratch notes across the table.

Max glanced from the notes to Sia's bouncing calves, then up to her furious eyes.

"Harry and I, we were not lovers, Artemis," Sia said.

"My bad," Procter said. She clicked open a pen and crossed out *former lover.* Then the Chief tied up her hair with a rubber band and said, "Imagine this: You two are acquainted by chance through one Harry Hamilton. He's suddenly got a billionaire hard-on for horses, and sure enough he's invited Maximiliano here up to Palo Alto for a little chat. Old Harry's also brought his former Lyric employee and friend Sia along. The meeting I mentioned in my albeit brief cable is in"—Procter checked her watch—"three hours. At this meeting you two and Harry have a nice talk about horses and what he might buy from San Cristobal. Maximiliano, at the end you say: Why don't we all head down to San Cristobal for a scouting trip? You both also happen to think the other is peachy. You all go down old Mexico way: wine, tequila, tacos, bareback horse riding, whatever-the-fuck. And then Sia comes up with a great idea. Anna and her husband should come down to Mexico for dinner instead of visiting London. They are filthy-rich Russians, and jetting down to San Cristobal for a few days should be easy. Hell, it's gotta be easier for them to get documents to visit Mexico than the U.K. these days. We're doing them a favor. Plus, unlike everything else Sia does in London, this way I won't have to read in the Brits."

Procter opened another Coors. "You two play Romeo and Juliet and we access Vadim's tech, Max, according to the usual playbook. The San Cristobal two-day special. Hell, maybe check if we have any angles on Vadim? Peek into the blast furnace, see what gets him going, assess his recruitment potential." She paused, drained half the can while looking around to read the energy, then steamrolled on. "Now, before anyone gets all bothered, starts complaining about the risks and blah blah blah, well, let's agree on a few terms. One, this is temporary. No need to convince the Russkies you're sweet on each other for all that long. Two, we own the turf. It ain't the Russian badlands, it's Mexico, and the hacendado here is a friend. The Russians are playing our game, an exploratory tickle across their Slavic belly hairs puts your platforms at little risk. Plus we're not exactly getting face time with loads of Russians these days, Ukraine and all, and when we can, we take our shots. Access to Putin's money would give us beautiful opportunities for fuckery and general mayhem. Now I'll shut up. Max, what do you think? Are you game for this?" She finished her Coors and opened another, which foamed and ran down the sides and over her fingers. Procter did not seem to notice.

He looked to Sia. That Procter had not asked Sia's opinion, that she was addressing Max, that it was a request of him and an order to her, he could see that all of this had rankled Sia, because her right foot had begun bouncing on the floor and she was fidgeting with her sculpted hair and avoiding his eyes. "Sia," he said, "you've been developing Anna. For how long?"

"The meeting next week is our first," Sia said.

"You haven't met her?"

"No."

"And she reached out to you?"

"Yes."

"Why?"

"My law firm, my NOC platform, we hide dirty money. Crooked little operation out of London. Anna's interested in our services for a few of her clients. And probably for Vadim."

"But why *you*?"

"A good deal of my business is filthy Russian money." Her tone was sharpening with each response.

"And what was going to be your angle? To develop Anna, or Vadim?"

This time she gave only a glare.

Max put up his hand and took a sip of mescal. "No matter. Time for that later."

An exasperated spurt of air escaped Sia's nostrils. She flicked a forelock of dark hair from her face and turned away toward the window, swinging her left leg across her right. He caught the gloss of rage in her eyes and felt that she was comfortable fighting, maybe even enjoyed it, and that she disliked him, immediately and on principle. And maybe on specifics, he could not be sure.

He had the picture, anyhow. Sia got credit—and thus promotions, pay bumps, and prestige—for recruitments above all. She hadn't started working Anna, and Procter had just offered Sia a supporting role in a scheme to help *him* work Vadim. He was stealing her kill.

"What do you think, Maximiliano?" Procter asked. "A little prep trip with Harry and Sia, then the Russians come for the two-day special?"

And though Sia's dress stretched past her knees, he sensed from her frustrated, bouncing calves and her bearing and her height that her legs were athletically muscled and also quite long and if they approached the color of her face they would be pleasantly tan. He looked to Procter and said, "I am happy to help. The plan is a good one."

He turned back to Sia in time for another audible sigh from her flared nostrils. "Artemis," Sia began, "if Anna is as highly connected as we think, why in the hell do we see her as a path to Vadim? She is a valuable target on her own. And I'm best positioned to work that target."

Procter plucked the tab off the Coors and twirled it in a flourish toward Sia, who had fallen silent. "Go on, hon, finish your thought, you won't offend old Artemis."

"I don't think we have to do it this way. I can develop Anna myself. I don't need"—she glared at Max—"to shuttle Anna halfway across the world to a Mexican ranch. I can work her in the U.K., in Europe, hell, I can work her in Russia if necessary," Sia said, shooting a sidelong glance at Max.

"She's a fine target," Procter said. "I agree. But she doesn't, far as we know, manage Putin's money. I want the money. Vadim Kovalchuk is the one who sees where a good chunk of the President's cash goes."

"Give me a shot with Anna," Sia said. "Let's see how that goes first."

Procter shook her head. "Why? My way is direct. Need me to diagram it out, hon? Plus, if Anna ends up being a valuable target on her own, you are right there to work her. A wingman helps you, Hortensia. And, look, I'm not asking you guys to bone or anything. Just kiss each other on the cheek and maybe hold hands in front of them."

Sia poured herself a few fingers of mescal and sat back in her seat. She took a few agitated sips and sized Max up with a scowl.

"And I know you love horses," Procter continued. "You're a ranch girl, Sia. Horses are *bueno*. Am I right?"

Sia glared at Procter. "Yes, Artemis, you know I love horses. I grew up around horses." Sia turned to Max. "Is anyone else down there in on the CIA connection?"

"Just my father, but he is not well. Early-onset Alzheimer's. He lives in a separate house on the property, tucked away from visitors. Discretion will be in order around the staff."

There was an awkward silence.

Procter looked back and forth between them. "All good with the plan for the Harry meeting and the next few days?"

"Yes," Max said. "Good."

Sia grumbled her assent.

He stood and shook Procter's hand, then offered his to Sia, who accepted the handshake with a wonderfully firm grip and a look of faint disgust.

Adios vaya con dios, Procter said, in her rotten gringa Spanish, as the loadmaster shut the door. Max parted wordlessly with Sia at the bottom of the airstair, setting out for his own car and the trip to Harry Hamilton's office, admiring how she walked and that she did not once glance back at him.

————

MAGGIE GELLER HAD ARRANGED LOADS OF BIZARRE MEETINGS IN HER twenty-seven years as Harry Hamilton's long-suffering executive assistant. A formal powwow between Harry and the King of Jordan and a Texas rancher. A boisterous afternoon for Harry, Bono, and a homeless man from Berkeley. A long weekend at Harry's place in Jackson Hole with a Russian businessman who would later be strangled to death in his bathroom, and one who would merely be shoved from a hotel balcony. The pair she now ushered into Harry's office were less bizarre, but eyebrow-raising nonetheless. They'd passed a silent twenty minutes in the anteroom outside Harry's office as if steeling themselves for an ambush, or perhaps a grim session of couples therapy.

Following closely at Maggie's heels was Hortensia Fox, a Lyric alumna and longtime Hamilton protégé who had run off to London to make even more money. Harry enjoyed younger women, and years earlier there had been nasty suggestions that the two had been lovers. Then, Maggie had paid the rumors little mind. But she now reconsidered. Harry had invited Hortensia to fly across the world to join him on one of his impulsive trips. This time—and even battle-hardened Maggie had struggled to wrap her mind around this part—this time Harry was scouting for racehorses. In Mexico. The opening salvo, perhaps, of his third or fourth midlife crisis.

"Mr. Hamilton," she had said—for she refused to call him Harry— "horses?" The intonation was incredulous, yet polite. He'd eased into his desk chair, avoiding her eyes, and said yes, yes, he was a goddamn billionaire and was getting bored. Horses, he said without conviction, now, horses were interesting.

"But Mr. Hamilton," she protested, increasingly concerned for his safety, "have you ever ridden a horse?"

He laughed. "That's the beautiful thing. All these rich-prick owners, they don't ride the horses. They just pat the animal down after it wins a race. I'll fit right in. I am fucking going to love horses."

The horses were the reason for the second guest, a handsome man by the name of Maximiliano Castillo. He ran a horse-breeding and -racing operation outside Monterrey, Mexico. Harry had asked Maggie to invite him to Palo Alto for a chat. Harry insisted he'd taken an interest in a few of Castillo's horses. Hortensia and Maximiliano shook hands with Harry and they all sat. Maggie quickly closed the door, grateful—as always—that though she suffered the unpleasantness of arranging the meetings, she did not have to bear the ordeal of actually participating in them.

Part II

RAZRABOTKA /
DEVELOPMENT

- 12 -

San Cristobal

H ARRY'S PILOT CIRCLED SAN CRISTOBAL A FEW TIMES SO SIA COULD take it in. The Big Bend ranches of her youth were large but drifted toward run-down and shabby, and it was not uncommon for the property's centerpiece to be a one story, two-bedroom rambler with a corrugated steel roof and peeling paint. But, floating above San Cristobal, through the thin clouds Sia glimpsed hacienda-style barns with matching terra-cotta roofs and a sprawling U-shaped mansion with a glittering swimming pool. There were at least four, maybe five barns, meaning San Cristobal could be home to over one hundred Thoroughbreds. As the G800 began its descent, one detail more than any other hinted at San Cristobal's grandiosity: painted white fencing ringed the entire property and divided the pastures, paddocks, and barns. Maintaining miles of fencing was a headache for any rancher; countless hours of her youth had been spent repairing fence line with her sister on the family's ranch. But ensuring it was painted? Well, that was unimaginable in the Big Bend. Harry, sitting across from her, looked up from a magazine and peered out a window. "Damn," he said.

Memories of home dissipated as the plane touched down. A waiting driver ferried them to the main house, where Max would join them for dinner that evening. They wound around a terra-cotta-roofed stable and then along miles of the white fencing, mares and then yearlings studying the cars as they passed. Lush brown grass carpeted the pastures, the creamy fence paint was immaculate, and the approaching hilltop house was three stories of stone twisted in a lovely chaos of pillared breezeways and balcony gardens and towering palms. Lots of ranchers had land, not many had palaces like this. The place was grand and beautiful, and Sia's experience with grand and beautiful places was that they were usually owned by pricks.

There was the predictable moment in which the attendants led Sia and Harry to the same bedroom. Harry laughed and, as usual, strolled inside without correcting the mistake. When this had first happened years earlier, not long after she took the Lyric job, Sia would flush and snap at Harry for allowing the rumors to linger. Now she calmly explained the error and the rosy-cheeked attendant led her to a stately bedroom with vaulted ceilings, exposed oak beams, and a fireplace the size of a car. She walked into the bathroom: marble, ornate tilework in the steam shower, a dial that controlled heaters in the floor. She held one of the towels and smiled. Her dad had liked to say he was going to steal the towels when they stayed in nice places. Sia remembered that line when she was playing rich: on some Greek isle, a Knightsbridge mansion, or here, on what felt like a feudal farm in northern Mexico. This was a steal-the-towels kind of place. She stuffed one in her suitcase.

———

WHEN HARRY ARRIVED IN THE LIBRARY, MAX THRUST A TUMBLER OF scotch in his hand and, following Procter's instructions, spent the next thirty minutes explaining the farm's bloodlines, stakes race performance, and breeding philosophy, should anyone question Harry about this visit upon his return. Max produced a thick leather book emblazoned with San Cristobal's crest to show the pedigree charts for the yearlings he was so generously offering to Harry, instead of taking them to the sales in Keeneland and Saratoga. Harry twice tried to tell Max it was unnecessary. "I know Artemis would appreciate your effort, and I really do think this place is the tits, but Artemis isn't here and I'm fucking famished. Just sell me the damn horses you've got in mind," he protested.

Sia had heard enough of Harry and Max sparring about the pedigree charts. "I'll have a look," she said with a note of charm, then snatched the book before either could protest. "It's fine," she told Max with a flippant wave. "In real life he wouldn't read the charts anyhow. Would you, Harry?"

Harry laughed, looking out one of the library's picture windows. The view fell down a gentle hill toward a red-roofed training barn. "What the hell am I going to do with these animals once I've bought 'em?"

Without looking up from the book, Sia said, "You'll figure it out, Harry, that's why we love you."

———

AS SIA HAD EXPECTED, THE CHARADE QUICKLY EMPTIED WHAT remained in Harry's shallow well of patience. They toured the training barn, the breeding shed (it was not in use—"I don't wanna see that shit," Harry growled), and one of the yearling pastures. Harry was buried in his phone while the grooms led out the three yearling colts that he was involuntarily purchasing. Harry's amused smile and silence greeted the breeding manager when he asked if the tech tycoon or his friends had any questions or concerns. Though, near the end, he did perk up to briefly watch a horse walk on an equine treadmill submerged in water and another dip into a saltwater bath. "Fucking horses have it better than I do," Harry quipped. At sunset they clinked glasses of champagne on a vine-draped veranda under stone arches overlooking a rolling pasture. The unseasonably warm air tickled Sia's nose with agave and pine. And though Harry was facing the pasture, Sia heard a soft belch and the clatter of his champagne flute meeting a stone table. Harry's drink had disappeared in a single pull.

Thanking Max for his hospitality, Harry announced that he felt like shit, and declared that he was going to bed. "Stay, Sia," he said, "enjoy yourself." He shook Max's hand and left. Max whispered something to the headwaiter, who, with several others, soon returned from the kitchen carrying plates of green salad and *cabrito al pastor* ringed by a spread of tortillas, chopped onions, cilantro, and limes. The headwaiter plunged another bottle of champagne into an ice bucket and then opened a bottle of red, which he left on the table after Max completed the wine ritual.

Max thanked him and the waiters departed. They were alone, the sun was ten minutes above the horizon, and in the fading light the white adobe glowed pink. Then Sia's mind switched tracks. The picturesque setting, the lively spread of food, the disdain for Max that had been festering throughout the day—she banished it all from her mind with barely a thought. Time to work.

"Give me your pitch for Vadim," she said in a military voice.

"I have a stallion here, Smokey Joe, who is half brother to my senior sire, Rex." Sentence punctuated by stabbing his fork into the platter of goat meat.

"Senior sire?"

"My most valuable breeding stallion. Smokey Joe is a stallion with a distinguished racing record. He won the Travers just a few months back, during his three-year-old campaign. He's had a medical complication. I won't bore you with the details, but he won't race again."

The race meant nothing to her, but she held her tongue.

"The point being," Max continued, "he'll be put to stud. His pedigree, conformation, and stakes performance would make him an extremely attractive purchase for anyone prospecting for stallions. And based on what I know of RusFarm's pedigrees, they should be interested. I would typically offer this type of bloodstock at auction, or send him to stand for breeding in Kentucky, but there are private sales all the time. Vadim will be keen. Particularly since Vadim's Russian pedigree makes it tricky for him to do business in Kentucky or the U.K."

They ate in an uncomfortable silence broken only by the sound of busy cutlery. Sia grew increasingly agitated that they were sacrificing opportunities to prepare their story. The ops plan required that they share and memorize a few basic facts and anecdotes about each other before any Russians arrived. It did not have to be much, merely enough to demonstrate the intimacy of a weeks-old relationship. "This is quite the setup," she said. "Horses have been the family business since the sixties?" Now she was using her lawyer voice.

"My grandfather started the horse business in 1963," he said. "Before that it was primarily a cattle operation."

Sia allowed herself—clinically—to think about how she might feel in this moment if she were a different person: The wine, the lanterns, the brilliant stars, the moonlight casting down on the rooftops and the adobe, and the occasional whinny of a horse. She studied him. Handsome, with dark brown eyes and hair about her shade of black. Well-cut khakis, nice boots, ostrich, weren't they? The top two buttons of his shirt were undone, revealing the outlines of a built chest. Did he actually work the farm? She wouldn't have believed it possible—exhibits: the jet, the house, the staff—but he looked strong and vital to her, like a man who took care of himself and worked outside with his hands. The corners of his mouth were slightly upturned even when his lips were shut, making him seem perpetually on the verge of laughter. She wondered why there wasn't a girl.

They made a list on a napkin—later ripped to pieces and flushed down Sia's toilet; she had insisted on the appropriate tradecraft—of all the topics one covers on a first date, ticking through it like a corporate punch list.

She started with her family. Mama was South African, her side owned and operated a wine farm outside Cape Town. Dad was a Brit. They'd met during study-abroad semesters in Austin, married, and settled in Texas, down in the Big Bend country. Sia was born during a Cape Town sojourn, where she'd earned South African citizenship, an asset that years later made her case an interesting one for the CIA's NOC program. Her American citizenship and the paper trail to Texas had been expunged during the process of joining Langley. Hellish Texas summers were dodged at the wine farm in the Cape Town winter, she explained without enthusiasm. She had planned to stop there, but heard herself volunteering, "Mama wanted me and Daisy to learn Afrikaans."

"Daisy?" Max looked up from his plate with a grin.

She felt herself blushing and wanted to tell him off, none of his damn business. But she supposed that now it was. After all, she'd offered the story. "Lousy flower names were Dad's idea," she said, making a face. "I still don't understand why Mama agreed. Anyway, during those trips we spoke only Afrikaans. Hence the accent. When it came time for university,

Grandpa, who had gone to Cambridge, said he would pay for me to go there if I studied law. And I did, because I didn't have any better ideas."

Back on track, she confidently ran through her relationship with Harry, Lyric, the move to London, and the work at Hynes Dawson. The one lapse aside, she delivered it all like a formal briefing.

When she had finished, Max asked if she wanted more wine. She shook her head, turned her chair to face the veranda and the rolling pastures. Her chin pointed to their list. "Your turn."

———

THE CASTILLO FAMILY HAD JOINED UP WITH CIA DECADES BEFORE MAX'S birth. Like so many foreigners who decide to work for the Agency, Max's grandfather Arturo had studied in America: four years at UCLA in the late 1950s. It was in the United States that Arturo watched his first Thoroughbred race, at Santa Anita, and fell in love with the horse business. It was also in the States that Arturo met a man named Hoyt, a talent spotter for the CIA. At first Arturo had no clue of Hoyt's true employer. By the early 1960s, Mexico's Dirty War had begun. Guerrilla groups, many Marxist-inspired, were recruiting peasants and farmers. Armed groups appeared in the mountains outside San Cristobal. They harassed the ranch. Stole cows. Burned barns. In 1963, they shot two ranch hands repairing broken fence. The Mexican regime cracked down. Cycles of violence and repression ensued. And the cattle operation was struggling. Threatened by bandits and bankruptcy, Arturo feared for San Cristobal, and Hoyt pitched him: Work for CIA, help us keep tabs on the inroads made by the Communists in Coahuila, in exchange for weapons and cash. Arturo took the deal, thinking it would last a few years.

But the Castillo family and the CIA, it seemed, were natural partners. And everything, in the end, would be bound up in the land itself.

San Cristobal's present twenty-three thousand acres had once been part of an even vaster Mexican hacienda: a sprawling estate granted to the Castillo family by Charles III of Spain in 1781. By the middle of the next century, it would be one of the largest private landholdings in the New World and would run, north to south, for more than one hundred miles through mountains, grasslands, and Chihuahuan high desert. The lack of mineral wealth made the land suitable for few profitable activities save for the raising of livestock and horses. And the arid climate meant that the tracts of land had to be immense to support the animals. Just like your neighborhood to the north, in the Big Bend, Max said. Anyhow, the hacienda shrank with the strictures of the colonizing legislation following Mexican independence from Spain, and again with an appropriation in 1866. It was a minor miracle, Max explained, that the ranch now approached the six square leagues legally permitted by the independence government and that San Cristobal had survived the revolutionary land reforms of 1917. By his grandfather's time San Cristobal was a cattle operation. There were no Thoroughbreds, no racing.

Sia cut in with an unpleasant smile. "You normally run through this on a first date?"

"Usually not. The women tend to hail from Monterrey. The land is the family and the family is the land," he said. "And most of the women I've been fortunate to know, well, they've known the land." He shrugged nonchalantly and sawed off a large bite of steak. "But if you'd prefer—"

"No, no. Keep going. It's good. Deep background." She shot him a sardonic smile.

When people lost interest in the ranch, Max typically lost interest in them. Also he despised the little smirk. He poured himself another glass of wine. But by the eighties, he continued over a generous sip, the clubby world of Thoroughbred horse-breeding and -racing had transformed into a glitzy, cosmopolitan club for the global billionaire class. CIA was interested in many of the owners. Max's father, Angel, was now in on the CIA connection. Hoyt put the question to him and Arturo: Would they take CIA seed money to start an operation? If it failed—as most Thoroughbred operations do—fine. But if it grew, they could build a global Rolodex Langley might flip through. That was 1982, two years before Max's birth.

In the end they succeeded for two reasons: money and luck. CIA pumped in seed capital, and the Castillos acquired top-of-the-line pedigrees at the big U.S. auctions. They built a stable of high-quality bloodlines. Over time, they won races. Then they sold breeding rights for their stallions. The virtuous circle spun around. And all the while Arturo and Angel worked for CIA.

"When you were living in Texas," Max said, with a glance toward her hand clasping the wineglass, "did you work the land yourself, or did you hire it out?"

"We had help, of course, but I did all of the jobs," Sia said. "I fixed water tanks, I strung up fencing—ours was just the barbed wire hung on knobby cedar, not this stuff—I hunted coyotes and snakes and hogs, I cleaned the barns." Her hands were indeed veined and her grip had been strong, but she was an English lawyer with an Afrikaans accent and he wondered if this might be pleasant bullshit.

"Same," he said. "I was raised on the land. I awoke before dawn to work in the pastures and stables. I fed and groomed the horses, I fixed miles of broken fencing and painted it, too. I've frozen in midnight pastures waiting for mares to foal. My earliest memories are of running through the stables and watching the horses on the training track. My mother taught me to ride. There are owners in this business who keep their distance from the animals. The Castillo family does not. We are horsemen and ranchers."

Sia glanced at the glowing pool and gave him that smirk again. "Horsemen and ranchers, eh?"

"I am a simple man, Hortensia."

She put up a hand. "Do. Not. Call. Me. That."

He mocked surrender. "Of course, of course. I'm sorry."

He tracked her angry gaze searching around the veranda, the pool, and the house. "The marriage of this place with CIA," she said, "is not what I'd call simple."

"I would. None of this would exist without CIA. The hacienda would have been picked apart, the land sold off. This house—built mostly between 1783 and 1787—would be a hotel for rich gringos and *chilangos* up for a weekend in the country. This place is a joint venture. The business is horseflesh. And when CIA asks for help, I try to accommodate. Simple, as I said."

"Our ranch almost killed my dad," she offered. "He said it felt like a prison."

That didn't strike Max as bullshit. "That's because the land is alive. San Cristobal might as well draw breath. And living things have their demands, don't they? When I was young it felt like it might swallow me. I wanted to study at UCLA, like Grandpa. Maybe go to New York after school. That never happened."

"When did they break the news about the CIA to you?" Sia asked. "I know I'm out of character here for our little date. Just curious. Seems like a complicated conversation."

He drank more wine. "You want the story?"

"Sure."

On the night of his sixteenth birthday, Max told his mother and father he wanted to go to L.A. To his surprise, there was no fight, no resistance. Clenched teeth from Papa but no words. The next morning Max's father woke him early. Before dawn they were riding in silence through the western pasture. They stopped at a creek to water the horses. Max had not asked why they were here. Mouths were best kept shut around the old man.

"We are taking a trip in a few days, Maximiliano," his father said. "To Washington. You, me, and your grandfather."

"Why?"

"To learn."

When his father pulled the rental car off the GW Parkway, Max yelled for him to turn around. Signs said this was the CIA. A mistake, Papa! We have business here, his father had said. Max looked to his grandfather in the passenger seat. The old man put a hand on his and nodded.

It would be Max's first and only trip inside CIA headquarters at Langley. There was a closed-door awards ceremony with the Director. The talent spotter Hoyt, wearing the green badge of what Max would later learn was a contractor, shook his hand. He gave Max's grandfather a framed copy of the assessment cable he had drafted on Arturo in September 1963. His grandfather had been encrypted JY/COWBOY. His father, JY/MUSTANG, in 1978. The Director presented them with a plaque that could not leave Langley. From the windowless events room they were whisked to the Agency dining room, which had been emptied for the celebration. For most of the day he felt as though he were watching a movie. This was someone else's father and grandfather. When Max had managed to focus during the ceremony, he felt proud, mostly.

But on the way to lunch, scudding his too-big dress shoes along the Langley marble, the lies blossomed in his gut, and that pride swelled to anger. They had betrayed him.

Hoyt sat next to him in the dining room, which Max later realized was a setup. Max and his father did not get along. Hoyt was the perfect deliveryman for a message from two generations of Castillos and the CIA. At first the rage made him comfortable ignoring the guy. Max picked at a salad and an overdone steak and mostly stared at the treetops out the window.

"Pissed off at your old men?" Hoyt finally said in perfect Spanish. "I'd be, too. You should be. They made choices a long time ago. You're the one who will live with the consequences."

Max chewed his steak and said nothing.

"It seems to me," Hoyt said, "that you've basically got two options. Run away. Or make it your own."

"I already told them," Max said. "I'm going to UCLA like Grandpa, then New York. I'm not going to die on the ranch."

"Not going to live there, either, huh?" Hoyt said. "Sounds like the running-away option."

"I'm not running away."

"What would you call it, then?"

"Leaving."

"Well, I suppose that's right," Hoyt said, "technically. But we both know the difference between leaving because you're drawn to something you love and leaving because you hate where you are."

"It's that one, then. Hating where I am."

Hoyt took a forkful of fried potatoes and a bite of steak. Grimacing, he wiped a slimy piece of gristle on the rim of his plate. "Sometimes the food here is not so good," he said. He washed it down with sparkling water. "Max, I've known your grandfather since 1959. I met your father for the first time when he was three days old, and you when you were eight or so days in the world. I've walked around every acre of San Cristobal, I knew it when it was still a cattle operation. I've ridden the horses, I've suffered under your mother's cooking. Not that ours is much better." He nudged his chin toward the steak.

Max smiled at that one.

"Let an old man tell you something he shouldn't," Hoyt continued, "something they"—he jerked an elbow down the table toward the Director—"whitewashed from those fancy remarks I made about your two old men just a bit ago. Something to give you an idea of the difference San Cristobal and the Castillo family have made on the course of history: Ten thousand people. At least. Maybe more."

"What?"

"I think at least ten thousand people are alive today that otherwise would have died if your family did not work for the CIA."

Max's first instinct was to call bullshit on this, but he was starting to like Hoyt, despite everything, and he wanted to hear him out.

"Since the 1980s there have been a few nasty Middle Eastern terrorist groups that like to incite mayhem. Bombings. Hijackings. Kidnappings. Palestinians, a group of wackos called Al Qa'ida. Now, the guys doing the bombings and killings typically aren't involved in the horse business, but a lot of the rich guys who write the checks are. Financiers in Saudi, the Emirates, Egypt. San Cristobal sells and deals in horseflesh with guys in those places, doesn't it? Your dad tells me he's brought you more into the business. These countries ring a bell?"

Max nodded.

"Well, you think it's easy for CIA officers to get access to clandestine financial networks over there? Understand where the money is flowing, that kind of thing? In fact, it's hard as hell. We need a different way in. A creative way."

On his suit Max wore a pin with the San Cristobal crest. His grandfather had given it to him in the CIA lobby. Hoyt gently poked it. "Now, this is creative," he said. "Imagine a Saudi is interested in touring a first-rate horse operation outside Kentucky. He might be invited to San Cristobal. Or you might visit him and spend time in his home, at his facility. You might learn about his family. His friends. His beliefs. He leaves a phone in his room at San Cristobal and we have ways of getting inside. You see where I am going?"

Max nodded. Hoyt again poked the pin. "It would seem to me, Max, that we're back to our original choice: Run or stay. You run, I think, to make something for yourself. You stay to be part of something bigger than yourself."

After lunch they met a few of the officers who had used the intelligence Papa and Grandpa had provided. Max sidled up next to Hoyt in the hallway afterward.

"Did Papa and Grandpa spy on Mexico?" he asked.

Hoyt shook his head. "When the CIA's relationship with San Cristobal started, yes, we talked with your grandfather about some of the groups targeting the ranch and the government. But since the early 1970s—so almost thirty years—we've had an arrangement in which we do not ask your father or grandfather to provide intelligence on Mexico."

"What would happen if the Mexican government found out?"

"They wouldn't like it."

"Because we are traitors."

Hoyt put a hand on his shoulder. Max spotted his father looking at them. When their eyes met, his father turned away. "Ten thousand lives," Hoyt said. "Remember that. But, hey, here is an idea, don't take my word for it. Try it out for a while and see if what I'm saying makes any sense. Your old men brought you here today because they want you in the tent. They wanted you to see the San Cristobal legacy and get the information you need so the decision makes sense here"—Hoyt pressed a finger into his forehead—"and here"—then his heart.

"I should try being a CIA agent? And if I don't like it, I quit?"

"Well, yes, basically. What's wrong with that? But the words are important, Max. It is true that when I started working with your grandfather he was a CIA agent. Or asset. Either works. He did things on our behalf. But he was not a CIA officer. He was not an employee of the CIA. Make sense?"

"Yes."

"I am suggesting something different in your case. I want to bring you into the family, as it were. We have decades of history with the Castillos. We know your family better than most of our own officers. CIA has a group of people, like your family, that work for us. We can teach you everything our officers get. You learn the business inside and out."

"What happens if I say no?"

"Nothing. We part ways as friends. You go to UCLA and New York. Make a new life for yourself."

"And if I say yes?"

"Then we get started."

———

MAX FINISHED, AND SIA EMPTIED HER WINE. "IF PROCTER HADN'T vouched for you," she said, "I would assume that story was horseshit."

"Sometimes I wish it were."

Max stood up, then, with his hand outstretched, gestured for her to follow, guiding her around the pool toward her room. She'd offered no openings tonight. Her guard was up—she was working, focused, edgy. As they walked, he said, "Procter mentioned you still ride horses?" In his experience women who loved horses loved San Cristobal and they usually loved riding horses with him. And he had only loved women who knew their way around horses.

"Yes, it has been a while, though."

"Tomorrow we can get up early for a ride before you fly out, if you'd like. It would be good for you to see more of the operation. Before you call Anna."

"Sure."

He said good night outside her room and was a few steps down the hall when he heard, "Oh, Max, I almost forgot." She had the list in her hand when he turned around. "Since we've just begun dating," she whispered, "I assume you don't have a girlfriend? I'm single. Just got to make sure you're on the market."

"No girlfriends," he replied. "And, Sia, my god, I would not have agreed to this if I did." *And he heard Alejandra explaining that she was going through with it, that this time was different, it had to be a clean break, and a real one, for once in this long, complicated, sordid love. That after her wedding she could not come around anymore.*

"Anything we would have covered on our first few dates?" Sia asked. "The weighty tortured stuff. Past marriages?"

"No."

"Kids?" She feigned a grave tone.

"No."

"Severed engagements?" *And then he heard Alejandra's feet pattering along the tiles, closing the distance from the bed to the bathroom. Her soft skin glowed in the moonlight. She shut the door and changed, and when she came back out she wasn't his anymore.*

"Unfortunately not," he said. And with a good-night, he turned and was gone.

———

AT SUNUP THEY WERE IN ONE OF THE BARNS. SIA WAS GRATEFUL FOR the coffee Max had brought along, and sipped it slowly as she watched grooms put the tack on the two horses, both mares. "Yours is Rosa. I will ride Penelope," Max said, gesturing to the other.

Sia put her hand on Rosa's muzzle and spoke gentle words to the animal. She could sense Max watching how the horse took to her. The animals were intelligent, they were noble, they could sense fear or discomfort in their human counterparts. But Rosa, Sia knew—could see, actually, in the glint of the horse's eye—right now felt none of those things. The groom accepted her coffee, and Sia swung herself confidently into the saddle.

They rode between the fencing of the pastures until they came to a flat, grassy expanse that veined out into several trails. Rosa's energy became palpable: this one wanted to run. Sia trotted the mare up alongside Max. He carried himself well on a horse. Comfortable, assured. Not like so many horse owners, who were afraid of the animals. So he had been honest about that in last night's monologue.

Dew glistened on the grass and everything smelled earthy and wet and yet clean. Sia's life was a rotation between her office, client dinners, airplanes, and her flat, and she realized she'd lately forgotten how much she missed country where the sky had no ceiling and the land unrolled in all directions. It made you feel wild or free or vulnerable or all of it at once. A sky this open conjured many emotions.

It was interesting that, unlike last night's speech, he was not narrating. He seemed to be letting the land speak for itself.

Two or three times Sia felt his eyes on her. And though she was accustomed to the admiring glances of men, these looks were different. He did not seem to be admiring her so much as studying how her body merged with the horse. His gaze was now focused on how her legs gently squeezed the mare's ribs and sat in the stirrups. Her legs were tools for horsemanship. How was their craft? She felt self-conscious—it had been a while, after all—but this quickly dissolved to frustration. Why did she want him to approve of her riding? As they came to a neck in the trail that led up into the mountains, he seemed to read her agitation.

"You are either not happy with the ride," he said, "or with Procter's arrangement. And the ride, I feel, has been beautiful."

"Is that a question?"

"No."

She nudged her mare forward up the trail. The path was wide here, ample space between the boulders, and he pulled alongside as they climbed.

"I understand your position," he said. "You fear that I've stolen, or am stealing, your kill. But I can assure you, Sia, I am not hungry. I have no interest in the meal, only the hunt. And I do not mind hunting with you. We might even enjoy it."

"Not hungry," she repeated, grip tightening along the reins. "Sounds about right. You get a bonus and a pat on the back from CIA if we get access to Vadim's computer or recruit him, but I live in a different world.

I need to get promoted. I have a hall file inside Langley. I have to fill out expense reports. I have to return to the U.S. Treasury the difference between the paycheck from my law firm and my GS-13 salary. While living in central London. You don't have to worry about any of that. You don't need this. You could have told Procter *no gracias* and there's not a damn thing she could have done. I do not have the luxury of saying no. And I'm hungry because I eat what I kill. What I don't get is why you even—"

And there was a rustle and a rattler slithered from the stones across the trail, and Sia's mare spooked and snatched the bit and she caught a blur of Max doing the same, tearing away up the trail. Sia's connection to the animal was lost, but she'd been atop a terror-stricken horse before and taught by her own cracked bones, and she jerked the right rein to force the mare into a slower circle, steal back control, then she yanked tighter, gutter Afrikaans seeping through clenched lips, struggling until the rein was almost to her knee and the mare's corkscrew was slow and tight and thank god she'd not been bucked. The horse whinnied and the mare's nostrils rifled with hot breath and Sia brought her mouth to the mare's ears and encouraged her and stroked her head. When she finally looked up, Max was still in the saddle, in control, and he was looking approvingly at Sia as if she'd passed some unspoken test.

"Goddamn," she said, trotting her mare toward him.

"*Pinche vivoras,*" he said, spitting in disgust. Fucking snakes.

13

Moscow

CHERNOV STOOD FROM HIS DESK TO RETURN THE FILES TO HIS SAFE. He'd been reading since well before dawn: yellowed folders sealed by red wax since the days of Brezhnev, bound notebooks from the Yeltsin years, documents typed in the time of Putin. He had studied Agapov's files with great attention to detail. He memorized names, phrases, years. He had read reports filed by Agapov's schoolteachers at Leningrad Secondary School No. 211. He had reviewed the full slate of tests, psychological exams, and party evaluations from the Higher School of the KGB in Moscow. He had read every report Agapov filed while *rezident* in London. He had reviewed pictures of Agapov's family. Daughter, Anna. Deceased wife, Galina. Son-in-law, Vadim. No grandchildren. Odd.

Chernov's office had a window overlooking Lubyanka Square. In the center stood the statue of Felix Dzerzhinsky, returned from the leafy park where it had been retired after the Soviet collapse. The blood spent in Ukraine had tugged back some reminders of the old ways and Iron Felix, happily, was one of them. The professional revolutionary and founder of the Cheka was dusted in snow. A gaggle of children pulling sleds circled him, parents following behind. But Chernov was not paying attention, he was spinning off the dial on the safe, gathering his coat, collecting his thoughts for the battle with Agapov that would take place behind the Kremlin ramparts that afternoon.

There are two metro systems in Moscow. One, official and frenetic, boasts cavernous stations piled with arches, patriotic friezes, stained glass, statues, and marble, each a chandeliered testament to the Soviet Union, a people's palace filled by warm, oily air. The second, D6, unofficial and quiet, boasts merely secrecy and the privilege of access. Seven stories below Moscow, occasionally parallel to the official lines, sometimes running through tunnels first carved in the time of Ivan the Fearsome, D6's five lines connect the most sensitive installations in Moscow: airfields, VIP bunkers, an underground city, the headquarters of Russia's military and security services. Unused for decades, the war has breathed new life into the bunkered world of D6. Now its lines are running. One of those makes the short trip from FSB headquarters to the Kremlin.

The elevator doors opened to the spacious D6 station below the Lubyanka. Chernov's black shoes squeaked over a mosaic of six flinty-eyed men in uniform, each celebrating the glorious evolution of Russia's security services: Leninist Cheka, Stalinist NKVD, Stalinist OGPU, Stalinist MGB, Brezhnevian KGB, Putinist FSB. They'd had to skip a few iterations—the floor simply was not large enough. Chernov eased into one of the quiet train's red leather seats.

Less than five minutes and he was at a station just northeast of the Kremlin near Staraya Ploshchad'. Chernov shuffled up the stairs and escalators. He skipped the metal detectors but left his cell phone in a locked cubby. He showed official credentials to three different gatekeepers, all sturdy, unsmiling women in their forties and fifties—the foundation of all Russian bureaucracies—who dutifully checked them against their lists. On the third floor he entered a warren of offices comprising the Presidential Administration. Like an imperial court, Russian power spreads outward, in rings, with Putin's Kremlin office at its center. Though, in the twilight of his reign, he is often absent, preferring instead his estate on the Black Sea at Idokopas. Goose, however, is not often absent. Goose is eternal.

Goose had summoned Chernov to his office: a vaulted room with heavy wood-paneled walls and a ceiling caked in elaborate floral plasterwork. A long lacquered table sat in the middle of the office, ringed by chairs upholstered in gold fabric. Two Russian flags flanked the massive desk forming the official roost of the Secretary of Russia's Security Council. An aide, watering the ferns while Goose worked, excused himself and ducked out. Chernov took a seat at the table to wait. Goose removed his reading glasses and rolled up a report. His face was craggy, bony fingers rolling and unrolling the papers, lost in thought.

The aide reappeared with a tray of teacups and a platter of *pryaniki*. He set the tray on Goose's desk and scurried out. Goose picked several of the glazed honey spice cookies, tapping his foot on the plush blue carpet as he ate. He licked his finger, then wiped it across the plate to gather crumbs. He put another *pryanik* in his mouth. "Tell me how you think Agapov will play it," Goose said at last.

"He will refuse," Chernov said.

"Of course. Then?"

"Then he pays."

"Yes. Then?"

"It depends how he pays."

"No blood."

"Then I think we have the daughter to deal with. He trusts her. He will hand his affairs over to her if he's sidelined."

"Good," Goose said. "The damn fool." He took three frustrated sips of his water, then thrust his jaw at the door and asked: "How long has he been waiting?"

Chernov looked at the wall behind Goose's desk—a clock for every one of the eleven time zones in Russia, plus Washington, London, Berlin, Damascus, and Beijing.

"Three hours," Chernov said.

Goose returned to his papers. "Let's give him one more."

———

CHERNOV MADE PHONE CALLS AND SMOKED CIGARETTES IN AN ADJOINing office. When Agapov's hour had expired, he returned to find Goose still poring over papers. Chernov slid a single chair in front of the desk, the one with the stubby legs they used for guests.

Snatching up the brown secure phone, Goose barked at an aide to send in Agapov.

Chernov took a seat at the long table. Goose remained at the desk. Agapov flung the door open, pushing past a startled aide, who immediately slinked from the room. Agapov approached the desk, eyed the chair, and stayed standing. The man was coiled up: fingers dug into palms, jaw set, a bluish vein rising on his splotchy neck. "You keep me waiting four hours, Goose? You prick. We may hate each other, but we can be decent about these things. We're all busy."

Goose steepled fingers over his mouth and looked beyond Agapov to address the plants at the office's far end. "Why do you want to see our President, Andrei?"

"That's my business."

"Is it?" Goose said with genuine incredulity. "My god. Why don't you sit? Some tea?"

Agapov tapped on the short chair's wood back. He smiled at Goose. Goose smiled crookedly at Agapov. Chernov smiled to himself.

"Well, I'm going to have a cup," Goose said. Agapov remained standing as Goose called for tea. He stood waiting for the aide to arrive with the tea. He stood while Goose steeped the tea. He stood while Goose stirred in the sugar. He stood while Goose set down the spoon and wiped his hands. He stood while Goose took his first tentative sips.

Agapov was still standing when he turned to Chernov and said, "You are Konstantin Konstantinovich Chernov, yes? The one who stole from my bank. That you?"

"I am," Chernov said. "And as I told your man at the bank, it was not theft. We all belong to Russia, Andrei Borisovich. The gold is Russia's. And Russia will do with it what she must."

Agapov laughed sadly. Shook his head. So did Chernov. He smoothed his tie. Waited for the boss to jump in. He felt pity, not anger. Agapov was blind. Soon he would be severed from the Russian body. And there was no worse fate than being torn from Russia's embrace.

"Why do you want to see our President, Andrei?" Goose repeated.

"Let's just get down to it," Agapov said. "I've spent four fucking hours groveling in your waiting room. I have things to do. So tell me: What do you want? What are the terms of your next shakedown?"

Goose brought his fist to the desk. His cup teetered and spilled. Tea ran into his papers and off the side. The corners of Agapov's mouth curled upward, as if he might laugh.

"Shakedown?" Goose said, wagging a finger. "No, no, no. We are asking all patriotic Russians to contribute to the war chest. And what angers me, my old friend, is that you know how this works. You know it well. For god's sake, you and I did our part to break the old oligarchs twenty years ago. And now you, you, Andrei Borisovich, are acting like one. You are withholding wealth and resources from the state. It's a goddamn capital call, Andrei, and you're not answering."

"Who is asking, Goose? It's not the state. It's you! You said you needed my shipyard. I sold it to you for 10 percent of its value—"

"Lies!" Goose yelled. "All that rust wasn't worth half of what I paid."

"You mean what your son paid, eh? And you're out of your mind, Goose. We had bankers and consultants put a price on it and you gave me 10 percent of that."

"Bankers," Goose sneered. "I'm supposed to trust a pack of European bankers to tell me the right price?"

Agapov released the stubby chair, folding his hands at his waist as if worried he might break something if they got loose. "You took the shipyard. You sent this one"—he freed a finger to jab it at Chernov—"to steal my gold."

Goose stood and pointed across the desk. "Andrei Borisovich, that gold was moved from your bank as part of a security precaution. It's in bunkers out east with the rest of our strategic reserve."

Agapov laughed again. "Still in Russia, is it? Not squirreled away in nameless shell accounts in the Caribbean by your crooked bankers and lawyers? You're telling me the money is in the Rodina, and that the *khozyain* approved of the transfer?"

Goose righted the teacup. "That, my old friend, is exactly what I am telling you."

They stared at each other, Agapov pondering whether to challenge the lie.

Goose leaned forward, palms on the desk, eyes far-off and cold. "Here is how it is going to be, Andrei Borisovich. You will sell us Rossiya Industrial at 8 percent of whatever your bankers say it's worth. You will sell off your shares in Bank Rossiya at the same discount. You will sell me your landholdings—Moscow, Piter, Sochi. As part of that I want the horse farm. You will convince your son-in-law to participate in that sale. You will sit quietly somewhere like a good boy. That's the offer. That's the final word."

Agapov took a step toward the desk and began yelling, "What does the *khozyain* think about this, Goose? If he approves, why keep me at a distance? I could be down in Idokopas tonight. I could hear it from his own lips!"

Goose again pounded the desk. "I have been charged with collecting from our boyars, Andrei Borisovich. You are a boyar! You will pay your share!" Final slam of his bony fist.

"I cannot help but notice, Goose," Agapov said softly, "that none of the others are receiving punishment quite this severe. Am I suffering because I took Galina from you, made her happy so she didn't spend her years getting knocked about in your kitchen?"

Goose's lips curled into a wretched smile. He laughed. He pointed the sugar spoon at Agapov. "You, my old friend, are a fool." He clanked the spoon on the silver tray. "This conversation, cheery though it's been, is done. What's your answer? And my god, man, you know what happens if you say no. So say yes. Say yes and be done with it."

Agapov buttoned his suit coat, smoothed his tie, ran fingers through his white hair. "Galina would say no. I say no. The answer is no, Goose. No."

Goose put his forehead on the desk and spoke to his shoes. "Galina's dead, you stubborn fool. And if she weren't, she wouldn't have you committing suicide like this. She'd be sensible. She'd see reason."

"The way she did when you'd smack her?" Agapov said.

They looked each other over, eyes crackling with energy and violence, until Goose waved Agapov out and slipped on the reading glasses to bury himself in his papers. But Agapov did not witness his formal dismissal. Having already made a few nasty gestures at Goose, then Chernov, he'd spun around and was marching for the exit, where he paused, giving the Putin portrait an almost imperceptible nod before he slammed shut the door and it slipped, tilting slightly on the wall.

14

Moscow

Anna Andreevna Agapova: *Sia, hello, how are you? I've just seen the notes between the assistants and thought I'd call directly. Mexico might be possible, yes, but let me confirm those dates with my husband.*

Hortensia Fox: *That's lovely. Spur of the moment, I know, but when I learned of your husband's connection to RusFarm I thought it was all too perfect to pass up.*

Anna Andreevna Agapova: *Yes, of course, of course. Your boyfriend, Max, he runs this San Cristobal that you mentioned in your email?*

Hortensia Fox: *Yes. Maximiliano Castillo. We met through a friend who convinced me to come down to Mexico to help him scout horses.*

Anna Andreevna Agapova: *San Cristobal seems quite the place, from the photos.*

Hortensia Fox: *Yes, it is. And I must say, I spend most of my life in dreary offices and stuffy London restaurants. The fresh air's a tonic. And the weather right now is a bit better in Monterrey than it is in London.*

Anna Andreevna Agapova: *To say nothing of Moscow or Petersburg!*

[Both callers laugh]

Hortensia Fox: *Spot on, spot on!*

[Laughter thins]

Hortensia Fox: *So, what do you say? We ride horses in Mexico, make a weekend of it?*

Anna Andreevna Agapova: *Schedules are always challenging, but I will see. More to come.*

Hortensia Fox: *Fingers crossed. Talk soon!*

[Anna Andreevna Agapova terminates call at 7:46 p.m. MSK]

———

ANNA SANK DEEPER INTO THE BATHTUB OF HER GRAND, SOULLESS Ostozhenka apartment, flicking bubbles from her nose, staring at the crown molding. Pastoral scenes of trees, deer, a fox. The woman had beaten her to the punch with the Mexico invitation, which both maddened and intrigued her. Maddened because it delayed the inevitable squeeze inside the Rodina. Intrigued because RusFarm, not the offices in Piter, might actually be the best place from which to do the squeezing. She let more scalding water into the cooling tub and replayed it all again and again until she felt she could defend her performance to her father.

Anna rinsed the suds from her body in a cool shower and toweled off, wondering if she might be able to keep Vadim out of this. She did not think so. Her father would insist that Vadim join.

She wanted brandy for the next part. She poured a glass of Laubade, aimlessly flipping through a magazine to put it all off. It was sad to treat fine brandy so shabbily, but she did, downing it too quickly and waiting on the bed's edge until she could savor the airy, disconnected feeling. She had debated doing this in person, but she was impatient. And he would be less dodgy and disagreeable on the open line. He would not ask so many questions.

She called Vadim. It went to voice mail, which she rarely left. But this time she did, and she said it was urgent. Please call back. He did, ten minutes later.

"What's the problem?" he said.

"Nice to hear your voice, too," she said.

A sigh. "What is going on?"

"We've been invited to Mexico for the weekend."

A laugh, a real one.

"I'm serious," she said. "To San Cristobal. The horse operation. The lawyer's boyfriend is apparently the owner. Makes good sense for the things we are working. Dear."

"Someone down there tried to get a meeting with me maybe a year or so ago," he said. "Didn't happen, but San Cristobal has a reputation. I would like to see it."

"Can you get out of Piter for the weekend?"

"I will see," he said.

Anna had wandered from the bedroom. For her birth control she filled a glass with water, clanking it on the countertop. "I'm sure she won't mind you leaving her for a weekend. What's her name again? The one you set up with the Kamenny apartment and the French bulldog?"

"Aliona does PR for the bank," he said. "She works for me."

"Well then how can she afford Kamenny?"

He just moved on. "It's this weekend?"

"Yes. I'll join you in Piter and we can go from there on Friday morning."

"What else?" he said.

"That's it."

He hung up.

ANNA OWNED TWO APARTMENTS IN MOSCOW. THE FIRST, PERCHED ATOP a glittering glass box on Ostozhenka, was where the mail arrived, where she infrequently entertained her father or, God help her, Vadim. Her monstrous apartment's interior was ultramodern; white and straight-lined, like an insane asylum, she thought. There was a portrait of the President hanging in the lobby.

Anna packed a duffel bag and changed into jeans, a white sweater, and scuffed Nikes. She slipped on a beanie and wound a scarf around her neck. She looked at the Moskva coursing below her windows. From her safe she removed the cell phone they did not know she had. She dialed. He answered right away—she liked that about him.

"We missed you last night," he said.

"Who is we?" she said.

"I missed you."

"Jean Martel at ten?" she said.

He whistled. "I have work in the morning."

"So do I," she said. "I won't keep you out too late."

"I hope that's not true."

"You will bring the board?" she asked.

"Of course." A pause. "I am feeling like I might win tonight. I just wanted you to know. I had a dream about it."

"You won't, but the warning is kind." She hung up. She thought for a moment of how angry her father would be when he realized she had not phoned with an update. But she could do this no other way.

INSIDE HER SECOND APARTMENT, ANNA UNPACKED HER SUITCASE AND turned up the heat. Two stories of brick, tilting toward the neighboring building, with wood floors, soft light, and a crumbling fresco of angels above the door. It had been a pre-Revolutionary mansion for a forgotten Muscovite family, built when Piter was the imperial capital and Moscow was a sleepy backwater filled with old money. The owners had been unlucky: the family was arrested and then shot after the Revolution, the apartment became communal, and then the new occupants were all arrested and shot during the Terror.

There was a large stone fireplace and windows that were stuck, either open or shut. The heater could not outrun the cold. Shivering, she slipped on a fleece under her sweater, reapplied lipstick, and considered herself in the mirror. Her eyes were softer here, she thought. She tucked a pack of Dunhills in her purse and went outside.

She smoked as she walked, taking her time, though an undried tangle of hair was crunchy and her fingers were freezing inside the mittens. Zigzagging under arches and through courtyards, Anna strolled in a cloud of smoke and frozen breath along the Street of All-Holidays. This was Moscow between the seams of the skyscrapers and the colossal Stalinist avenues and the brutal Brezhnevian concrete. It was lamplit and snug, an eclectic pocket of the Russian world that had not been demolished into glittering nothingness by the property developers. There was a bar at the far end of one of the neighborhood's courtyards, a low-hung place called Jean Martel.

Though she knew it was not really so, here she felt new, clean. When Anna, girl of nine, had asked how it had been under the Soviets, her father fed her some folksy, useless saying, but her mother told the truth. She said that life was a game of lies. We pretend to love the state, she told Anna, and the state pretends to care for us. We are all bound up together in a grand project to destroy each other. And because this game is about deception, it must be played alone. But something must be true, Mama, she had insisted. Mama just gave her a sad smile.

Anna slipped into the warmth of Jean Martel and found Luka seated in their usual spot. On the table was a bottle of Armenian brandy and a knife jutting out of a lemon. Luka was arranging the chessboard. The owner had tried to re-create the feel of a White Russian émigré bar in Jazz Age Paris: gilded bronze mirrors, murals of sugary winter scenes in Imperial Piter, flowery sconces that might have been yanked from palace walls in a rush to flee the Bolsheviks. But the tables were dusty, the mirrors were cracked and smoky, the murals were faded. It was empty save for an old drunk and a young couple at the bar.

She tossed her coat on a chair and sat. Luka poured her a brandy, squeezed in lemon juice, and handed her the glass. For a beat she held his gaze with a smile. Then she took a drink.

"White or black?" he asked.

"Black."

He rotated the chessboard. "As I said, I had a dream where I won. Prophetic, maybe. Who knows?"

"In your dreams we play chess?" Under the table she playfully jabbed his leg.

He smiled, scratching his hair. "I have a pure mind, Anya."

Long ago, in a now-faded life, Anna had played chess competitively, as had Luka. They had met by chance in a department store, both buying boards. She had liked his blue eyes and unkempt blond hair and that he dressed casually, unlike an employee of Bank Rossiya or the SVR. He did not have Vadim's brown eyes and dark hair. He was confident, but he did not carry himself with menace like the men who ruled her life. In the checkout line he asked her if she'd like to play a game sometime. Since then, they'd played hundreds. Anna had the edge by a wide margin.

He moved his pawn, she mirrored. He moved a second, quickly, alongside his first.

She clicked her tongue. "You are predictable."

She moved a pawn next to her first move in the middle of the board, consuming his space. The beginning of an aggressive counterattack.

"And you are not, Anya," he said, thinking.

He defended well, they traded queens, he developed knights perfectly, she poured another glass of brandy and watched as he wriggled from several traps and, eventually, took the game.

He beamed. "The dream was true." He held out his hand, she took it, and he kissed hers.

"Your drama is sickening," she said, reaching for her scarf. "Smoke with me."

They bundled into the cold and smoked on a sagging bench outside the bar. "I saw some news about the bank," he said.

She blew smoke into his face with a scowl. "The rules, Luka."

"I know, I know," he said, waving the cloud away. "I just wanted to say I am sorry if you've gotten pulled into it. That's all."

She stood and stubbed out the Dunhill in a pile of black snow. "Again."

Two more games unrolled in silence. She took both handily. Then he collected the bottle and they tramped into the midnight cold, strolling down the Street of All-Holidays through the dull lamplight and the smog hissing from pipes. They passed a young woman marching, head down and brisk, not a glance their direction. Though if she had, Anna considered what she would have seen: a handsome man, hair peeking from under his cap, bottle of brandy swinging inside the pocket of his greatcoat, mittened hand clasped tightly to that of a blonde clutching a folded chessboard under her other arm. They were laughing. They looked happy, like people without secrets. She liked to think they weren't secrets if he didn't want to know.

———

HE KISSED HER NECK AS SHE PUT THE KEY IN THE DOOR. SHE TURNED to give him a kiss on the lips and said, Let's get a fire going because it's going to be too damn cold in here. The door opened with a creak.

He turned on the gas and she lit the fire and they got distracted because in the bedroom on the hunt for the blankets he'd kissed her neck again and she shivered with him behind her, reaching for his hair, running her own lips across his cheek. He was kissing the nape of her neck when she pushed him off.

"Focus, Luka, we need blankets," she said. "I can see my breath."

On her tippy-toes Anna searched shelves in a musty closet while Luka ran his hands over her bottom and between her legs. He tried to slide down her jeans. She swatted his hand away and said: "You could reach up here, you know that? It would be easier."

The corner of a blanket peeked at her from the top shelf. As Anna strained for it, her jeans slid below her bottom, replaced by gentle kisses. "I can't help," he said. "I am distracted."

The blanket went around her shoulders, and she led him by the hand into the living room. He turned off the lights and they slid out of their clothes and onto the couch in the warmth of the fire. She pulled the blanket around herself again, hemming it on her waist above naked legs.

For most of her life Anna had been a stoic practitioner of mechanical sex. She'd come to believe that piece of her had vanished along the way, somewhere between the limp affections of a probably gay college boyfriend and Vadim's erratic attention, which swung wildly from chilly disinterest to blazing, unhinged desire, shot through with violence. But with Luka it was not mechanical—it was fun and easy. Even the first time when, expecting the robotic, she'd discovered instead that Luka's appetite for her was ravenous, that he was curious to discover what she liked, that they could move together in rhythm.

Luka fluttered kisses over her. She tugged at his hair. He looked up at her. "I want you," she said.

He grinned. "Not yet."

He returned to kissing her until she yanked at his hair and he was up, forehead gently pressed to hers, slyly teasing until she smiled wickedly and grabbed his waist and guided him inside. She held his eyes for a beat and kissed him. He laughed.

"What's so funny?" she said.

"I won," he said. "I can't believe it."

"One of three," she reminded him. "And that one? Just barely." He angled to find a good spot and she told him when he had, gripping his shoulders to bring him close.

He was moving well now. It had been too long; everything was wound so tight. Anna rolled her head back onto the armrest. She watched the shadows of the flames dance on the ceiling, and she forgot the operation, the world, her family, as she felt her body melt into a pool.

When it was done, they lay naked above the blanket to cool off. He was rubbing the back of her scalp while they watched the fire.

"Sleep here," she said at last.

He switched off the fire and rolled the blanket over them. She snuggled into him. They were sticky, but she was exhausted and he smelled like their sex, which she liked. Her last thought before sleep was that he'd beat her in chess. She'd lost. And after, she'd brought him to her apartment and made love to him as if it didn't matter. As if he were safe.

15

San Cristobal

HOME FIELD ADVANTAGE MATTERS IN THE INTELLIGENCE GAME. On its own turf a spy agency can wire a target's hotel room for audio and video, it can own his laptop and phone, it can break into his room—perhaps even lawfully—to search his possessions, it can direct immense surveillance and support resources to watch his movements. And so, when a clancomm—clandestine communication—message from Sia Fox landed on Procter's desk at Langley, relaying that Anna Agapova and Vadim Kovalchuk had agreed to visit San Cristobal, Procter's hoot of excitement carried to the most distant corners of her Moscow X fiefdom. Two days with a Putin moneyman happened maybe once a career. All stops would be pulled.

"I want you to approve me flying an Access team down to do a spot of prep at the rancho," Procter asked Bradley over the green line phone. "Most of the place is wired up, of course, but we've got Russians coming and, color me crazy, but they'll run a shade more suspicious than our recent Emirati guests." They didn't need the lock pickers. It was Max's house, after all. No, they needed the Access guys that prepped rooms for the breaking-and-entering ops.

Most of San Cristobal's full-time employees paid little attention to the flurry leading up to the arrival of the serious Russian buyers. The chef designed the menus and sent the staff to shop for the food and alcohol. Max summoned the ranch manager, the vet, the trainer, and the breeding manager to the library for a discussion on Vadim's interest in Smokey Joe, which had been relayed to San Cristobal by a team of RusFarm agents and lawyers. The stallion, cared for more intently than most humans, did not see his grooming, breeding, diet, or exercise regimen change in the slightest.

Amid the hubbub, the only person who noticed that Max held a face-to-face meeting with an American A/V consultant was the farm's bedraggled IT manager, who defiantly sniffed at the slight but was privately saddened at his exclusion.

Two days before the Russians landed, the new girlfriend, Sia, arrived. One of the housekeepers gritted her teeth at the sight of that foreign woman—*puta!*—wheeling her suitcase into Maximiliano's bedroom. If the old *hacendado* still had his wits, he would slap Maximiliano across the face and send this temptress packing, tail between her spread legs.

————

SIA WATCHED THE RUSSIAN'S JET SLIDE THROUGH THE CLEAR BLUE SKY and kiss the runway. Vadim emerged first, smile and a wave in their direction. Max and Sia waved back. Anna appeared next, then a man Sia did not recognize. Perhaps one of Vadim's bloodstock consultants.

The couples greeted with handshakes and kisses on the cheek. Sia had seen a handful of pictures of Vadim and read the thin biographical information the CIA possessed. But, as she met him, feeling his handshake, his eyes on her, absorbing the garrulous, almost authoritative persona he adopted around Max, these few seconds in the flesh offered more than any of the desktop research ever could. Vadim Kovalchuk, she thought, recalled several of her wealthy clients, a profile she called the High School Quarterback. Handsome. Comfortable. Patriotic. Authoritative. Able to develop political relationships to advance his own standing. Successful in business. Anna, she thought, was colder, aloof. A challenge to read.

The attendants scurried into the plane for the luggage. "Anna," Sia said, "perhaps you and I ride together? Give the boys time to get acquainted?"

"Of course," Anna said.

Max and Vadim hopped into the lead G Wagen and set off for the house. Sia waved Anna into her vehicle and they sped off, following Max. "This will be such fun," Sia said. "How was the flight?"

"Easy. Thrilled we could make it." Anna was looking around the farm. "Beautiful," she murmured, "absolutely beautiful."

When the convoy came to the fork in the gravel road, Max turned left toward the barns, instead of right toward the house and dinner. "Huh, okay," Sia mumbled to herself. Their driver followed.

"Vadim is impatient," Anna remarked casually. "He has his eye on a stallion, and I believe made this known to your boyfriend."

The G Wagens parked outside the training barn. Because of the change of plan, the trainer, the vet, and the grooms were absent. The stallion barn was long, with two rows of stalls and a path tracing around them so the horses could walk inside. Max spoke as they toured. He recited pedigrees by heart. He ticked through the specific place on the farm where several had been born. He quoted the track times for Smokey Joe and a few of the higher performers.

The flustered groom entered the barn just as they reached Smokey Joe's stall. The horse poked his head through the yoke cut into the door. As his name suggested, the stallion was smoky gray, albeit with a spot of white running down his nose, which Max gently stroked. Sia noticed that Vadim made no move to touch the horse, nor did he crack so much as a smile. The groom led Smokey Joe out of the stall toward the round pen where they would watch him walk.

Thoroughbreds are designed for two traits, speed and stamina. By those measures, Smokey Joe was a masterpiece.

According to the just-arrived trainer, the stallion stood 17.1 hands high. He was built for power, with well-muscled shoulders, long bones in his upper hind legs, and generous hips. A long neck cantilevered his fluid stride, which was twenty-five feet, only a foot off American Pharoah and four feet off Secretariat and Man o' War. He could cover more than fifty feet in a second. As the horse was paraded in front of them, Sia saw the swagger of an animal uncomfortable standing still.

The trainer told Vadim that Smokey Joe had won two smaller races and the Travers, the Mid-Summer Derby up in Saratoga, but had some moderate tearing in the suspensory ligament on his right hind leg that would not heal. Smokey Joe wouldn't be racing again. Time to be put out to stud.

When the trainer had stopped speaking, Vadim regarded the horse for a moment, then spat into the sand. "I've read all the paperwork your people sent over. I'll give you two million for him." Sia caught Anna gritting her teeth at the break in decorum.

Max smiled generously. "Please, Vadim," he said, "let's not bore everyone with the details. Let's have dinner. Back to business later, eh?"

Vadim looked at Max, mental gears turning, debating a fight. Then he smiled, put up his hands. "Sure, fine," he said, his eyes flickering mirthlessly, "of course. But before dinner, let's swing by one of the fields."

They drove to the closest paddock and strolled down to the fence, toward a group of mares congregating to watch the cars. The fields glowed bright orange.

One of the broodmares pricked up her ears as they approached. The mare stood behind the horses that had gaggled around the fence, but she nudged them here and there until she had a spot directly facing Anna.

Sia watched as the mare held the Russian's eye contact. Anna took a step closer, then another. Then the mare stuck its head over the fence. Anna gently put her hand on its muzzle. The murmurs of Max and Vadim's conversation floated behind Sia. Turning her head, she saw the vet and one of the trainers staring at Anna and the mare, whispering to each other.

Then Anna was dropping herself smoothly on the other side of the fence.

Sia could not hear, but she saw Anna whispering to the horse, and as she did the mare's ears prickled and its left fluttered downward toward Anna's hushed voice. Wasn't this the same mare that Max had ridden when the snake had spooked their horses?

"Do you have a knife?" Anna called back to the vet. The vet, stunned, said yes and handed her a small, folded blade through the fence. Anna knelt into the grass,

The mare's head bobbed down to meet Anna's. The Russian was still whispering to the horse. Sia turned back. Max's face was a strained mixture of enchantment and alarm, but he did not move or ask why she had the knife. Sia watched the Russian gently lift the mare's left front foot from the ground. The mare did so, but to Sia this looked less like obedience and more like enjoyment. Anna used the knife to clean and inspect the foot. Anna set down the mare's foot with her right hand. Then with her left she felt the mare's loins and hips.

The light was fading, but Sia could see Anna's lips moving as she talked to the horse. Still on the ground, almost under the animal, Anna shifted to her right and lifted the mare's right hind leg. She was vulnerable, a spooked horse away from disaster: Putin's moneyman's wife getting her head kicked in on a CIA-run farm in Mexico. The thought evaporated quickly, though, because Anna was directly under the horse, lifting the right hind leg to examine the foot and the bone structure. She set it down and crouched underneath the mare to her offside. Anna ran her hands from its thigh to its rump and across its back to the mane. She positioned herself in front of the mare, and looked the animal dead-on.

Then Anna stepped back. A large step for a short woman. She stood still. A dog barked up at the house. A motor growled on the other side of the barns. Vadim was muttering. Anna and the mare stood at attention for what seemed like minutes, though it must have been seconds.

Anna took another step back.

The horse took a step toward her.

Anna stepped back. The horse stepped forward.

Anna and the horse stepped forward at the same time. Sia heard whispering but could not make out the words. Anna seemed to caress the horse's muzzle and Sia thought she caught a glimpse of the Russian pressing her own forehead onto the animal's. Daylight had vanished from the field, the details of Anna and the horse gone along with it. But in the gathering darkness Sia saw two shapes: a woman and a horse, each sizing up the other.

16

San Cristobal

NEXT MORNING, FROM THE DRIVER'S SEAT OF A BOUNCING PICKUP, Max sent a text message to a contact named Charles: *A/V clear to work for next four hours.* He texted the security manager, head butler, and the chief of the household staff and told them to expect a couple guys who would be out to provide a quote to upgrade the smart sound system. Slipping his phone into the cupholder, he smiled at Vadim jostling in the passenger's seat.

———

CHARLES WAS IN FACT ARTEMIS PROCTER, WHO CALLED A CIA OFFICER named Patrick, who was with a stocky guy called Pete in a restaurant outside San Cristobal. Patrick and Pete were specialists from Access, CIA's break-in crew. There were teams focused on auto locks, on mechanical locks, on electrical, on security systems. They worked out of a classified warehouse in the D.C. suburbs that Max had visited once, before Procter had sent him on an op to Dubai. Master keys clotted an entire wall of the building. The keys were reverse-engineered by testing locks for vulnerabilities, some of which were bizarre. One of the guys had shown Max how to break into a hotel safe by inserting a paper clip between the 3 and the 4 on the keypad and then punching the 8. It was the mechanical equivalent of hacking software.

Patrick paid the bill and they jumped into the truck to head for San Cristobal. At the gate, he gave the name of the A/V cover company. This one was going to be easy. Photo the room, image a few pieces of gear. No hostiles. Piece of cake.

And holy crow, this place was nice. He'd done the breaking-and-entering work at more than a few mansions, but this whole complex was just a first-cabin kind of place. Patrick swung a backpack onto his shoulder and greeted the butler, who said that the hacendado had requested they begin in the guest wing. In tow behind the butler, Patrick indulged his guilty pleasure: ticking off things that would be interesting to steal (though, Scout's honor, he never would). As the butler guided them through the wing before taking his leave, Patrick filled his mental getaway car with an oil painting of a rich Mexican lady, a few boxes of cigars from the walk-in humidor, and a marble statue of a horse. "What are you smiling about?" Pete prodded. But Patrick never did answer.

On the door and inside the room they checked for countermeasures: double-sided tape, hair, anything left behind to signal to the Russians that someone had entered. Patrick ran a radio-frequency survey to see if Vadim or Anna had hidden a camera or microphone to keep tabs on the room while they were away. Nada.

Pete pulled an extendable tripod from his bag and stuck his camera on top. He punched a button on his remote and the camera rotated to snap pictures of the room. A laptop was right there on the desk. Patrick removed the imaging hard drive from his bag and plugged it into the laptop. Just two minutes later it blinked green. He flipped open a purse and took pictures of its contents. He discovered an iPad, gently removed it. He pulled a second imaging drive out of the bag and plugged it into the iPad. They found another laptop in Anna's suitcase and imaged that, too. No phones. Not a surprise. People took those everywhere. They snapped pictures of every medication, scrap of paper, and ID card. They reviewed the photos to be sure everything had been returned to its proper location.

Leaving the room, Pete took the drives in one bag, and Patrick, fake contractor's bag in hand, continued his tour of the house toward the receiver in one of the living rooms. In a sitting room a horse figurine covered in faux–gold leaf caught his eye. Checking that he was alone, he unzipped the bag and slid the figurine inside. He looked at it for a moment. Then he set the golden creature back on the end table's mahogany pasture and started toward the doors.

———

WHILE PATRICK WAS FANTASIZING ABOUT ROBBING SAN CRISTOBAL OF its treasures—and actually robbing the Russians of their data—Max and Vadim, his would-be and soon-to-be victims, both stood under a patch of scrub tree on the edge of a wheat field holding twenty-gauge Benelli shotguns. The barrels were still warm but they had fallen silent, despite the doves continuing to stream into the field to feed. One of San Cristobal's yellow Labradors was retrieving some of the last hour's haul.

"The business with the stallion," Vadim said, watching the dog lope back into the field before quickly returning with a dove in its mouth.

"*Eso chingón*," Max said, patting the dog's head. He slipped the bird into the game belt slung around his waist.

"You offered two million dollars," Max said, watching the dog dart off. "Too low, my friend. Smokey Joe's stud fee will start at twenty-five thousand, maybe go as high as forty thousand, with his performance and pedigree and the few recent sales I know about. You've already done this math. And so have I. So two million is a no, my friend."

From his pocket Max slid Vadim the San Cristobal card embossed with the QR code. The Russian turned it over in his hands and wrinkled his brow. "Fancy. What's this?"

"The math. A report for you. Our stallion offerings and prices and recent comps. I make a point of not bullshitting my guests. I am a straightforward man. And you will see that you are fantastically low. The numbers show this. Two million does not work. But if that is your budget, the report will show you some excellent bloodstock well within your range."

Max caught a violent flash in Vadim's eyes. His adrenaline surged until he remembered that the chamber of Vadim's shotgun was empty.

The Russian, at any rate, apparently had more sense than San Cristobal's recent Emirati victim. The card, acknowledged with a grunt, disappeared into Vadim's pocket.

While Vadim reloaded, the dog returned with another bird, depositing it in Max's hand, where it flopped as a wing tried to flit free. Max snapped off its head and tucked it into the dump pouch.

As the dog took a break for some water, a group of five, maybe six doves appeared above the trees on the field's opposite side. Vadim aimed the shotgun and fired twice. The birds flew on, unharmed, to land in the field. "Fucking hell," he said. He balanced the gun on his shoulder and treated Max to a smile crossed with bared teeth.

"What was the name of the horse my wife met in the field last night before dinner?"

Max watched the dog bound across the field. "Penelope."

"Her information is on this card as well?" Vadim said.

"No. That is limited to the horses for sale," Max said.

"I will give you four million for Smokey Joe if you throw in Penelope."

A few streams of birds flew in above the trees. Vadim nodded to Max: *Your shot.* He slipped two shells into the Benelli, aimed to miss, and squeezed the trigger. He had Vadim twenty-one to six—but who was counting?—and he was starting to suspect the lopsided score was frustrating the Russian. Four million was also climbing toward Smokey Joe's market value. Unlike Sia, he wouldn't be returning cash to Uncle Sam.

"Four is still too low. And Penelope is not for sale."

"Come, now, my dear Max. Everything has a price."

"Not my mother's horse."

"Ah, I see. Perhaps I speak to your mother, then?"

"I'm afraid that's impossible. But even if she were alive, Penelope would still be unavailable."

Vadim looked off into the field. "I am sorry to hear about your mother. And you are a good man, honoring the dead. Though our parents"—he clicked his tongue—"sometimes their desires poison the children." Vadim fell silent. Then he turned back to Max and said, "Four-point-five for Smokey Joe and Penelope."

Fucking prick, Max thought. He slipped two more shells into the Benelli. In quick succession he shot two birds out of the air. The dog darted off at his whistle.

"Penelope," Max said, "is not for sale."

Vadim was fishing a water bottle from the cooler. "Where are the girls?"

"Riding."

"I mean the entertainment."

Max held his eye contact; the guy was serious.

"None this time," Max said. Unlike the Russians, CIA preferred—generally—not to use hookers during the recruitment dance, even if it was now clear a few might have accelerated the developmental work.

Vadim looked at Max as though he were insane. Then he laughed. "When you said we were going hunting, I thought you meant we would also sneak away for a few hours to have some fun. Maybe have a look at that filly who brought us the bottle of mescal last night? We can't grow tits like that in Russia. Too cold, I suppose. Fucking shame."

The girl was Antonia. She would turn sixteen in three weeks. The twenty-eighth, if he was not mistaken. Her mother was Martina, one of the housekeepers. Martina's father had been hired as a groom by his grandfather in 1972.

Breaking this gringo fuck with a winding trail ride into a driving rain—now, that would be entertainment. Max took in the western horizon. Clear skies, even-keel barometer behind his temples, sun. *Pinche sol.* He spat.

"I generally prefer women to little girls," Max said.

"Oh, you are blind, my friend!" Vadim said, an edge creeping into his voice. "Nothing little about that one. Anyhow, you come to RusFarm and I'll show you a good time." The Russian stared off across the field and they hung there in a hostile silence.

"I rather enjoy owning a farm," Vadim finally said. "I was raised in Petersburg, my family had a dacha in the country, but there were no animals. I did not think I would care for a horse operation, but I am having great fun."

The dog had returned, its job done. Vadim seemed to be waiting for Max to ask why he was enjoying the country life, but the question never came. Max was just scratching the dog's ears.

Vadim coughed and went on. "I have found that the horses show us who we are."

"How is that, my friend?"

"You are a horseman, you must understand."

"There are many opinions on the subject of horses."

"Here is mine. Petersburg Knight is our senior sire. We have him breeding on a full book of three hundred mares each season. He's at it five times a day. And you know what I think? He loves his job. A little twinkle in his eyes when he trots off."

Max whistled. "A book of three hundred mares? Too many. Talk to your breeding manager. And five times a day? Too much, even for a fertile stallion. Two, maybe three times. That's better. Sustainable."

Vadim ignored this. "The stallion is strong. So he fucks. That simple."

"This is all you've learned from the noble horse?" Max thwacked Vadim's shoulder. The Russian's face twitched in anger, but Max's smile was genuine, even friendly. And, as tended to happen with customers of Vadim's type, the confusing contrast was sufficient to coax a wary, submissive smile onto the gringo's face.

Max handed Vadim a box of shells from the truck. The Russian slipped two in the Benelli and scanned the empty sky. They should have been spreading out along the field's edge for more shooting, but Max wanted to keep him talking, change the subject.

"How'd you and Anna meet?" Max asked.

"Schoolmates," Vadim said, "since secondary." A long swig from the water bottle.

"Young love," Max said.

Vadim chuckled, but a darkness crept over his face. "How much do you know about Russia, Max?"

"What I read in the newspaper."

"Well, the damn newspapers lie. Russia was pillaged after the collapse of the Soviet Union and we've been building it back ever since. I help run a bank that enables Russian companies to compete and operate all over the world. Yankee sanctions be damned. My father has passed, but the bank was his creation. He was one of the people who recognized in the nineties that we needed strong leadership to overcome our problems. And he had known a man named Vladimir Putin since they were young boys growing up in Piter."

"I'm sorry about your father."

Vadim shot at a single dove, missing terribly. "Thank you. I've made peace with it."

"And, Piter?"

"Saint Petersburg. And I suppose that you, as a Mexican, will understand this next point: Russia in the nineties was chaos. You had your cartels here. We had our Mafia oligarchs running things. My father, an honest banker, had a hard time in this environment."

"My grandfather also had to defend our land and our business during the Dirty War," Max reciprocated. "And my father had to navigate peace with the cartels. Lawlessness, the enemy of the businessman."

Vadim slapped his shoulder. "Exactly right. But in Russia what that meant was my father, a businessman, had to forge alliances with the security men, the former KGB guys. My father found Andrei Agapov. Or should I say Major General Andrei Agapov. And General Agapov had a daughter, Anya. My father made his expectations clear to me."

"It was an arranged marriage?" Max asked.

"Not formally. At least no one ever said it that way. But, over time, my father impressed upon me that my place in the business hinged on marrying Anya." Vadim shrugged.

A wind had kicked up, and the skies over the field were empty, the doves having gone to roost in the scrub trees to wait out the breeze. "What did Anna think about that?" Max asked. He was scratching the dog behind the ears.

"About what?"

"The marriage."

That set the guy's eyes to searching Max up and down, as if reviewing opportunities for violence. Then his countenance lightened, doves flew from the trees toward the decoy spinning in the field, and Vadim plucked two from the sky. The dog hustled out to collect them. Vadim slipped the first into the dump pouch on his belt. The second flopped to the ground from the dog's mouth. He continued, "Like you, Anna tries to honor her parents. Even if what her father wants is not good for her."

The dove uselessly flapped a shot-through wing and tried to walk. Vadim's lip curled while he stared, eyes glued to the wounded bird. "Five for Smokey Joe. And Penelope," he said.

Vadim loaded a shell into the shotgun and began to level it at the struggling bird.

Max put up his hand. "There won't be anything left if you do that."

Vadim lowered the gun.

Max stared him dead-on and took a step into the Russian's space. "You are my guest. And I've told you that I don't bullshit my guests or clients. But you must presume that I am in fact bullshitting you, Vadim, otherwise you would stop making offers on the mare. Would you like to make another?"

Vadim's mouth spread into a sly smile, pointing downward at his gun. "I would love to, but Penelope is not for sale, Max."

They stared at each other for a sticky moment; Max again entertained the disconcerting thought that the Russian would doubtless find it amusing to shoot him. And this time the shotgun was loaded.

"What interests you about a fifteen-year-old mare with a so-so pedigree anyhow?" Max asked, cooling the conversation. They began walking toward the dove.

"Because my wife wants her," Vadim replied.

"The mare would be a gift?" Max asked.

"Yes," Vadim said. "A gift for me."

Max's face screwed into a grimace. Then he stooped to pick up the bird and pop off its head.

17

San Cristobal

ACROSS THE HACIENDA ANNA BROUGHT PENELOPE TO A COMFORT-able canter as the hilly pasture descended into a flat expanse of dirt and bunchgrass. There had been no need to ask for the mare. After the auspicious greeting in the field, Anna had arrived in the stable to find a groom readying Penelope for their ride.

Anna shut her eyes, felt the wind whipping through her hair, and then leaned back slightly to communicate with Penelope as she had with her old horse. Penelope slowed to a trot. Sia caught up and pulled alongside. A mild sun beat down on her face and the land stretched open in every direction. They had covered much of the hacienda that morning, though they had been careful to avoid Max and Vadim's hunting grounds.

At a creek they stopped to water the horses. Sia had a flask of whiskey in her saddlebag. She poured some into a collapsible stainless steel cup and handed it to Anna. They sat on the ground in the shade of a walnut tree. Anna liked this unpretentious side of Sia. Camping cups and whiskey and horses. The opposite of what RusFarm had become.

"Your clients," Sia said. "Can you tell me more about them?"

"In general terms, yes," Anna said. "No names, of course."

"Of course."

"Three are particularly keen for your services. Two are in natural resources: one in potash, the other in timber. But there is a third, and I will share the name only because it is Vadim. It is me."

Sia sipped her whiskey. "I see."

"I think between the three pots there is perhaps a hundred million we would like to move out of Russia. Each client has certain objectives. For example, the timber baron is keen for exposure, through beneficiaries, of course, to the European and American real estate markets. As are we."

"And you are ready to start the process?" Sia asked. "Because there are a number of things I would need—"

Anna was shaking her head. "Moving money out of Russia is a bit delicate at the moment, as you must know. Reputational risks, and all. I've been asked, first, to get a sense for you and Hynes Dawson. Then, after everyone is comfortable, we can move forward. Once that happens, perhaps in a few weeks, you might come to Russia for a more in-depth conversation?"

Anna thought she glimpsed a spark in Sia's eyes.

"Of course," Sia said. "So tell me what you want to know."

"We understand your firm's reputation," Anna started in, "that Hynes Dawson is effective at structuring client finances in ways that maximize flexibility and security. And secrecy. It's—"

Sia cut her off. "See, that's the bit I'm still puzzling over, Anna. The secrecy. Because I don't understand how you found us. We don't advertise. There is no website. Hynes Dawson is a word-of-mouth operation. Doubly with Russians. So which mouth told you about us?" Sia smiled thinly over her cup and then took a drink.

There was a pause. A breeze washed them with the scent of dust and hay and the musk of the horses.

Anna took a generous sip of whiskey. "Vassily Platonovich Gusev," she said.

Then, setting the cup in the grass between her legs, Anna thought: Will your greed win, Sia, or will you call me on the lie?

———

"VASSILY GUSEV," SIA MURMURED. "HMM. THE KREMLIN BIGWIG? GOES by Goose, I think?"

Anna stood to stretch her legs. "I will speak plainly, understanding you cannot break client confidences. You have doubtless seen reports in the British media about a feud between my father and Goose. Let me say this: They are wildly exaggerated. And they further ignore the truth that in Moscow it is challenging to keep secrets about money. The fixers and facilitators speak to each other. We heard about Hynes Dawson from some of Goose's men in Moscow. That is where the glowing reviews about you and your firm originated."

Vague, Sia did not say. *And why bring up the media reports? Why that fake dramatic pause before mentioning Goose's name, you little Russian liar?* So many questions, but instead she plucked blades of grass. They'd been watching Mickey Lyadov in London, Sia figured. Anna was hunting for Daddy's lost gold. Then Sia said, "I cannot speak to whether Goose or any of his associates are Hynes Dawson clients, of course."

"I know. I am not asking that question. But you must understand that my clients and, quite frankly, my family, care deeply about your discretion and your ability to anticipate Russian needs. The environment today is . . . complicated. There are those who would like to put hands on this money, or to publicize its existence outside Russia."

Sia gestured to the horses and the stream and the field. "We're alone. We can be frank with one another."

"I want assurances that you have personal experience dealing with Russian clients, Sia," Anna said. "Rich ones. Powerful ones. Men like Goose, with thin patience and complicated financial empires to protect. A track record of delivering that protection."

"You have a reference for me, do you not?" Sia asked. "From one of Goose's men in Moscow. Nameless fellow." She arched an eyebrow and gave the Russian a smooth smile.

"I do, I do," Anna said, staring her dead-on. "But I like to look potential partners in the eye when they say it. My father's disagreements with Goose are not what the papers say, but it's no secret that they are not close. A reference from a Goose moneyman means you're the best. It does not mean I can trust you."

"I have extensive experience offering Russian clients the services you're requesting," Sia said. "I know what I'm doing. I keep my fucking mouth shut and I don't ask questions. I do the work. That's how we build the trust."

"Fair enough. But my clients are keen for one little detail, Sia. It matters greatly to them. They must know if you arranged Goose's structure. You personally. We know his moneymen use Hynes Dawson. You were referred to us. But my clients want this certainty . . ."

Their eyes met. Anna's were cold blue; hard, and remote.

Then each woman gave the other an unkind smile.

Sia tapped a finger to her nose. A quick nod.

Sia poured more whiskey and raised her cup. Anna did the same. They downed the whiskey, mounted the horses, and left the shade of the scrub trees, winding through the pasture.

This one is Russian intel, Sia thought as they rode toward the main house. Got to be. She's trying to work me, but she's on my hook. She's playing my game.

———

AFTER LUNCH THEY SAT IN THE LIBRARY WITH MESCAL AND STILTED conversation until Max suggested he and Vadim raid the walk-in humidor. They collected a box of Gurkhas drenched in cognac and took them poolside. Half their cigars were gone before anyone spoke, and once or twice Vadim flicked ashes into the water. The Russian launched into an unsolicited monologue on the leadership style of his President, then another on the wisdom of Moscow's bloody foreign adventures. His eyes stalked young Antonia carrying a stack of towels across the veranda toward the guest rooms.

Sia and Anna emerged from the library to join them, and thank god, someone else could speak to this man. As if reading his tired mind, Sia struck up a conversation with Vadim about the Mexican weather. Max stood and strolled under a vine-draped archway. The weather. The pressure was building in his temples. And through the bright afternoon sun he saw a hazy rim of clouds appear off in the west, just beyond the mountains. The sky above was pale blue. One or two thin linen clouds scudding along. But a disturbance lurked. He blew a jet of smoke up into the arches and sensed Vadim behind him.

"You said Smokey Joe has begun his new duties?" Vadim asked. "Something about a mare sent up from Brazil?"

"Yes. She's arrived in the last week. I've got a contract to send her back once she's in foal."

Cigar clenched in his teeth, Vadim said, "When's his next performance?"

Max checked his watch. "You've seen all the evaluations, Vadim."

Vadim smacked Max's shoulder, ejecting the cigar from his fingers. Embers popped when it skidded across the stone. When Max picked it up, Vadim was smiling. "But my dear Max, before I buy something," he said, "I like to see how it fucks."

———

THERE WAS A BRIEF DEBATE OVER WHETHER ANNA AND SIA WOULD TAG along. Anna had scolded Vadim for insisting they all should go, have a time of it, but he would not listen. Hand in the air toward Anna, Sia graciously said she would of course be delighted to observe the courtship. Max stepped aside and phoned Roberto.

"*Sí, patrón.*"

"Where are you?"

"The yearling pasture. Dealing with a fence."

"Get Penelope and Rosa ready in the next thirty minutes. Pack jackets. Nothing else. No guns."

Max pictured the old man's eyes slatting in the direction of the mountains.

"The pass, *patrón?*"

"The sun is shining," Max said.

Roberto chuckled.

———

MAX DROVE THEM TO THE SHED. THE BRAZILIAN MARE WAS A TWO-year-old bay called Midnight. Grooms excused the poor teaser stallion who, having sniffed at Midnight's hindquarters to stoke interest, was no longer required. Grooms whistle when foals urinate, teaching the horses over time to do the same on cue. Wearing vests and helmets—just in case she kicked—they now whistled as they led Midnight into the narrow, padded, three-sided enclosure. She'd been fitted with felt boots on her hind legs to protect her and the stallion. A twitch set onto a long pole was applied to Midnight's nose and held down by one of the grooms so he could maintain control of the animal. Another lubricated her, tied up her tail, then lifted her right front leg to prevent her from kicking. Smokey Joe trotted into the shed.

"I have found," Vadim whispered to Max, "that, like us, some stallions are naturally roguish and irascible in the breeding shed. No foreplay. Rough mounting. Biting."

"Only if you let them," Max said. "The grooms here are attentive. We don't tolerate that. And Smokey Joe is a gentleman."

Upon entering the shed, the stallion nuzzled the mare.

One groom helped guide Smokey Joe, two more were moving the animals here and there so the coupling would occur in a clear space and the horses not smash into a shed wall. The vet, like Max, watched Smokey Joe. The stallion covered the mare, placing his forelegs onto her back. A groom guided the stallion with the focus of an astronaut docking rocket modules. In a few seconds Smokey Joe went stock-still, raised his nose into the air, and curled back his mouth. Then he thrust again, his tail flagged upward, and it was done. Vadim clapped. Anna and Sia, Max saw, were deep in conversation and had perhaps not even watched. Smokey Joe lingered by Midnight in a brief afterglow that unceremoniously ended when the grooms led the stallion from the shed.

"Five-point-two for Smokey Joe," Vadim said.

"You are still low."

"But for god's sake, Max, he did not even bite!"

Max glanced toward Sia and Anna. They were smiling, the body language companionable. He strolled from the shed with Vadim, the women trailing behind, enjoying whatever they were chatting about.

Max looked up at the sky. He spat. Turned to Vadim. "How about you and I take a ride?"

———

THE RAIN BROKE THROUGH WHEN THEY'D CROSSED THE GRASSY PAS-tures and the edges of the salt pan and reached the path tracking up into the mountains. They'd not been elevated a thousand feet when the shoaling clouds kicked Vadim's common sense in the teeth and he asked Max about the weather and Max shook his head. Said most likely not until well past midnight. Vadim was not short and his mare was not fifteen hands high, but he'd still thrown all his weight into the left stirrup when he climbed into the saddle, callously tossing his right leg over to knock the poor mare square in the ribs. Most of all, he rode with the fear of a man who had not trusted a horse before, and, Max figured, probably not many people, either. The Russian's grip on the reins was either flaccid or strangling, and he sat tentatively without connection to the animal. Then the storm had arrived. They put on the jackets from the saddlebags, but the rain came in cold sheets that invaded the canvas and soaked into his ribs and boots. The negotiation, too, had washed away, forgotten.

They curled up the old Comanche trail into the mountains. Water coursed down the path, running through the exposed roots of the crooked and withered pines.

"Max, for fuck's sake," Vadim shouted from a few lengths back, "can we make it down tonight?"

"The trail is flooding," Max called through the rain. "Can't risk the horses. Ten minutes up, there is an overlook with rocks. Shelter. We will wait it out there."

The mountain water ran brown and red under Penelope. He leaned close to the animal and thanked her for making this wet and unpleasant journey. When they reached the overlook, they positioned the horses against a wall of rock that shielded their backs, at least, from the rain. They kept the horses bridled, holding the reins because there was nothing to tie them to. Vadim pulled his phone from his pocket and grimaced.

"There is never reception up here, I am afraid," Max said.

"Can we go down?"

"The trail is a river, Vadim."

Hours passed in silence, their hands stuck on the reins, bodies alternating between the saddle and standing alongside the horses. Before dark the wind shifted to whip the rain against the rock face. Every few minutes Vadim fruitlessly checked his phone. After nightfall the rain stopped and Max began whistling an old tune about horses. The clouds had disappeared with the storm and the sky was starlight and an incandescent moon. He could hear Vadim shivering in his coat. Still holding the reins, Max dozed off in the saddle.

Max woke to the flutter of doves and the first crease of sun breaking above the eastern rim of the hacienda. Vadim sat in the saddle, eyes closed. Their coats ran with dew. He nudged Vadim's shoulder. The Russian's eyes opened, and for once Max did not see fight in them. For several minutes they sat in silence.

"The number is six-point-two," Max said. "And it is final. I cannot negotiate below market rates. You must understand this. That is the price. That is the price for Kovalchuks. For Maktoums. For Kentucky men. For anyone else. It is fair, it is based on the stud fees you will earn from his conformation and pedigree and his racing record. You know this. Or your people do. I hope we can do business. But if we cannot, there are no hard feelings. I rode you hard and put you away wet last night, and for that I offer my deepest apologies. Weather breaks all kind of crazy ways off these mountains and sometimes it is impossible to predict." Max turned and spat.

Vadim slowly extended his hand, tilting his head downward in a slight nod. "Six-point-two."

Max hauled him up. They shook hands.

"Well," Max said, "let's head back. Celebrate."

———

AS THEY RODE, MAX FELT PENELOPE'S BLOOD TWISTING AND SURGING through the veins and arteries on her back. Her breath rifled through her nostrils and she arched her head side to side because she wanted to run.

They took the last grassy expanse of the western pasture at full gallop, Max careful to keep Vadim always a few lengths behind, and he coaxed Penelope to run as his mother had, leaning forward, the gentlest hammer of his heel into the vault of the mare's ribs.

They arrived at the hacienda by lunchtime.

Anna and Sia were reading by the pool. Max and Vadim carried with them the smell of mud and sweat and horse and perhaps worse. Vadim had brought them to a stop on the way back to take a shit. Vadim's eyes were raw and red-rimmed. His hair was mussed and oily. He'd shivered himself to sleep on a horse. He'd overpaid for the damn stallion.

Sia shut her book and stood to greet Max with a kiss on the cheek. Her lips were soft and warm on his skin.

Anna's eyes seemed to shine in amusement. She did not stand to greet her husband. She flipped to the next page with a flourish and buried her eyes into her book. "My dear," she said, "what happened? You look unwell."

Vadim's mouth had just opened for a retort when Max saw his father walk from the living room, through the open doors, and out into the courtyard. He wore gray sweatpants and an oversized blue T-shirt and sandals with socks. Vadim looked confused. "Papa?" Max said. "Are you okay?" He spoke in Spanish.

"Are you my new handler?" his father said in rapid-fire Spanish, pointing at Vadim. "Because I don't know you. And you don't look like a CIA man."

18

San Cristobal

S IA COULD MAKE OUT MERE SHREDS OF THE SPANISH, BUT SHE WAS certain she heard *CIA*.

Max's dementia-stricken father, freshly wandered out of his guest cottage, was confusing the Russian target for a new handler. Sia's eyes darted between the two Russians to see if either could understand.

"Where's Hoyt?" he shouted at Max in Spanish. "I want to talk to Hoyt." Max was up now, trying to frog-march his father back into the living room. The old man wagged a finger at Vadim. Max was muttering and whispering to him in Spanish.

Max finally hustled his father into the house and out of sight. Sia heard more yelling, doors slamming. Anna's mouth hung open. Holy hell. Had she understood the Spanish?

When he returned to the patio, Max went to the bar and poured himself a generous mescal.

For a long moment all four of them stood in silence. Sia studied Anna and Vadim. If they had understood the Spanish, would they say something? Max broke the silence. "My father has Alzheimer's. He lives in a house on the property. He wandered off."

Max downed the mescal.

Fuck, Sia thought. Had a lunatic blown her op?

Vadim went to a cabinet, took down a glass, and smacked it onto the stone bar. He slapped Max's shoulder and smiled when he filled his glass. But the smile did little to hide the fact that Vadim's face was unkind.

And it was not because of what Max's father had said. No, she did not think either Russian understood. It was something else. The eyes were not knowing. They were angry. What had happened on the trail?

"We're here to drink with you, Max," Vadim blurted out, his glass raised. "To your father. And your farm." And they did. In the afternoon they rested. Then they had two bottles of wine at dinner. Mescal in the stallion barn afterward, where Anna and Sia broke off for a drunken smoke.

When they returned to the barn, Max and Vadim were propped against Smokey Joe's stall in silence. Max seemed relieved to see her. As the four of them strolled out, Vadim stopped. He went back to stare at the horse. He was gripping the door, shifting his weight from foot to foot.

"All right, Max Castillo," he shouted, "we have our deal for Smokey Joe. And only Smokey Joe. But there is one more thing. A condition. You both come visit RusFarm. The four of us, we'll make a weekend of it. Come see us in Piter. And soon."

Vadim held out a wobbly hand.

Max stepped forward, looked at Vadim's hand for a beat, then shook it.

They popped open a celebratory bottle of champagne and chatted near the pool, dance music bouncing from the speakers nestled under the stone archways. Max and Sia said goodbye to the Russians, who were leaving first thing in the morning. See you in Saint Petersburg, Sia called as they went to their room. In her head Sia began drafting the cables, considering ways she might increase the odds that Langley would approve of that. Max had closed on the damn horse during their ride, they had successfully exploited the Russians' tech, but judging by the hateful eyes during his toast, the odds of further developing Vadim Kovalchuk were low. On Anna, though, Sia thought there might be angles. That Vadim's invitation had included Max added a layer of complication. After all, a solo visit would be simpler, cleaner. But Sia could work with this setup. There was a path forward. And after two days with valuable Russians, that was a miracle all its own.

In the bedroom Sia's guard fell and she collapsed, exhausted, onto the bed. She was sliding into sleep when she heard Max hiss: Get up, get up, come on, Sia. Up. His laptop was open, and though Sia was only half-awake, her brain dim from the night's alcohol, she heard the strain in his voice and was instantly up and alert. The surveillance program was open on his computer. They could see the entire guest suite: shower, bathroom, closets, sitting area, multiple perspectives on the bed and the built-in desk. Anna and Vadim were standing on either side of the bed speaking in hushed Russian. The surveillance program produced a clunky real-time translation.

Anna: What do you mean by that?

Vadim: I mean there is something off with them. They are lovers? They do not seem intimate to me. They seem like business partners.

Anna: You are angry with him because of the sale?

Vadim: Oh, it's play money, who cares about all that?

Anna: You do, Vadim.

[Five-second pause]

Vadim: I care that I spent the night freezing my balls off in the fucking mountains.

Anna: Maybe she is after his money?

Vadim: If that's the case, he should be screwing her brains out in return, screwing anything he likes, actually. And do you think that is happening? Yesterday when we went hunting there were no girls. There are always girls on trips like this. Always. And when I made a joke—a joke, Anya—about the maid, he soured. Scolded me, the fucker.

Anna: Give me a break.

Vadim: I am serious. You are not capable of intimacy, so how could you see?

Anna: Ah yes, you are quite the lover, I forgot, Vadim. So sensitive.

Vadim: Fuck off, Anya.

Anna went into the bathroom. Max expanded two of the surveillance shots. One, Anna, sitting on the toilet in her underwear. Then she got up, snatched a pill from her cosmetic bag, and swallowed it. The other shot showed Vadim on the bed's edge. They seemed to be waiting each other out. After a few minutes Vadim went into the bathroom, shoved Anna aside, and began rifling through her cosmetic bag. He held up a bottle of pills and shouted something at Anna, who shook her head. Now the Russian was much too fast for the program to translate. Vadim was dumping pills in the sink. Anna came at him, he again pushed her away. Arms folded across her chest, she leaned against the wall to watch him work. Then he chucked the cosmetic bag into the shower. More pills and a toothbrush and makeup cases and brushes spilled across the marble floor. Max was shaking his head.

Max slid the laptop to Sia and began pacing the room.

Sia returned to the screen. Anna was watching Vadim's tirade with an expressionless face. For a moment they glared at each other in silence, then Vadim said a few more words that escaped the translation program. He was pointing at her, motioning with his fingers: *Spin around.* Anna said something, but the words were too soft for Sia to hear even through the mics. It was, Sia thought even then, as if the Russian spoke to herself.

Then Anna slid down her panties and turned to the wall.

Sia shut the laptop and joined Max at the window. She whispered, "What did you do to him out there?"

"Nothing he does not deserve." Then Max, taking a candlestick into his grip, battered it once twice three times against a table. *Pinche*

ruso, she heard him hiss while he worked. Fucking Russian. After, Max
calmly righted the scuffed candlestick, gathered up a few splinters from
the table, and threw them in a wastebin. He sat on the edge of the bed
to slide off his boots, muttering curses in Spanish. "You take the bed
tonight," Sia said. "You need the rest."

He put the boots aside and started unbuttoning his shirt. "Only if
you join me. The couch is uncomfortable. You won't rest. It's a big bed,
and I'm a peaceful sleeper."

And a fast one, Sia thought, returning from the bathroom to hear
the slow, heavy breathing of sleep just moments after he slid under the
covers. Sia climbed into the bed, but sleep would not come. Her mind,
her building anger, was fixated upon what was occurring in the Russians'
bedroom. Her thoughts were only broken when she turned to look at
Max. True to his word, he was a deep and tranquil sleeper, ramrod-still
over on his side, and she was bothered that she noticed, or thought of
him at all, or thought of Anna's plight, for that matter, because that suggested something other than apathy, and apathy had so far been a good
and loyal friend to Sia Fox.

19

San Cristobal / Langley

NEXT MORNING SIA WOKE TO WATCH THE RUSSIANS' PLANE ASCEND and vanish into the fog. Max was still asleep in the bed. She collected a cup of coffee from the kitchen and went to the patio to nurse her hangover. The fog had rolled in thick, the morning cold and wet. She pulled her robe snug to the chill. An older housekeeper scowled at Sia when she passed. Max joined her, and for a while they sat in silence. Slate-gray clouds were swirling around the hilltop. "Let's walk," he said finally.

They took a damp trail from the house into a western pasture, snaking along a length of the same creek where Sia and Anna had watered the horses.

"We have something to work with," Sia finally said when they had stopped. They paused to watch a small group of javelinas—wild hogs— rooting around a patch of yucca on a hillside. "Anna is not a sullen victim," Sia said. "There's something running just beneath her surface. She's headstrong, willing to take risks. No telling what she does if presented with a way out. And there's no way in hell that Vadim is the angle here. Any disagreement?"

"None," he said. "And it's *you* with the bead on Anna, Sia. You've got a reason to visit her in Russia. This worked. Just not in the way we expected."

They watched the javelinas for a while longer, then turned back. Sia was savoring a lovely smack of adrenaline. Anna was their prey to chase. And now Sia, not Max, would be the lead hunter.

Back in the house, Sia drafted the cable. They sat on couches in the old chapel. Max watched horse races as she wrote.

Sia summarized the major events of the past two days, opting to leave out the parts about Max's father and the breaking of Vadim on the trail ride. A good NOC knew what to exclude. She finished with a statement that they stood by to accept the invitation to join Anna and Vadim in Russia. She penned every word and phrase to guide Moscow X and the Seventh Floor leadership toward that outcome. And though Deputy Director Bradley was considered operationally aggressive, more than anything Sia feared Seventh Floor hand-wringing and subsequent inaction. Plenty of good ops were stillborn thanks to Langley's diddling, though this one, run through Moscow X, admittedly stood a better chance given Procter's reputation for bureaucratic bulldozing.

When she'd read and reread the finished cable, she showed it to Max, who nodded and said fire away before turning back to the races. She sent it, then she took out her phone to sort through her overgrown inbox. Lawyer was her real day job, after all.

Max had arranged for the San Cristobal jet to ferry her to Mexico City for the return flight to London. He drove her to the airstrip, parking on the edge of the apron.

"If Langley gives us the green light," Sia asked, looking up at the plane, "will you be in?"

"It depends, I suppose."

"On what?"

"On what Procter asks."

"Fair enough. But what do *you* want to do? You can say no, right? You've got choices."

He shrugged. "I might like to see RusFarm."

Max carried her bag up the airstair and into the plane. They said goodbye with a hug. Then he kissed her cheeks and began walking down the aisle.

"Hey," she said.

Max turned around.

"Why would you want to see RusFarm?" she asked.

"Call it professional curiosity." He smiled.

Sia caught his eyes break cover for a fleeting moment as he turned to descend the stairs before he was gone. That curiosity, she thought, taking her seat, well, that was anything but professional.

———

DUE TO THEIR BOSS'S FAVORABLE PERSPECTIVES ON SECRECY AND deception, Procter's minions in Moscow X ritually eyewashed every scrap of intelligence created by her NOCs. Eyewashing, or obscuring the true source of intelligence, even to those inside the CIA, was one of Procter's favorite parts of the job. And so she doctored the reports from Mexico so other CIA officers would not be able to trace them back to Sia, Max, Vadim, or Anna.

In the early evening, two days after the conclusion of the San Cristobal operation, Procter visited with George, one of her senior techies, a gaunt man whom she had poached from NSA. George sat in a windowless office inside the Moscow X spaces. Light beamed from the dozen or so computer terminals to reflect off George's pasty skin. So far, the news on the technical operation had not been promising.

Procter eased into a chair alongside George. The techie, picking at an uncooked blue raspberry Pop-Tart, did not notice the Chief until she squeezed his shoulder. "The news, Georgie," she said. "The news."

"There is no good news," he said, with some measure of enjoyment, which made Procter angry. He brushed Pop-Tart crumbs off his hands.

"Tell me."

"Vadim's laptop and tablet are for personal use. I am sure of it. No work email. No connections to the Bank Rossiya network. He's not even conducting RusFarm business on it. Nothing. Vadim is, I think, adopting security protocols like we do when we go overseas for short stints. Nothing work-related travels with him."

"Anything interesting on the personal side?"

"Just the pictures of him, girlfriends, emails to girlfriends. There is a mountain of that on his machine."

"You've run searches on the chicks?"

"I have on the ones I can identify. So far, I can't find anyone of importance inside Russia. They are assistants, hookers, department store clerks. No one with an angry and influential husband, if that's what you're after."

"It is very much what I'm after."

"So that's the bad news," George said. "I cannot conduct even basic reconnaissance on the Bank Rossiya network, much less access any of Putin's financial information that may live on it."

"Goddammit," muttered Procter. "Same on Anna's?"

"Same," he said. "Personal use. Spare. Not many pictures. Her web search history is thin. The laptop model is three years old, but if you'd told me she'd only had it for a week, I would believe you. You know what they say about people who travel with tech like this, right?"

"I don't like riddles, Georgie. They agitate me."

"You're either a terrorist, a criminal, or an intelligence officer."

Without asking, Procter pulled George's second Pop-Tart from the foil sleeve and took a generous bite. "I hope Anna is only one of those, Georgie, but my money's on two."

———

THREE DAYS AFTER THE RUSSIANS DEPARTED SAN CRISTOBAL, MOSCOW X had woven a tapestry of ten eyewashed operational cables that Procter disseminated to all of two people at Langley: the Director, who probably would not read them, and Ed Bradley, who most certainly would. Procter didn't trust many people. In fact, she frowned on the concept and did not like the word, but whatever you called it, she had it with Bradley. And Ed would decide whether they were going to continue the adventure in fortress Russia.

One hour after she sent the cables, Procter received a summons to Bradley's office.

"Artemis, I've got five minutes," he said after she'd taken a seat under the launchers. "Then I need to prep for dinner with the SSCI Chairman."

"Woof," Procter said. Two thumbs down.

He tapped his nose, then said, "Bullshit eyewashed reports aside, let me make sure I have this straight. We have an open invitation for our officers to visit a Thoroughbred horse operation outside of Saint Petersburg run by one of Putin's moneymen."

"That's right."

"And his wife is a banker. She contacted one of our NOCs in London."

"Yes."

"And the traces all check out?"

"Correct."

"And your NOC thinks they have a recruitment play with her?"

"Yes. Her husband, the moneyman, he's abusive. Unsurprisingly they do not like each other. It'll give the pitch some lift."

"Can we stall and bring them out of Russia again?"

"Doubt it."

"Why not?"

"Because the Russian wife-beater bought a six-million-dollar horse from one of my officers and drunkenly insisted their next visit happen in Petersburg."

Bradley laughed. "I mean, Artemis, good lord."

Procter tried a smile. She'd been practicing.

Bradley flipped through a few of the papers. "The NOC ... true name is Hortensia Fox."

Procter interrupted. "Sia. She goes by Sia. Gets pissy when you use her Christian name."

"All right, Sia gets a call from a member of the Agapov clan weeks after helping their rival Goose stash money. Coincidence?"

"Hell, no. We're getting sucked into the toilet bowl of Kremlin power politics. Which is good, because we don't have any idea what's jammed in the pipes, besides shit, of course. But I do think Anna wants something from our NOC. Hence the outreach."

"The info on what she's done with Goose's money?"

"Probably. Has to be, right? Russians are counting on Sia being greedy, willing to collect fees by working both sides."

"Right. Holy hell." Bradley steepled hands over his nose. "What is the best-case on this from a collection standpoint?"

"The best angle here is that Anna can help us get access to the tech Vadim is using to manage Putin's cash. We struck out on this one in Mexico, unfortunately. The tech the Russians brought was clean. Throwaway gear. Nothing useful on it, no wormholes to helpful networks."

Bradley folded his hands behind his head and creaked back in the chair. "What's the worst-case?"

"If this Anna is an intel officer, she probably wants Sia inside Russia so she can work her. Things can always go badly."

"And the Russians sometimes lack patience in these matters."

"True, true, fucking true. But Sia suspects this Russian chick, Anna, is different. Sia thinks Anna might be trying to recruit her, considers herself an artist, usual bullshit. My money is Anna is SVR or working for them, though we don't yet have any hard proof. Daddy was KGB First Chief Directorate, though. It would make sense."

"Reading between the lines here," Bradley continued, "am I correct in thinking that if you sent them to Saint Petersburg, you would lead the Russians to believe they were gathering intelligence from our NOC lawyer along the way?"

"It would be the only way to guarantee her safety. She would have to be authorized to give up information on Goose's money. That's got to be what Anna wants. And if it is, we give it to her. Why the hell not?"

"This is quite the tightrope, Artemis."

"I know. It's the job, man."

"Sia's got the business connection to Anna," Bradley said. "Why send Castillo at all? That's not normally how we use him."

"I think asking Max to tag along would be helpful," Procter said. "He can keep Vadim busy, give Sia space. He and Vadim can do horsey shit together. Whatever the hell. And shit, Ed, you and I both know Max can say no. Probably will say no. Worst-case, Sia goes alone. Best-case, he goes along as wingman, gives her some cover."

Bradley's warm smile hid the skepticism she felt settling over the room. Guy had probably flashed those teeth to a hundred fucking agents over the years—the evergreen kind of operational smile you wound up bringing in from the field and turning on your friends and family. "Right now," he said, "no bullshit, what are the odds Sia recruits the Russian? Put a number on it. Humor me."

"Seven percent. Normal odds with Russians are sub–one percent. We've got more to work with here."

Same smile. "Seems high. Does Sia want to go in? She obviously understands the risks."

"She's a hot-shit NOC. She's tough as nails but also wants to prove it. She's got an adrenaline complex. Hell, yes, she wants to go inside. She wants a Russian scalp."

"And I presume that you think we should send them in? Even with the risks and a seven percent chance of success?"

Procter picked at her teeth and thought about that. "Absolutely. Our job is to collect, not sit on our tushies and hope sweet intel moseys our way. We're not getting many bites at Russian intel officers these days. If we have a shot at primo Russian ass, we should take it."

Bradley rapped his knuckles on the table and stood to put on his jacket. "Pass my regards to the officers. And get them into Petersburg as soon as you can."

20

RusFarm / Moscow

ANNA'S WORLD REVOLVED AROUND ONE MAN: VLADIMIR PUTIN. BUT Anna had met him only three times. Twice at birthday parties for Vadim's father and once at a Chekists' Day celebration at Yasenevo. Each encounter had lasted no more than a few seconds.

She'd come to think of Putin as many things all at once. An all-powerful Tsar and the cheerless manager of an unruly system larger than himself. A despot and an issuer of vague, sometimes ignored guidance. A new public idol and a private source of jokes and snickers. He was former KGB Second Directorate, after all. A thug, not an artist like the foreign intelligence men around Papa. Like the rest of our country, she thought, he is proud and insecure, aggressive and pitiable, strong and weak. He was everything, he was nothing, but sometimes you had to give a damn about him because he was the center of the Russian world. The *khozyain*. Master. Without him the world did not spin. His existence was neither good nor bad. It just was.

Now, though, it was the *khozyain's* absence that moved the tides. Papa had shared bits of his nasty discussion with Goose at the Kremlin. Enough for Anna to understand that Goose, at present, had the freedom to grind them to bits.

Anna now walked with Papa and Vadim inside the RusFarm stables. The stables, they all had agreed, were an unlikely place for Goose to have mics. Papa was running hands through his hair and biting his lip, blinking too much, overfull of a manic energy that was rubbing off on the poor horses, who whinnied from the stalls. Anna leaned against a stall door and watched as Vadim scraped manure from an Italian loafer. Her father, shutting the stable door, said to Anna: "How long?"

"They will be here in five days," Anna said. "Maybe a week. We are still working to confirm her boyfriend's schedule and the delivery of the stallion."

Her father grunted.

Vadim said, "Maybe we try working the Mexican boyfriend, the horseman," he said. "More opportunities for leverage."

Papa gave few quick agitated pulls on his knuckles. "The lawyer's got Goose's financial information. Who gives a shit about the Mexican?"

Vadim was kicking straw around with his loafer. "I do. I want his farm. Excellent land and bloodstock. A solid investment. A pipe for moving money in and out of North America."

He had a point there, she hated to admit it.

"Oh for god's sake," her father said, smacking Vadim's chest in exasperation. "Don't get distracted. We need the dirt on Goose, everything else is noise. Understand?"

Vadim was looking at the straw. Sullenly sweeping it around.

"Vadim Yurivich," her father said, "tell me you will let your wife run this operation. Tell me you understand."

Vadim clenched his jaw and looked away. "I understand, Andrei Borisovich," he whispered.

"Good," her father said. "Now, Anna, what is the plan?"

She told them.

When she had finished, she watched Vadim sulk from the stables, excusing himself with a lie about urgent business in Piter.

Her father turned to her. "It's a good plan, my dear. A good plan." He put a hand on the muzzle of a curious horse, head peeking from the stall. "There was a detail that stood out to me in your report from Mexico. You wrote that the lawyer and the Mexican interact a bit—"

"Robotically," she said. "Yes, I did write that."

"And why do you think that is?" he asked.

"Several reasons," Anna said. "He could be a prudish Catholic.

There was not much physical contact in Mexico, for example. They did not seem ... familiar. Or perhaps they are using each other for connections. "

"The Mexican is an attractive man?" her father asked.

"Handsome," Anna replied. "Wealthy and handsome. The lawyer is attractive, too."

"Two attractive people in a new relationship should behave a certain way," her father said. He made a crude gesture with his hand. "If things appear strange ..." Her father trailed off, stuffed his hands in his pockets, and jutted his chin in the direction of the house. "In a few days you'll have another chance to check them out."

"We will have eyes all over the farm," Anna said, "we will know if they behave as they should." She made the same nasty gesture, and her father laughed.

———

THE FOX FUR WAS SOFT ON ANNA'S NAKED BACK AND BOTTOM AND LEGS. She was flushed and sweaty this close to the fire, the shadows licking the ceiling's peeling plaster. Luka returned from the kitchen with two beers. She took hers with a kiss. They drank watching the flames.

"How was your trip?" he asked.

"Fine."

"What did you do?"

"Not much." She cocked her head onto his shoulder and drank some of the beer. He liked to drink beer after sex and now she did, too.

"I think I am falling in love with you, Anya," he said.

She sat up with a laugh and shoved his shoulder. "Shut up, Luka." A swig of beer.

He laughed, then his face darkened and he shook his head. "I am in so deep." His voice was measured, determined.

"What are you talking about?" She could feel the skin around her eyes quivering.

"I think about this place all the time." He motioned around. "I think about you. I worry about you."

This nonsense. "I can take care of myself."

"I know, that's not what I meant."

"Then what did you mean, Luka?" She stood to face him. "Eh?"

"I mean, Anya, that I have seen every inch of your lovely body tonight and there are little bruises where there should not be. And—"

She smacked the bottle on the mantel. "Stop," she hissed. "We have rules, Luka, or have you forgotten? We don't talk about these things in here. This place is separate, it is sacred. We don't talk about my lousy other life, my shit husband, none of it. What the hell is wrong with you tonight?"

She stood over him, arms akimbo. He took a frustrated sip of beer, set down the bottle, and stood to face her. "I know you do not like him, but I do not like sharing you. I wish that you and I did not have so many secrets."

"There must be secrets, Luka."

"My mother and father said the same thing," he said.

She watched his eyes in the glow of the fire. They were confident, unwavering—eyes that knew what they wanted. "What are you saying?" she asked. "You want my secrets? The dirty laundry? You want to know more about Vadim? My father? Maybe more about the money? The horse farm, the villas, the apartments? The war my family is in now, with thugs who want to slit our throats?"

He started toward the pile of clothes, hastily stripped off as soon as they had entered. He tossed aside her bra to gather his boxers and began slipping them on.

"Right, sure," Anna said. "Go ahead and leave. Easier that way."

He looked sad. Not angry, not violent. Sad. "I am not leaving," he said.

She stood there naked, watching him dress. He shuffled into the bedroom and shut the door. She finished his beer and dragged a blanket onto the couch. She shut her eyes.

———

HOURS LATER, SHE HAD NOT FOUND SLEEP.

The fire was dead and the room was an icebox, the heater whining in a vain struggle against the cold. Outside, the Street of All-Holidays was still in the glassy winter night. Anna did not know what to do about Luka, but she knew life without him would be blacker, and that was enough for now. She went into the bedroom and lay down beside him. He turned and sleepily kissed her lips.

"I will tell you a story," she said.

SIX MONTHS BEFORE SHE FINALLY FLOWERED, ANNA ANDREEVNA Agapova heard rumors of her marriage to Vadim Yurivich Kovalchuk. It was 2002, she was fifteen, late to bloom, and the old apartment was still a well of sad shadows, though it had been almost five long years since her mother had died. Her father had recently retired from the SVR. Unlike many of the former KGB officers that had collected around the new President, Papa had not left the service for business in the nineties: he had stayed to work his way onto the executive third floor at Yasenevo. He'd retired in 2000, Anna remembered, two years after Mama died.

Through his pension and the banal graft of the Russian bureaucrat, Papa had provided a comfortable existence. He'd rustled the funds to purchase the abandoned *konezavod*, a Soviet horse breeding facility, that would later become RusFarm. But he was hungry and unmoored after her mother's death, and he threw himself into business upon retirement. Though he was not rich, Andrei Agapov had ample political and security connections. And so he had become close to Vadim's father, Yuri, a successful banker with ties to Putin.

Her father took her on a walk in the woods near the old house on the farm property and asked what she thought of Vadim. He was three years older, and not a friend—they had spoken perhaps once or twice, even though they went to the same international school. He was attractive and popular. His family had money. Even then Anna understood that they were peasants in comparison to the Kovalchuks. Vadim, a Year Thirteen preparing for university, seemed to occupy a different world than prepubescent Year Eleven Anna Andreevna. Her father's questions were innocent enough. Is he a nice boy? What is his reputation? Why don't you go and speak to him at school? She'd had little to say; she didn't know him.

Next month the Kovalchuk family came for a visit.

Anna had been that most horrendous of creatures, a fifteen-year-old girl, and her recollections from the first part of that weekend mostly involved not giving a shit about anything. She was quiet, shy, drawn inward. Years later, the SVR psychologists would link this to the death of her mother. Her mother had been the only person she had ever witnessed standing up to her father. If Anna was out with him and they ran into one of his colleagues, the men were always deferential, practically bowing, and they laughed at jokes she knew were not funny because her mother did not laugh at them at home, and sometimes told him not to say such things in the house. But Mama was dead, and Anya was a sullen teenager who would have been perfectly happy to sulk around the dacha all weekend, avoiding the Kovalchuks and her father, wandering into the forest to read a book. Vadim ignored her. Fine. She did not care.

She first heard the word *marriage* from the lips of Vadim's mother. Anna, of course, should not have. She was on a flat rock in the woods, T-shirt off, a lizard basking in the sun. She was near enough the walking path to eavesdrop on an angry conversation and sufficiently cloistered behind tree trunks and bramble to remain out of view. Anna had grown accustomed to harsh language in the years after her mother's death, even if it was mostly the brandy-fueled rage of her widower father, who had only come to understand how much he loved his wife after her death.

But Vadim's mother said it, Anna heard "marriage" clear as a summer midnight in Piter, and it was obvious the Kovalchuks were skeptical about the match. Anna remained flat and still on the stone as they passed, until the conversation drifted into the bright sky and she could hear no more. The day was warm, but she'd never felt colder. Marriage? She could not fathom why her father would suggest such a thing.

When confronted, Papa did not deny it. He said simply that nothing was decided and please be quiet, Anya, you are making a scene. They were all down on the pebbly beach by the lake. She demanded to speak with her father; he suggested they take a walk. That vein bulged on his neck. She told him how she heard. He muttered to himself. Then he cracked his big knuckles and told her to speak. Out with it.

I will choose my own husband, she said. He did not respond to this. He instead asked what Anna wanted to do with her life. She was fifteen, he'd never asked this question before. She was taken aback, but she did know the answer.

"I want to do what you did, Papa," she said.

At this he stopped walking and shook his head. "Why in the world would you want to do that, Anya?"

"I've seen the way people look at you," she said. "They respect you, Papa. I want that, too."

The answer seemed to deflate him. She did not know why. He should be excited to hear his only daughter wanted to follow him, yes?

The Kovalchuks, he said, thought she was not being sociable. He hissed at her to go speak with Vadim.

She found him alone on the beach. Her eyes were wandering down his muscular chest and the thin trail of dark hair that wove from his navel down into his trunks when, sensing her stare, he rolled to face her. He tried to smile. He looked bored.

"Do you ride horses?" she asked.

"Yes," he said.

"Want to ride with me?"

At that time the Agapovs had two horses. Anna's was Anastasia, a white Andalusian. The second was Sophia, a reddish brown Budyonny. She had been her mother's. Anna trusted both horses more than most people and she was intrigued to see that Vadim agitated them. And Vadim, despite claiming that he rode horses, did not seem comfortable, either. She saddled them both and watched him struggle to mount Sophia, who stood nearly sixteen hands high. He said he did not need the mounting block. Twice he nearly fell, cursing, before he awkwardly swung himself up, jabbing his left foot into Sophia's near side. Anna used the mounting block because she was short. And sensible. She led them onto one of the paths in the forest.

"You've heard what they're talking about?" Vadim asked.

"A little."

"What do you think?"

"I think it's stupid."

He shrugged. "I think they just want to see if we get along. I'm going to Oxford next year. There will be English girls." He laughed.

They both ducked to avoid the trunk of a pine that had fallen onto a cat's cradle of tree branches overhanging the path.

"Where do you want to go to school?" he asked.

"Lomonosov," she said. "Like my parents."

He scrunched his nose. "You want to work after college?"

"I am going to join the SVR, like Papa."

Now he laughed, and it was even worse than just laughing at her words, he laughed because he thought she was joking. Anna decided the horses were right. She did not like Vadim Kovalchuk. He tried to recover when he saw that she was serious.

"I thought you were kidding," he said.

"Why would I be?"

"There aren't many girls working in the SVR."

"So?"

"Hey, look, I'm just saying, there aren't many. Ease up. I'm not trying to pick a fight."

"What are you trying to do, then?"

He sighed. "Forget it."

They rode in silence until the forest became low rolling pasture. Here, her mother had taught her how to ride at full gallop. Vadim pulled alongside.

"Maybe a race to the first little hill?" he asked.

"I don't think so. You don't know how to ride horses."

His mare whinnied and began to startle as if in agreement. "First to the hill," he said. Then he wrenched the reins and hammered his heels into the mare's side.

Anna's only instinct: Do not lose. She brought Anastasia to a gallop and began to close the distance to Vadim, now three or four lengths ahead. He was working Sophia too hard and offering none of the encouragement the mare had grown to expect. Her mother had been a gentle and loving master; on its current rider the animal smelled fear. If Sophia did not trust him, the mare would not give him her all.

The mare began to spitefully slow with each of Vadim's hard jabs to her ribs. Anna began closing the distance. Three lengths, then two, then one. In control, she thought, for the first time all weekend. The warm summer wind rippled through her hair as they pulled alongside Vadim, whose eyes blazed with an impotent rage. She looked ahead, away from him, and as the gap widened, his curses at the mare grew louder, and made Anna wonder if he meant them for her. When they cut through the grass and galloped over the hill she was grinning. And she was still grinning when she slowed to turn around. She wanted to see the defeat on his face—she liked seeing people lose to her—but when he reached the hill, his mare quickly shed speed and did a little buck and Vadim was not ready, so he slid right over her mane and spilled into the grass. Anna laughed, trotting over to the boy Vadim until she'd found a spot where her triumphant face blotted out the sun, casting shadows across his eyes.

————

WHEN SHE HAD FINISHED TELLING HER STORY, SHE PUT HER HEAD BACK on the pillow and shut her eyes. The clockless minutes rolled along, the room quiet except for their breath, and she was nearly asleep when Luka said, "I wish I had known you then."

Anna smiled, eyes still closed. "We were mercifully spared each other in youth."

There was a comfortable silence. "What are you thinking?" he said as he stroked her face.

Her eyes opened and her lips parted into a mischievous smile.

He laughed like he did when she put him in check, and dropped his head back on the pillow. "You are a hard woman, Anna Andreevna."

She rolled onto him, kissing his lips, his neck, his forehead, his lips. When he was ready, she drew him inside to let the feel of him rise through her. There were no secrets from his body. It told her the truth. For a moment she held him there, locked in the stillness. The first traces of dawn were painting the window frost when he slid Anna onto her back. Her legs knotted around him. Their rhythm soon made her warm. Shoved out the cold and left a thin line of sweat on her hairline and damp flaxen curls brushing the pillow. He was moving well, her pleasure building so fast, her body coiling up, readying to unwind in those lovely rolling swells. He responded steadily, gently, and firmly. When she made a noise he would kiss her and his lips tasted like the beer. And he was just bonded to her eyes, watching what he was doing to her. She held those eyes. She wondered what her body said to him. If there were secrets. If it told him the truth.

21

St. Ives, Cornwall

THE VACATIONERS RENTING BEASLEY COTTAGE MOSTLY KEPT TO
themselves. Hired cars came and went throughout their week of
occupancy, and many of the locals, bored in the late autumn low season,
tried to keep track of what they assumed to be a party of rich Londoners
out for one last getaway before winter descended. The proprietor of the
wine store, Shelton, observed that the group's anchor appeared to be the
couple, Max and Sia, whom he met when they stopped in for supplies. A
getaway, Sia told him when he asked why they'd come to St. Ives in the
off-season. She was a lawyer in London, she said, and carried the faint
lilt of an accent that Shelton could not place. He liked how she held eye
contact. Something about her seemed inaccessible, though, which Shelton also liked, and which explained why, despite his sizable inheritance
and modest good looks, he remained a bachelor at fifty-one.

Initially he thought they were business colleagues. A nosy man who
took pride in prying, Shelton one evening mosied behind them around
the store, noting the wines they purchased and inquiring about whether
Max worked at the same firm as Sia. He swore he'd caught a flash of
alarm or concern in Sia's eye, he could not be sure because it was gone as
quickly as it came. Max put his hand on her shoulder. They were dating.
He was from Mexico. Met through a mutual friend.

There was another woman who came to the store only once. She was
short, with a wild spray of curly black hair, and did not respond to his
greeting. She purchased only sweets. Her energy made Shelton uneasy,

which made him talkative. Assuming the sweets were for her children, he inquired how many she had brought to St. Ives. The woman did not respond. Shelton tried to smile, but he saw that her bright green eyes glimmered only with violence.

"THAT GUY AT THE WINE SHOP IS ANNOYING AS SHIT," PROCTER SAID when she returned to the safe house. She dropped a bag on the table, packages of colorful sweets spilling out. She nodded to the mess, said it was for everybody. Max opened a bag to be polite.

Procter had arrived from Langley on a circuitous itinerary through four countries in the Schengen. Sia canceled client dinners and work meetings and a trip to Paris. Some R&R, she explained to an inquisitive— and unhappy—Benny Hynes. Max flew in from San Cristobal. Three days of carefully timed beach walks, shopping, and relaxation in St. Ives, aided by two countersurveillance teams, had so far turned up no hint of Russian watchers.

There are only a few countries in the world in which a NOC would be ill-advised to travel with clandestine communication software embedded deep on their phone or computer. Russia is one of them. So a techie showed up at the cottage and stripped the software from phones, laptops, and tablets. They would be black in Russia. No communication with the CIA during their trip, save for a single thread: a daily proof-of-life message. Max would call a Monterrey cell phone number in Kentucky. The phone number belonged to one of San Cristobal's agent buyers. The agent was a Moscow X officer. Sia would call a Hynes Dawson executive assistant on a line monitored by Langley.

Max had met with some shady people in shady places, but he'd never been inside a place like Russia, where the surveillance would be a stifling blanket. Procter, who had served in Moscow, explained how it would feel. They'll have the usual stuff wired, she said, bedroom, bathroom, closets, hallways. Maybe the stables and shit. Hell, look at what we did in Mexico. But in Russia it'll be one hundred times worse. You will never be alone. And for their intelligence services it's not just about surveil-

lance to understand and learn. It's about intimidation. Make you think
they control everything, so they control you. Freak you the fuck out so
you make a mistake on the street or something.

One of Procter's techies ran a show-and-tell of devices used by the
Russian services. Cameras flat as paper with the circumference of a pinhead, powered by strontium batteries with a usable life far longer than
any intelligence operation. These had been adhered to the clothing of
CIA officers in Moscow, did not come off in the wash, and communicated
back to the FSB in hard-to-detect, sporadic bursts. They could be stuck
onto their clothing, saddlebags, or even the horses themselves.

Unlike Mexico, Procter barked, the Russians really will be on their
home turf, so they can toss considerable flesh-and-blood surveillants at the
operation. Every RusFarm employee would be an informant. Additional
SVR or FSB resources would likely circulate around the property. If they
went on a ride, or got in a car, the Russians would have eyes on the rabbit.

A geriatric with thick white eyebrows spent an evening at the St.
Ives cottage. His grandfather had apparently been a Count in the court
of the last Tsar. He gave a crash course on the manners and etiquette
of Russian high society. His CIA affiliation was never explained. Most
of what he said was common sense—look people in the eye, good posture, don't put your hands in your pockets, eat more than you should.
But some tidbits were useful: don't show the bottom of your feet, point
with your whole hand (not your finger), men should use a bone-crushing
handshake, do not whistle indoors (bad luck), leave a little food on your
plate to show that you have been satisfied. By the end of the evening Max
suspected the man had no CIA affiliation at all. He wondered, in fact, if
Procter had hired him off the internet.

Max and Sia spent hours reviewing satellite imagery of RusFarm
and the surrounding countryside. They memorized routes if they had
to escape. An attentive imagery analyst discovered a small enclosure
tucked into the woods alongside a barn. Dogs. Running was probably
a bad idea. If it comes to that, Sia whispered to Max, we're already
cocked up.

Because it had been years since either officer had received any hand-to-hand combat training, Procter flew out an instructor to drill them. For a morning Max and Sia sparred in the living room, Procter and the techies their audience, watching in pure delight. They imagined the items and furniture that might be in each room at RusFarm and visualized how it could be used as a weapon. Some were obvious: kitchen knives, farrier's tools, fireplace stokers. Others, less so. Purse handles, the instructor said, were excellent for strangulations. Procter nodded knowingly. Throw a light wooden chair hard against a wall, the leg comes off, you've got a club. Maybe you've even got a few sharp ends on there, the Chief said, punctuating the sentence with an unsettling stabbing motion.

Each day, Max and Sia walked the beach to work out a system of signals and code words to communicate under the surveillance crush. Most centered around warning of danger, triggering the escape routes, or alerting the other to progress with Anna.

On the third afternoon they were on the beach walking toward the village. It was warm for November. A mild wind brushed against Max's back, and the water was a brilliant aquamarine. A few families had scattered across the beach. Two children flying a yellow kite were shrieking in delight. Hands clasped, wine in hand, their parents cheered them from beach chairs. Max, oblivious to the joyful scene, was instead trying to get a read on Sia.

Throughout the St. Ives sojourn she'd smiled little, laughed even less. The flickers of energy between them in Mexico had grown dim. Meals had passed joylessly—clouded not by anger or apathy, he believed, but by the slipstream left by Sia Fox's journey inward, her mind sweeping aside all but the operational considerations, her body conserving energy for the task ahead. And though Vadim's suspicions had thrown Max a pristine operational justification to suggest they address them in bed, he'd not cast out so much as a hint. This was partly because she'd slid clean into her armor. There was also pride to consider; his quiver to influence Alejandra's decision had been full but he'd shot none of it, he'd wanted to keep the fight for her level and fair, and he'd done that and lost. But he could look himself in the eye. He wanted to take Sia Fox to bed after a day on horseback at San Cristobal. Not after lectures in some stale operational theater. Unless, of course, she asked.

"How are you feeling?" he asked.

"Like we've got the codes down," Sia said.

"I mean about the op."

Sia stopped for a moment and looked out over the water, hands on her hips. "That we have a good angle with Anna. That we have a shot."

He'd expected the determination, but her voice ran with another edge. And he thought he knew what it was. "You should get your head checked," he said. He was grinning at the waves.

"Langley shrinks take care of that," she said, lips pursing into a wan smile. "They say I'm fine. And, hey, you're here, too, aren't you? So let's not get drearily clinical with it, Max, because unlike yours truly you can just go home. Shall we plumb those depths, eh? You want to tell me why you told Procter you'd stick around, when you possess a stable of reasonable excuses to head back to the ranch?"

"Because I'm having fun," he said.

Sia's eyes were fixed on the kite's checkerboard pattern of bright yellow and black. Loose forelocks of her dark hair danced in the breeze. Her hands were on her hips, fingers tapping away at her coat pockets. Lips frozen in that slight smile. She picked up a rock and cast it into the waves. Then, for the first time in days, Sia laughed.

———

WHILE DEBRIEFING THE OLD MAN'S PRESENTATION ON RUSSIAN ETI-quette, Procter brought them back to the topic of booze. "Do you understand how much they will force you to drink?" Procter asked. "In Mexico you could at least control it. In Russia? No way. They are going to push drinks on you all day. You will have to conduct this operation in a semi- or fully intoxicated state. I need proof that you can perform."

A techie—relishing the moment—removed a few boxes of Clif Bars from a knapsack. "Your blood alcohol content is determined by many variables," he said. "One is your gastric emptying rate. It takes time for your stomach to break down protein and fat, so we want to keep those in your system." He slid the box to Sia and Max. "The Office of Technical Service has doctored these bars for you. A special OTS recipe. They have the fat content of four Big Macs. Use them wisely." The techie also provided packets of an electrolyte and vitamin powder that they could mix into water.

Procter went into the kitchen and collected three bottles of vodka. She led them through the Russian vodka ritual. Nothing will be mixed with the booze, she said, pouring everyone a glass. You will drink it straight and chilled. The techie's foot started bouncing in agitation. There will be zakuski, Procter said. And again, as if on cue, one of the techies-turned-waiters brought a plate from the kitchen. There were pickled cucumbers, cabbage, and mushrooms. A tomato and cucumber salad. Cured herring on open-face black bread.

Procter offered a toast in Russian, which Max did not understand. Everyone drank, then took a helping of zakuski.

"It is considered rude," Procter said, "not to finish the bottle." She poured again. Max tried one of the doctored Clif Bars. He could only get half of it down. He thought that would be fine, since it was two Big Macs. Sia stomached a single bite.

After the second round, Max took a hunk of bread and a pickled cucumber.

After the third round, he tried the fish.

After the fourth round, he had more bread.

After the fifth round, he finished the Clif Bar and gagged in his mouth.

After the sixth round, he tried a bite of the salad.

After the seventh round, he tried the mushrooms and listened to the techie throwing up in the bathroom.

After the eighth round, he sat down and forgot to eat.

After the ninth round, there was snoring and he realized Sia had passed out on his shoulder. Procter was on the couch opposite Max and Sia, watching, drinking vodka from the bottle.

That was the last thing he remembered.

- 22 -

St. Ives

MAX AWOKE TO THE HEAD-RINGING CLATTER OF THE TECHIES stumbling from the cottage. One, seeing Max perk up, waved goodbye. He looked around. Sia was asleep, upright, and slumped into to him. They were still in their clothes. Procter came in from the kitchen wearing a red velour tracksuit. Mug of coffee in hand, hair wet from a shower, the Chief looked spry despite consuming her own bottle of vodka. "Shake her awake," Procter said.

Max nudged Sia's shoulder, but she did not respond. "You there, Hortensia?" Procter said, snapping her fingers through the air. "Yoo-hoo, Hortensia, yoo-hoo." Sia yawned, eyes still shut. He felt her jerk upright when she sensed she was leaning on him. Then Sia opened her eyes and scooted over.

"I have watched the surveillance footage from Mexico about twenty times," Procter said. "Vadim and Anna's argument, the dumping of her birth control pills, the rough sex, all the parts you know. But there is one thing we need to talk about."

Sia now sat up straight.

Procter gave a knowing smile. "You guys know already. You're pros. I don't have to say anything, but I'm going to say a little bit because we're about to send you into the bear's den." She made a weird clawing motion with her hand. "And if I don't say something and you get disappeared, it will be on my conscience forever. And my conscience is squeaky fucking clean. I don't plan on you sullying it."

Procter took a long drink of coffee. "Our friend Vadim has his suspicions about your relationship. At least, he did in Mexico. And weeks have passed. Now, listen, I don't want to know shit. And I sure as hell don't want anything—including this discussion—appearing in cable traffic of any kind. Before or after Saint Petersburg. Clear?"

Max and Sia nodded.

"What I want is a solution. Fix the problem. We cannot have the pervy Russians working the cameras seeing you guys in separate beds, or holding hands like you think the other person has a fungus. I'm not saying you guys need to bone. But you need to *act* like two people who want to bone. So, tell me, what's the plan?" Procter twirled her hand toward them in a flourish.

"Maybe she pretends to be on her period," Max said. "No sex."

"Oh for fuck's sake," Sia said.

Procter's face twisted into a wiseass grin. "Sure, vaquero, why not?" Then she made a fart noise and shot two thumbs down. "Oh wait," she continued, switching to a horrendous Russian accent, "let's say my name is Igor fucking Russkie and I'm the poor bastard watching every minute of the video feeds from your room. Vadim comes to me and asks if you two are banging, and Igor fucking Russkie says *nyet*, boss, *nyet*, it's that time of the month, his bushy Slavic brows twerking at the hint of menstruation. And Vadim, who seems to, one"—Procter counted this with her fingers—"not like you, and two, thinks you are full of shit . . . well, what does he do? He figures she's got tampons or pads or something, right? They're in the trash? He has someone check that out, some poor guy rooting through the damn garbage on a truffle hunt for Sia's bloody tampons. He doesn't find them. Then Vadim thinks maybe she's flushing them down the toilet. That bitch is wrecking my septic system. He has Igor fucking Russkie review the tapes of the bathroom. Do they show Sia flushing tampons down the crapper? If the tapes do not, Vadim now has an interesting thread to yank. Why did they lie to me about her period, of all things? Then, you—we—are in a bad way, vaquero."

Sia's lips pursed into a thin smile. "Couples go two days without sex. We'll sleep in the same bed. Do a better job acting."

Procter shifted to Max. He nodded. "What she said."

"Good," Procter said. "Now I need to catch a plane." She hugged Sia, shook Max's hand, then wheeled her suitcase out the door. This was their last CIA contact before they went inside. Procter stuffed her bag in the trunk. She turned to Max and Sia, who were standing in the doorway.

"You're the best of us," she said. "And I'm proud of you both."

———

THAT NIGHT A THUNDERSTORM SETTLED OVER ST. IVES. THEY'D BEEN apart for most of the day: running, reading, napping off the terrible hangovers. Max motored the rental back from town through a driving rain. He'd gone out for bread and wine. Shopping bag in hand, he darted over the drive through the downpour, and regretted it

The soaked bag gave out when he flung open the door, and Max followed the wine bottle as it rolled along the foyer's stone tiles toward the living room. He found Sia watching sidelong raindrops pelt the windows. She wore a white silk robe stenciled with a black jaguar. She turned to face him, drained wineglass in hand. Her eyes were serious, cold.

"If it comes to it," Sia said, "it will be important that it works. And that we work well together. That our performance immediately quashes all doubt."

He stooped to pick up the wine, set it on the coffee table, and took a seat on the couch. She was looking right through him. "That," he said, "is a very sensible plan."

He motioned for her wineglass. When he'd filled hers and then his, she sat on the couch opposite and crossed her legs and that robe ran right up her thigh and the underwear was lacy and white and there was a dazzling contrast with her sunned skin and he'd happily taken the bait with a sticky glance, because Sia knew damn well what she was doing.

"You like my legs." Her tone was still sterile. Operational.

"That," he said, "is a silly question."

"It wasn't a question. So, then, Maximiliano, tell me. How do you want to play it?"

He drank in his wine, and then glanced at her leg, still brandished in a manner that should have been playful but instead felt clinical. "Vadim was suspicious because we were acting," he said. "It would be easier if we were not acting. If we had a rhythm."

"Or if we had actual practice acting."

"Practice. A rhythm. Call it what you'd like."

"You've not made a move or suggested a thing since we got to St. Ives," Sia said.

"Is that a question now?" Max replied.

"It's a question."

"Not for lack of interest. You've been in a different world since we arrived here."

"We're professionals with an op to run."

"Of course. But I must say that the requirements of our profession . . . they are not normal, are they?" he said slowly, measuring the weight of his words. "Our work makes strange demands, even if sometimes they are enjoyable."

She stood, undid the belt, and let her robe fall. Next to the floor was the underwear. Her breathing was even and unbothered. And though he'd admired them he'd not grasped how long her legs were. She showed him her backside, pointing out a mole on her left buttock in case Max was asked to prove he knew her body. Then she turned to face him, arms slung across her chest.

He took off his gray sweater and slid down his jeans and boxer briefs. Her gaze wandered around his frame. She came toward him, stopping a step away, eyes cradling his as she put a cool hand on his chest and brushed fingers over his skin.

She took him into her grip and drew him closer until their lips were an inch apart, their eyes still locked. He felt her nipples, stiff from the cold, pressed into his chest. Her eyes were hungry, and in her hand he was quickly well-grown.

He caressed her hips and thighs and his hand wandered to find her wonderfully ready for him, but when he kissed her lips they were still and dispassionate. He gently nudged her toward the couch, but she did not budge, her hand kept them planted. And she kissed him, open, slow, and wet, but then she withdrew and he saw that her smile was crooked and her tongue was sliding along her lower lip as if she'd tasted him for the purposes of future testimony. The look she'd given him on Procter's plane in Palo Alto now flitted back and it said, I'll break you, maybe have some fun while I do. Max had walked into a trap, and the worst of it was he'd gladly stumble in again. And she damn well knew it.

Sia was smiling down at her handiwork.

"My god," he said in Spanish, "you are an evil woman."

Then, looking up to meet his eyes, Sia gave him a comradely slap on the shoulder. "This works," she said.

Stock-still and unsatisfied, he watched her casually collect her robe and underwear. Her countenance had brightened, and when she sashed the robe she was humming a soft melody. Then she padded upstairs and called down a peppy good-night from the landing, where she gently shut her bedroom door.

———

NEXT MORNING HE AWOKE TO THE DISTANT CRASH OF THE SURF AND a rerun of Sia's robe falling to the floor playing on the back of his eyelids. As he showered and shaved, Max realized that fragments of that otherworldly experience were now stamped into him: the come-and-get-some look in her gray eyes, the long legs, the floral smell hovering around her lips. While dressing, he twice paused languidly to imagine her shrugging from her robe.

They walked the beach once more before departing St. Ives. The cold was biting, but the same family was there, children flying the yellow kite, parents sunk into the chairs, deep in their coats and wine.

The children ran past, and an idea arrived as the kite crossed overhead.

Yesterday he might not have considered it, but he felt a growing sense of partnership with this closed-off woman. He wanted them to win.

"I have something that might help you recruit Anna," he said. "Soften her."

"Tell me," Sia replied.

"Penelope," Max said. "We bring my mother's horse with us to Russia."

23

Moscow

THE BLUE LIGHTS ON THE MERCEDES FLASHED AS CHERNOV'S CAR tore through Rublyovka, the traffic parting like water. The driver weaved from lane to lane, the tendons in his hands flickering from clutching the wheel as if it might snap. The string of villages along Rublyovka had been an escape from the city since the days of the Romanovs. Unlike central Moscow, the air was not scarred by the scent of peat fires and benzene. What it smelled like was money. There was a mall with a Bentley dealership and Prada shops to entertain the women kept in this zoo. The homes were gated and gargantuan. Few were visible from the main roads, but through the windows of the Mercedes Chernov did make out one painted a sugary pink, like a dollhouse.

Had any Rublyovka residents been sufficiently foolish or impoverished to walk in such frigid weather—and in this glittering enclave there were no compatriots meeting that description—they would have paid no mind to Chernov's speeding government car. Many senior officials had homes here: Prime Ministers, the Defense Minister, oil tycoons. The KGB had once owned much of the area, and many of its parcels had been bequeathed to its principal successor, the FSB. Everyone used the *migalka*, the blue lights, when they were speeding.

The gate guarding the road to Goose's state dacha slid open. With a wave, Chernov's driver jetted past a handful of Federal Protective Service officers standing guard, down a narrow road flanked by towering pines clothed in fresh snow.

Chernov stepped into the cold and looked toward the golden domes of the khaki-green chapel that Goose had built at his estate. Chernov wore a black Zegna suit, as he often did for meetings with Goose. The style had become popular in the service after the *khozyain* wore a similar vintage while delivering a speech during the Chekists' Day celebrations at Lubyanka. He crossed a gravel, tree-lined path toward the church, careful to walk in its center to avoid sullying his loafers in the slush fretting the edges of the trail.

He swung open the chapel door and was greeted by panels of stained glass soaring above the altar, depicting comrade soldiers raising the Soviet flag over the rubble of Stalingrad. He crossed under an archway decorated with a mosaic of citizens holding a banner that read CRIMEA IS OURS. On the next archway he ran fingers along a frieze in which a collection of angels watchfully protected Russian soldiers forcing peace on restive Georgia. He joined Goose in a metallic pew fashioned from a melted-down Wehrmacht tank, captured by the Red Army while beating the Nazis back from Leningrad. For a while Goose was quiet. The boss tugged absentmindedly on the fabric of his pants and sometimes shut his eyes, as if in prayer, or, perhaps, pain. Chernov waited for Goose to speak.

"It is time," Goose said at last. "He's left us no other choice."

"Retribution action?" Chernov asked, surprised.

"No, no, no," Goose said. He was staring through the stained-glass hammer and sickle. "We've got one restless nobleman. There is no need to upset the rest of the herd. Nothing heavy. He's a former KGB general, for god's sake. Uphold the law so they all understand how to bend the knee."

To destroy Agapov, his master of course had to consider the politics. But morally, really, there would be no boundaries, no limits. And how could there be, when Russia was the source of the divine and he was the state's sword?

ARRESTS DEMANDED MOUNTAINS OF PAPERWORK. THANKFULLY THE documents cataloguing Agapov's criminal promiscuity were simple to collect because one cannot live in Russia without breaking the law—it is an ensnaring thicket, ingrown and contradictory, making everyone a criminal. The trick is merely finding the right law. Chernov viewed those without formal criminal records as worrisome examples of FSB negligence and inattention. He was fond of the proverb of Stalin's NKVD: Your lack of criminal record is not to your merit. It is our flaw.

Chernov opened the case file on his computer. This was not public—it was protected under a State Secret Privilege decree withholding the documents from the accused, the Prosecutor General, and the courts. To feed the file, the FSB had compiled reports describing Agapov's various infractions. Chernov flipped through these from the desk of his spartan office overlooking Lubyanka on a clear, frigid Moscow morning, when even the sunlight was cold. In the files he reviewed evidence of embezzlement of state funds, elaborate mirror trades inside the conglomerate's financial arm, falsified tax rebates. Some of the intercepts between senior Agapov allies included thinly veiled references to bribes of officers of the Federal Tax Police. None of this was abnormal; indeed, it was already well known. But Chernov still required the papers. Even Stalin had insisted on papers.

He phoned Evgenia Yegorova, the chairwoman of the Moscow City Court. They called her the "Iron Lady," but it had not always been so. To bring the old judge to heel, Chernov had once picked up her husband at his home on his birthday to take him shopping for a nice car. Yegorova would later call it a kidnapping. An uncharitable characterization. Chernov drove him to a dealership and told the trembling man to pick out any car. It was his birthday, after all! A smack on the back.

"What if I do not want a car?" the man had stammered.

"You do not want a car?" Chernov said. "We will be shocked—and devastated!—that you refused a birthday gift." Chernov ran a hand over the glossy hood of a jet-black 7 Series. "This one is nice," he said. "You wouldn't consider turning down a gift from Goose, would you?"

Yegorova's syrupy voice answered on the third ring. Chernov explained the case. He spoke in concepts, theories. He did not yet use names. They discussed possible sentences: a ban on business activities in relevant sectors, a fine of twenty times the amount of his bribes, and twelve years in a prison camp with hard labor. When—if—he emerged from Siberia, Agapov could wait tables to pay off the legal bills.

"What do you think the sentence should be?" Chernov asked.

"What do you want it to be?" the judge asked, sounding very bored.

24

RusFarm

O N ANNA'S FIRST VISIT TO THE LAND THAT WOULD BECOME RUS-
Farm, the barns were rotting and the dormitories were decrepit,
sagging skeletons. Every usable piece of lumber, metal, and tile had been
carted off in the last days of the collective.

Anna had liked it better back then. Her mother kept the renovated
farmhouse, once an old dorm, small and cozy. Vegetable plots dotted
yards that spread into a sprawling birch forest veined by streams and
walking paths. They'd put up a stable for their two horses. Anna had fond
memories before life had wilted. Then, of course, they had not called it
by the ridiculous name: RusFarm.

It had been Vadim who insisted they raze the old farmhouse. She'd
said that was the one thing she could not abide, too many memories of
Mama here. Please, we don't need the big house, and we don't need it
here. We need a place to entertain the President when he comes, Vadim
had said. We knock down the old house, build back a big one. "Have
you seen his palace at Idokopas?" he had asked with the condescension
of those with secret knowledge. I've heard about it, she answered, and I
don't want my mother's house bent into a macabre castle. She knew the
khozyain liked things that others had, wanted them a bit bigger or better. You had a large house, Putin's had to be larger. You had horses, he
wanted a few more, and they'd better be faster than yours.

Vadim had not listened to her. He could not listen. In those days he
was always checking his watch, grimacing at the threats, a dismissive

nod here and there, then he said he had to return to Piter for meetings. He told her this was how it had to be. President's wishes and all.

The *khozyain* himself had suggested the name, Vadim claimed. Rus-Farm. He said the name would bring international recognition; to foreign ears it would ring of Russia without the thicket of Russian. She could barely speak it aloud.

Now, for a few days, she had to pretend that she cared deeply about this place. There was an audience; and it was not only Sia and Max.

Anna sat in a living room in front of the crackling fireplace with Vadim and Grigory, the SVR Line OT tech donated to the operation. They were reviewing the current security system's coverage and deciding where to place the new cameras. A mounted bear head presided over the conversation from above the fireplace, dead eyes regarding them with a hint of embarrassment. Vadim's voice was raised, his foot drummed the floor. The conversation about Max and Sia's bedroom had made him testy.

Anna pointed to the bedroom on the floor plan and waved a hand, cutting off Grigory. "Vadim, do you have eyes in there?"

Without answering, he kicked his feet up on the coffee table and began flipping through his phone. Anna snatched a glance at the table, paws on the end of the legs. It was expensive, a recommendation from the Italian decorator Vadim hired. Purchased, she imagined, before he had bedded her.

"My dear," Anna said, "I know that this is your whorehouse, and has been since I quit helping around here and went back to Moscow. But it is my operation, and I need you to tell me if you already have a camera in there." She jabbed her finger on the floor plan.

He slapped his phone on the table and tugged at his ear. "Yes. I do."

"Where?"

"One in the ceiling above the bed."

"Perfect," Anna said. "One less for Grigory to install."

They went through each room on the floor plan to determine whether they required audio, video, or both. The old farmhouse had eventually been replaced by this hulk of a hunting lodge, overfull with gaudy glitz: everything was slathered in gold, marble, crystal, and lined with dark wood. The rooms—and there were so many—were stacked with opulent baroque furniture. RusFarm was a dark metaphor for her life: abounding luxury, lacking any semblance of soul.

Grigory and Vadim started arguing about whether to place cameras inside the bathhouse. "The steam can be hard on some of the cameras," Grigory said. He ran his hands over the floor plan. "But we will need at minimum two inside each room. We can put them in the wood. Make it look like the head of a nail. Simple."

Grigory was pointing to the women's side of the bathhouse and Vadim was again shifting in his seat. Anna rolled her eyes. "Are the women's baths already wired, Vadim?"

Vadim smirked at his reflection in his leather shoes. Anna smiled genially at Grigory and smacked her hand on the floor plan. "Well, how about that? We're already half done!"

———

ANNA PICKED UP THE PHONE IN THE GRAY BOX OUTSIDE THE KIRISHI morgue. The chief medical examiner buzzed her in, met her in the hall, and led her to his dank office. Dasha was waiting. The woman had nearly qualified for the Russian Olympic team in 2012. She had been tapped to help with this operation on account of her physical talents.

There were five decedents present, the chief medical examiner said, five choices, unless you plan to create a few more. His lips threatened a smile, but Anna could not tell if he was joking.

"Only two are suitable," Dasha said. "Both male. Without witting kin. And not so fat." They reviewed pictures of each in the files.

"Him," Anna said, pointing to Kiril Alexeivich Bogdanov.

"Why him?" Dasha asked. "He's a bit heavier than the other."

"He is handsome," Anna said. "And you are pretty enough. The other is too ugly to be your husband."

"Maybe he was rich?" Dasha mused. "He was plain but he had money. A Forbes. He took me shopping, put me up in an apartment."

"Does he look like he was rich to you?" Anna asked.

"Perhaps you dress him in an expensive suit? Give him a watch?" the chief medical examiner said. "Put a nice cologne on him. Make him smell rich, and cover the preservatives?"

"It's his face," Anna said. "He is poor in the face. And not so handsome."

They walked to the coolers. The halls smelled of formalin and mold. There were signs everywhere: (ALL BODY PARTS MUST BE SIGNED OUT! PLEASE PLACE BODIES IN COOLER FEET FIRST!). Even the hallway floors sloped gently toward drains. Kiril was on a gurney in one of the body refrigerators. The chief medical examiner wheeled him out and unzipped the bag. Dasha practiced lifting him. She'd been a weight lifter; she was sturdy and strong. She could lift him above her waist. She set Kiril back on the gurney like she was spreading linen across a table.

"My poor husband," Dasha said, caressing his cheek.

The chief medical examiner zipped Kiril up and wheeled him to the refrigerator.

"Taken too soon," Dasha said.

———

ANNA RETURNED TO THE FARM TO REVIEW THE MANSION AND THE grounds with Vadim while Grigory and his men finished installing the cameras and microphones. In the movie theater they watched techies place cameras in wall sconces. Outside, they strolled through one of the gardens. Two men on ladders fiddled with floodlights mounted on tree trunks.

They walked the snowy stretch of road chosen for the pitch, Anna pointing to a few bare birch trees. "Put the bigger, obvious cameras in those," Anna told Grigory. They passed the barking Alsatians. Anna instinctively stuffed her hands in her coat pockets. She did not like the animals because sometimes they bit the staff; one had sent a gardener to the hospital short two fingers. Leaving Grigory to work, the couple trudged back toward the house.

"I will need as much time with her as possible," Anna said. "The best thing you can do is occupy Max."

"I have a few ideas," Vadim said.

They circled around the fountain in the drive at the mansion's front.

Above them rose a statue of a rearing stallion, its ears and flowing mane stretching skyward as high as the eaves. In summer, water would gush from its mouth. This absurd place; a gimcrack Versailles in the Russian woods. She spat into the dormant fountain as they passed.

"It is important, Vadim," she said, "that none of your ideas sow chaos in their relationship. It will be difficult to recruit this woman if her relationship is in distress."

Vadim's lips firmed into a tight smile. "And why would a few days here put any stress on that relationship?"

She turned to him. "No whores. No staff"—she put air quotes around this word—"to service you in the bathhouse. Tension in their relationship accomplishes nothing. Understand?"

He ignored this. "Their match is still strange to me, Anya. What is he doing with her?"

Anna reviewed the mansion's watchful façade. That any union might be more than a coupling for money, power, or sex was clearly lost on her husband. But she could not risk him storming off, so she merely chided, "My love, have we finally discovered a woman you do not find attractive?"

"She is attractive enough," Vadim replied. "But, still . . . they are too polite."

"We will watch them in the bedroom," Anna said. "To check." She didn't necessarily disagree with Vadim. Something was off. But the way she was going to run this op? Well, it simply would not matter.

"Good," he said. "And I will behave. And I will make sure Max behaves as well. We will steam. Perhaps go shooting."

"Just keep him busy," she said.

A truck rattled into the circle, coming to a stop at the foot of the marble steps. The driver rolled down the window. "Hi, Dasha," Anna said. "Did the farmer give you any trouble?"

"No, but he asked why I only wanted the blood."

"What did you tell them?"

Dasha dangled two fingers over her top teeth to mimic fangs. "Vampire," she said.

Part III

ZAKHVAT /
ENTRAPMENT

25

RusFarm

SIX-MILLION-DOLLAR THOROUGHBRED STALLIONS DO NOT FLY COM-mercial from Mexico to Russia. Nor do they fly direct. Smokey Joe and Penelope's route was hopscotch: by trailer from San Cristobal to Mexico City, air to Miami, two days of rest at a quarantine stable outside Coral Gables, then a transatlantic jump to London for another stable sojourn and the collection of Sia Fox before the final leg to Petersburg. The chartered 737 was outfitted for equine air travel: stalls replaced seats; bits and bridles and tack hung where the overhead compartments had been; the stale smell of recycled air was now that of hay and dung.

It was bad luck not to accompany the horses. Before Max had been born, Papa once had passed on traveling with a prized stallion they'd sold to a Lexington operation; the horse spooked, tranquilizers were ineffective, and the wildling animal was put down somewhere over south Texas. Since then, Castillos had flown with their horses.

The boarding process was always the same: the mare Penelope went first, into a stall in the tail. Then a groom slathered Vicks VapoRub into Smokey Joe's nostrils to prevent him from snatching Penelope's scent, and he was led onto the plane near the front, into a stall without sight lines to the mare. Though Smokey Joe was well behaved, no chances could be taken: an impromptu breeding attempt at thirty-five thousand feet would imperil not only the honor of Max's mother's cherished mare, but the aircraft's structural integrity and the lives of all aboard. Xylazine was administered to the horses, mescal to Max and the Mexicans, and an Ambien for Sia—the evening prior had been a Hynes Dawson all-nighter. She awoke to the bump of the runway. The plane was taxiing at Saint Petersburg's Pulkovo Airport.

Two black Rolls-Royce SUVs, one hitched with a horse trailer, rushed toward the plane. An airstair knocked into the hull. Max leaned into a window to scan the tarmac, face taut.

An attendant unlatched the door and one of the men outside poked in his head. He scanned the plane until his eyes came to rest on Sia. Then he smiled. "Welcome to Russia. Mr. and Mrs. Kovalchuk are sorry they could not be here to greet you." A customs officer shuffled past him into the plane. Document checks could be nail-biters, but Vadim had arranged for an arrival through what is known in Russia as the Green Corridor: Max and Sia would receive only a cursory document check. This officer would not search their bags, nor image their electronics. He quickly reviewed their passports and visas; he did not glance once at Penelope or Smokey Joe's proof of vaccine. Then, with a curt nod, he vanished to the warmth of his car and sped off toward the terminal.

A biting wind rocked the airstair while they deplaned, the sky a charcoal-gray sheet smothering the sun. The grooms led Smokey Joe and Penelope down the ramp and into the waiting trailer. Sia flipped up the fur-lined hood and drew herself farther into her black coat.

No comms to Langley.

No diplomatic immunity.

No lifeline. They were alone. Black.

And in mortal danger. She wanted to be nowhere else.

———

THERE HAD BEEN A FOUR-MONTH WINDOW BETWEEN LEAVING LYRIC and joining Hynes Dawson in London. Sia fed friends and family the tale that she would fill this fleeting corporate freedom with travel. Cape Town, of course, but also a few spots for pleasure: Rome, then maybe an adventure in Alaska. I'll rent an RV. Drive up there and get off the grid for a month or two.

Sia went to northern Virginia for TOTT when her family thought she was in Alaska. Tier One Target Tradecraft. The big leagues, the premier training program given to NOCs and case officers deploying to the hardest of the hard targets: Russia, China, Iran, North Korea, Belarus. Class sizes were small. Just six in hers. She got in because they thought she'd be traveling regularly to Moscow.

Day one was in a classroom: all six of them, one instructor for each. She was paired with a graybeard named Jon, who was also her course's overall lead instructor. Thirty-one years in the service, most of it crawling around Russia House. Snow-white hair on account of the Russians dousing him in luminol during a Moscow tour. The classroom was a red-brick colonial in the D.C. suburban sprawl. This place doesn't really matter, Jon said, because you won't be in desks, you'll be on the street.

TOTT washout rate is fifty percent, he said, in turn looking all six of them square in the eyes that first morning. We take it seriously because if I pass you and you're a fuckup, an agent dies. You design a shitty route, we fail you. You don't spot the ticks, we fail you. You mistakenly think you're covered in ticks and you abort, we fail you. And yes, you improperly document anything about anything, we fail you. This is all about the security of our assets. They're number one, and we're going to make sure you don't get them killed when we release you into the wild.

TOTT wasn't what the SEALs got. This wasn't BUD/S—though at a few points Jon and another instructor jumped from a van, bagged her head, and spirited her away to their phony jail. Which was, in fact, the actual local lockup down in Madison County, Virginia. There the instructors had successfully imagined the interior of a gulag: from the adjoining cells rose a constant chorus of screams, and the raunchy smell came courtesy of what she later learned was ten pounds of oysters left to cure behind a radiator. Three days in that cell, and they brought in a vagabond named Lucy—who may have been an instructor, Sia never did find out—a tweaked-out lady who insisted, ad nauseam, that Sia confess her crimes and just spare them the trouble of putting a bullet through her head.

Each night during TOTT she was sleep-deprived, and her body

screamed for relief from the near-constant motion of the day—usually covering twenty or thirty miles by foot or bike on her planning runs or scouting trips. There was never time to eat. She was always hungry.

TOTT was about pushing their ability to multitask to the absolute limit, to manipulate their physical environments, to create opportunities for operational acts in places where they would be watched constantly. It meant Sia's mind hummed twenty hours each day, every day, as she prepared and planned seemingly simple operational tasks in a zone spanning the entirety of the Washington, D.C., metro area. They rented an apartment for her in Clarendon. Her fictional office was in the District, off Dupont. The trainers mimicked the tools of a hostile intelligence service in the nastiest operating environments: Beijing, Moscow, Havana, Minsk, Tehran. The District's blanket CCTV coverage was in play. The service, Jon explained on the first day, had wired her apartment. They'd beaconed her car. They had her phone and had vacuumed up every shred of the telco data.

Abductions, arrests, and interrogations could happen at any time. The legends came out in drips: officers who had dissolved to tears under the interview room lights, those who had successfully fled the snatch teams (role-played by the FBI guys, the Feebs), others who had attacked the guards, the dopes who agreed to meetings with hostile CI officers (their instructors, in role) and were immediately flunked from the course.

The only certainty was that TOTT would end in eight weeks, and that they would either pass or fail. There were only two grades.

And it was here that Sia learned that the old tradecraft was truly dead and gone.

Faded light pouring through the dirty windows, Jon held up his phone. Average of seventy-two apps on here, he said, all spewing digital dust, pairing with dozens of unseen sensors and towers. Now they don't have to catch you running the surveillance detection route. They thread this all together and catch you later. Then they kill your agent.

They dispersed after day one. In TOTT you walked alone. That was good. She was good alone.

Each week Jon brought a new task to her apartment. Find a foot emplacement site. Brief encounter site. Cache site, then drop ten grand there for the agent. Signal site, then lay down the signal. She planned, she wrote it up, she submitted her plan to Jon, she executed the operational act. Sometimes Jon interrupted her, tried to break her flow to see how she'd respond. Agent changes the meeting time or place or, hey, we've got a volunteer we need you to meet tonight! They once nabbed her ten minutes before she could lay down the signal, pillowcase over the head. A nasty female instructor pushed her around, leaving a collage of bruises on her wrists and ribs. Again they trundled down to the Madison County lockup, and this time she spent the night chained to the radiator belching the dead oyster smell.

Her last task was to find a site for a brush pass with an agent on April 11 at 2213 hours and to carry out the act. How hard could it be?

Sia cased, she planned, she lost five pounds that last week because she wasn't eating or sleeping and her heart was just hammering away even as, to the outside world, she appeared calm, even serene. No sweat, no tremors, no looking over her shoulder, no head on a swivel—normal dreary lawyers did not perform street tradecraft, they did not walk around Moscow coming to pieces. They were boring. She looked boring. But in her mind there was always a fire drill.

On the day of the meeting, Sia forced down a single piece of dry toast in her apartment. She took the metro into Dupont to her "office"—a concrete building belonging to Johns Hopkins University. Inside her head was chaos: cataloguing everything, scribbling mental notes on the entire world. She had lunch at a Mexican place east of Kalorama and took a coffee nearby. Normal boring lawyer taking a long lunch break.

But Sia was not a normal lawyer, nor was she a normal trainee. Normals would think about it something like this: I show up at that site with coverage and I get tossed. And not just from TOTT. My deployment is toast. I fuck this up, and my career is gone. But not Sia. That day she only thought about winning, about beating Jon and his surveillants. She did not once consider failure, even as a remote possibility.

From the coffee shop she returned to the office. Jon was outside on the street in his car, tapping on his iPad, whispering into an RF earpiece. Normal. He was the maestro for her opposition, she was not to acknowledge his presence. She shuffled around her office until five p.m., then back to her apartment. She'd not detected any of Jon's street surveillants, but then again, they had her phone and car and apartment. They knew where she was. Time to change that.

At home she put on workout gear, collected a duffel bag—packed in the darkness of her closet—and set out for the gym. During TOTT, she had visited every day after work. The duffel bag—which held her phone—got shoved into a locker. Sometimes she lifted weights. Sometimes she swam. Sometimes she ran.

Tonight, she lifted weights for twenty minutes and then went for a run. Out, into the spring air. No phone, no car. Dressed for the outdoors: yoga pants, light jacket, ball cap. In the first week she'd been casing signal sites and realized she was in a skirt and blouse. *Can't be traipsing around the muck in Rock Creek Park in a skirt, can we, Hortensia?* Jon said during the debrief. Her route would have appeared random to any watchers, as if she were making it up on the go. But she'd spent days planning it; every turn, every stop to quickly catch her breath. She knew every camera along the way.

She catalogued while she ran: faces, vehicles, clothing, minuscule changes to the environment. A white-brick home had newly painted shutters; there were freshly planted flowers outside another; a garage door was open that was usually shut. She'd run segments of this route dozens of times during the course: evening, morning, rain, sunshine. She had to feel the street, each segment of the surveillance detection route had to speak to her, whisper if They were hunting her.

Two hours into the run she'd reached Crystal City and the leafy neighborhood bordering the park where the brush pass would take place. She'd never felt so dialed in to the world in all her life; every color, every sound, every smell was absorbed and processed and catalogued. This was flow, she was running well, she was going to fucking win. *The world is humming, I see it all.* She'd designed a provocative zone—a PZ—near the park. The PZ was where *she* would hunt the surveillance. One last check before the meeting. Tonight she planned to stop, look into a dumpster, and then jump in. That should be enough to draw in any watchers.

Sia cut out of the neighborhood, down Twenty-Third Street, along a row of shops and restaurants. She turned right, back toward the park, and ran—faster now—by a drugstore, a low-hung strip club that looked like a steak place, and into a parking lot shared by a gas station and a kebab joint.

And there were two black sedans idling right smack in the middle her PZ. Damn thugs of Jon's, assholes blowing up her flow. Same as the night they bagged her and roughed her up. No need to dumpster-dive tonight. The opposition had shown themselves already, daring her to act. Fine. Let's play.

This was the game: Losing surveillance without surveillance thinking they've lost you.

Winning meant manipulating the environment so she could clear a few seconds of space to perform the brush pass and walk away.

She jogged toward the park. She'd chosen it with surgical care. It was slightly sunken, almost a bowl, ringed by pines and firs. Two walkways led from the parking lot. Both crested uphill before spilling down into the park. No entrances on the other sides. Uneven coverage from the streetlamps and the lights over the soccer fields. If she could reach the top of the path before Jon's guys stepped from their cars, she would have ten seconds—precisely ten seconds—to conduct the brush pass. If the agent—and tonight Jon was playing the agent—was late, she would abort.

She ran through the parking lot, ascended the walkway, and snaked through a crowd of teenagers milling around after a soccer game. Then she was at the crest, under the trees. She heard the slam of car doors, thought, This is it, I am going to fucking win. And she was on the downslope, running into the park, counting down from ten, and she could see Jon ahead on the path, in the shadows.

He is alive in the shadows, she thought, like I am.

And as she slowed to accept a thumb drive, tucking it smoothly into her jacket pocket, she counted past three and felt something right then, for the first time since joining CIA, a tug back to a few halcyon nights of her youth, when she'd walked to the edge of herself and found that was where she was most alive.

Under the smothering blanket, beneath the all-seeing eye of their surveillance, she had won a tiny foothold from which they would lose the entire battle. And these thoughts collided into a sensation of pure joy, a feeling that later she would tell Jon was as though she were a god. Alone, all-powerful, all-seeing, the keeper of all secrets, the winner of all battles for now and forever. Amen.

26

RusFarm

MAX'S MOTHER HAD SHOWN HIM A HORSE HIS FIRST HOURS IN THE world, and when she died he'd spent his first hours without her riding one. He'd been on horseback alongside friends and enemies and lovers and people whom he could no longer recall. He'd been on a horse, riding with his father, the day the old man first hinted at the relationship with CIA. It was rare to discover a Thoroughbred operation he disliked, and unprecedented for the disdain to arrive with the property line.

But a hollow feeling struck at the precise moment they crossed through RusFarm's brutal iron gate. Soiled stone walls had been etched with images of rearing stallions glaring through hateful eyes. Thick, naked trees guarded the road, breaking the weak sunlight. As they drove deeper into the farm the road darkened, and the trees seemed increasingly to twist in pained, almost manic contortions. Max saw no evidence of a connection between the farm and the world outside the fence. There was no movement out there, no noise, no animals. The woods were dead except for the faint whiff of smoke and petrol floating on the air, the menacing smell of an unseen, gathering army.

The forest surrendered. And when the house came into view his emptiness curdled into fear. We should leave, he thought, we should get away. And it was not because he feared them nabbing him as a spy. There was something else. Something he could not name but only feel: the absence of good, a dark energy pulsing from the mansion.

They circled around a horse fountain nearly the height of the mansion itself, stopping at the bottom of a marble staircase. He reached for the door handle and realized that his fingers had become cold even with the car heater rolling.

Vadim and Anna greeted them with cheery kisses in a gloomy foyer. *Might we stay in a guesthouse?* Max wanted to ask. The bags disappeared, ferried away by the silent staff. Sia, he thought, seemed unburdened. Oblivious to the weight of this place.

Anna's face brightened at the sight of the trailer. A cluster of Rus-Farm grooms were assembling to greet Smokey Joe. The arrival of a six-million-dollar horse was a rare occurrence, even to an operation as stupidly rich as RusFarm.

"It is so kind of you to bring her," Anna said, pecking Max again on the cheek. "I asked them to stop here before going to the stables. I am going to say hello." She walked down the marble steps and into the cold. The trailer was enclosed, heated for the winter, with separate compartments for each horse. Anna opened the door to Penelope's section and stepped up. Before she disappeared inside, Max caught a glimpse of something that made him wonder if, despite all odds, Sia might just have a chance with this one. Anna was smiling.

Vadim clapped his hands. "How about a tour?"

———

THAT EVENING THE WIND BEAT THE WINDOWS AS CLOUDS ERASED THE moon and stars. From the bedroom window Sia watched a driving snow. The cold had grown so biting that during the tour her body sweat had frozen in a filmy layer on her skin instead of passing through her clothing to dry. She'd taken a hot bath and then a scalding shower and still she felt chilled and soiled.

She snatched her phone from the nightstand and typed out her sign-of-life message. In what appeared to be an email to an executive assistant at Hynes Dawson, she inquired about several client transactions, including those of a Greek shipping magnate. The message would be routed to Procter, the mention of the Greek the signal that all proceeded according to plan. The message whooshed away. Sia picked at one of the CIA-doctored Clif Bars. Max emerged from the bathroom dressed for dinner in a dark cowl-neck sweater, slacks, and boots. She wore a black dress and pumps.

As best they could, they walked a straight path to the dining room, driven by the unspoken yet clear conviction that this was not the kind of house you should explore. The design was bewildering; halls zigzagged, some rooms were windowless, linked not to hallways but nested inside other rooms.

At the end of a hallway Max stopped, hand to his lips. They had not spoken since leaving the bedroom.

Sia stopped and listened to murmurs on the other side of a door.

She caught Vadim yelling, then Anna's shouted reply. A bottle clinked into a glass. A pit turned in Sia's stomach, and she did not know why. She smoothed her dress and pushed past Max, shoving open the heavy door. A bear head was mounted above the fireplace. Anna and Vadim were standing in front of a blazing fire, drinks in hand, argument midstream.

"My, my," Sia called out cheerfully, "did you get the party started without us? Sorry to barge in. We got lost, if you can believe it!"

The evening began with a round of the vodka ritual before moving to the dining room. Three iron chandeliers that recalled medieval torture instruments were strung above a table that to Sia's eye had to be more than twenty feet long and was creaking with a spread of food that made her queasy. The display included a dish called chicken Rodina, which, before the war, Anna whispered to Sia, had been known as chicken Kyiv. The two couples sat across from each other at one end of the table. Vadim was good and drunk, goading Max to keep up. Wine and vodka *stopki* were filled and refilled. Each round, the butlers brought new frozen glasses. The empties, Sia thought, were doubtless carted away to collect fingerprints and perhaps DNA.

"It is nice to have people from outside Russia at our table," Vadim said. "These visits have become more rare because of the lies about our country. The propaganda? My god." He downed a vodka and called for cognac. The switch in alcohol the suicide move, Sia figured, meaning that in a half hour he either intended to be asleep or moving on to cocaine. Anna did not seem amused.

"For example," he continued, "this business about Russians poisoning dissidents in Poland. Some of my friends have stopped reading the Western papers, but I still do. Important for business. And do you know what I saw in the *Financial Times*? Leaks from CIA claiming that our President himself ordered the attacks." Vadim shook his head and picked at his food. "The Americans will stop at nothing to tar us.

"What is the view from Mexico on this, Max?" Vadim asked.

Max shrugged, pulled more chicken onto his plate. "Traitors get what they deserve."

Vadim grinned.

"Please, we are not political people," Sia said. She shot Anna an imploring look.

"In Russia everything is political," Vadim said. "Everything that matters, at least." He turned to Sia. "Well, what do you think?"

Sia chewed on a toast point slathered in foie gras and pretended to consider her answer. "I think Russia probably did it."

Vadim's laugh catapulted a cord of chewed duck over his plate. Anna smiled darkly and shook her head and clucked her tongue. "My god," he said. "Really?"

"Yes. Why shouldn't I think that?" Sia said. Procter's coaching on dealing with Russians: don't show weakness, stand your ground. "As Max said, traitors get what they deserve."

Before Vadim could respond, the doors swung open and a herd of kitchen staff arrived with a large Napoleon cake and a fresh bottle of vodka sweating in ice. Each piece of cake, Anna explained, was twelve layers and accompanied by a chocolate horse, diminutive cocoa Emperor Napoleon riding atop. The left foreleg of Sia's chocolate horse snapped off as the plate slid in front of her. The butlers refilled *stopki*.

As Vadim droned on, Sia took a bite of the cake and thought about what they would do tonight. She had never really seen this job as a job. It was more like a life, and because it was a life, she rarely thought of it as strange. Your life was your life. It was normal. But now Sia granted herself a moment to consider the insanity of this situation. The risk she was taking. But that quickly evaporated into a hit of adrenaline, and her mind focused, readying for the game ahead.

Anna cut Vadim off, said they should all get some sleep. "It's well past midnight. Their bodies think it is morning already."

They were walking from the dining room when Sia said, "Wait. One thing." Strutting back to the table, she picked up the chocolate horse and bit off its head. She watched Anna's mouth curl into a knowing smile, as if she were accepting some unspoken challenge. Sia licked her fingers and slung her arm through Max's for the walk upstairs.

————

STUMBLING INTO THE ROOM, THOUGH, HER THOUGHTS WERE NOT OF romance. They were, insanely, of paperwork. CIA officers had to write cables to document sexual encounters or secure approval for relationships with foreign nationals. And though Max was an FNO, he was also a Mexican citizen and the damn bureaucracy rendered that a gray area.

She disengaged from the bureaucratic mental gymnastics and took stock of Max. He was sitting on the edge of the bed, silent, and she slid down next to him. There they sat, trading glances for a heady moment, sharing a signal that had not been planned, no tradecraft, nothing operational, just two people wordlessly communicating that it was time to put to bed the Russians' suspicions and iron out whatever creases remained in their partnership, and that it all must unspool under surveillance, memorialized for all time in the archival records of the Russian security services.

There were operational justifications, even Procter had said as much, but Sia had also felt Max's desire in St. Ives. She'd not done this in a long time, work and all, and had felt stifled, like she was denying herself. Which she was: she'd only managed to stop in their practice session because she'd been so strung out readying herself for this trip and wanted to beat him, establish some control, and that had been enough to wrestle down the hunger. But now she was telegraphing the desire coursing through her. And all the reasons to stop were operationally foolish. Max had her underwear down at her ankles. He was kissing her legs and then she had his hair tight in her hand to guide him and there should have been liftoff, weightlessness.

But her desire vanished. She looked down at Max. Around the room. The cameras were everywhere, the house was heavy, she was with a man who was, in the end, a professional colleague. And the watchers would be sitting with them at breakfast tomorrow, working off hangovers, smug in the knowledge that they had watched them screw. A switch had flipped off. She wanted to slink under the covers. Instead, she hiked her dress up farther and lay back on the bed.

One of the can lights seemed to peek down at her and she thought that was where she would put the camera. She looked away, she could not help it, she could not look at the watchers. She wanted him. But she could not look at him now. Her eyes were closed when he started. It felt at first like some cosmic embarrassment she might never shake.

But as he worked, her appetite returned. He was strong, he was feeling for what her body liked, and Sia let the curtain between theater and reality peel back a bit. She put her hands on his shoulders, on his chest. They kissed, and she liked the taste, how he smelled of cedar and salt. The flow was lovely—assured arms cradled her back and head and kept her close, their foreheads gently touched, his eyes watched her closely and she saw that he was in the moment, and soon she was, too.

After a while she pushed him back and patted the bed. He lay down, and she slid onto him. Tossing her head back, getting that hair out of her eyes, she began to move, and soon there was a familiar electricity surging through her. He opened his mouth, but she pressed a finger to his lips. "No," she said. "Not yet."

———

THROUGH THE NIGHT-VISION-GREEN OF THE SIX CAMERAS WIRED INTO Sia and Max's room, Anna and Vadim watched an act that recalled riding a horse at a substantial gallop. There were frequent profane outbursts; three times Sia gripped his shoulders and rolled back her head and shuddered. It made Anna miss Luka.

"Do you think those are real?" she asked Vadim.

Vadim shrugged. "If not, it's a convincing performance."

"Well, what do you think of them now?"

Again, he shrugged.

Anna's thoughts settled on Vadim's camera in the ceiling. A snide comment rolled to the end of her tongue, but when she turned to deliver it, Vadim was gone.

27

RusFarm

THE NEXT MORNING THE MEN DISAPPEARED TO THE BATHHOUSE. SIA and Anna hitched a horse trailer to a Rolls SUV and loaded up Penelope and another mare for a ride on the eastern rim of the property. A few trees had fallen, Anna had said, blocking the trails near the house and the stables. They carved through a hilly pasture at a slow trot, the depressing sky thick with clouds filtering weak morning light.

This conversation had to appear fluid and natural. And yet Sia had planned and rehearsed every word in St. Ives. For a while they rode in silence. Sia sized up Anna and saw that Max had been correct about Anna and Penelope; the Russian's eyes and countenance had softened since breakfast. The entire world, Sia thought, seemed gentler the further they trotted from the house. Sia looked over the tack and saddlebags and wondered where they'd hidden the microphones. She cast the thought aside. It did not matter—at least not yet.

"The farm is beautiful," Sia lied.

"It is, thank you," Anna replied. She was murmuring to the horse.

Sia smiled. "Does she understand Russian?"

Anna laughed, and it caught Sia off guard. Laughter was rare from this one. "I'm teaching her," she said.

In St. Ives, Procter had delivered the blunt challenge: co-development, a dance for two, each woman working the other. I love co-developing Russkies, Procter had said, because if they date, they consummate. That's why the Russian services won't do it if they know the person on the other end is CIA. Their people go for dinner with us, and soon they're dropping the old metaphorical britches. So how do you get them to the table? Well, you start by inviting them.

"On the flight here," Sia said, "it struck me that I don't know much about your family. Maybe you'd tell me a little about them?"

Sia watched the Russian closely, Anna lost in thought. They'd stopped atop a hill with a commanding view of a valley unrolling below. A finger of open land parted the trees. They nosed the horses down the far side of the snowy rise. Hooves crunched over the snow. Sia steadied her mind, readying it to transcribe every word, every pause, every unsaid thing.

"Family," Anna said, looking into the middle distance. Her chuckle came out soft and sad. "Papa is ex-KGB. Now in business. He's all the things you'd expect—overbearing and clever and deceitful, and often he's kind." Anna patted Penelope's haunch.

"My father taught me to ride," Sia said. "Did yours?"

Anna grunted. "It was my mother who taught me. She passed when I was young. For me there have been two seasons in life. One with my mother, and one without. My mother encouraged me, she drew me out. She had a light spirit. A lot of Russians remember that period only as a time of chaos. But for me it is also joy. It is me on horseback with my mother. She wasn't like my father. Or the Kovalchuks. Or any of them, really. She wasn't even like me. She was different."

"What do you mean?" Sia asked.

Anna laughed. Words seemed to float around her lips, but they never did come. They rode on for a few minutes, the silence broken only by hooves shuffling through unpacked snow. The air hung with the smell of the wood and the musk of the horses, and Sia thought all of this would be just beautiful had it not been for the reality that they were in a sandy ring, circling each other with knives.

"How was your mother different?" Sia asked. "Not to pry."

Anna held the reins and regarded the sky, as if expecting snow. They were folded among the trees. "Do you ever feel like a piece on someone else's game board? Moved around so somebody else can win? My mother was not like that. She did not play their games."

"I suppose everyone feels that way at times," Sia said. The unwelcome thought of CIA and Procter flashed quickly through her mind. She continued, "My grandfather said he would pay for my college but only if I studied law. He wanted a lawyer in the family. My father had the lousy idea to name his daughters after flowers. Hortensia? Hell, I've been playing someone else's game from day one."

"What is your sister's name?"

"Daisy."

Anna gave a wicked smile.

"Is that what it's like with Vadim?" Sia said. "You're playing his game?"

Their eyes met, each of them sizing up the other. The skin on Anna's face was pulled tight and a cord pulsed in her neck as if she were grinding her teeth. The Russian looked away first.

"My father wanted to make money after my mother died," Anna said. "So I helped him forge a partnership with the Kovalchuks by marrying Vadim. It was Papa's game, not mine. And Vadim likes his women with their mouths shut and their legs open, so…" She sucked her bottom lip into her teeth and grew silent.

"Not so good at his game, are you?" Sia said.

A shadow fell over Anna's eyes. "But what other game is there to play?"

"Your own."

Anna brought Penelope closer to Sia and said, "There is no such thing."

But the Russian's shining eyes betrayed the lie. There was another life in there. And it was the one calling the shots.

Anna pulled a few lengths ahead. Silence fell over the woods. Sometimes you let it sit, Sia thought. Sometimes you wait.

———

ANNA CURSED HERSELF FOR SHARING, FOR BABBLING ON ABOUT HER family. She never did that—with anyone. Even Luka. Instead of drilling into Sia and finding a desire to protect a loved one, or a need for money or sex or power, or—better—some strange, unacceptable addiction, Anna seemed to be tunneling into herself. She wanted to stop this and ride. Just ride. She let her frustration echo through her mind. Then she imagined treating it to an appropriately disgraceful Russian death: heaving it right off a building to die on the street below. She had an operation to run. A family to protect. Prey to hunt.

Anna stroked Penelope's mane to clear her mind. The snow was picking up. Perfect timing. "We should be getting back," she called.

———

THEY MADE FOR THE STABLES AT A QUICKENING PACE, HEADS DOWN, bearing into the snow through narrowed, blinkered eyes. Anna pulled alongside Sia as they slipped from the trees and brought the horses to canter in the open pasture.

After a few minutes, Anna fell a length behind Sia.

Then Sia heard a shout and a yelp.

Turning her head, Sia saw Penelope riderless. Anna was spread motionless in the snow. Sia halted her horse and dismounted. Anna was sitting up, clutching her lower back, cursing.

"Stepped in a damn hole," she said in English.

The snow fell harder now. Sia wiped her eyes in frustration. An injury meant less time in the saddle, less time to develop the Russian. "Can you ride?"

Anna stood, hobbled a few steps, let loose more curses. Shook her head and looked around. "We are close to the truck. And it is warmer than yesterday, even with the snow. Let's walk."

They led the horses toward the Rolls. Sia guided both into the trailer and tied them up. She closed the trailer gate and went to the passenger-side door. Anna was already in the seat. "Can you drive?" Anna asked. She winced. "Back spasms."

"Of course." Sia guided the car along the rutted path, which soon necked into the main road back to the house. Anna groaned and shifted in her seat with each bump. She was searching her pockets, cursing in Russian.

"Maybe just sit still," Sia said. She was hunched over the wheel, trying to squint through the snow.

"My phone," Anna said. "My phone must be in the saddlebag. Can

you call Max and have him tell Vadim to ring the doctor? I need someone to look at my back." Sia fumbled in her jacket pocket for her phone,
accelerating the Rolls as she began searching for his name in her contacts, eyes glued to the screen.

Then she sensed a shape in front of her in the road. Anna screamed.
There was a loud thump.

Something bounced onto the hood to collide with the windshield;
there was a shock of dark hair, a tan coat, a man's contorted face. Sia froze
for a moment, watching things unfold. Blood spattered onto the glass.
The man bumped over the roof. Sia slammed on the brakes. Through the
rearview she saw the man roll off the passenger side of the car. Horses
whinnied. The windshield was soaked in blood.

She started to get out of the car, but the Rolls slid forward until she
pressed the brake again and remembered to put it in park. She stumbled
into the road. The man was motionless, facedown in his own blood.
A woman held his head in her lap, alternating between weeping and
screaming in Russian. Oh God, oh God, oh God, Sia began mumbling.
Anna had hobbled out of the car. She was muttering in Russian. The
woman picked up her phone. Dialed a number. Began screaming again
in Russian.

"Dead?" Sia called out. "Is he dead?" She knelt by him in the snow.
The woman, still howling into the phone, pushed her away. Sia shoved
her back, told her she wanted to take the man's pulse. But the woman
was hysterical—Sia twice more tried to check if the man was alive, and
twice more the woman forced her away. The woman was shouting into
her phone, yelling at Anna. Sia slumped into the snow by the Rolls while
the woman spoke with Anna.

Blood dripped onto one of the tires along a red trail running from
the Rolls's roof. *Plip-plop-plip.* There was so much of it, as if the impact
had burst the man open. The warm blood hissed and steamed as it kissed
the snow. *Plip-plop-plip.*

The sirens summoned the instinct to move, to get off the X. An
ambulance. How had they arrived so quickly? Two paramedics jumped
out. They took the man's pulse—she saw grave shakes of their heads. The

woman was pacing, muttering, cursing, pointing at Sia and Anna. One of the paramedics slipped a blanket over the body. They put it on a gurney. Then a police car arrived. Anna, hands on her head, approached the car.

Sia ran a finger through the blood in the road. It seemed real. She wanted to get up, but her legs would not move.

After a few minutes, a second police car arrived. Anna and the new police officer exchanged machine-gun Russian, Anna gesturing from the car to Sia to the man and back again. Then the two police officers broke off to talk. Anna sat down by Sia.

"The first one is road police," she said. "The second is the criminal police. He will take us to the police station. It is in the village just outside the farm."

"Can you talk to them?" Sia asked. "Tell them it was an accident."

Anna nodded. "I have." She turned to the sheet-draped body. "I know that couple. They live just off the property. They are always trespassing."

Sia's mind swam. She had been panicked and nauseated when she saw the dead man, but now a different feeling gnawed at her. One to which she was not accustomed. Fear. Whatever they wanted, she would give it to Anna. Had to be Anna. She could not go to a police station. My god, she could not go to a police station in Russia.

One of the police officers returned and told Anna they had to load up into the patrol car. Someone would come from the house for the horses. Anna said she was sure this would be routine; all would be fine. Anna again spoke to the officer in Russian and then whispered to Sia that he had agreed she could come along to translate. Sia slid into the car; the driver locked the doors. Anna sat with her in the back. Time ceased flowing at its normal pace. Sia did not know if the drive took one minute or thirty. The Russian was patting her thigh with a stiff hand. Perhaps Anna was trying to appear reassuring, Sia thought, but something about it felt cold and sinister. Pat-pat-pat. *Do what I say, girl, it seemed to say.* Pat-pat-pat. Sia considered different off-ramps: a nice bribe, perhaps, or Anna persuading the police to let her go. In all of them she was at Anna's mercy.

And that, she now realized, was terrifying.

28

RusFarm

THEY STOPPED AT A TWO-STORY CINDER-BLOCK BUILDING. THERE was no light in the windows, no sign, no cars parked in the gravel lot. This was the police station? The officer led them into an office with a desk, a computer, and mismatched metal chairs. He snapped Sia's picture. With Anna translating, he filled out a pink form with Sia's biographic data. He asked Anna to send Sia's documents and belongings from the farm: passport, visa, UK driver's license, phone, computer. He fingerprinted her. He wrote down Sia's account of the accident, frequently stepping out of the room for hushed phone calls.

After one such call, he brought them to a new room, cold and musty, with weeping cinder-block walls. The table and chairs were scuffed metal. This, she knew, was an interrogation room. Same vibes as the TOTT mock-up in Madison County, Virginia.

Where were the other police officers? Nothing about this felt official, but was that helpful? Probably. Maybe. Who knew? She was in Russia. They could do with her what they liked, official or not. The cold of the room seemed to settle into her bones.

After a particularly shouty phone call in the hallway, the police officer joined them at the table, running his hands through his hair with the frenetic air of a man being squeezed for results by his superiors. He asked Sia to again recite her testimony. When she had finished, the police officer spoke, punctuating his final sentence by pressing a finger into the back of the cell phone lying on the table. He waved for Anna to translate.

But before she could, there was a knock at the door. The police officer disappeared into the hall. She heard hushed voices, footsteps, the shuttering of unseen doors.

Then another man entered the room. Tall, dead-eyed, well-dressed in a dark suit, blond hair slicked to his skull. His shirt was pressed, his tie was worked into a clean knot. He spoke to Anna for a minute, then waved for the translation.

"This is Captain Ivanov from the Federal Security Service, the FSB," she began. The three letters sucked the air from Sia's chest.

Anna continued, "He says that he understands you are at RusFarm as our special guest, and that this was an accident. But he would like to speak with you about something that came up when the police ran checks on your employer. He would like to talk to you here, tonight."

The door opened. The second police officer entered. He carried her purse and suitcase from the farm. He put her laptop and phone on the table. The FSB officer dismissed him, then spoke to Anna before waving for another translation.

"Something important has come to Captain Ivanov's attention," Anna began. "He says that if you can help him find it, we will keep your case out of the courts. We might resolve this informally. Pay the wife, that kind of thing."

Sia stared at the laptop. The computer was here, in Russia, for exactly this moment. It gave Sia something to offer. She could again draw full breaths into her lungs; her numb hand reddened and warmed a little. The space let a brief thought flash through Sia's mind: *Not gonna tell Procter the whole story.* This was the kind of debacle that got you put on ice stateside, doing biweeklies with ops psychologists, polygraphers, and cement-eyed security guys itching to get to the bottom of things. The end of a promising career.

Then, though she already knew the answer, Sia asked a question because it would have been strange not to. "What does he want with the computer?" she asked.

Anna translated for Captain Ivanov, who explained, then gave Anna another curt wave.

"Access to Hynes Dawson documents and correspondence," Anna said. "He believes that there may be information in your files revealing illegal financial activities conducted by senior members of the Russian government and several high-profile businessmen. He understands the most unusual nature of this request but asks that you please unlock the laptop and guide him through the files of interest."

"You are working with them, aren't you?" Sia whispered in English. "Tell me what's happening, Anna, please. What is this? I don't understand what is happening."

The FSB officer snapped at Anna, who nodded and put a hand up. "Please, Sia," she said, "no asides to me in English. Speak to Captain Ivanov."

"What happens if I do not cooperate?" Sia asked.

Anna chatted with Ivanov about that. The conversation ended in a long shouting match that did not quite seem right to Sia.

"He says," Anna said between her teeth, "that if you do not cooperate, the FSB will encourage the criminal police to pursue an investigation. They will jail you in Kirishi tonight, in Piter after that. Confiscate your passport. Let the system work it out."

"Anna," Sia said, "you must be able to do something."

More chatter with Ivanov. Anna shook her head. "I might be able to help as the case progresses," Anna said. "But for now this is the captain's offer. I am sorry."

The first police officer opened the laptop and plugged it in. The second brought steaming Styrofoam cups filled with tea. Sia watched the laptop boot up and stared at the screen demanding her password. She did not move.

Ivanov dismissed the policemen. In English, he said, "Go."

She waited.

He said something in Russian to Anna. Then he pointed to Sia. Anna scooted her chair closer. Those chilly blue eyes did not leave her own.

And Sia knew this was the true version of Anna, the one she'd glimpsed earlier on their ride. The deep one. It was cold and terrifying, but it spoke in a soothing voice, it promised to do whatever necessary to help Sia out of this jam with the FSB.

Anna, Sia thought, was pretending to translate for the FSB officer. Or was that right? Who was in charge?

Sia's left hand shook. She could not get warm. A ringing kicked up in her ears and she could barely hear the questions.

Anna began with a statement that the FSB believed Hynes Dawson had helped several Russian businessmen establish foreign bank accounts overseas, in violation of Kremlin capital controls. The question mark arrived with an eyebrow raised at Sia.

"Yes, that's right," Sia heard herself say.

The FSB, Anna continued, is especially interested in the activities and associates of a man called Vassily Platonovich Gusev. Known as Goose. We discussed him briefly in Mexico. Do you know him as Goose, Sia? And Sia said, Yes, yes, I do. I will tell you whatever you want about him.

And then Anna's lips were moving, but Sia was staring through the table and her ears were ringing again and she didn't hear a damn thing for a while.

"Mikhail Lyadov?" Anna said. The Russian was frustrated, as if she'd repeated the name a few times already.

"What?"

"Do you know Mikhail Lyadov? Calls himself Mickey around London, we're told."

"I do. I know him. Micks. He's a client."

Her left hand was shaking again. She mashed it into her leg to see if it would stop. Instead, like a marionette, its movement made her thigh shiver.

"Goose stole a large quantity of gold," Anna said. "Too much to ignore."

"I see." My hand, Sia thought. I cannot make it stop shaking. She was suddenly aware of her constant blinking. Her breathing was labored, each draw from her lungs forced painfully through the straw of a tightening throat.

"But you already know that, of course," Anna said. "Mickey Lyadov helps Goose move money overseas and then wash it. Hynes Dawson establishes the legal structure. You have the documents, yes? Articles of organization and incorporation? A diagram of the whole system? The bank accounts—locations, balances, wiring information, perhaps log-in credentials for a few? The lists of individuals authorized for the accounts? Captain Ivanov says he wants all of it. You'll give him everything, tonight, and in exchange you get to leave Russia."

"Anna, please, I'll be disbarred. I—"

There was a winding, translated presentation of nastier alternatives: FSB-led criminal investigations, Lefortovo, a Siberian labor camp.

Anna often said the words "official paperwork" and more than once stated flatly that future discussions would be presided over by FSB officers who are *not friends of my family.* The fiction that Ivanov was pulling the strings grew thin. She felt that Anna was in charge, but she could not really be sure, and in that uncertainty her mind flitted to dark places. Anna had played this one rough. The training brought neither comfort nor the semblance of a plan. Her mind pondered failure, not victory. Sia's longtime companion, that hammer in her chest, was disturbingly silent. Sia tried to snuggle deeper into her coat, but she could not get warm, no matter how much she shivered or rubbed her shoulders and arms.

In the end she logged in to the computer. I will do whatever you want, she said.

She gave them everything: The hidey-holes for cash that had once been Andrei Agapov's gold. A vast financial empire scattered to the four winds by Sia Fox, Hynes Dawson, and the Swiss bankers.

She showed them the few accounts for which she had power of attorney and might conceivably move funds herself, without authorization. For emergencies, Micks had said. In case we need something done quick.

I have never been colder, she thought. Sometimes her fingers shook when she pointed at the screen. She asked for a heavier coat, or maybe a blanket, and she thought Anna told the first policeman to bring one, but he never did. I'll never be warm again, she thought. Winter is buried in my chest.

Sia's left hand quivered through the night, she could not make it stop, and Anna grew impatient with her because the shaking fingers made it difficult to type. Sia did note that through it all Anna sat up straight as an arrow. The little bitch's back was fine, her fall from the horse a perfect dive.

The idea of convincing this psychotic Russian to cooperate with CIA dissolved into an absurd fantasy with each dollar, euro, and ruble uncovered. You are a fucking fool, Hortensia, she thought, for believing that was possible.

A shadow often veiled Anna's eyes, and Sia had the vague sense the Russian was disappointed, or perhaps she didn't know what to do now that she'd gotten what she wanted.

But as Sia gave them everything, she considered that, though Anna's hands all evening had been folded primly on the table, they might as well have been cinched around her windpipe, strangling the life clean out of her.

29

RusFarm

WHEN THEY HAD FINISHED, AFTER SIA HAD BEEN FERRIED BACK TO the main house to stumble upstairs, Anna stepped out of the old administrative building. An ambulance was idling in the parking lot. Anna found Dasha grinning from the driver's seat. Blood streaked her greatcoat.

"How did I do?" the gymnast asked.

"A perfect toss," Anna said. "Ten out of ten."

"Did we use too much blood?" Dasha asked. "Perhaps too many balloons?"

"It was the right amount," Anna said. "It was perfect."

The balloons had been a nasty business. Dasha had filled and fashioned them into a necklace that could slip under the late Kiril's greatcoat. Her smile faded, and she now looked a little sick. The putrid scent of pig's blood in the truck could not be helping.

———

FROM RUSFARM'S FIRST-FLOOR OFFICE ANNA AIMLESSLY SCOURED THE bookshelves, eventually arriving at the hulking cabinet where Papa kept some of his more interesting weapons. It was always unlocked. There were no children around, her father had once explained. Why bother? And then his little twist of the knife, "Though I would appreciate an excuse to lock it. Maybe two." She ran her hand over the case with the lipstick tube. She thought of shooting with him the night he had brought her into this mess. Then she closed the gun cabinet, swiveling her chair to face the window and consider the evening.

Sia. She'd been fearful after the staged accident but had soon regained a confidence, apart from that shaky hand. It struck Anna as a performance. And not that of a lawyer in a courtroom.

Of someone trained for this type of stress.

Someone like herself.

The office door opened. An eye roll on instinct, expecting Vadim.

"Anya," her father said, "what do we have?"

"Papa."

Her father sat, and her face must have spoken her mind, because he frowned. "What's wrong, Anya? Tell me."

Her mouth wasn't yet open when he tilted his chin toward the window. Headlamps blotted the fountain in the circle. Six cars, she counted. Blue lights flashing under the grill. The FSB.

"Expecting company?" her father said.

———

WHEN SIA SLIPPED INTO THE ROOM, MAX'S PINCHED VOICE INDICATED that he knew something terrible had happened, but when he asked about her night with Anna, she said only: "We had a lovely time. Jovial." (*I gave her the information on Goose.*) What Max could not ask was how that had happened, nor why Sia's left hand seemed to be shaking uncontrollably after such a jovial evening. The codes were clunky, Sia had sworn up and down to the supposed FSB officer, through Anna, that she would not tell Max what happened, and she certainly could not do so now, here inside their Rodina and under the crush of the RusFarm cameras.

Now Sia's eyes were shut to show the cameras she was asleep like a sensible, if battered, houseguest, but her mind was at work. This op was thoroughly blown to hell. She'd screwed for the cameras. Anna had then turned the actual screws on her. And who was that dead man, anyhow? She lay beside Max—also awake—unable to say a word about any of it because of the surveillance feeds, those slimy camera eyeballs stuck on her skin. The room itself seemed to crawl around her, its dark wood

212 - David McCloskey

walls pressing down on the bed. She imagined the Mongol horseman, dying quite badly in the painting hung above the dresser, twisting his head to smile at her.

She opened her eyes at Max's nudge. Headlights down in the front circle. They went to the window. For a moment Sia blinked in confusion. Six cars. Blue lights, the telltale sirens—government vehicles—probably FSB. Why would they come back?

Oh god, a paddy wagon.

"We are dead," she whispered to Max, forgetting the microphones. We are dead. This is the kind of place where people die.

And then Sia was outside her body. She was perched on the bed canopy watching herself stumble to the nightstand and her phone. Alongside Max she was readying emergency signals for Procter, fumbling with the numbers, wondering if instead they might break open the windows and jump. We are not high enough, we will just shatter our damn legs. She fought to focus on the numbers, but her eyes bounced through the room, searching for a good place to sling up a bedsheet noose.

———

THE HEADLIGHTS GUIDING CHERNOV'S CAR LIT UP A GIGANTIC STONE statue of a horse, twisted around the circle, and came to rest on a man stepping gingerly into the beam. He held up his hand to shield his face and waved Chernov's lead car forward. The tires sputtered over snow. The man leaned in to meet the driver's window. Chernov held up his credentials.

"I need to speak with Andrei Borisovich. I understand he is here tonight," Chernov said.

"Who are you?" the man asked.

"Lieutenant Colonel Konstantin Konstantinovich Chernov. Internal Security Directorate. You are Vadim Yurivich Kovalchuk?"

"Yes."

"Tell me where Andrei Borisovich is."

"Why are you here?"

"The state's business," Chernov said. "God's business. Where is he?"

Chernov's boot tapped into the fresh snow. He brushed Vadim aside and looked up at the darkened house. Snow glowed on the roof. Smoke curled from what must have been five, maybe six chimneys. "Where is he?"

Vadim pointed toward a lamplit room on the first floor. "The office," he said.

Chernov drew in a frigid breath. He expelled it upward, toward heaven.

30

RusFarm

PRECISELY FIFTEEN MINUTES LATER THE GOVERNMENT CARS departed. Sia returned her phone to the nightstand.

Then came the crash of toppled furniture from a room below.

Glass shattering.

The dull thud of more falling furniture.

Shouts from Anna, then Vadim.

When the fighting whimpered and then died, Sia assumed they had merely relocated the combat to their bedroom on the far side of the second floor, down yet another maze of halls, well out of earshot.

Sia texted Anna. She and Max were wide awake on the bed, every word worth saying impossible to speak aloud. When after a while Anna did not respond to the message, Sia rolled onto her stomach and shoved her face into the pillow.

ANNA PICKED HER SPOT CAREFULLY TO AVOID THE BROKEN GLASS, ceramic shards, and the chaotic sprawl of decorative books she'd thrown to the floor. She examined one of them, done up like a first edition of Grossman's *Life and Fate*, banned by the Soviet regime. Fitting, she thought. RusFarm's copy is a hollow, painted, decorative box.

She tossed the book onto one of the overturned shelves.

They had arrested Papa.

That night, Anna had obtained from Sia evidence that Goose had stolen; she had accounts and amounts and the belief that the *khoz-yain* was in the dark. But what difference did it make, without Papa to deliver the message to the *khozyain* and with the FSB so clearly under Goose's control?

Innumerable lost chess matches had attuned Anna to this feeling: the turn of your stomach when your loss is inevitable.

But in chess you can resign.

Now, she did not know what to do.

And had Vadim been involved? Had he told them Papa would be here? He must have, she thought. She did not know, but she knew.

I should not go up to the bedroom, she told herself. But she was already walking upstairs. I should get some sleep and think on it. But she was clenching the doorknob. I should turn around. But then she twisted it open.

Dull moonlight shone through the window. Vodka fumes invaded her nostrils when Anna shut the door behind her. Then man-sweat mixed with the lavender of the plug-ins vainly masking the scent of mold. Vadim sat on the edge of the bed. Her eyes adjusted to the dim. He was still clothed. He lifted a bottle to his lips and stared ahead. Anna stood still by the door.

"You pointed to the office," she said. "You pointed at me, your wife."

Vadim's lips pursed. He gave a scratchy swallow. "What's your point, Anya? What was I supposed to do? Fight the FSB myself? Come on." Pull of vodka.

"We have material in this house that Goose would like to see. You opened the home to them. Then you stood on the stairs and did nothing. Did you bring them here? Did you help them?"

"What are you saying, Anya?" He smiled weirdly, baring his teeth. He stood and took a wobbly step toward her.

She stepped forward to meet him, grim smile on her lips. The boozy smell was muscular; he was soaked in it.

"Anya," he repeated, "what are you saying?"

She looked him dead in the eyes. "I am saying, Vadim, that you are a coward and a traitor to our family."

He lunged for her arm. She dodged and punched him in the nose. Boxed an ear. Could not control herself and smacked the other. Stepped back. He had a hand on a throbbing ear, the other cupped over his mouth to catch the blood running from his nose.

Then he rushed her. She sidestepped but not fast enough, because he snagged her by the sweater and shoved her against the wall. She kicked a shin. Drove a knee into his balls. Bit his neck. He howled, retreating to compress the teeth marks. Anna searched for a weapon. An alarm clock on the nightstand. She ripped the cord from the wall and tried to smash the clock on his head. She missed; got a shoulder. He fell onto the bed.

"Stop it," she hissed. "Stop it, you lunatic." Her fists were up, she was bobbing like a boxer. Their eyes met for a moment, and she did not like what they said.

Get away.

She made for the door. Her hand was tight on the knob when she felt a sharp pain on the back of her skull. Her head snapped forward and she heard the bony smack of her forehead connecting with the corner of the door, and in the next frame she saw carpet fibers and she could only hear from one ear because the other was smashed into the rug. The ear turned to the ceiling collected Vadim's cold promise that he would spare her face the embarrassment.

Pain surged through her stomach.

Then her ribs.

Her thighs.

She screamed, grunted, cursed. Tilted her head to see what was happening. Vadim was sitting on her legs, punching rhythmically, each blow landing below her shoulders. She tried to raise an arm. He swatted it away. She tried to flip over, a turtle slinking into her shell. He pinned her shoulders, keeping her exposed. Her eyes held the gilded ceiling and she wondered if she might die. The pain exploded on her skin, tunneling deep into muscle and bone. She thought of Luka and her mother and the mare Penelope and she was riding the horse, the wind whipping her hair.

At full gallop, Anna rode into the black.

31

RusFarm

WHEN SHE WAS TEN, A CAR STRUCK SIA WHILE SHE WALKED ONE OF the county roads along the ranch. She'd been listening to music on her sister's CD player. Never heard or saw it coming. One minute upright, next she was pancaked in a bar ditch unable to open her eyes. That terror had receded from her life. Until tonight.

Now when she closed her eyes Sia saw the blood coating her windshield, Anna patting her thigh in the back of the police car. This bitch is SVR. She is one of them. I am certain now. Anna had been working her from the get-go. Anna was a Russian version of Sia.

Sia got up to use the bathroom, anxiety riding through her. She'd just slid back into bed when the knock came at the door.

——

BY THE TIME ANNA REGAINED CONSCIOUSNESS, VADIM HAD VANISHED. Her stomach was an angry smear of bright reds and splotchy whites. She could move her arms and legs, but when she tried to sit up her midsection would scream and she would buckle. Up on the gold-leafed ceiling she blinked at the lions and cherubs and elk dancing along the molding.

What now?

Deep into herself she went, searching for a refuge from the pain, for wisdom, for any guidepost that might lead her home. Anna imagined that she rode on horseback alongside her mother. They were in the fields and it was summer. The grass was bright green, and some patches stretched to the mare's haunches. They rode in silence until Anna's rage had consumed itself and she could, at last, speak. She told her mother about Papa's arrest. About Vadim. About Luka. About this strange South African, Sia, whose handling of the feigned car accident had raised all manner of questions in Anna's conspiratorial mind.

Her mother asked: Can you keep on living like this, Anya?

I won't.

Won't? Or can't?

Both.

What then?

Anna said she did not know.

Her mother offered: Your hand is weak, Anya. But you know that. What do you have now, with your father arrested? You are cleaned out, yes?

Her mother pointed toward the mouth of the birch forest. The sky was gathering dark clouds into a storm and the wind was picking up. The mare whinnied, beginning to worry.

Her mother asked: What about Sia? You think she is more than a lawyer? Her mother drew her collar against the wind, patted her horse, picked up the reins, and folded her arms in her lap.

I don't really know who she is, Mama.

Her mother shook her head with a smile. Yes, you do. You know exactly what she is. You simply will not say it aloud. Even to yourself. And that's fine. But what do you think that woman wants?

Her horse whinnied again and Anna stroked her mane, thinking. Information, she said. Maybe about the money, the bank, the SVR. She could want many things. I do not know.

That's a start, Anya, her mother said. A good start. I suppose she could also be keen on knowing more about Goose, don't you think? Her people, if she is what you think she is, well, they do not like Goose, do they? Her people want certain things, we want certain things. I wonder if we might share a common enemy. Now I will ask again: How can she help you?

Anna thought about that, riding behind her mother through a pale golden field.

Anna blinked, looked away from the gilded ceiling, and struggled to her feet. At the doorframe she paused to suck in a full breath. The pain was sharp, as though a rib were stuck in her lung. Perhaps one was. In a fog of pain, she put on her coat, her hat, her mittens, a scarf. She hobbled down the halls, sometimes halting to lean into a wall or to clutch her stomach.

At Sia's door, Anna took a labored breath. Then she softly knocked.

———

THE FIRST, FAINT LIGHT OF DAWN BURNED THROUGH THE WINDOW. Another knock.

Another.

Sia opened the door.

Anna was stooped; with her left arm she held her chest. She limped into the room, peering at Max, who was now sitting up on the bed.

"Anna, what happened?" Sia said.

"Put on your coat. We are going for a ride."

"Anna, what happened?" Sia asked again.

"Get your damn things, Sia."

Sia slipped into leggings, jeans, two sweaters, and her overcoat. She exchanged looks with Max on the way out. She wondered if he would send the emergency signal; there was no time to plan.

They walked to the stables, Anna stopping twice to paw at her stomach, to moan, or to catch her breath. Anna directed them to Penelope's stall. Their arrival had stirred the mare from the deep sleep of a horse lying down. The horse stood and nosed her head through the yoke in the door. Anna put a hand on her muzzle. Then her face.

"I cannot ride alone," Anna said. "I think we are small enough to ride together. She is a large mare. And I'm under fifty kilos. Have you ridden bareback?"

Sia nodded.

"Good," Anna said. "Take us into the woods."

"It's got to be ten below out there, I—"

"The woods," she said. "It is not a question."

———

SIA LED PENELOPE AT A SLOW TROT BECAUSE DAWN LIGHT WAS ONLY just building and Penelope's movements sometimes made Anna cry out in pain. But were the cries genuine? Or another performance? Anna guided them across snowy pastures and plowed roads. The Russian sat in front of Sia on the mare's strong shoulders. It had been more than twenty years since Sia had ridden without a saddle. It made her feel close to Penelope; the warmth of the mare's back and skin on her legs. Anna's hair smelled salty, and her neck was sprouting a nasty red bruise. She refused to answer Sia's questions about what had happened. But the bruise made it easy to guess.

Sia brought Penelope to a halt. She wanted to see Anna's eyes for this, but there was no way they could dismount—and Sia was not sure Anna would be able to climb back on. They sat at the mouth of the forest, birches towering above. Sia closed her eyes and inhaled the cold air.

"Anna, I can see the bruise on your neck," Sia said.

"Go deeper into the trees," Anna said.

They rode on through the birches, into snow piled so deep it nearly reached her dangling feet.

"Away from the roads," Anna said at last. "There are cameras."

"Cameras?" Sia asked, playing dumb.

A snicker. "Please, Sia. My god. What did you bring from the stable?"

"Bridle and reins."

"Nothing else? No bags?"

"No. Anna, what's—"

Anna yelped in pain as she pawed her right hand back to touch Sia. She ran her hands over Sia's jeans. She slipped her fingers into Sia's coat and over the sweater. "Where is your phone?"

"I left it in my room."

"Anything in your pockets?"

"Anna, what's going on?"

"Do you have anything in your pockets?" she repeated.

"No. Nothing."

Anna leaned back. The mare stopped. "I need to see your eyes, Sia."

Sia gently clutched the Russian, turning her until Anna's back was spread atop the mare's mane. Anna only cried out once. Then Sia pulled Anna upward until they were sitting on the horse, bareback, knees knocking, facing each other. They fidgeted and jostled into position; Anna was cursing in pain.

Then Anna unbuttoned her coat. "Lift up my sweater a little," she said.

Anna's milky skin was gone. A patchwork of fiery red bruises now covered her stomach. Sia gently tugged down the sweater. Anna winced.

"Damn him," Sia said. "Can you go to the police?"

Anna looked at her in pity. "There are policemen in Russia," she said, "but there is no security. Not from someone like Vadim."

Light now began to fill the birch forest. Sia found herself losing the script, the plan. All of it seemed so distant. Was Anna making this up?

"I would like to have a frank discussion with you, Sia," Anna said. "I will start. We staged the car accident, which I think you know. The FSB officer who spoke to you, well, he works for me. For my family."

"For the SVR?" Sia whispered. "Or the FSB?"

Anna's lips curled but she did not answer. "My family is in a war with Goose. He is a powerful man, a former director of the FSB, now the head of the Security Council, but you know that. I have been trying to find money he stole from us. Money your firm helped him hide. Tonight he had my father arrested. Did you see the cars? Hear anything? Of course you did."

"I did."

"We are losing the war, I am afraid. I am losing. They've robbed us, deprived us of access to our President. They've taken my father. And my own husband is knocking me around. He might even be working with them. Goose probably cut a deal with him to sell out my family."

"Why are you telling me this, Anna?"

"Because I know who you are."

"And who is that?"

Anna patted the horse. "We are the same, aren't we? In a way?"

Sia arched an eyebrow.

"Oh please," Anna said. "You and I have been fencing for a while now. I suppose we could keep at it, but I am too angry. And tired. And out of options. What I realized this evening, during your little chat with my actor of an FSB officer, is that you are no lawyer. Not a chance. Or, more accurately, you are not merely a lawyer. You are a lawyer like I am a banker. Which is to say, partway. Or not at all, depending on how you see things. What I could not figure was why Langley would send you into Russia. I was puzzled. Then I realized. Bait. You knew what I wanted, and you were going to let me have it if it gave you a chance to reel me in. Instead, I cleaned your hook. Do I have it mostly right?"

During the training they told you not to unzip your cover, ever, without formal approval from Langley. You keep the fiction running, never say what you are. But Anna knew what Sia was. And Sia now knew what Anna was. Lies would risk Anna wriggling from the line. Still, Sia did not trust this clever bitch.

"Let me see the bruises again," Sia said.

Anna shot her a cold stare.

"You tossed a body onto the windshield of a car and tried to blackmail me," Sia said. "I want to make sure it's not makeup or paint. Or maybe I should ask how your back is doing after your little spill earlier, when you could not drive?"

Anna unbuttoned her coat and again lifted her sweater. Sia ran a finger over the red-raw flesh; Anna winced. Sia poked a rib; Anna yelped, cursed her in Russian, eyes bright with anger. Sia tried to think of a reason for this elaborate charade. If Anna's people suspected Sia was CIA, she thought, they would simply snatch her up. That Anna was here at all, that she had taken them into the woods, far from the cameras and microphones, suggested that Sia may have snatched a miraculous victory from the jaws of Russian intrigue.

"What do you want?" Sia asked.

"I want to speak with someone in your service," Anna said, buttoning her coat. "Someone senior. I believe we share a common enemy. I could provide information on this enemy."

"And if I did have a contact," Sia said, careful with her words, "what would I tell this person about your ability to travel?"

"If you did have a contact," Anna said, "I would say that I could travel in the next few weeks. I have operational reasons. But the men who arrested my father are tightening the noose. It will have to be quick, efficient."

"Do you ski?" Sia said, still not quite able to believe they had arrived here.

"I do, but it might be hard at present." With a sour smile, Anna waved a hand over her bruised stomach.

"Can you create a reason to travel to Switzerland?" Sia asked. "Maybe a few days on bank business, tack some personal time on the end."

Anna's eyes wandered to a bird fluttering in the trees. "That is possible."

"There is a little village in the Jungfrau," Sia said. "Gimmelwald. You know it?"

Anna smiled thinly. "I do."

———

SIA RETURNED TO HER ROOM AND PUT HER HEAD ON THE PILLOW. ANY minute they will come, she told herself, grinding her face deeper into the down. She never did fall asleep. When she turned to look at Max his eyes were wide open.

In the morning she showered, packed, exchanged a quick signal with Max on her success. (*Brilliant conversation on our ride last night. Just brilliant.*) Every cell in Sia's body yearned to flee—from this house, from this farm, from Russia. But there was a final scene to this twisted theater: a send-off breakfast. Hand on the doorknob, all tidy and smiley and ready for the world, Max put his arm around her shoulder and pulled her in for a hug. He kissed her forehead. The embrace made her feel light; for a still moment she did not think about her arrest, she did not think about Anna, she did not think about what they had done.

The RusFarm chef and kitchen had been working all night, through the entrapment, the arrest, and the beating. In the vast dining room, Sia discovered poached eggs, dried salmon, white truffles (flown in that morning from Italy, one of the butlers boasted), and a raisin cheesecake, among other platters Sia never learned about because she and Max asked where Anna and Vadim were, and the butler explained that, unfortunately, the Kovalchuks had been called to Piter on business and would be unable to join them this morning. Their charter, the butler said, was ready and waiting at Pulkovo. Sia looked around, waiting for hard men to pop from the walls with clubs and grave expressions and an urgent summons to Lefortovo. "We'll skip the breakfast, then," Max said.

The Rolls that greeted them in the circle drive did not pull the horse trailer. They stood in the cold at the top of the marble steps, glancing at each other, debating a protest. Penelope, after all, remained in the stable. The driver was already hustling their bags down the stairs. Max looked at his phone and had turned back to the house when Sia's hand touched his shoulder. She shook her head. *Please*, her eyes said, *please listen*.

"*Pinche ruso*," Max said. Fucking Russian. He spat. Slid the phone in his pocket. Took a last look up at the house. They got in the car.

Sia granted herself a glance through the back window: at the rearing stallion statue covered in light snow, and at the house itself, those windows still watchful and alert, its facade pressing down as if it might crash onto the escaping car. Sia closed her eyes as they slid through the woods, and when they'd passed the hulking gate, she felt something deep inside her release, as if she'd been underwater for days and had just now surfaced to suck in her first full breaths of air. All the while she waited for the blue lights. They will do it at the last minute, she told herself. Watch until the very end, draw out the suffering. The terror-stricken ride to the airport was quiet.

On the tarmac at Pulkovo, the engines whined to life and from her seat Sia overheard the bemused and clueless equine charter pilots explaining that this would be their first route without a horse. Twice Max called Vadim, twice she urged him please let it go, twice it went straight to voice mail. Sia watched the ongoing tremor in her left hand with a dark fascination. This had never happened. Never. But there it was, vibrating. She held her fingers tight. Released them. Still shaking. When the tarmac let go of the wheels, she scanned for the chase cars, again clutching her fingers. The vibrations jumped to her eyelid.

When the plane banked over the water, Sia searched the sky for Russian fighter aircraft, and when she saw none, damn eyelid fluttering like a springy roller shade, she sat for an eternal moment, hand on her chest as if pressure might slow her heart. When she knew they were at last in Finnish airspace, Sia retreated past the empty stalls to the bathroom and put her head in her hands.

Dear god, she whispered to herself. Dear god.

32

St. Ives

THAT FIRST NIGHT BACK IN ST. IVES, THEY GOT FANTASTICALLY drunk; not in the style of a party, but in the sad manner of those drinking at the same bar but entirely alone. There was no joy, no revelry. It simply had to be done. Next day the clock told Sia that she first opened scratchy, bloodshot eyes at 12:17 p.m. An hour later, she had managed to sit up. An hour after that, the specter of vomiting had departed. The cottage was quiet; the door to Max's room was still closed. As a bright sun beat the curtains and the surf battered rocks, Sia opened Max's door and found him smiling grimly at the ceiling, eyes shut.

"Morning," he said without opening his eyes.

"Afternoon, actually," she said. "We overslept."

"We slept the right amount," he said. "Artemis here yet?"

"No, and that's good. Because we need to talk."

They went for a jog to sweat out the alcohol and clear their heads. Through the town they descended on Harbour Beach. Low tide exposed a stretch of sand and rocks that created a bridge to Portminster, so they could cover a mile on the beach before turning around. It was a slow, wheezy run, but Sia pressed them on until they'd done five laps and her skin ran with boozy sweat. After, they knotted windbreakers around their waists and trudged along the cold beach as the afternoon puttered on. They found a spot and sat in the sand. Classical music rang from one of the Victorian villas on the wooded slope. Tendrils of smoke rose from the chimneys.

They watched the gulls and sandpipers until an old man with a stained canvas jacket and a knobby walking stick asked them if they were okay. What energy were they giving off that had compelled the old man to ask? Yes I'm fine, she said, and Max nodded. The man moved on. When he was a speck in the distance, Max finally said, "Tell me."

She did. Every detail, every scrap of conversation. Everything that she'd done and that had been done to her in Russia. She had not planned to be so truthful. There was certainly no point in telling Max things that she would not tell Procter, but she could not help herself. In the end the only detail she omitted was her shaky hand, quivering even now in St. Ives. When she was done recounting the discussion with Anna in the woods, Max whistled and slapped her shoulder. He pumped his fist, said, Yes, Sia. Hell, yes. She accepted the congratulations with a grimace and a glance at her wobbly hand, which she quickly tucked beneath her leg. Anna's pelt had been costly.

Max, a loner operator himself, instinctively understood her. He stared at the waves. "What do you want to tell Procter?" he asked. "How should we write it up?"

———

CAPE TOWN. HORTENSIA ROSE FOX, GIRL OF FOURTEEN, SPREAD HERSELF flat in a dusty ditch, waiting for the headlights to pass overhead. Two weeks into the annual South Africa pilgrimage, and she was still, as Grandpa would say, in the adjustment phase. The city was laid back, too much like the Big Bend. She was also fighting with the language— like every summer—screwing up pronouns, the little roll of the *r*, the switching of tenses. She found the speech slow as the city, and when Sia practiced with Grandpa or Mama she'd go too fast and her language mistakes would pile up. She was tired, though she knew that in a few weeks she would again dream in her mother's Afrikaans. She also knew she sounded foreign and dumb, which made her jumpy and angry, which made her impulsive. Which explained why she was alone, in this ditch, on a stranger's farm in the dead of night.

The headlamps painted the vines above and jerked onto the road leading away from the farm's main house. Sia crawled into the vines and stood, hunched so her head did not peek too far above. The night was clear; the moon was bright on her path; she wondered if anyone would see her. She crossed the vineyard, flushed with pride. She did not feel anxious, she did not sweat, her breathing was even. No moment in her life had ever been more vibrant or alive. She did not once ask why she was doing this insane thing; she knew already, and understood that no one would understand. The consequences were not unclear. They were merely irrelevant; a dim possibility at the end of a tunnel that would not be traveled. The peppery smell of Cape scrubland filled the air, the darkened peaks of the mountains rose above the gabled, thatched-roof farmhouse, the vines bristled against her arms in a gentle breeze. Light shone through a few of the farmhouse windows. That should have made Sia pause, but instead it contributed to the challenge and tweaked even higher the adrenaline that seemed to thicken in her veins and ball in the back of her mouth.

The vineyard's edge shoved onto a rolling lawn in front of the house: the first place where things might go haywire. Though, she told herself, I do not much care if they do. There were sensors and lights here, she knew. She'd seen them while scouting the farm, which blessedly did not boast exterior fencing. Minor obstacles, she would outrun them.

She counted: One, two, three . . .

Then she was sprinting across the lawn toward a grove of trees, eyes darting between the ground and the trees and the house. A light on the farmhouse clicked on, painting her in white. She looked away. Clack— another cast light onto the lawn. She ran faster, dove into the grove, snuggled behind a tree, and realized she was smiling. She caught her breath, listening to the still night until the lights shut off. Then she got to the ground and crawled forward for a view of the farmhouse's front door, which was now opening with a light creak. A man stepped outside, peering into the night. His head turned here and there. He stood still for a few moments. Then he went inside and the lights clicked back on.

She was just outside the fingers of the light, snug in the darkness of the trees. The figure reappeared on the stoop, whistling, and Sia's heart fluttered. A dog? She had not thought there was a dog. It will tear me to pieces, she thought, what do I do? She put her head into the dirt and again realized that, though her heart was beating faster, her thoughts were clear, she was not sweating. I am in the darkness, she thought, I am hidden. But the man must have been whistling to himself, or to the night, because no dog arrived. The lights extinguished. The man went inside and shut the door. I should be relieved, she thought, but I feel the same. I feel level.

Dusting herself off, Sia ducked down a low rise through the trees. The stables were at the base of a hill that hunched over the barn like a breaking wave. The doors were not visible from the main house, but someone was clearly up and awake and would see any lights. Sia considered this problem as the grove thinned and the stables came into view. Six stalls, old wood. Two beautiful horses. Lights be damned, she thought. She made her way to the rock she'd spied three days earlier, when she'd cased the place. She picked it up.

Rock in hand, she ran down the rise toward the stables. The overhead light flickered on. She did not even look, just took the rock to the meager padlock, striking, bashing, clubbing until the latch holding it gave way, screws tore from the wood, and it clanged to the ground. She slid open the door and marched to the stall of the mare she had ridden one week earlier, in daylight, with the full sanction and approval of the farm. She trusted the mare. The horse, awoken from its light sleep, watched Sia move quickly to put on the tack. She led the horse from the stables, gently, but with confidence, and swung into the saddle with a posture and certainty that told the horse she knew what the hell she was doing. She took off up the road, toward a fork where she would turn away from the house and planned to ride, wild and free, through a field on the northern rim of the vineyard. But a motor had kicked to life up at the house. And now more lights were flicking on.

Sia put the mare to work, not with abuse but with a gentle strength. She maintained contact from reins to bit. Not too much, just enough pressure for control. She pressed her legs into the mare's ribs. The horse broke into a gallop toward the fork. They moved quickly, banking left, the headlamps still absent, Sia's thoughts still clear, the night perfect because she was going to get away with it. She turned to see a car starting down from the house. But she was well clear of the headlamps. They can't see me, she thought. She looked back to see if they went down to the stables or followed her along the road.

They chose the stables.

Sia galloped into the pasture.

For a few luxurious minutes Sia bathed in the moonlight, savoring the victory of the criminal requiring neither grace nor pardon because she would never be caught.

Then something rustled under a nearby fence. The spooked horse took the bit in a mad sprint, breaking her control over the animal. This was the only time she'd been afraid that evening. Later, back in the Big Bend, she would practice reining in a startled horse, but that night in Cape Town she'd not had much practice and her mind and muscles could not work together to contain the mare.

When she should have yanked on the left rein, pulling it into her knee to send the animal into a slower circle to shed its speed and regain control, Sia instead fruitlessly yanked back on both, with insufficient strength to calm the wild mare tearing through the open pasture at a frightening torrent. In a few seconds the mare bucked, sending Sia thudding into the field with such violence that she thought she heard the crack of bone.

The mare took off toward the house. Sia was spread on the ground wondering if she could walk. Her left side was raw. Bruised or cracked ribs, she did not know. Her arms and legs seemed to work, but the three-mile walk back to Grandpa's farm seemed impossible. For a while she just waited for the farmer to find her. The problem was actually worse, she realized, thinking about it more. She'd ridden deep into the pasture; the march to Grandpa's farm would be a few miles longer than her walk earlier that night. And it would be a slow one, she could tell as she stood. She might reach home before daybreak, but her sister would be awake, up and writing in the cottage they shared during the summer. Would Daisy snitch? She hadn't last time. Or the time before.

She limped home: through the pasture, vineyards, tree cover where she could find it. It is strange, she thought, how good I feel even though I am wrecked. She huffed the last mile along the road, senses up, knowing that if the farmer drove down here and saw a dirty girl running and clutching her left side, well, he was going to stop and ask questions and probably call the police. She turned up the long, leafy drive toward Grandpa's farmhouse, cutting left to cross the small bridge running over the stream.

Through a curtain of trees the little guest cottage came into view, the lights on, her damn sister awake and alert and no doubt gravely attuned to the morality of things. Sneaking in was pointless, so Sia flung open the door. Daisy was sitting at the desk in the common room. Her sister did not look up, did not speak. She was scribbling in her notebook. In the bathroom Sia examined her bruises. Red-raw, but she did not think anything was broken. She showered and changed into clean clothes and in their bedroom found Daisy sitting on her bed in the morning light.

"What was it this time?" her sister asked in English. "Another car with the keys left inside?"

"Don't worry about it, Daze," Sia answered in Afrikaans. "I didn't take anything."

Daisy's eyes narrowed to slats. "Uh-uh," she said. "Right."

"I'm serious."

"Don't you think it's weird?"

"Maybe."

"Do you even think about it?"

"Not so much."

Daisy flopped back on the bed with a laugh. "You sound like a psycho. You know that, right?"

"Something happens to me when we come here, Daze."

"That's crap," Daisy said. "I know for a fact you've taken stuff back home. From Porter's. Stupid stuff. Gum. Nuts. Bottled water."

"This is home, too," Sia said, switching to English without knowing it. "We've got two homes, so we've got none." She glared at her sister but didn't deny the shoplifting at Porter's. So what if she had?

"Sure, whatever, Horty," Daisy said. "Whatever."

"Daze, are you going to tell Mama and Papa?" Sia asked in Afrikaans. "Grandpa?"

Daisy was at her notebook, scribbling. "I'm not going to tell anyone."

"Then what are you writing?" Sia asked.

"Nothing." Daisy closed the notebook, stuffed it in the drawer, and went into the bathroom to take a shower.

Sia listened to the running water and eyed the desk. Might need to steal that notebook, she thought.

———

SIA TURNED FROM THE WAVES TO LOOK AT MAX. "HERE IS HOW I THINK we write up RusFarm."

There were elements of the visit best left in the shadows, she said, free and clear of the cable traffic. Anna's attempted blackmail and their performative sex sprang immediately to mind. No benefit to sharing if we want to stay in the field, she said. Nowhere for them to reassign us anyways—we can't just change offices like the Langley drones. And there is definitely no upside if we think we're on the cusp of Anna crossing a line, producing something useful. The balance is delicate, Sia said. We should tell the truth, but not all of it. We don't want to lie, it's simply that there are extraneous details best left on the cutting room floor, for everyone's sake. Because how could they understand what it was like out there for us, really? The pressure we faced. We made decisions in the moment with the information we had, she said. Plus the odds of Langley getting intel from the Russians that contradicts our story is pretty much nil. Anna is running this thing unofficially. She will not say a word on the phone, Sia said. There will be no intercepts spinning a different tale.

Sia did not know how Max would take this, but as she spoke, carefully watching his eyes and his body, she came to believe that maybe they were not so different. That, like her, something ticked inside his chest—though perhaps not as overgrown—propelling him forward not despite the risk, but because of it.

Max listened; he stayed quiet. When Sia was done, he said, "If Procter ever found out, the consequences would be steep. Particularly for you."

"And how will she find out? We're the only ones who know. If we tell her, everything grinds to a halt," Sia said.

"And you want it to keep going," Max said.

"I think we can win," Sia said. "But tell me what you think."

"Oh, we can win. On that I have no doubt. But is it worth the risk?" He shrugged, picked up a stick. "I do not know."

With the stick Max scribbled in the sand. Does he know what he wants? Sia wondered. He could go back to his ranch, but something was keeping him here, and though she felt his attraction to her, she did not think that could be the only reason. Perhaps, she thought, he does not want to go home.

And she could sense then that he trusted her, and she, him. And that was a strange thought indeed. Perhaps her body had known for a while, but this was the first time her head could attach words to it, and had she been a different woman entirely, in a different profession and place and country with a different man, she might have said so. But instead Sia remembered that RusFarm bed, and she still could not figure which compartment should hold the feelings gathering inside her, which in the days since had flitted from shame to denial to stoic acceptance to a lingering desire that began the cycle anew.

Max stood, wiped sand from his pants, and held out a hand to haul her up. "I want my horse back. Let's write it up as you say."

She extended her sole steady hand. "Thanks," she said. And Max pulled her up.

On the hike back they bought watery coffees from a windblown café. The cottage came into view as they rounded the path atop the hill. A blue Prius sat in the drive. Procter had arrived.

33

St. Ives

THE CHIEF HAD STOPPED FOR GROCERIES AND THANK GOD NEARLY all of it was pre-made. They found her in the kitchen, pulling from the scorching oven with bare hands a cooking sheet without a hint of pain. What she did drop hints about, with zero prompting and an equal amount of preamble, was the nosy proprietor in St. Ives. The man's tendency to snoop, in Procter's estimation, made him a borderline sex pervert (her words). From a culinary standpoint, though, he had steered Procter well: there were containers of fresh bucatini, thick tomato sauce, crispy oil-fried meatballs, and a salad with squash and carrots sprinkled with chickpeas and toasted almonds.

The perverted proprietor had suggested pairing the food with a few bottles of Chianti. But Procter said that when she was acting classy, she was a white wine kind of girl and so poured for herself a sweet white blend she'd bought as well. That it would pair awfully with the pasta did not concern the Chief; neither, apparently, did the £3 price tag (still visible on the bottle), nor the Technicolor label inhabited by a cartoon fish family. Sia noticed Max staring at the bottle while Procter poured.

At the dining room table, Procter immediately fumbled a meatball and it rolled off onto the floor, leaving a saucy trail behind. Then she picked it up and ate it. "So, tell me everything," Procter said, mouth full.

"Of course," Sia said. "Where to begin?" She started with the "light pressure" Anna had applied, then barreled on to Anna's father's arrest, the beating, and the final dance on horseback, where she had emerged victorious. If Procter was excited, it did not show. She focused mostly on the meatballs, scraps of which she occasionally picked from her teeth. When Sia had finished, Procter sat for a moment, using her fork to roll a half-eaten meatball around her bowl.

"What'd you give up in the end?" the Chief asked. Looking up from the bowl, Procter watched Sia's body language with those bright green eyes.

"I gave her the computer and explained how Goose's finances are structured. Showed how they turned the gold into cash and where it is now."

"And the squeeze?"

"Gentle," Sia lied. "Anna is, or was, playing a long game with me. I think she wanted information on Lyric, too, on Harry Hamilton and all that. On the first afternoon we went riding, she told me Goose and his guys were making it hard on her family. Might I help? I said I would but of course I can't break the law."

"Of course," Procter said. "Obviously."

"Then Anna hinted that if I did not help, I might be arrested. She did not say arrest, but it was implied. I cooperated. I explained things."

"And then Daddy gets arrested, hubby smacks her around, and we've got a new ball game on our hands," Procter said. "Holy hell." She put a whole meatball in her mouth. "She never said she was SVR or FSB?" Procter asked after she managed to swallow.

"Not in those words. She implied SVR. Did not confirm."

"You never said CIA?"

"No. But she knows. Like I said, she asked for someone from my service to meet with her. Someone senior."

That elicited a grunt from Procter, who twirled pasta on her fork and turned to Max. "What'd Vadim have you doing?"

"Drinking, sauna, repeat," Max said. "But the atmosphere was tense. He's pissed he overpaid for the stallion, and he disappeared to fucking Petersburg on the last morning, left the RusFarm people with instructions to hold on to my mare."

"You've called him since, I presume?" Procter asked.

"Right. He dodged my calls the morning we left Russia. When we get here, he picks up. Tells me he thought the mare had been included in the sale. Which is bullshit. But it gives him an out so he doesn't have to call it theft. Vadim Kovalchuk is a shit. He's tolerating this dance because it's Anna's op and I guarantee that someone on their side had a word with him about playing nice. But he had to pay me back for the rough ride I gave him in Mexico. It couldn't be otherwise with him."

"What's the horse's name?" Procter asked.

"Penelope," he said. "She was my mother's horse."

"I'm sorry about that," Procter said. "We'll mention it to Anna in Switzerland, see if she can help shake things loose."

"She's got about the same influence over that prick as I do," Max said.

"Even so," Procter said, "we'll give it a shot." Then with her customary abruptness she smacked the table to signal a topical shift and said, "Tell me about the creepy-ass farm and the surveillance crush. No detail too small."

The Chief poked for a bit on that, until, with Max in the middle of a debrief on their dinner with Vadim and Anna, Procter poured herself a gigantic glass of the sickly sweet white wine and gave a nudge toward the bedroom. "Did Vadim's sexy suspicions return?"

As agreed on the beach, Sia let Max field this one. "We put on a more convincing performance," he said.

Procter nodded her head. "Uh-uh," she said. "Okay." She eyed them both. "You feel good about things?"

Max said yes.

"Hortensia?" Procter asked.

"I feel good," she said into her bowl. "He's not suspicious. No one is suspicious."

"Bueno," Procter said. And she let it drop.

In the kitchen Sia explained the rudimentary comms plan she had built with Anna on horseback in the woods. They would meet her in Switzerland. The Chief said she wanted to look into Anna's cold Russian soul, see if they had a beautiful thing going. The glint in Procter's green eyes suggested that her hopes for the case exceeded the mere exploitation of Vadim Kovalchuk's financial networks for intelligence-gathering purposes. There was a bigger play here, Sia intuited, and the Chief was keeping it close.

During her career Sia had learned that you often did not want the full picture. Headquarters animals wanted as much information as possible because knowledge—the more secretive, the better—was the preferred weapon of bureaucratic combat. But for the loner NOC in the field, knowledge meant more secrets to spill when drunk or high or in a Russian interrogation room. The headquarters aquarium was a safe place to swim; NOCs navigated the open ocean. And the open ocean before Sia Fox had whipped into a maelstrom. Still, she had bled for this case. She took a cautious step into the waves.

"What do we want her to tell us?" And more importantly, Sia asked, "What do we want her to *do for us?*"

"Well," the Chief said slowly, "kinda depends on your read of Anna's motivations here. What does she really want?"

Sia thought for a moment. "Anna's in a tough spot. Husband is a beater, dad's in prison, she's got another clan after her family's business empire, threatening her position in society. Underneath it all is a stubborn woman who does not understand how to depart the field without beating her opponent or being beaten herself. She wants to win. And I think she cares how she wins. That matters to her."

"So she doesn't just divorce the guy and run, because she wants to beat him, beat Goose, on and on," Procter said. Not really a question.

"I think so," Sia said. "She would see fleeing Russia as a loss. Same for divorcing Vadim, which would weaken her political standing and make it more difficult to help her father. But she's no fool. She would rather win dirty than lose. And doing nothing will mean losing."

"So here are the cards on the table," Procter said. "Anna Agapova doesn't want money. Fine. She wants to control the environment around her. Well, that's good, because we could come up with a few ideas for how that environment might be re-swizzled to align more happily with the interests of our great republic. She'd like to see her husband's brainpan drained bone-dry. Well, maybe we take some of Putin's cash and her husband gets blamed for it. She'd like to schwack a few of her daddy's enemies. Well, we'd like to see a putsch in Moscow, even if it's not real. Dial up the paranoia, spill a bit of blood. We're careening toward Stalinism anyhow, why not have some fun on the way? Say, is there an ideological play here, hon? Maybe she hates the system, wants to hack at the beams from the inside, help old Uncle Sam toss a few wrenches in the gearbox because, well, old Sammy is swell and a beacon of hope and all that sugar?"

"She's a Russian patriot," Max offered.

Procter flicked a dismissive hand through the air. "They are always patriots. Always. I've run Syrian patriots. Russian patriots. Saudi patriots. French patriots. Always love their country. The question is if they want to change their country."

"I do not think Anna wants a new kind of Russia," Sia said. "I do not think she cares one way or the other about Putin or the system. She doesn't like what's happened in Ukraine, but neither will she lift a finger to change it. She does not believe Russia should be a democracy. I don't think she believes that is even a possibility. To Anna, Russia simply is. The corruption bothers her not at all. She wouldn't even call it corruption, I think. It's business, it's how the country works. She sees herself as outside all of that, by the way. She is rich on paper, but she doesn't care about the money. She works. She is a worker bee. Like me." The last words had tumbled out of her and raised one of Procter's eyebrows.

"So, Hortensia"—Procter ignored, or did not notice the flash of anger in her eyes—"you didn't answer my simple question. What does Anna Andreevna Agapova really want?"

Sia clasped her hands at her waist. Damn left one was still shaking, though less vigorously than in the plane or on the beach. "She wants to burn things down. Play her own game."

Procter let loose a loud whoop. "That, my dear, is a woman I can do business with."

———

THAT NIGHT PROCTER BANGED OUT A CABLE TO THE COUNTERINTELligence trolls, and soon they had received a cryptonym. In all official comms inside the Restricted Handling compartment, from here on out and through all eternity (amen), Anna Andreevna Agapova, banker, long-suffering wife, burdened daughter, horsewoman, likely SVR officer under non-official cover, future conspirator, spy, and traitor, would henceforth be known as GT/PERSEPHONE.

PERSEPHONE.

The Chief—whose fascination with Greek mythology fueled Sia's suspicion that the codes were not, in fact, generated randomly—cackled at the name. Perfect, she said. Too fucking perfect.

Later, in her room and in bed, Sia looked up the myth.

PERSEPHONE. Queen of the underworld. Goddess of the dead, of life, of grain, of destruction. There were many stories and interpretations. The one Sia liked best had it that the goddess ruled nature. In it, she created and destroyed. That seemed about right, Sia thought, her daydreams thickening into sleep. The PERSEPHONE case was going to make her name, that much was certain. And if she was not careful, it would destroy her.

34

Washington

PROCTER DID NOT BELIEVE IN THE AUTHORITY OF TITLES, NOR DID she give a hoot about the supposed pomp of a SitRoom meeting with Deputy Director Bradley and the National Security Adviser (NSA), James Piper. But Bradley had insisted she come. He said it was her intel—it was—and he wanted backup in case Piper drifted into the weeds during the discussion, which he usually did.

Procter followed Bradley inside the West Wing and down the stairs. The posted menu for the Navy Mess advertised a crab bisque, which sounded pretty damn good. The stairs spilled into the low-hung warren of conference rooms collectively known as the Situation Room. As it happened, a matronly staff secretary guided them to the main SitRoom, a space that Procter had always thought a bit cramped and dumpy, even by her standards. The ceiling was low. The chairs were blocky and ate up the legroom.

Bradley joined Piper at the main table. Procter took a seat in the backbenchers' row and tucked her black lock bag under the chair. It contained no paper; instead, she had loaded the bag with sleeves of Ritz crackers to ward off late afternoon headaches. Piper studied her like she was a weirdo alien. Bradley said for god's sake Artemis, there are only three of us. Rolling her eyes, she pulled one of the gigantic leather chairs from the table and plopped into it. The chair was too big. Made her feel like a teeny person. Piper and Bradley exchanged pleasantries. Procter tuned out.

Piper was an old Europe analyst from the State Department's Bureau of Intelligence and Research. She'd met him a few times when he'd been NSC Senior Director for Europe ten years earlier. Piper, she remembered, was pretty fucking weird. She saw a packet of wipes on the table in front of him and remembered the tic.

As if on cue, Piper removed a bottle of hand sanitizer from the pocket of his slacks to squirt a generous portion on his hands. Miracle this guy hadn't lathered himself into oblivion during the pandy. He was short and wiry, with close-cropped hair, thick hipster glasses, and a boyish face that she found irksome, that weird mouth moving in ways that made her angry. He had grown up in State/INR, worked on Europe, and had left the intelligence community to play politics. The portrait, to Procter, of an all-around loser.

"The Russia red stripe PDB this morning got some attention," Piper said. "Wanted to bat around a few of the President's questions about our options."

Debman had tried to make her read the piece, mostly because it had hung on a few bits of intel Anna had provided during the visit to RusFarm. Procter had refused. She'd been meditating, plus the analysts used such dopey language, she never could understand what they were trying to say. Piper had the memo in front of him; Procter glanced at the title of the President's Daily Brief article. "RUSSIA: SIGNS OF FACTIONALIZATION EMERGING INSIDE PUTIN'S INNER CIRCLE." Actually, she thought, that's a pretty good one.

"The finding signed after the Ukraine invasion gives us pretty broad leeway from a covert action perspective," Piper said. "Of course, we left a hell of a lot of mother-may-I's in there, make sure you Langley boys don't go hog-wild on Mr. Putin." Piper flashed a weird smile at Procter.

"But like I said," Piper continued, "POTUS this morning started to riff while reading this piece. He pulled me aside after the meeting and asked me to run a question by you."

"What is it?" Procter interjected. Her head was hurting. She considered, then decided against, the Ritz crackers. Too noisy. Too bad.

Piper straightened his notebook on the table and arranged three pens so they were spaced equidistantly. "POTUS wanted to know if any of the sources in the piece this morning might be able to help us aggravate Putin's domestic situation further. I know we did some of this thinking after Ukraine. You guys wrote up some ideas, we mostly did nothing."

Nothing, Procter reflected, was a generous interpretation. Moscow X had come up with a menu of beautiful options. They'd all been ignored.

"Has the risk appetite changed?" Bradley asked.

"Maybe," Piper said. "The President was encouraged by signs of cracks inside Putin's regime. He wants real operations to take place to widen those cracks. His words. My question is whether you have the access to do so. The source in the piece this morning was interesting. Made me think perhaps we've got an angle here."

Bradley rubbed his jaw. "Artemis and I have a few ideas. Things we might consider if we really wanted to tweak Vladimir Vladimirovich." Bradley laid his hand on the PDB memo and turned to Procter. She'd come up with the concept, after all.

Procter said: "Preamble. This idea is not about Russia becoming a friendly country, a democracy, or whatever. Not in the cards. There was no chance of it even in the nineties, but now? No way in hell. What we should aspire to instead is a divided Russia. Weak. Inward-looking. They want to attack their neighbors? They want to divide us? Well, I say fuck them, two can play this game. This idea is about chaos."

She took her time explaining the concept and its supporting operations, peppering her speech with historical and criminal analogies to demonstrate its logical precedents. It was one of those ideas that seemed intelligent both when you were drunk and then again after you'd sobered up. Smart before the Russians drug you and blast pictures of your pieces and parts all over the web, and still going strong a few months later. A damn good idea. Creative, but not constructive. Quite the opposite. Procter told Piper how PERSEPHONE might act as the linchpin. She explained PERSEPHONE's motivations for working with CIA and how they perfectly aligned with the mayhem Moscow X hoped to visit on Mother Russia.

Piper tapped a pen on his notebook and appraised Procter with cautious curiosity, as if she'd been bused to the SitRoom from a zoo or, perhaps, an asylum.

"Let's say Putin survives all of this," Piper said.

"Which he probably would," Bradley interjected. He shot Procter one of the disapproving stares she'd come to expect when she was on a roll.

"Yes, fine, he survives. He's hobbled," Piper said. "He's having to spend more time shoring things up internally. Does he suspect us? Have we hidden our hand?"

"Of course he will suspect us," Procter said.

"Hell," Bradley said, "Putin *already* thinks we are running ops like this. It's baked into his paranoid psyche."

"But how does he respond if we *actually* do it?" Piper asked.

"I'd say use your imagination short of nukes and another massive land war, and that's the limit," Procter said.

"Then why in the hell do we do this?" Piper said, throwing up his hands. "We hit him, he hits back, it will spiral and spiral and never end. Or end in darkness for both countries."

"Well, I suppose we could continue letting him think we suck," Procter said. "That we're dickless and will just let them do whatever they want. Savage Ukraine. Microwave our brains—"

Bradley cut her off there. "Artemis, thank you. Here is the issue, James. The Russian mentality is to poke and prod and jab until they get a response. They will go as far as we let them. If I may, we need to draw a line, jab them right back, force them to reassess their approach. This could be a way to do that."

Procter had her own analogy. "I think of it this way, guys. We are playing a game with the Russians where both sides stand facing each other. Every few minutes the Russian guy punches us. Shoulder. Ribs. Junk. Face. Wherever."

Piper wrinkled his nose, halfway suppressed a sneeze, cleaned his hands again. "What if we don't punch them?"

"They still punch us," Procter said. "That's the thing that we don't get. They still fucking punch us, man. And they do it hard, working toward the softer parts because they can get away with it and it gets them off."

"And if we punch back?" Piper asked.

"Then they punch back. Maybe harder. Maybe softer. Maybe, just maybe, they stop going for the crotch and face. They punch the shoulder a few times. We can take those."

"So your best analogy for U.S.-Russia relations, Ms. Procter," Piper said, "is of two individuals punching each other in a fight without end?"

"That is exactly my view."

She stood to grab a piece of candy from the jar on the table and slid back into her seat. Bradley's face had tightened. His fist was pumping into a ball.

Piper tapped his fingers on the table, thinking. "Ed," he said, "we're going to get the Lawyers' Group working on language for a Memorandum of Notification to give you the authorities to get this done and protect your people. The existing finding won't stretch that far. Gang of Eight notice, of course, but let me know once the Hill gets agitated and I'll make some calls to prevent about two hundred teenage staffers from being read in to the edgy stuff." He stood to end the meeting.

Bradley was thankfully occupied with the evening readbook on the ride back to Langley. Procter consumed an entire sleeve of Ritz crackers as they sped along the Potomac. With the darkness gathering outside the Suburban's windows, she enjoyed a colorful daydream set to the deep, rich music of Tchaikovsky's *Swan Lake*. Her fantasy was again chaos in Moscow: protests, fires, bullhorns, tanks cruising the Stalinist avenues. As the car clanked onto the headquarters compound, Procter briefly nodded off to the sultry image of a mob overrunning the Kremlin to set it aflame.

35

Moscow

SIX DAYS AFTER THE ARREST, ANNA VISITED HER FATHER IN BUTYRKA. A prison-fortress since Catherine's reign, red-brick Butyrka had once held Dzerzhinsky, founder of the Cheka, seed that would spawn the KGB, before he escaped amid the chaos of the Revolution. Like a good Bolshevik, once in power the spymaster built his service in the image of the Tsar's and set to filling Butyrka with enemies of the new state. The opponent was different, the methods the same.

Anna broke eye contact with the Dzerzhinsky portrait crookedly hung above the door and tried to banish from her mind the shouts and grunts escaping from the next room. Those, like Papa, arrested by the FSB for political crimes were typically locked up in Lefortovo. Goose had chosen Butyrka intentionally, Anna knew. It was part of the general prison system and not under FSB control. That meant murder, rape, drugs, guards on the take of the prison gangs. Her father's wealth and the guards' corruption would doubtless allow him a private cell with a television and shower, but Goose had arranged for Butyrka to send her father a message that at any moment he might be fucked—literally—for his insolence.

The door creaked open, screams from next door rushing in. A guard led her shackled father to the table. He put his hands on the cold metal and smiled.

The guard left them alone except for the cameras and microphones.

Papa's skin was whiter, his creases deeper, eyes emptier. His nose was still crooked from Chernov's blow.

"You look well, Papa," she said. She did her best to smile.

He laughed. "My god, it is good to see you, Anya."

She put a hand on his. The shackle was so cold. "I am sorry," she whispered. "I am so sorry."

He grimaced to suppress whatever it was he wanted to shout. He glanced toward a camera blinking from the corner and began maniacally tapping a foot to the concrete. "I cannot believe he did it."

Anna wanted to talk strategy, to check her instincts on the moves, but the cameras made that impossible. And she knew he would never approve of what she planned to do. They had been checkmated, she had no choice, but he would not see it. He would feed her nonsense about how there was always another move. But it was a lie. Sometimes there was nothing to do but turn over the board. About to lose? Flip it over and see what happens. Imagining a chessboard midair, she thought of Luka and wondered if she might run away with him. Take some money and get out. Where would they go? What country would accept a prominent Russian whose papa had just been arrested on corruption charges?

She did not know what to say to him. They stared at each other and around the room and listened to their unseen neighbor's howls. He looked at the wall knowingly. He'd been in that room, in both positions. He understood places like Butyrka. When the noise stopped, his eyes settled on her. Anna wore a heavy turtleneck sweater to cover the bruises, now an ugly quilt of blues, blacks, and sickly yellows. Her father could not see them, but he sensed something. "Did they hurt you?"

She shook her head but found herself wanting to cry. She prayed that he could not tell. He looked her over and then shook his shackles, clinking them on the metal table.

"For some reason," he said, "I have been thinking about a party in London a long time ago. I believe it was Independence Day, because it was steaming hot. You were maybe nine or ten. Do you know what I am talking about?"

"No," Anna said, "I don't think so."

Her father's gaze remained fixed on her even as the yelling next door picked up again.

"Well, it is a simple story, but amusing. At least to me. They had lugged in several coolers filled with ice cream and popsicles for the celebration. There was a line. A proper Soviet breadline for the sweets. You were waiting by yourself. There was a boy, the son of someone in the *rezidentura* or the embassy, I honestly do not remember. He cut into the line, directly in front of you."

A thin smile parted her lips.

Her father continued, "I watched you stutter-step to the left. Then you swung a savage little uppercut into his ribs." He shadowboxed the move, chains jangling. "No words exchanged, no warning. He almost fell over, turned around, saw it was you. Do you remember now?"

"After I hit him, the boy told me to leave him alone, said he could do what he liked," Anna said after a moment.

Both of her father's fists pounded the table in delight. "She does remember after all. What did you say next to make him run off, tail between his legs?"

"I didn't say anything," she said.

Her father smiled.

"I just broke his nose."

He slammed the table in joyful laughter. "And I was proud of you, Anya. So damn proud. Well, here is a piece of wisdom from an old man who remembers watching his daughter fight a punk long ago." He stopped to smile up toward the camera. "Someone disrespects you, you hit back. We are in the middle of it, Anya. You played boys' games when you were a girl. And as a woman you still play with the men. You have insisted on it. If you want to keep playing, you fight. There is nothing else."

He was staring right at the camera. Could not help himself. Papa smiled. Then he turned back to her and continued, "I will have the lawyers work up papers giving you power of attorney to control Rossiya Industrial in my stead, to manage my shares in the bank. Everything. To ensure we don't get picked apart and keep the decisions in the family. I want you to have control. You will not actually run the businesses, but I will make sure that they cannot be bought or sold without your approval. At least while I'm in here."

"What do you want me to say to them, Papa, about the offer?"

"*Ot tyurmy i ot sumy ne zerekaisya*," he said, looking away from her to deliver the message directly to the camera above the door. What comes will come. We accept prison and poverty. "The answer is no."

───

IN THE YASENEVO OFFICE OF HER FATHER'S OLD FRIEND, SVR THIRD Deputy Director Maximov, Anna looked over the pines toward Moscow and her body felt pinned under the weight of this city in winter. Her mother had died in February, and this feeling brought her back to that black winter. Maximov, hand cradling his paunch, leaned back in his chair and began to pick something from his teeth with the other. He was reading Anna's report about the operation against Sia. The last time she'd been in this office had been to start preparing for it.

When he had finished, he wiped something collected from his mouth onto his pant leg and joined her at the table. "We can speak freely in here," he said. "How is he holding up?"

"Fine." She didn't want to talk about Papa.

Maximov smoothed his red tie over his gut. "I worked with your father for more than two decades, and not once did I see him give up."

"He is a proud man."

"And a stubborn one," Maximov said. He leaned across the table. "I know you. You have already played this out, Anya. Do you think I should take this report to the *khozyain*?"

"No."

"And why not?"

"Well, to start, can you get a meeting with him?"

Maximov smiled. "Well, that depends. Without Goose?"

"Without Goose."

"No," Maximov said. "I cannot. Your father was sometimes able to get those meetings alone. But now . . ." An aide carted in a tray with the tea service. Maximov filled his cup to the brim with sugar and then doused it in black tea.

Anna filled hers and took a sip. The bone-white cups were embossed with the symbol of the Russian state: a double-headed golden eagle. A freakish bird looking both East and West, flying against itself. I am this bird, Anna thought. I am all Russians.

As Maximov stirred in more sugar, Anna set out on the tightrope. "There is a case in Geneva I handle. A banker. I have postponed two visits there since Papa pulled me into this." She motioned to the report.

Maximov blew steam off the surface of the tea. "I know of the case. What about it?"

"I should go see him in Geneva."

"I see." Said as if he did not want to know why she was lying.

"I am going to meet with him, but I am worried that Goose might be suspicious of the travel."

"What are you asking, Anya?"

"I want a paper trail in channels you know the FSB will see. Cables alerting the Fifth Department to the dates and purpose of my travel to Switzerland."

He took a sip and smacked his lips and the table met his cup with a loud clatter. He wiped a few spilled drops with a napkin. Maximov watched her for a moment, and she could see the questions flashing in his eyes, but then he said, "You write the cables. I will make sure they get around."

36

Falls City, Oregon / Palo Alto

O N THE HELIPAD AT LYRIC'S PALO ALTO CAMPUS ARTEMIS PROCTER marched through the rotor wash of a chrome helicopter. The ambient interior light and hardwood finishing beckoned her to join one of Harry Hamilton's executive assistants seated inside. The woman knew Procter as one of Harry's security consultants. "Quite the fucking chopper," Procter said.

"Mr. Hamilton is not at HQ, unfortunately," the woman said as the pilot shut the door, "but he'd like you to join him on site. Have dinner."

"Where is it?"

"Oregon. Timber forest."

Procter hooted. "Sure, whatever."

Procter fell asleep to the helicopter lurching skyward and she woke to the woman nudging her shoulder. They had set down in a clearing.

The flaps of a white pavilion billowed against parked logging machinery. The table inside creaked under a barbecue spread. Bottles of Tito's vodka chilled in a trash-can-turned-ice-bucket. She saw a foil bin full of corn dogs and she'd never turned down a corn dog in her life. She took several. She filled a clear plastic cup with vodka and started in on the dogs.

She was finishing her third, the afternoon sun waning, when Harry arrived. Harry flicked on three space heaters and began to make a plate. He offered her a cocktail; she handed him her empty. His eyebrows knitted at the large cup, then arched at the three corn dog sticks, which Procter had stripped bare.

"Those big cups are for Coke," he said.

"Yeah, I know what they're for," Procter replied.

He filled the cup with Tito's and gave it to Procter. Then he sat and started to eat.

"I was just in Hong Kong," Procter said. "Paid a short visit to a shady crypto brokerage called Polycoin Investments." She winked and clicked a finger gun his direction at the threatening name-drop. Polycoin was a private cryptocurrency trading operation backed by Hamilton. Harry thought his involvement was a secret.

Harry gave Procter a chilly look. "And how was that?"

"It was real pleasant, Harry. Nice way for you to buy and sell big blocks of crypto without people knowing what you're up to. And strangely enough, it's the kind of thing I'm interested in, as of late."

Harry grinned as he chewed, wiped his fingers on a napkin. He took a long sip of vodka. "The thing I have always respected about you, Artemis, is that you don't beat around the bush."

"True, true," Procter said. "Not a bush-beater. Never been accused of that."

"So," Harry said, "my good friends Artemis and Ed have in the past few months asked me to buy racehorses from a Mexican stable. And now I learn you've been out in Hong Kong sniffing around my preferred crypto shop."

"What does it make you think, Harry?"

"That I wish I knew what the fuck was going on."

Procter put back her vodka. "Here's the skin," she said. "We're setting in motion a nice little slice of intrigue. We're going to put some bad Russians in hot water. Fuck them over a bit. The kind that has you walking like a cowboy for a few days."

"Who's the sore one in this analogy?" he asked. "Actually, don't answer. I'm getting another." Emptied cup in hand, he eased up from the chair. Procter tipped her own in his direction, which he again refilled to the brim. Gonna be lights-out on the helo to San Francisco, she thought.

"Does this Russian have the intelligence services at his disposal?" Harry asked, returning with the drinks.

Procter's scowl said: *Try again, man.*

Harry rolled his eyes and sat down.

"You're the indispensable fucking man, Harry," Procter said. "I know you know that. Now, you ready to hear what I want?"

"Yes, for god's sake," Harry said.

Procter held him in a dead-eye stare. "I want you to buy crypto from Polycoin. In big blocks."

"How much?"

"I don't know yet. But a lot. Maybe hundreds of millions."

"Holy shit, Artemis," he said, wiping grease off his hands.

Procter noticed his feet tapping, and he was rubbing his knuckles over his lips like he did when he got all hot and bothered by an idea. "I presume that these Russians will find their way to Polycoin at some point."

Not a question. Procter ran a finger around the rim of the cup and didn't say a word.

Harry smiled. "How much should I expect to get back?"

"Assuming the bottom doesn't fall out of the crypto markets over the next few months, you should get back most of it. Hell, you might even make a little money. But if it swings the other direction we'll find a way to compensate you for some of the loss. Black budgets, well, they help. Lord knows they help. Now, we both know crypto is a big scam, it's a Ponzi scheme after all, right? No fucking underlying value. You're trading away with Polycoin, Harry, because, well, there's money to be made before it all falls apart. But that's a bit distant, so we've got time to pull this thing off, run our little op, and you get the money out the other side. I'm obviously not financing it this way because I've got a lady boner for crypto. I just need a way to vaporize a bunch of money, get it out of the currency markets real quick, and I don't much care what it's worth on the other side. I just care that I can move it and hide it."

Harry looked at the tent ceiling and tapped his fingers on the table.

"One more thing," Procter said. "You say yes and I can promise you a nice letter from POTUS and a ceremony at Langley thanking you for your service. Medals and plaques and shit you can't take from the building. No glory for you, of course. But you'll know what you did. And that, I think, is what matters to you, Harry. You could be a simple billionaire who likes buying forests and drinking million-dollar bottles of wine on his yacht while he parties with women much more attractive than himself. But you're not that guy. You're Harold Hepburn Hamilton. You're no summer patriot, no sunshine soldier. You live for this. And, like me, you are sick of the Russians pooping on the United States of America."

They regarded each other for a moment. In the distance a tractor engine rumbled to life. The vodka bottles crunched and settled in the buckets as the ice melted.

Harry took a deep breath and shook his head like he knew he was a big sucker. He held out his glass over the table. Procter smacked it with hers. They worked the logistics over another pour of Tito's. Then Procter stumbled back to the chopper and took off, bound for Palo Alto.

———

NEXT MORNING PROCTER WALKED FROM HER PALO ALTO HOTEL TO AN abandoned WeWork building in a leafy office park. Signs advertised that it was available for rent, which was no longer true. HLK Solutions, a CIA front company, had secured the lease. The building bore all the hallmarks of a commercial sensitive compartmented information facility, a SCIF: stand-alone structure, good fiber connections, plenty of room for hardware.

But the facility also had some hair on it. They'd found feces, and then, eventually, the responsible parties: raccoons. The roof leaked. They discovered hypodermic needles jammed in an espresso machine the size of a commercial oven. Procter thought one of the exposed concrete walls had been tagged by vandals, until she realized the message read: STRIVE TO BE BETTER, TOGETHER. WeWork propaganda. She'd had the team run black paint over that one. To cap it all off, the drained pool behind the building looked like one of the places the Taliban used to kill people.

She punched the code and went in. Meandering down a hallway, she clicked into another room. This had been open-plan workspace in the

WeWork days, filled with cheap desks for what Procter imagined had once been a sizable horde of tech bro douchebags. Now it was the command center for Procter's operational brainchild. She dumped her purse on a table and watched the team of techies bustle around. A guy in shorts and sandals and a Mickey Mouse hat was peering into the toaster with one eye shut, scraping a knife around.

Apart from George, Procter knew not one of their names. She had asked exactly zilch about what she imagined to be their bizarre backgrounds. George's instincts were impeccable when it came to nerds, and George had handpicked these. But, man, these kids were pasty as hell. Skin almost translucent. Like shrimps, Procter thought. She 'had half a mind to install a few tanning lights, keep them alive long enough to get this done.

Procter cracked open a Jolt and strolled to the other corner of the room, where the FINO guys had congregated. There were three of them, former bankers who spoke banker language. One, Procter remembered from the cable traffic, had been a NOC who'd run a dirty bank in the Caymans. They dressed like idiot bankers. One of them was actually wearing a pin-striped suit.

Procter knocked on a closed office door. "Fucking busy," a voice called back.

"That's the kind of uncouth behavior that got you in the Penalty Box in the first place, Snake." Procter shoved open the door. A short, muscular man in a tight red polo grimaced when his door slammed into the wall. His funnyname in cable traffic was Gerald B. SNAKERSON. Everyone called him Snake. Procter did not know his real name. Snake was a senior ops officer with a glorious recruitment record and an equally abysmal managerial streak. Like Procter, he was serving time in the Penalty Box. He'd been COS Stockholm, managing a team of case officers that had recruited a startling number of Iranians. Problem was, Snake was also bedding a few of the case officers, one of whom was married.

"Pop in," she said, tossing back the final sip of Jolt and taking a seat. "I was in the neighborhood. Working on the crypto angle. Figured I'd swing through and see how goes the move in."

"Good, it's good," he said, recovering his composure, but still obviously annoyed by Procter's materialization. "We've mostly got the talent we need." He ticked through the roster. Procter promised she would send Debman, her Moscow X analyst.

Setting her empty Jolt can on his desk, she asked him to fire up the WINKELVOSS tool. "Give me a demo." Ten months earlier, a joint CIA-NSA operation had implanted a worm on a piece of equipment the FSB used to monitor Russian telecommunications traffic. The tool gave CIA the ability to make the FSB see things in the data that had never happened. Want to make it appear as though a case officer running a surveillance detection route sat idle at a café for two hours? Or that, say, a group of senior officials close to Putin all traveled to the same dacha at the same time, perhaps in the dead of night? WINKELVOSS was the answer. It had so far been used sparingly; Langley feared they might not have more than a few bites at the apple before the FSB put two and two together and uncovered the malware.

They wound through the main room toward George's desk in the corner, collecting the guy in the Mickey Mouse hat along the way. "Show me, Georgie," Procter said.

"So," George began, his six monitors flickering to life, "let's say we land on five coup-plotters to frame. There are three ways we can sprinkle them in damning digital dust. Suspicious financial transactions. Suspicious comms. Suspicious travel inside Russia. Vadim's laptop, if we can get into it, will help with the money. WINKELVOSS is the answer to comms and travel."

"What exactly do we want Putin to believe?" asked the Mickey Mouse guy. "I mean, how seriously do we want him to take the challenge?"

Procter turned to him, shock blossoming across her face, as if she'd assumed he was incapable of speech and had preferred it that way. A crocodile smile spread across her lips to show most of her teeth.

"The idea," she said, "is to make Putin think a nasty little cabal is coming for the crown, that a few of his boyars are fixing to snuggle his head onto a pike for display on the Kremlin ramparts. We want him to see that this cabal is meeting, conspiring, spreading hush money around.

The goal here, Brian"—she was winging it, no idea what his name was— "isn't merely a whiff of smoke, it's a fucking five-alarm fire that a coup is imminent, a signal that Putin should rip up the floorboards hunting for traitors. They'll be imaginary, of course, but oh so real in the steroid-and-chemo-drug fever swamp of his mind."

"So he does have cancer," the Brian guy murmured.

Procter put a hand on his shoulder and said, but these are all really good questions, Brian, and squeezed until he made a noise. "Rich and powerful Russian pricks killing each other," she concluded, "is the name of the game."

Brian, whose name was in fact Chris, nodded uneasily and took a slow, casual step away from Procter. George sipped his Jolt and continued, "So, we decide on a few big meetings for this group. Places and times where they are all together, that way once the FSB starts digging, it will look weird."

"Show me," Procter said.

George opened a map of Moscow. Procter pointed at a spot along Rublyovka. "There," she said. "Goose's estate." George clicked on the plot. "And let's say he travels there from his office."

George traced a series of roads from the Kremlin to Goose's villa. He entered start and arrival times. He punched in the phone number and a date and hit enter. Up came a new map. Blue dots were the cell towers the phone pinged on the fake route. George tapped on the screen. "This is oversimplified because we haven't created all of the fake data, but it will show any FSB unit investigating that this phone traveled from central Moscow to Rublyovka in the middle of the night on December twentieth."

"You beautiful nerd," she exclaimed, slapping George's back so hard he yelped.

"Make sure you include everything you need from her in the ops cable," Procter said, speaking excitedly. This was getting good. "We've got one shot in Switzerland, then she's gone."

37

Moscow / Geneva / Gimmelwald

ANNA SLEPT SOUNDLY AND WOKE EARLY WITHOUT AN ALARM. IN her silky pajamas, she took a breakfast of toasted rye and black coffee alone in the Ostozhenka apartment, flicking mindlessly through the news on her phone. Padding into the bathroom, she gently peeled off her pajama top and examined the sickly green and yellow splotches on her ribs. She grazed fingers over her stomach and found the muscles less tender than the day before. Four ibuprofen went down with a glass of water.

Opening her closet safe, she withdrew the tourist passport she would use for Geneva. Many Russians had left during the operation in Ukraine, never to return. Artists. Writers. Ballerinas. Journalists. Academics. Many still would kill for her passports and state-approved travel to leave the Rodina. But she had not once considered fleeing. How could she? Luka was here.

She could not bring herself to pick up the phone she used for him, which also lived behind the locked safe door.

———

ANNA SLEPT ON THE FLIGHT TO GENEVA. SHE MET THE DREARY SWISS banker over lunch at the Beau Rivage. They discussed his dealings with the American financial authorities and Washington's perspective on the sanctions against Russia. The banker droned on about the various Russian yachts, scattered in ports across the Mediterranean, that he expected to be impounded. Her reports, she thought, would be of certain interest to SVR and, critically, reduce the chances anyone might press her on the two-day sojourn tacked on the back end of the trip. In the late afternoon she got her nails done and fell asleep after two glasses of wine in her room. Next morning, she took a circuitous walk through the downtown and along the water. The Geneva weather was a warm relief from the tightening grip of the Moscow winter. She watched the plume arcing from the fountain in the center of the lake, spouting high into the cloudy sky. Anna sported a long skirt and boots with a cashmere sweater and a white jacket she had not worn in Moscow since September. She bought a new pair of Louboutins on the rue du Rhone, stopped for a long coffee, then trudged back to the Beau Rivage in a zigzag route including a few reversals that, to any practitioner of street tradecraft, would have been considered extremely provocative. Outside a boutique on the rue du Marché, Anna spotted a man riding a Vespa whom she thought she may have seen earlier in the day, near the fountain. She assumed he was part of their countersurveillance team, but could he be SVR, or FSB? Both had reasons to watch her. She filed the profile for now. She had more time to confirm.

In her hotel room she packed her suitcase and sat on the edge of the bed, considering a hasty return to Moscow. Again, she thought: Is there another way? And, again, she could not imagine one.

She had told herself she would not visit the old neighborhood. But five minutes later she found herself calling the front desk for the bus schedule and the man said in French, Mademoiselle Agapova, please let us take you in a car? In the choppy French she had practiced here during her first four years of marriage, her first four years employed by the now-shuttered Bank Rossiya branch in Geneva, she explained that she preferred the bus. She had always taken the bus. The phone reported a long, metallic sigh.

On the bus, Anna daydreamed. Luka was here and they drank coffee atop twisted sheets in the slanted morning light. Vadim did not exist. The SVR did not exist. Life was sunny fields and warm wind. The dream popped at the screech of the brakes.

The village bustled in the lunch rush. She bought a warm butter-and-salami sandwich at a bakery she had visited every day in her old life. She had loved the bread and for some silly reason she expected the taste would be cheerful, but instead it drew her back to this horrible season and became dry in her mouth. She tossed the sandwich in a rubbish bin and continued her march to the villa. Ten bedrooms, expansive views of the lake and the Jura Mountains. Vadim had chosen it. They had been rich Russians, young and ambitious. Here, she had once thought, here we can work things out. Here we can find our way to love.

From outside the front gate she could see the windows of their old bedroom and the windows of the room that soon became her own bedroom. Here, in Geneva, she had decided a marriage bed shared with an ensemble cast of tarty women was not one worth protecting. They'd mostly stopped making love, and she'd secretly begun taking the pill to defend her uterus if Vadim tried. Here Maximov had dangled the SVR job and then she'd said no on account of her father and Vadim and the then-powerful voice of the Good Daughter and Wife, keen to please the boys to their faces even though the blast furnace of resistance was already roaring inside her. Anna had hoped her visit now would conjure a righteous certainty in her choices, but instead this felt like she was snooping on a dead woman's life, and she turned from her old home angrier at herself than at them.

She returned to the village and the bus, which, at 3:07 p.m., was precisely on time for its departure to central Geneva. She collected her suitcase from the Beau Rivage and checked out at the front desk. "Where to next, Mademoiselle Agapova?" the clerk answered.

"A few days of skiing," she said.

———

FRIDAY WAS A CLASSIC HYNES DAWSON LATE-NIGHT BURNER. DOZENS of client calls, a few interviews with prospective hires, document reviews—the mass crank-turning on the associates at the bottom of this pyramid. The blinking, too-early November Christmas tree brought little cheer; it was instead a reminder that the world outside the firm might be joyfully anticipating the holiday season instead of toiling in a glorified sweatshop. An associate on one of Sia's teams noticed that the boss, usually quite serene, now seemed pretty tweaked. She was texting a lot in meetings; her sculpted hair was a little mussed; one hand now seemed to be shaky. Might be coked up, the associate thought. God knew everyone needed the energy.

At two-thirty a.m. he knocked on Sia's office door to explain that he had sent her everything she'd asked for and was going home. The boss was sitting there in the light of her computer. Weirdly staring at the screen. Zoned out. The associate knocked again and Sia sat up straight. "What's up?" she mumbled.

"Sent you the Sandalwood files," he said. "You okay?"

"Yes, yes. Just tired. As we all are." She'd not turned her head to look at him.

"Course," he said. "Night, boss."

———

THERE WERE DOZENS OF DIRECT FLIGHTS FROM LONDON TO GENEVA, but Sia's travel pattern to Switzerland required obfuscation: multiple legs and modes, the use of cash wherever possible. In the morning she packed a bag with winter gear and rode the Eurostar to Paris, the TGV Lyria to Geneva, then on to Interlaken, where she spent the night. Next morning she caught a blue-and-gold-painted train that trundled up into the Jungfrau. As the train rumbled into the mountains, Sia fought the urge to sleep. Her left hand had stilled, but she was struggling to shake the fatigue.

The train clipped by alpine churches and timber chalets with shutters and windows trimmed in reds and greens. Lugging a suitcase to the Hotel Staubbach in Lauterbrunnen, she checked in, dumped her belongings, and put her cell phone and laptop in the safe because they could not travel with her to the meeting.

It was the opening day of Lauterbrunnen's Christmas market. Sia bought a cup of hot chocolate and sat on a bench, forcing her mind to focus on the meeting. Jon, her old instructor, had once asked her how many meaningful ops she thought an officer would land in a lifetime. Five, she had guessed. One, he corrected, just one that will really make a difference. And this, she knew, was hers. From the cone-spired alpine church beneath the falls came four pleasant dings of the bells. Her bus would soon arrive.

She was the lone passenger. Though the drive was only fifteen minutes, she greeted the bus driver with, "Wake me up at Stechelberg." He gave her a cold stare, as if he did not understand her more than passable French. She took her seat and the door shut with a hiss.

She woke to the driver poking her shoulder, muttering about the schedule. He looked frustrated, as if this were not his first attempt to wake her.

Stumbling from the bus, she boarded the Schilthornbahn cable car, and the glass box swung skyward. The bus and cable car ride acted as a channeling mechanism for what had become a multi-day surveillance detection route. She'd been alone on the bus; she was alone on the cable car. She'd been alone on the trains. Her body might be calling for rest, for endless rest, but she would not bring hostiles to this meeting. She would not fail Anna.

Gimmelwald was a farming village perched on the gorge high above the valley floor, a winding single road dotted by timber homes, accessible only by cable car. High, neat stacks of firewood were piled for the winter. The village possessed a serene, bone-deep quiet that Sia found unsettling. No cars, no rumbling motors, just the distant ring of cowbells announcing the gathering night. She passed a small grazing herd as fog curled over the village.

It quickly became so thick that Sia nearly banged into the sign. Stopping about two feet in front of it, she saw that it read MOUNTAIN HOSTEL. But it had not been one for years; it was now an Airbnb, rented for two nights by a Germany-based Airbnb user CIA paid to secure bookings on the Continent. Two floors, dark wood, nestled right on the edge of the cliff. There was smoke rising from the chimney and a warm golden glow dancing on the windows. Sia stamped her snowy hiking shoes on the mat and pushed open the door.

Procter was in a low crouch stoking the fire. The Chief wore white jeans and white furry boots with tassels and an oversized white sweater with strange, fuzzy poufs sewed onto the sleeves. A man Sia assumed was the polygrapher nervously watched Procter tending the fire.

"Well, hon," she said, looking Sia up and down, "you look a bit rough."

38

Gimmelwald

THE ROUTE HAD BEEN PLANNED WITH ONE OBJECTIVE ABOVE ALL: lowering the odds that Anna would be arrested and shot upon her return to the Rodina. A ten-strong CIA countersurveillance team had trailed Anna since Geneva to confirm that her compatriots were not watching her. In the glow of the fire, Procter told Sia that the team believed Anna was black. A CIA support asset had left instructions and the safe house address in Anna's Geneva hotel room just that morning. To make sure she behaved, Anna had been under CIA surveillance every minute since. They would follow her as far as Lauterbrunnen.

The instructions also included several specific requests. (*"At Lauterbrunnen, take the 7:08 Post Bus toward Stechelberg Schilthornbahn"*). Some developmentals would buck your authority by ignoring directions, an easy, annoying way to pretend they were in control. Since RusFarm, the Moscow X analysts had corroborated several of Anna's reports; she was producing, but would she keep it up? No one expected outright control of her, but if CIA was going to send Anna back inside Russia as the linchpin of an op with risks this spectacular, well, CIA wanted as much proof as possible—even if it was thin gruel—that she would follow simple directions. That she could deliver.

———

ANNA CAUGHT THE DIRTY YELLOW BUS AT LAUTERBRUNNEN AT PRE-cisely 7:08, bumping along the valley floor toward Stechelberg. What are you doing? she said to herself, again and again, as she peered from the window at the sheer cliffs rising above. Jumping from one of those might be easier than the path ahead. When the cable car creaked to a stop at Gimmelwald, Anna stepped into the crisp air, taking in the smell of hay and mud and the metallic tinge of new snow. The only sounds were the jangle of cowbells and murmurs from a hotel a few hundred meters up the hillside. The old hostel was shrouded in fog. She knew it was at the edge of the gorge, but she could not see down, much less across the valley to the peaks and cliff faces beyond. She could barely see the sign. Chimes jangled, announcing her treason. No, she said aloud, it is not that. It is my answer to Them.

She pushed open the door and a flurry of snow followed her in.

Sia was drinking coffee on the couch. A muscular woman with curly black hair sat next to her. The body language suggested that the new woman was in charge. The curly-haired woman stood to greet Anna. She was quite short, with electric-green eyes.

"Hi, Anna," the gravelly voice said in impeccable Russian. "My name is Lulu. I do a lot of work on Russia. Sia has told me so much about you. How much time do you have?"

"I have the evening and tomorrow morning through lunch," Anna said. "My phone is in my room at the lodge."

"Good," the woman calling herself Lulu said. "We might all camp out here tonight, then. Give us more time. Much to do. Much to do."

"You find your way here okay?" Lulu asked, switching to English. "We know you're a pro, but we need to ask. You know how it goes."

"Other than your team watching me," Anna said, "the trip was perfectly fine." Anna poured coffee from a pot in the kitchen and took a seat on the couch. "What do you mean by 'pro'?" A wry smile parted her lips.

Lulu appeared to be attempting a grin. "I mean that, for a banker"— the word rolled out in disgust—"you seem to know which way is up."

Anna nodded. Good enough.

"How'd you get here?" Sia asked.

Anna explained her route, though they already knew. They'd had countersurveillance on her since Geneva, she was sure of it. "And you?" she asked. The CIA women described their path to Gimmelwald. Anna liked it. Careful, conservative. Not clowns. Good.

Lulu continued: "Sia told me about what happened at the farm. What your husband did. I'm sorry about that. We want to find a way to help, and we think we have some common interests. I also wanted to convey that we were gripped by the information you passed to Sia about the men around your father and Putin. That is the sort of thing our *customers* find fascinating."

Lulu hunched forward and picked at a cuticle, keeping an eye on it as she spoke. "But right now our organization is operating in what might be fairly termed a deficit of trust with your people. There are really no boundaries left at all. I know you have an agenda for speaking with us. We've also got some ideas that could be disruptive to our common foes. And we'd like to move fast. I'd like you to sit for a polygraph so we can accelerate our basis for trust. You don't have to, you can walk, but if you split, well, we're done."

Anna creaked forward in the wooden chair to pluck a few almonds from a tin on the coffee table. "Before I do that, I want to know what you have in mind. You both must know, and you must tell your *organization*"— said in disgust—"that I am not interested in the fall of Putin or a change in the Russian government." They nodded in understanding, but it struck her as a hollow gesture. How could they really understand? How could they know what that meant to her?

"The war in Ukraine has been poorly managed," Anna continued. "But I have no wish to see Russia brought to her knees. I have no interest in changing the system because I do not, quite honestly, believe another system is possible. There would be new faces, new names given to institutions, but nothing would truly *change*. And I will not tell you about *my* organization, you must know this right now. It is off-limits. You want the org chart, you want me to put something in a computer at my office, you want to know about operations in America?

No. I will not share it. I am not a traitor to Russia, and I will not be made one."

The Lulu woman's face was twisted in thought.

"Maybe you tell us what you want, Anna?" Sia asked.

"I want help disposing of my enemies. Goose. Perhaps my husband."

"Understood," Lulu said. "And I have an idea for how we might do this. But I have a question for you: Are you open to helping us access your husband's computer?"

"For what purpose?"

"I want to see where the money is. And I might want to move some around."

"Whose money?"

Lulu smiled. "C'mon."

"My father owns a great deal of that bank," Anna said. "He has since Vadim's father passed. I will not let you wreck it. If I am going to help you, you will tell me what you are doing."

"Your father owns a good amount of Bank Rossiya, does he?" Lulu asked.

"You know this."

"And how much will he own when Goose finishes his shakedown?"

Anna folded her arms. Lulu leaned closer and put a gentle hand on her wrist. "We have a price here, Anna. We need money for our little idea to work. And I think it should come from the bank. But here is what I can promise you: None of this will be traced back to you or your father. We will pin it on our common enemies."

Anna withdrew her arm. "Perhaps you are trying to entrap me."

Lulu laughed. Said she was paranoid.

Anna switched to Russian and set into her. "Paranoid, eh? Look at what your sanctions have done to Russia!" She smacked a palm on the coffee table. "Ordinary people are back living off their potato patches as they did in the days after the Soviet collapse. Our travel is restricted. We are pariahs in Europe. A good Russian should be paranoid about your intentions, Lulu, because you lie just like we do."

Sia put up a hand. "Maybe we spare each other the speeches? And stick to English? Arguing is counterproductive, don't you think? We all want the same things here."

Anna shook her head and clicked her tongue. "No, Sia, we do not. Not really. I could ask you why it is that you want to help me settle a few scores. Should I ask that? I do not think I will, because I do not want to know the truth. Or maybe I should ask, because you would just lie to me, eh? Feed me some garbage to get me on board. Perhaps I hook you up to the polygraph tonight as well?"

Anna took a big sip of coffee, smacked her lips together, and stuck out her tongue. "This is awful. I am making tea."

In the kitchen she rummaged around for a kettle. "Are you recording this meeting?" Crouching, she found it in a lower cabinet.

"No," Lulu called from the living room. "You have my word."

Anna grunted. She filled the kettle at the sink and put it on the stove. Lulu's word meant nothing.

She returned to the living room. "How widely known is my name inside your organization?"

" 'Bout five people," Lulu said. "Tightly compartmented."

The kettle began whistling. Still standing, Anna gripped the back of the couch. "I am a patriot. I do not think you truly know this. Maybe as Americans you are incapable of understanding. I do not care that Putin rules our country. The Russian system has always been this way. One person at the top, everyone taking what they can. The activists and protesters mean nothing to me. I am a Russian patriot—"

Lulu put up a hand. "Like I said, I am not trying to dress you up as an American cheerleader. Believe me, I know you're not helping us light the path for democracy in the Rodina. How about this: You hear me out. I tell you our idea, which has been approved in concept by the highest levels of my organization. We chat about it. If you like what I have to say, you take the poly, then we get into the details over cognac and Swiss Miss."

Anna found a bag of black tea. It bobbed and waterlogged and finally sank as she steeped it. She returned to the living room. "Tell me what you have in mind."

Lulu did, in a speech so aggressive, so fevered, so bold that Anna wondered how her American mind could have possibly birthed it. What it recalled, Anna thought, was a proper Russian conspiracy. Anna listened. Occasionally she would nod; sometimes her eyes narrowed in grave concern. She did not interrupt with a single question or comment. When Lulu had finished, Anna pushed aside her drained teacup. "Give me the polygraph," she said. "Now."

39

Gimmelwald

THE POLYGRAPHER HAD BEEN CACHED UPSTAIRS. ON LULU'S CALL, HE sauntered down, introducing himself as Morris. He was beefy with shaggy brown hair, offering a clammy hand and a sheepish smile. "Ms. Agapova," he said, "we'll flutter you quick, have it done in time for schnapps. Right this way."

The upstairs bedroom faced the gorge, but she could see only fog out the window. Morris gestured to a wooden chair in the middle of the room between two twin beds. She sat. He dropped onto one of the beds and began punching keys on his laptop. He slipped two pneumograph tubes around her chest. He wrapped a blood pressure cuff around her left arm. Then he put finger plates over her right pointer and middle fingers to measure her galvanic response—the sweat that would seep through her skin on this emotional ride.

He told her to relax. And strangely she was relaxed. She'd once chatted up an SVR operations officer who had run American cases, including a low-level CIA support officer who stole documents for the Rodina. Her colleague said it was tricky to polygraph intelligence officers for two reasons. One, they knew what to expect. Two, deception was more common because they inflated their access, puffing themselves up for bigger stipends and escrow payments. This was a game. She could win at games.

They covered the ground rules, set the baseline, and previewed the questions. Then Morris began.

Q: *Is your name Anna Andreevna Agapova?*

A: *Yes.*

Q: *Are you a Managing Director at Bank Rossiya?*

A: *Yes.*

Q: *Are you an officer for a Russian intelligence service?*

A: *Yes.*

Q: *Are your superiors, or is anyone else in Russia, aware of this meeting?*

A: *No.*

Q. *Have you been sent to this meeting at the behest of a Russian intelligence service?*

A. *No.*

Q. *Are you able to gain access to your husband's computer?*

A. *Yes.*

Q. *Do you intend to provide truthful information to our organization?*

A. *Yes.*

[Polygraph terminated. 8:47 p.m. CET]

Anna removed the plates from her sweaty fingers and the scratchy pressure cuff from her arm. Morris had trotted off to speak with Lulu and Sia. Had she lied? It bothered her that she did not know.

When Morris returned, he said they had to run through it again.

"Which question is the problem?" she asked.

"All of them," he said.

They did it again. He left, and this time his absence was longer. Anna grew tired, and that, she knew, was the point.

Morris returned with one of the chairs from the kitchen. Flipping it around, he scooted it a bit too close and eased his gut against the seat back. He folded his arms and looked beyond Anna into the gray gathered outside the window. Morris's breath stank like a bar at daybreak. "Ms. Agapova, did you tell anyone about this meeting?"

"No."

"No one?"

"No one."

"No one in your family? Father, husband, dog?"

"I don't have a dog."

"Anyone at the bank?"

"No."

"Boyfriend?"

"No."

"Girlfriend?"

"A little kinky, Morris?"

Morris scowled. "Girlfriend?"

"No."

"Anyone inside the SVR?"

She wrinkled her nose. "No."

"GRU?"

"No."

"FSB?"

"No."

They ran the poly again.

When they'd finished, Morris told her to hold tight. He collected the laptop and left. Anna unhooked the tubes, plucked off the finger plates, unwrapped the cuff. She spread out in one of the twin beds and shut her eyes. *Should I worry? I'm not even sure if I lied.*

———

PROCTER AND SIA WERE SMOKING AT ONE OF THE PICNIC TABLES OUT front. Sia had mindfully positioned herself to hide the trembling hand from the Chief, and had already burned through two cigarettes in a bid for warmth. She was now on her third. Morris trudged outside. Procter took the last drag of her cigarette and stamped it in the snow. "Well, Mo? Let's have it."

He sat at the table and yanked up his hood. "I think she is telling the truth that she's not told others about this meeting. That she's kept this a secret."

"That's good," Sia said. "Gives us leverage."

"She still flickering bullshit on the other one?" Procter asked. She lit another cigarette and pulled the hood of her banana-yellow parka over her head. Procter shoved hands in her pockets, dragging and expelling smoke with the cigarette clamped between her teeth.

"That's right," Morris said. "She is consistently uncomfortable with the question about telling the truth."

"Occupational hazard," Sia said.

Procter grunted. "But you don't think Moscow knows she is here?"

"Can't be certain, of course, these things have to be—"

"Morris, I don't want the lawyer-speak. A few weeks back I had to amend a damn covert action finding with lethal authorities and I've had lawyers on my back like baby scorpions riding their mama. Not interested. I just want to understand if you think Moscow knows she is here."

"That question is no longer eliciting a physiological response."

Procter rolled her eyes. "Whaddya think, Sia?"

Sia tossed her cigarette and stretched her legs. "I think we've got enough to move ahead. We've got corroborated intel. Validated motivation. Reasonable fodder for asset validation. Poly is pretty decent. Things aren't pristine, but it's worth the risk."

"It's a day-old pantie," Procter said. "Not clean, but it gets the job done. And when it comes down to it, you have no choice." The Chief flicked the cigarette into the darkness. "Let's get to work."

40

Gimmelwald

PROCTER POURED COFFEES AND TEA. MORRIS WENT TO BED UPSTAIRS. Sia fed a few more logs into the fire and they sat in the living room fighting sleep, trying to squeeze every minute, every piece of information, from Anna Agapova. PERSEPHONE. There was a long list of questions from the Moscow X analysts on the SVR. Current operations, priorities, org chart. Procter ceremoniously read the questions to Anna, then fed the papers into the fire. "Nothing on your organization," Procter said. "That's fine with us."

As the night dragged on, Anna explained her understanding of Goose and his allies. They covered Vadim's friends, his enemies. Her father's friends, his enemies.

On the dregs of the third cup of coffee, Sia returned to the topic of Vadim. "How much money does he manage?"

"I don't know. Hundreds of millions. Maybe more."

"And it belongs to whom, exactly?" Sia asked.

"Are you familiar with the concept of *obschak*?"

Sia shook her head; Procter nodded.

"It's a cash box," Anna explained. "A common till for a criminal gang. The leaders know what they own, but nothing is held in their names. This is the structure with the money he manages. He oversees a pot owned collectively by Putin and other bosses inside the regime. They feed off the cash from the bank and the industrials. There are other *obschak*, of this I am certain, but Vadim runs this one."

"He does this work from the bank?" Procter asked.

Anna shook her head. "The money originates from the bank. Once they skim it off, they like to keep it separate. The bank has systems, processes, IT managers, FSB active reserve officers. Not that anyone would bat an eyebrow, it's the President's money after all, but it's better if everything is managed out of sight. Vadim has a laptop at home he uses for *obschak* business. It's in the Petersburg apartment, in a safe in our bedroom closet. Access might be possible."

"Now, how would that work?" Procter asked.

Anna explained. Sia thought there was a decent chance she'd be shot, or might shoot Vadim in the process, just because. Procter had started to tip a bit of cognac into her coffee. The Chief tapped her foot as Anna spoke. She seemed to be enjoying herself.

"Once I have access to the computer, what do you need me to do?" Anna asked.

Sia explained. They covered the product the CIA techs should use for the pop-up, how Anna should hide her digital tracks on Vadim's computer. How she should manage fingerprints.

Anna held her hand over her cup when Procter came by with the cognac.

"A Russian rejecting booze," Procter said, withdrawing the bottle. "Huh."

Anna made a nasty gesture to Procter, who laughed and ruefully shook her head. "More for me, then," the Chief said.

"Compensation for your risk," Sia said, with a cough. "We'd like to offer something."

"I do not want it," Anna said. "Besides, if you are trying to compensate me with money, you won't be able to afford me."

"You deserve something for the risks you are taking," Sia tried again. It was weak, but she wanted something to signal to Langley that they had a shred of control here.

Anna shook her head. "No money. Not even an escrow account in the Bahamas. Understand? I want you to write in the cable that I refused money. I want only to stop Goose and implicate my husband."

"Fine, hon. Just fine," Procter said. "Let's go through some of the homework."

Sia pushed her a piece of paper Procter had brought along. It listed every detail CIA sought on Goose and the men around him: addresses, associates, emails, phone numbers. Anna memorized the wish list, then it went into the fire.

Then Procter said: "Let's talk comms." Sia yawned at her watch: 3:08 a.m. Procter slid a laptop from her backpack. An Asus model, identical to the machine Anna had brought to Mexico. Right down to the streaky black scuff mark across the top.

Anna eyed it as if it were a bomb.

"I assume," Procter said, "that this looks a lot like the travel laptop you carried to Mexico. That right?"

Anna was running fingers over it. "Right."

"This is loaded with what we call a clandestine communications system. Clancomm," Procter said. "Am I also correct in assuming that your travel laptop does not have comms on it?"

"That's right."

"Is it an SVR laptop, or personal?"

"Personal."

"Good," Procter said. "You have this personal laptop in a bag over at your ski resort?"

"Yes."

"Anything important on it?"

"No. But you already know that."

Procter grinned. "Good. Toss it in a dumpster, bury it on the mountain. Doesn't matter. Just make sure that version doesn't return to Mother Russia." Procter jerked her head toward Sia.

"I'll show you how to use it," Sia said.

They practiced with grim determination because it was all about muscle memory and Anna would be blind inside Russia if she forgot a single step. A twenty-three-key sequence—letters, numbers, symbols. Random, no logic to it. Tough to remember. Anna spent an hour memorizing that first sequence. You forget this part, Procter said—anticipating

276 - David McCloskey

first light, she had drifted back to coffee—you are pitch-black. We can't see the beautiful words you're typing to us. Sia continued: Once you're into the partition you open a Word document. A blank one. Then you enter another sequence. Ten keys. They spent some time on that. It conjured a hidden button, which Sia clicked to demonstrate. Voila, Procter said. You're in. Messages travel to us in encrypted blobs.

Anna's jaw was clicking. "Ours is similar. Slightly less complicated."

"One more thing on the comms," Procter said. She slipped a small box from her bag and handed it to Anna. She opened it and found a statue of a horse.

"What is this?"

"Comms relay," Procter said. "Put it in your office at the bank. In front of a window. Like on the sill. You have an office in Petersburg, yes? With windows? We'd prefer Petersburg to Moscow."

"Yes. But why? What is it?"

"A comms relay," Sia reiterated.

Anna was unconvinced, twisting and turning the statue in her fingers. She rubbed the seam along its base.

Procter's face screwed into a dead stare for Anna. The Chief could get weirdly scary at times. "As Hortensia said, it's a comms relay. You put it in your Petersburg office in front of the window. And you don't tamper with it. Otherwise, none of this works and Goose remains frustratingly un-fucked by our organization. Understand?"

Anna stared intently at Procter, as if debating a challenge. Then she slipped the statue in her bag.

———

THEY TOOK COGNACS TO THE SNOWY DECK JUTTING OVER THE GORGE. The fog had lifted and the predawn sky was clear, carpeted by brilliant stars. The craggy peaks and snowy rock faces across the valley glowed under the moon. Off and on came the distant jangle of cowbells and the bleating of sheep. They sipped cognac and stared at the stars. Her dad had liked to say that the night sky made us realize how small we are.

Now it just made Sia tired. Her lids were hanging heavy when Procter said, "I'm gonna hit the sack for a few. Let's pick this up after breakfast."

Procter's footsteps crunched inside, the door swinging on its hinges with a metallic shriek. Sia had almost fallen asleep in her seat when Anna said, "I smelled cigarette smoke during the polygraph. You demolish the whole pack, or do you have a few more?"

Sia opened one eye. The Russian's face said she wanted to talk. In the living room Sia collected the remains of the cigarettes and Procter's lighter. She returned to the deck and they lit up.

The smoke shook her awake. Sia tossed one butt into the gorge and lit another. The Russian loosed long plumes of smoke that were sucked out over the valley by the wind.

"In your rush from the farm you left behind a horse," Anna said. "A horse I rather love."

"Can you persuade Vadim to give her back?" Sia said.

"I'm not sure I want to. And we have larger fish to cook."

"To fry."

Anna flicked her hand dismissively toward the gorge and took a long drag on her cigarette. "I am playing through the moves," she said. "Tell me when I get something wrong."

Sia leaned into the handrail. "Okay."

"I give you access to Vadim's computer. You take some of the money." Anna looked at Sia.

"That's right," Sia said.

"You move the money to other accounts. Some of that disappears."

"Still right."

"Then what?"

"How do you mean?"

"Tell me what triggers the chaos."

Sia tossed her cigarette into the gorge. She had another peeking halfway from the pack but, feeling her raw throat, she slid it back. Anna stuck out her hand; Sia surrendered the pack and the lighter. Anna lit another and dragged, long and deep. "The trigger," Anna repeated.

"We don't know the answer yet," Sia said. "It depends on what we find inside Vadim's computer."

"Meaning?"

"Who watches his transactions. Who will see the money moving and sound the alarm."

"And if no one is watching?"

"Seems unlikely, yes?"

Anna shrugged. "If I were the President, I might not want midlevel FSB officers watching one of my moneymen. What I am thinking, Sia, is if it turns out no one is watching my dear husband, it may fall to his unfortunate wife to sound the alarm. And I am running short of friends in Russia, as you know. They may not listen."

"Let's cross that bridge once we see what's on the laptop."

"I do not love this answer, Sia." Anna threw the cigarette off the deck and started inside. "See you in a few hours."

———

SIA WOKE TO THE SMELL OF BURNED GREASE. PROCTER'S CURSES WERE rising from the kitchen, along with smoke. She slipped on sweatpants and went downstairs to find the Chief scraping away at blackened strips of what had once been bacon. Procter wore a black tank top, and with her back turned, hunched over the stove, Sia could see imprinted across the Chief's lats nine simple stars tattooed in a line, the words IN HONOR inked above. A personal memorial wall on her skin. Sia had caught glimpses of the tattoo before, but she'd never seen the entire line, and she'd never been sufficiently foolhardy to ask about it. This morning would be no exception. The microwave clock read 9:46 a.m. Maybe two hours left.

Anna was sitting on the deck under a cloudless winter sky. Sia put on a jacket and filled a mug of black coffee and joined her. They sat in a comfortable silence until Procter called them inside. The breakfast, Sia thought, did not look so great. Burnt bacon, watery coffee, rubbery pancakes sired from a tattered box of mixture. There is no fucking syrup, Procter muttered. Sorry about that. Sia forced down a few pieces of bacon that had been spared the worst of the flames, but mostly she sipped coffee. Anna's plate was untouched. She filled a second cup of coffee with a generous heap of sugar and clattered the spoon onto the table. She nudged the mug at Sia. "We were speaking a few hours ago about the trigger for all of this. I have an idea."

"Tell us," Procter said.

"Maximov," Anna said, "third Deputy Director of the SVR. He is a close ally of my family. With the right information, he could intervene with the President. He might be able to compel the FSB to investigate, to run analysis on phone numbers and bank transfers, for example. We must make sure that, in the end, Maximov gets the information."

"Works for us," Procter said. "Let's go with that for now."

Anna turned to check the microwave clock. "I should be going soon."

Procter put a hand on Anna's shoulder. "Before you do, let's go through all of it again, just to be sure."

First Anna showered, changed, and lugged her duffel downstairs. Then they sat in the living room. Fog again folded over the village, shrouding the sunlight.

Anna accessed the clancomm partition on the new laptop. Again and again.

She described the plan for Vadim's computer and the website she would visit once she had access.

She repeated the information she would collect on the list of senior officials Procter and Sia had supplied.

She held up the horse figurine and explained that she would place it in the office at Rossiya headquarters in Piter. Her office had large windows.

Anna packed the laptop and figurine in her duffel. She shook Procter's hand and hugged Sia. Then she turned to leave, marching over the snowy path toward the village's only road, her white jacket disappearing into the fog.

"That bitch is ice-cold," Procter said.

"She wants to win," Sia said. "It's all she wants."

The bleating of sheep carried down the hillside; the two women turned back into the house.

"And I have the strange feeling," Sia murmured, "that she's going to get herself killed."

41

Moscow

LUKA WAS ALREADY AT THEIR TABLE AT JEAN MARTEL, CHESSBOARD arranged. He'd sliced the lemon. He was picking at black bread and oily herring mixed with onion and boiled potatoes. He grinned, but she did not notice; she just sat down, spun the board to play white, and advanced her first pawn. As she balanced her chin on her hands, her world was the board and the cognac. Tonight she wanted cognac, chess, and Luka, perhaps in that order. There was really nothing else right now that could make her feel good. Which was all she wanted. To feel good.

Over two games she made quick work of both him and much of the bottle. They played a third, and she won. Still working hard on the bottle. Eat something, Anya, he said nervously, you'll be sick. She told him not to throw her groove. They played again. A massacre. Maybe he wasn't trying? She yelled that at him. Three men seated at the table behind Luka scowled at her.

"Mind your own business," she snapped at them, and made a nasty gesture.

She'd started talking about another bottle, but Luka was packing up the board. Standing, she stumbled toward him, demanding another game. The bottles behind the bar rotated and shimmered. She steadied herself on a table. She gripped Luka's shoulder, but the world kept tilting.

Of the shuffle from Jean Martel to her apartment she would remember only fragments: dropping the chessboard, Luka sorting through the snow for pieces; skidding and falling on the icy sidewalk, smelly exhaust leaking from a grate into her nostrils. The Moscow night was smoke. Starless. Moonless. Smoke.

In the morning she was twisted in the sheets in her bra and leggings. The apartment smelled of coffee. Where was her sweater? Her shirt? Oh god, he'd seen the damn bruises across her stomach. Fuck. She sat up and held her aching head for a few moments. Only one eye would open to the light. *Where are the rest of my clothes?* Tiptoeing into the bathroom, she found her sweater and T-shirt hanging on the rack to dry.

"You got sick on them," Luka said. In the bathroom doorway he held a cup of black coffee. She slipped on the sweater to cover the bruises. They took a slow, wordless coffee in the living room as Anna tried to work out memories of the night before. She was angry with herself for even coming to see him. She'd vowed to wait until the bruises healed.

"Anya, will you tell me what happened?" Luka asked.

She turned away from him to look out the window. "Nothing," she said.

"Anya, please. I know we have our rules, but please, I love you. Please tell me what happened. Just this once."

Defiant sip of her coffee.

"Anya, I know they did this to you. *He* did this to you. Please, just talk to me. This is safe. I love you."

She looked into his eyes. Blue like hers, but warm. She hated herself.

"I fell off a horse," she said.

Then she shut her eyes because she could not bear to see his face. If she did, she would cry, and she would not cry for him.

There was shuffling, the door shutting. When she opened her eyes, he was gone.

———

EVEN IF LUKA FEDOROV HAD BEEN AN OPS-TRAINED OFFICER OF THE SVR or FSB, he would not at first have found much amiss during his march down the Street of All-Holidays. His eyes pounded the pavement, and he departed Anna's apartment at a pace far brisker than was normal, even for a harried Muscovite bearing down in a biting wind. He was angry, this was obvious even to the most junior of those watching him. Had Luka conducted multiple stops and turns, drawn out over a period of hours, and had he been a different man with different training, he might have eventually noticed the six-man team stalking him to his apartment. Each wore subminiature cameras snuggled into coat buttons and lapels.

The video, all understood, was not strictly necessary from a surveillance standpoint. They already had his face on several photos snapped the night before, both outside Jean Martel and from one of the fixed points in an empty apartment across the street from the Agapov girl's love nest. The face had been run through the FSB's databases. They already had his address, his employer, his phone records. No, the team followed and taped Luka Fedorov because the boss wanted options. When presented with video of themselves taped clandestinely, people tended to become quite frightened.

We stand for organized terror, the Chekists had once said, this should be frankly admitted.

As they had for the past two weeks, the surveillance team delivered the tapes and a clipped, written report to the Lubyanka offices of the Internal Security Directorate, where a clerk deposited them with Chernov. The apartment had been a bit tricky for Chernov's men to locate because it was not in Anna's name, nor her father's, nor any of the family's known business associates'. They knew of the Ostozhenka apartment, of course. And they had Anna's phone and every flake of digital dust it spewed, pinging cell towers and hundreds of unseen sensors all around Moscow. Establishing her pattern of life had been simple.

They also had her calls and messages through the FSB's bulk collection. And what Chernov's watchers quickly learned was that there were occasional periods—typically an evening and subsequent morning—in which Anna left her phone in the Ostozhenka apartment to trek across the city in an elaborate *obnaruzhit hvost*, a surveillance detection route, that belied detailed knowledge of the streets, parks, and CCTV camera coverage inside the Garden Ring. At first the mobile teams were not large enough to stick her; she was quite skilled and patient on the street, and sometimes after several hours she would vanish into the Moscow night. On one occasion she casually returned to the Ostozhenka apartment; aborting the meeting, Chernov believed, because she had spotted their surveillance. Where are you going, Anya, without your phone? She had made one mistake, it turned out, weeks earlier.

With access to her phone, FSB techies reviewed her call history to search for anomalies. They found a number she had phoned once, from her apartment. Who was that? They ran the number through a series of telco databases and discovered that the phone she dialed had been in the Ostozhenka apartment when Anna called. She had called herself. Chernov suspected that she had called the mysterious second phone with the first in a bid to hear the ringtone. The phone had perhaps gone missing under a couch cushion. He wondered if she had been drinking.

One mistake, that was all they needed.

They ran a historical analysis of the second phone and discovered that it lived in her Ostozhenka apartment. It did not leave Moscow. But on nights when Anna left her primary phone there, this second phone traveled with her. And it spent the night at an apartment building tucked into a warren of an old residential district near Novokuznetskaya that had survived Lenin and Stalin and Brezhnev and Putin and the *blagoustroistvo* that had raked over much of old Moscow, replacing it with highrises and boutiques and luxury stores. The tax records showed that the apartment was owned by a bizarre shell company incorporated in the Seychelles. Since this discovery, a team from the Seventeenth, the FSB's Operations Search Directorate, had entered the apartment to wire it with cameras and microphones.

Chernov poured more black tea. A knock stirred him from the reports. "Come in," he called.

Daniil, one of his lieutenants, plopped a stack of papers on the desk and took a seat by the window. He had a toothpick in his teeth, which he twirled with long, slender fingers. He was a major, but his boyish face looked no older than twenty. "Reports from one of our guys in Yasenevo," he said. "He pulled the cables. The travel was legitimate.

Approved. Went to Geneva. She runs an economic case out there. Looks like she is getting back to work."

Chernov grunted. Daniil motioned to the surveillance reports on the desk. "Did you see the video yet?"

"The boyfriend's walk? Yes."

"No, the video the boys took after he left. Inside the apartment."

"Not yet." Chernov raised a brow. "Why?"

Daniil plugged one of the thumb drives into Chernov's computer and clicked forward. Much of the evening, he explained, had been the Agapov girl sick, the boyfriend trying to comfort. The screen showed the boyfriend standing, Anna slumped on the couch. Nothing seemed to be happening.

"We need the sound on, boss," Daniil said. Chernov unmuted the video.

The boyfriend was asking what had happened to her. The report from the night before, Chernov recalled, had noted Luka Fedorov's audible surprise at the sight of something on Anna's chest. Then she'd been retching in the bathroom and the camera angles were bad. But when Anna told Luka that she fell from a horse, he got up and left. For a moment the apartment was still. The only sound the slap of a hockey match in the courtyard below.

Then Anna Andreevna Agapova began to cry. The sound took Chernov aback: it was surprisingly soft for such a hard woman, an operations officer, even if she belonged to the effete SVR. She was Andrei Agapov's daughter and heir. She cried for two minutes and thirty-one seconds. Then she got up and walked into the bathroom. Daniil killed the video.

"My god," he said to Daniil. "She loves him. She may not even know. But she loves him."

Daniil was smiling broadly. Chernov stood up to look down on the square. A light snow was dusting Dzerzhinsky.

"And people do things for love, boss."

Chernov thought about that. "Yes, they do, don't they? Stupid things, brave things, violent things. But they always do something. It just cannot be helped."

Part IV

$$=\!=\!=$$

TYAZHELYI / HEAVIES

42

Moscow / Saint Petersburg

FOUR DAYS AFTER SHE RETURNED FROM SWITZERLAND, ANNA DROVE to Yasenevo for debriefings. With the Fifth Department on the intelligence produced by her asset in Geneva and the ops plan for the case going forward. With Maximov on her father. With Grigory and the Line OT techies in the outbuilding where it had all begun, to officially close out the unofficial operation against Sia Fox. Documents were run through the acid-boosted shredders. Computers and phones were wiped. Equipment was boxed up. She said good night to Grigory well into the evening, explaining that she would close everything down. She made tea and sat in her office, sipping on her third cup, when at last she knew she was alone.

Grigory had ferried the surveillance equipment from RusFarm in black plastic cases and cardboard liquor boxes. Most of it had been stashed in his musty office, where it awaited return to Line OT inventory. Would Grigory raise a fuss over a few missing items? She thought not. Equipment broke or went missing all the time. She cracked open the door to his office. The boxes were in a corner.

She had paid scant attention to the equipment earlier because she trusted Grigory, and the surveillance piece of the op was simple. After all, they'd been operating at her family's farm inside the Rodina. But now she closely read the tags and descriptions affixed to the boxes and cases. She pushed past boxes of cameras that required electrical work—she would not have time to run wires or drill holes. Move. She came to one with more promising labels noting the models and quantities.

XRV-22-A—(15)

Pinhead cameras with an adhesive suitable for most surfaces (wood, marble, stone, plastic, aluminum, steel, etc.). Battery life: twenty-four to thirty-six hours.

PLM-1700—(6)

Small drives connected to a tangle of cords that gave them the appearance of jellyfish. The 1700 could be connected to phones and laptops to receive data from the cameras. She had used these before.

This would do. Move.

The bar of light seeping through the doorway illuminated her work. She stuffed four pinhead cameras and one of the jellyfish drives into her purse. Move. Over the tired, chipping floors. Out into the blustery cold, along the paths toward the parking lot. The pines creaked in the wind. The power plant hummed and belched exhaust. If they ask, I will tell them the truth. Move. As she walked, for some reason she fantasized about fleeing Russia with Luka. What would he say if she asked? He would say yes, she knew. She could not bring herself to think, much less say, why that was. She shoved it down to focus on her lines. On the theater. I am keeping an eye on my husband, she told herself, trudging through dirty snow toward a far row in Yasenevo's southeastern parking lot. Move.

ANNA STARED INTO THE SAFE IN HER OSTOZHENKA APARTMENT AND the phone and the laptop stared right back. Six missed calls from Luka, including two voice mails. She wanted to call him back, but she knew if she saw him, she would tell him what she was planning to do and then it would all be ruined. She was also feeling self-destructive and petty and thought that because the connection with him was so beautiful, she might strangle it a bit. See if it survives. She chucked the phone back into the safe.

The laptop. Moving quickly, making a mistake only once in the keyboard sequence, she opened the clancomm partition and sent a series of memorized phone numbers and addresses to Sia and the woman calling herself Lulu. Anna had gleaned them from a Kremlin directory Maximov had provided without too many questions. The women are CIA, a voice said. Quiet, for god's sake, she told the voice. I need quiet.

She applied lipstick, smacking bright red lips at her own reflection. She unzipped her cosmetics bag to make sure the necessary pill was still inside. She checked again that Grigory's equipment was snug in her suitcase. She picked up the box with the horse figurine Lulu had provided and wondered what the hell this was. Her lizard brain told her to smash it, but instead it went into the bag.

She wandered into the living room and calmly phoned Vadim, as if two weeks earlier he had not beaten her to a pulp. She did not think about that night now—instead she forced herself to remember a few of the pleasant memories. Newlywed vacations to Paris and the Black Sea when they had been fools and believed that in time the sharp edges of their marriage would soften. As the phone rang, she recalled a few instances of pleasant lovemaking with him. Paris: curtains billowing in a hotel room near the Pantheon, breeze on her sweaty skin. She fastened her mind into that memory.

"Anya," he said with surprise. "How are you?"

"I am well. I am calling because I have been thinking about things. Thinking about everything, really. And I don't want to discuss what happened. Not a word. I was angry about Papa. I said hurtful things because I was angry. I am coming to Piter today. I will be in the office for a bit. Then I thought we could have dinner. Palkin, maybe? We could just talk."

THE DAY WAS FRIGID BUT BRIGHT, THE PITER SKY CLEAR AND BLUE, SO Anna walked to Rossiya from the Moskovsky train station. She overshot

the bank to stroll south for a few blocks along the Neva, snow-covered
and fretted with ice, and stopped to watch the palace drawbridge rising.
The large white, blue, and red z painted on the bottom heaved skyward.
The war, it seemed, had conscripted even the undersides of bridges.
Anna crinkled her nose, stuffed her hands in her coat, and marched back
east, toward the bank, an elephantine neoclassical on Rastrelli Square.
Arriving, she scudded her case around the square, working up the courage. Anna looked up at the white-blue towers of the cathedral, down at
the few ramshackle kiosks hawking fruit and magazines. Before the war,
the square would have teemed with tourists, sometimes even in winter.
Now there were shoddy kiosks decorated with portraits of fallen soldiers, unsalted walkways, and a gaggle of beggars and drunks sleeping
in boxes, snug against the cathedral to break the marine wind.

She marched into the bank. Heads poked out of the cubicles when she
strode into her office. Waving off her waifish secretary, she shut the door.

Anna wiped dust from the keyboard and booted up the computer.
She slid a table underneath the window facing Rastrelli. On it she
clumped two old candles from her desk, a painting of ice skaters on the
Neva—she'd no idea who'd put it in here; could be wired, for all she
knew—and Lulu's spooky horse figurine, rearing on its hind legs. She
pointed the raised forelegs toward the square, then picked it up to run
her fingers over the seam on its base. She returned it to the table and
lounged back in her chair, tapping her fingers slowly on the desk.

———

THAT EVENING IN THE KUTUZOV EMBANKMENT APARTMENT, ANNA
poured a glass of wine and wistfully strolled about as if touring a new
home, checking the placement of security cameras against their original locations. Had Vadim installed a new batch, or covered some of the
gaps? She'd seen the plans; it appeared that here he had not opted for
cameras hidden above the beds. There would be room for maneuver in
the master.

She started in the closet. One of her shoe racks was level with the
safe where he kept the laptop. She found a pair of black Jimmy Choos

that matched the color of the camera and put those on the rack facing the safe. She stuck one of the pinhead cameras on the left shoe. Sliding over a chair, she stood on her tiptoes and stuck one pinhead camera on a track light that pointed toward the desk in the bedroom. She put one more on a light illuminating the abstract painting hung above their—his—bed. It was garish, violent. Harsh reds spattered across a canvas crime scene. Tippy-toe on the chair, she put her head a few feet back from the track light. The camera was not visible.

"I am keeping an eye on my husband," she whispered aloud. "Because I am a jealous wife and he is sleeping around."

Jellyfish drive inserted, she'd opened her laptop to check the camera placements when she heard a noise. The door? Vadim home early? Maybe nothing. She shoved the laptop into her purse and walked into the living room. Through the kitchen, the bedrooms, downstairs. She even checked the front closet. I am losing it, she thought, there is no one here.

The cameras had already sent the files to the jellyfish drive connected to her laptop. Opening one, Anna was treated to a clear view of the bed. The other showed the desk. Quality was high, even when she zoomed in. She set the laptop on the desk and began typing a test email to herself. Vadim was a fast typist. She clacked the keys faster and faster until the test message was nonsense, a garble of letters and numbers. She hit send and saw it arrive. She went to the door to listen for Vadim. Silence. Back in the bedroom she saw that a new file had dropped onto the jellyfish drive. A video of her typing on the computer. She zoomed in and saw her hands on the keys. Anna practiced freezing the video when her fingers struck the keyboard, then zooming in to see which specific letters and numbers and symbols had been compressed. Satisfied, she put the laptop in her purse.

Anna slipped on a white satin dress and knee-high black suede boots. She wandered to the living room for a pleasant, sweeping view of the frozen Neva. She had not seen his face since he'd beaten her. Would she be able to control herself? Yes, she said, of course you will.

She double-checked her clutch for the bottle of aspirin containing a single pill that was not aspirin. And it was not her birth control. It was flunitrazepam. A roofie. She zippered her clutch and went into the living room in time to hear the bolt click. She waited in front of the wet bar like a Good Wife, greeting him with a broad smile as he entered the apartment. He carried a gigantic bouquet of roses. She did not like roses. His briefcase clunked onto the hardwood. She forced that smile to stay open, white teeth shining brightly for her dear husband.

"Anya, I am so sorry," he said.

She went to him, pressed a finger to his lips, and kissed his cheek. "They are beautiful," she said. "Get ready. I will give them water."

In the kitchen, Anna clipped the bottoms of the roses and plunged them into a crystal vase. She poured two cognacs, handing him one as he emerged from the bedroom. They clinked glasses.

"I need to do a little work before dinner," he said, distracted by something on his phone. He disappeared back into the bedroom with a kiss on her cheek. Anna stood by the picture windows looking at the river. His safe beeped. His keyboard clacked.

The bright sun on the glass reflected her thin, wicked smile.

———

AT PALKIN THEY DRANK MARTINIS AND LAUGHED IN THE HONEY GLOW of the bar. They had burrata with radish slices and crab with beetroot carpaccio and Beluga caviar. They sipped a beautiful Boerl & Kroff champagne. They had wild boar dumplings and talked about old trips, finishing a bottle of Bellefont-Belcier over ox goulash and a chateaubriand steak, and Anna told him all about the case and said she was sorry for everything. He put his hand on hers. They talked about taking a trip, maybe another frolic on the shores of the Black Sea?

Anna slipped the flunitrazepam into his wineglass when he went to the bathroom. When he returned she asked him about his question. "Last time we were here," she said, "you had one for me. What is it? Please, tell me."

He was drunk now, and her reminder sent a jolt of anger across his face. He gulped down his wine and seemed to stare at her for a long time. Thirty minutes until the drugs kick in, she thought. Maybe a bit less.

"I wanted to know why you will not have my children," he said.

She put her hand on his and shook her head. "I've been a little bitch," she said. "Angry. Fighting you instead of with you. Maybe we try a different way. Maybe we start tonight?"

"But you're . . ."

"I haven't taken them since Mexico," she lied.

"Anya, what has happened?"

"Let's go home," she said. "Tonight let's be husband and wife for a change."

VADIM PASSED OUT ON THE BEDROOM FLOOR. ANNA HAULED HIM ONTO the bed, stripped him naked, and heaped his clothes in a chair. His phone went on the nightstand.

It happened fast: Opening her laptop, finding the right files—watching them to note the passcodes, checking constantly to be sure he slept. Her breath was thin and shallow; each pull of air demanded conscious thought. Safe passcode first. Four numbers. His birthday. Easy. Then the laptop. Harder, a random string of letters and numbers and symbols. She had to watch the video several times and wrote it down on a piece of paper because it was too long to memorize quickly. He didn't use the biometrics, thank God.

She retrieved the pinhead cameras in the closet and on the track lights. The one on the painting would be a little tricky. She shimmied onto the bed, careful not to rock her drugged husband, and plucked it from the frame.

She slipped everything in her purse and put on a pair of nitrile gloves. Then she stood there, briefly debating putting this whole thing back in the box. She thought about Luka and running away. Then she remembered her husband beating her senseless. Chernov smashing

Papa's nose in the back of the paddywagon during the arrest. Move. She took the piece of paper with the password into the closet.

She opened the safe and took out the computer and punched in the password and got it wrong. Shit, she said. Shit. Shit. Shit. She tried again. It worked. Her fingers dripped sweat in the gloves. Anna noticed herself swallowing. Throat scratchy as hell. It was all she could think about. Swallow, damn it. Her fingers were swimming inside the gloves. Would water leak onto the keyboard? In the web browser, as agreed with Sia and Lulu in Switzerland, she typed "Maktoum" and "Godolphin" and "GQ." The article Sia had mentioned came up. She clicked into it, scrolling down until she found a pop-up banner that made her chest twist and tighten. A Clive Christian fragrance made with Russian coriander. "What do you buy for Vadim?" Sia had asked by the fire in the mountain lodge. Cologne, she had said finally. A thoughtless bottle of cologne every Christmas.

Anna's cursor hovered over the pop-up. Then she clicked it. To her, it sounded like a gunshot.

That's it, Lulu had said. Simple.

The browser took her to the Clive Christian page. For a few seconds she just stared at the screen. You did it, she thought. You actually fucking did it. She cleared the last hour's history, shut the browser, and locked the computer back in the safe.

My god, what have you done? She bit her lip and swept the thought from her brain.

Anna listened to Vadim snore for a few moments and reviewed his naked body. Maybe stop it here? Normally she wanted only distance from Vadim. But she couldn't hurt him from a distance.

Anna extinguished the lights. For a moment she stood by the door, her eyes adjusting to the dark. In the bathroom she grabbed a washcloth. She removed her shoes. Her dress. Her underwear. She slid onto the bed and took him in her hands and began tugging into the washcloth. She evaporated from this room, into the sky, the heavens, a world away. This arm and hand do not belong to me, she thought. They are someone else's.

When it was done Anna dredged the washcloth between her legs. This might be when you lose it, she thought, acid lapping at her throat, but she swallowed it back down. The cloth went into the sink for him to discover in the morning. Still naked, she slid next to him under the sheets, expecting sleep never to come. The loamy smell and feel of his skin at first drew threads of nausea up her windpipe. But sleep did arrive, rather quickly, and Anna's last conscious thought was that she felt none of the fear or guilt that she had expected. Instead, she felt peace.

43

Saint Petersburg / RusFarm

THE APARTMENT DOOR SIGHED SHUT. ANNA WAS ALONE IN THE BED, pressed onto the sticky spot that made her stomach turn. She made tea. There was a single text message from Vadim sent ten minutes earlier. A winky smiley face. Her jaw tightened. She deleted it. Opening the laptop she had brought back from Switzerland, she entered the clan-comm partition and messaged that the comms relay was in place, that she had clicked on the pop-up, and that she awaited further instruction.

On her second cup of tea, her phone rang. Unknown number. Ignoring it, she spread herself buns-down on a bed in one of the guest rooms and wondered how and when she would get back to her real work at SVR. Would she be able to? What if she just soldiered through, did her real job? There were cases to run in Switzerland, Greece, France. And let your papa rot? the loud voice asked. The unknown number called again. This time she took a sip of tea and answered.

"Anna Andreevna," the voice said, "do you remember me?"

Her stomach sank. The tea balled in her mouth. When she could swallow, she said, "I do, Lieutenant Colonel."

"I would like to speak with you, Anya. May I call you Anya?"

"We are speaking right now."

"Not like this. Meet me at your farm?"

"We are speaking now," she said again.

He tsk-tsked and laughed, soft but menacing. "No, no. Come see us at your farm. We are already here. Why don't you come now?"

"I can come later this evening."

"I see." A pause, a sniff, crackle of the phone shifting ears. "Now, Captain Kovalchuk"—goddamn him, Anna thought—"I'll tell you how it is. You are in Saint Petersburg right now. RusFarm is a two-hour drive. I am generous. I will give you three. Every hour beyond, I take a leg off this Mexican horse I know you've grown fond of. What is her name? Penelope?" Then the line went dead.

———

THERE WAS A SILLY FIGHT WITH VADIM'S FAT FUCKING DRIVER OVER the Mercedes fitted with the blue emergency lights before she tossed her purse into the car and got in and checked to make sure the lights were flashing and she tore from the underground garage with that thing wailing and baying, the winter tires slurping and sloshing through the snow and ice and she flew south along the Neva, the factories and dreary apartments cracking the leaden sky of this freezing fucking place that had devoured them all, running on and on forever and ever without end. On the 105 she steered with her knees while she lit a Dunhill and cracked the window to blow smoke into the whipping wind. She flew past cars, honking, cursing, as the concrete blocks and dun tenements and chuffing smokestacks thinned into the vast Russian forest of birch and pine, of low brown hills covered in snow that unrolled from this windshield into eternity. Maybe you kill him, she thought, tossing the butt from the cracked window and swerving—another near-fucking-miss!—to avoid a turtle of a car plodding along at only a few kilometers above the posted limit. Dammit! She mashed the horn as she sped by. But she wanted more than one death and she worried that on her own she could accomplish only the one.

———

AT THE RUSFARM GATEHOUSE, A SHAKEN SECURITY GUARD POINTED HER to the stables. Inside, Chernov was watching a wary groom brush Penelope outside her stall. The horse whinnied at Anna's approach. Then she saw Goose. The old man wore an *ushanka* and a Loro Piana puffer jacket.

Vadim had the same coat. It cost upwards of €10,000, she remembered. The headwear was a Prada take on the traditional Russian winter hat. Like most of them, they did not resemble devils. Chernov wore a dark blue suit under his greatcoat. His white shirt was pressed. His cologne smelled of citrus. His tie was knotted in a perfect full Windsor. What they looked like, she thought, was her papa. Businessmen.

Chernov smiled at her, offered a hand which she did not accept. Goose did not turn to face her. He was watching the groom brush Penelope. "I know so little about horses," he said. "But they are beautiful animals. Noble." He turned to her. "It is not so cold for the first week of December, and we brought our boots. Let's take a walk, eh?"

———

ALL SLIPPED FROM EITHER FLATS OR LOAFERS INTO BOOTS, AND FROM the stables they snaked down the muddy road away from the main house. She kept pace with Goose; Chernov hung a few steps behind. Anna swung open the gate into a pasture. Enough snow and grass in here, she said, we can avoid the mud. They walked into the field and Chernov shuttered the gate behind. A wind had picked up, beating down on the snowpack, blasting occasional bits of ice into her eyes.

"Since I took over the Security Council, I don't get up to Piter as much as I'd like," Goose said after a while, "but I miss it. I grew up in an old communal just a few blocks from Yusupov Palace. No lights in the halls, green-painted mailbox, just like everyone else. Your father and I, we went to the same school. Number two-eleven. Played hockey together, fought each other, chased the same girls. Ended up at the Higher School of the KGB in Moscow. Came back to Leningrad and served together. Hell, I've known Agapovs all my life." He came to a stop. "Has your father said much about me, child?"

"Enough, I suspect."

Goose turned back to the horizon with a smirk.

"I loved your mother, Anya. I was devastated when Andrei stole her away. But I don't begrudge him now. None of this is about Galina. It's business. You are a banker. You are other things, but you are also a

banker. You must understand this, child. It is business. And it is important business, for what is Russia now but a fortress under siege? We have
a special mission in this world. And we cannot accomplish that mission if
Russia sinks into itself or if its pieces are snapped off. The embrace of the
Rodina, I must admit, can be smothering. Chechnya, Belarus, Abkhazia,
South Ossetia, the Ukraine. It is not easy. My god, it is not easy to hold
together the Russian world. The only way this can be accomplished is
through strength and purification, my child. And that means that boyars
must be loyal. The center, our state, it demands resources in these trying times. We must grow, we must prevail, you see this, don't you? We
require your father's production lines for electronics, robotics, weapons,
for god's sake, to defend the Russian world. Your father helped consoli-
date the cash flows twenty years ago. He knows, my god he knows. He
sat with me in the Kremlin just before his arrest and I saw that he knows.
But he is stubborn. I see him in your eyes. You are both stubborn. Your
mother was stubborn. Beautiful and clever, but stubborn. The government required the gold, child. But your father is blind. Do you know
what he told me when I visited him in Butyrka? He said it was his. His,
Anya, my god, it is not his. All of this"—he gestured around the rolling
fields—"all of this is Russia's. It—"

She cut him off. "Vassily Platonovich," Anna said, "is Russia profiting
from my father's assets and businesses? Or are you?"

Goose's eyes sparkled. He shook his head at the ground. "But there
is no difference, my child. No difference at all. Do you not see this?"

They walked for several minutes in which only the wind spoke. She
stopped on the low rise where the horse had bucked Vadim, all those
years ago. "What do you want?"

He turned to her straight on, pulled his bony right hand from his
pocket, and held up two fingers.

"The same things I wanted from your father," he said. "You will sell
us Rossiya Industrial and his shares in the bank at a steep discount." He
put down one finger.

"You will sell us your properties. Moscow, Piter, this farm." Second
finger down.

A gust of wind tossed snow across her face. She wiped her eyes. "This is the end of my walk. I am an old man," he said, turning back.

"This is what the *khozyain* wants?" Anna called after him.

Goose turned to her with a smile. Behind him, Chernov was also smiling. "You should ask him yourself," Goose said.

She stared at the rim of the birch forest swaying and cracking in the wind. The temperature was falling quickly, along with the sun.

"What is your answer, child?" Goose asked.

"Let me have the rest of the walk to think," Anna said.

He threw up his hands and set off for the house. When they arrived, Goose walked past his armored Maybach and up the marble steps into the mansion. Anna trailed him through the foyer, where he tucked his *ushanka* under his arm, and then into the living room, Chernov on their heels like a loyal dog. Goose warmed himself by the fire. "Circulation is terrible," he said, rubbing his hands. They had both come inside wearing muddy boots. This bony old crow and his attack dog traipsing through here like animals. This is worse than the shakedown, Anna thought. This is disrespectful. I'm an understanding woman, but this is too much, even by the rules of our ghoulish little game. Goose scraped some mud on the hearth.

Facing the fire, scraping his other boot, Goose said, "I hear you don't like this place. That they razed the old house for this new castle. Most of us old-timers preferred our buildings destroyed. Don't care for the memories. You're lucky you had a place with sweet ones." He scanned the room, bemused. "Your answer, child."

"If I agree, what happens to my father?"

Goose hung his head, clicked his tongue. "The Prosecutor General will make his case. The judge will rule. It is in the hands of the law."

Anna laughed. My god, the law.

"Well, Vassily Platonovich," she said, "that is disappointing, because you make the law."

"Child, I do not think you understand what will happen if you refuse us."

"But I do know what happens if I agree."

Goose blinked, eyes darted to Chernov, back to Anna. "Really? I know that your father has told you to say no to me, I understand that you are in a difficult position. But he has given you the authority to speak for him while he is in prison. You should exercise that authority now. Use your good judgment, because after this we cease to ask, negotiate, or even prod. After this there is only punishment. Do you understand, child?"

Anna wasn't listening to him anymore; she was looking at the muddy tracks. She was hustling toward the foyer to usher them out. She opened the front door. Winter rushed in, but she did not feel it. Goose put on his *ushanka*, prattling on about Russia, about her father, about good sense, and she could hear none of it, she was just looking at the damn footprints and they were at the top of the marble stairs when she began sizing them up and Chernov was on the phone with someone talking about the stables and a gift, Goose muttering this is a mistake, child, don't be stupid, but she couldn't help herself, she thought about doing it to Goose himself but she worried he would quite literally die and then it would all be spoiled.

Instead, she twisted to the side and gave Chernov a quick, snappy kick to the back of his knee. He went down the marble stairs, rolling like a log, grunting once or twice when his head struck marble. He came to a stop next to Goose in a pile of dirty snow at the bottom of the steps. The old man looked at Chernov, then up at her in wonder. Chernov stood. He put a hand over a gash on his forehead. He looked at the blood on his fingers. He laughed. Those eyes, she thought. They are bright with joy.

"It is only a war if you have weapons and soldiers," Goose said. "And you, child, have neither. But if this is what you want. Well, then so be it. Punishment it is." The driver, eyes popping from his head, had opened one of the Maybach's rear doors. Goose disappeared into the car.

Chernov hobbled around to the other side of the vehicle. He smiled at her: broad, eager, childlike. Her violence had made him giddy. "There is a gift for you," he said. "In the stables."

———

SHE RAN. THE STABLES DOOR WAS OPEN TO THE WINTER. INSIDE SHE called out, but none of the grooms answered. She slid shut the door. The horses were making a terrible racket, whinnies and cries and those

haunting trumpeting roars, haunches banging against the stall doors.
A panic. The animals had seen something. This gift, whatever it was,
maybe just the presence of Chernov or his men. Something was wrong.

She jogged down the line, peering in each stall until at last she came to
Penelope's. The stall was empty. Then, through the door's yoke, she saw it.

On the stall floor was a long gift-wrapped box. About the length of
a horse's leg. Oh god, she thought, please, god, no.

Anna opened the stall door. Another horse made a ghastly trumpeting call, and she shook and fell to her knees by the box, wrapped trim
and tight in a thick, creamy paper bound by a bright red bow. There was
a small note slipped underneath. Another roar. She opened the note,
teeth chattering.

It was blank.

She turned over the cardstock. Maybe her vision was so watery
she could not see the words. But no, it was blank. She set it in the hay,
slipped off the bow, and began unwrapping the box. A thin streak of
blood painted the paper as she worked. Where had that come from?
One of her fingers was bleeding. She licked the cut. The finger shook
on her tongue.

She peeled the paper from the wooden box and stood, looking down,
for the first time letting sink in what she had done. Maybe you take it all
back. Maybe you apologize. Slink off and let them win.

The top of the box was nailed down. She grabbed a farrier's tool-
box from one of the cabinets. She was so shaky it clattered to the floor.
Tools spilled, the horses whinnied and neighed. She found a knife and
brought it back to the stall. She wedged the blade into the gap between
the wood and pried until it gave with a creak. She could barely breathe.
She levered again.

The top popped off.

She looked inside.

The box was empty.

Her knife fell into the hay, Anna close behind.

44

Palo Alto / Purcellville, Virginia

Persephone's intelligence and the haul from Vadim's computer gave structure to Procter's fever dream. A shapeless conspiracy now took on blessed form. She had accounts, names, addresses. She had ideas the rat-faced lawyers and the hypochondriac National Security Adviser could now accept or reject. Procter flew economy class (middle seat: five-foot clearance from the lav door) to pay a visit to the team in Palo Alto.

On her first night Procter treated them to the Cicis pizza buffet for a little morale-booster. George, the lead techie, used Snake's absence to lobby for the team's cryptonym. He made eye contact with each person, then gave Procter a solemn nod. "We want to call ourselves the TROJANs."

Procter almost spat out a marshmallow from her dessert pizza. "Like the condoms?" she said.

"No," George replied, flustered. "Like a Trojan horse."

"Because this is a grand deception," one of the techie chicks said. Nora. Was that her name?

"Guys," Procter said, "in the end the Trojans get fucked by the Greeks. Seriously?"

TROJANs. They insisted, and Procter let them have it, though she could not shake the rubbers from her mind. Snake went nuts when she told him. He said those damn nerds had been bugging him about it for weeks. Why was she mucking around in his shit? But that was the point. Have to keep the subordinates on their toes, Procter knew, got to occasionally flex some muscle, splurge on a pizza buffet, show them who's boss. Otherwise they come for your head like a French king.

LIKE ANY FLESH-AND-BLOOD SURVEILLANT, THE PAYLOAD DROPPED ON Vadim's computer had stalked its target to understand its pattern of life, vulnerabilities, and dark heart. A keystroke logger sent compressed files to the TROJANs each morning. They saw what he typed into a few of the business logs on the hard drive. They had passwords. They had search histories. The TROJANs accessed thousands of legal documents. Articles of organization and of incorporation. Diagrams of the shell corporations and corresponding accounts. Reams of correspondence with law firms. This mind-numbing shit, Procter told Bradley, is precisely what we want. Not a single account, not a single document, bore Putin's name. That would have been insane.

Nora, perhaps the smartest cookie in this freaky jar, in a single afternoon downed a case of Jolts and executed the operation's essential deception. The TROJANs had to mask their activities from Vadim while leaving threads that investigators would later pull. Nora built an image of Vadim's computer as it existed before the CIA had access. Now there were two computers with the same data: the laptop in Saint Petersburg and the image on Nora's in Palo Alto. Then Nora built a layer through which Vadim could not see. Vadim's activities would be visible to the TROJANs, but the layer ensured that Nora's were not visible to Vadim. When they were done, Nora would destroy the image on Vadim's computer, replacing it with her own.

Access established, The TROJANs began linking a false version of Vadim to the real world of cryptocurrency. Vadim (Nora) created a ProtonMail account to correspond with private brokers and to research the various crypto denominations: Bitcoin, Dogecoin, Ethereum. Nora had initially protested this task, saying, "Who the hell doesn't know all this stuff anyway?"

"Vadim's an establishment guy," Procter said. "He doesn't know shit about crypto. He's the white-shoe type. Probably dresses like our bros over here." She pointed at a dark-haired FINO guy draped in a tan suit.

Procter directed Nora to a private crypto trading shop in Hong Kong. Polycoin Investments. "You work with them for the trades," Procter said. "They've got connections to the big mining operations, and they broker deals for crypto's heavy hitters: big institutions, family offices, whales. Polycoin is your place."

The FINO bankers sniffed out the money. As the lawyers had made clear to her a hundred times, screwing around with bank accounts was some heavy shit, because basically every financial transaction in the Western world cleared overnight through New York. Treasury had gone ballistic in the initial interagency meetings, griping that Procter's beautiful ideas would wreck global faith in the dollar and the U.S. banking system. They'd struck a compromise: Procter couldn't steal as much as she liked, and CIA had to be damn certain from whom they stole.

Debman and two Moscow X linguists were stapled to the bankers. In the mornings, Procter brought doughnuts. Watermelon Pop-Tarts in the afternoons. The FINO guys tracked Putin's financial network on a whiteboard network map. Lines of all different colors and thicknesses spiderwebbed between the nodes. On the right side Snake taped a picture of Putin falling onto the ice during a hockey match. Above, Procter scrawled PERSEPHONE's word: *obschak.* Cashbox. The communal pot used by the criminal gang of the Russian president.

During a late-night briefing, Debman said they finally had what Procter wanted: They had uncovered what they believed to be $684 million of Putin's cash under Vadim's management. They had account numbers. They had log-in information for these accounts at more than a dozen banks. Nearly half was inside Russia, at Bank Rossiya itself. Hard to reach. Nora wrote code to automate the emails and transactions that would launch V-Day (Vadim Day). The final apocalypse, when the TROJANs would slip their Trojan horse into the Rodina's digital bloodstream.

Procter was growing increasingly paranoid about leaks, given the number of Hill staffers and White House flunkies read into the covert action program. She wrote her final pitch longhand on yellow legal paper in illegible handwriting, packed the paper in a lock bag, and gathered her suitcase from the old WeWork office where she'd been sleeping. She assembled the TROJANs and told them how proud she was. Then she flew to Virginia to see Bradley.

————

PROCTER LANDED AT DULLES, BUT SHE'D FORGOTTEN IT WAS SATURDAY, so Bradley asked her to come out to his Purcellville farmhouse. Two Security Protective Officers, SPOs, doubtless bored senseless and deep into cups of terrible coffee, sat idling in a black Suburban at the end of the driveway. Procter waved to them as she clipped by in her Prius. Angela Bradley let her in. She was a bit icy, even with that sexy drawl, and Procter figured that, what with the riding boots and pissed-off demeanor, her visit had probably deep-sixed a happy morning on horseback. Seeing as this op was about to career into the Christmas holiday, well, Procter figured this inconvenience would soon be the least of everyone's problems. Bradley emerged from the basement, nodded grimly to Angela as if he'd just run over their dog, then poured two cups of coffee and guided them down to his SCIF, which he called the Box. Bradley handed Procter a mug emblazoned with the logo of Embassy Damascus. Her first Chief job, two hundred dim years ago. They greeted the SPO manning the basement and Bradley punched them into the Box.

The Box was half of Ed's old basement, a converted living room where his daughters had once watched movies and made out with high school boyfriends. Now it was cloven in two. The half that was still a living room had a single La-Z-Boy recliner. The SCIF portion contained a desk, two chairs, a computer, feeds from the home's security system, and a secure phone. They sat facing each other, knees nearly touching.

"Bottom line is we have eyes on close to seven hundred million dollars of Putin's cash under management," Procter said. "PERSEPHONE has given us the information we need to leave bread crumbs framing a group of conspirators. The Moscow X analysts think it makes sense, jibes with the available reporting, not just the stream from PERSE-

PHONE." She handed him a piece of yellow paper with the names on it. He squinted, said he couldn't read a damn thing. Procter snatched it back and read aloud the names. There was Goose and a couple of his minions, she said, Vadim, a few colonels with units around Moscow, some higher-ups in the FSB.

Bradley repeated the names, slowly and quietly, as if worried he might jinx the op. He took a sip of coffee. "Who's Chernov?" he asked. "Haven't heard of him."

"Konstantin Konstantinovich Chernov," Procter said, "lieutenant colonel in the Internal Security Directorate. Former Vympel operator who does bad things for Goose. PERSEPHONE says he's a bad, bad boy. One of these Third Rome neofascists who swirl Russia, God, and themselves all together into one sicko goop. Lawyers should be fine with it."

Bradley nodded his assent. "Tell me the story of the conspiracy."

Procter did, blending the names, duped travel courtesy of the WINKELVOSS tool, financial transactions, and a CIA-fabricated exchange on a messaging app into a gorgeous alignment of circumstances that could point only to a conspiracy against Vladimir Putin carried out by a small group of elite Russians. The conspirators CIA would frame had money. They had the right connections inside the praetorians, the military, the security services. They had mostly grown up together in Piter. Putin would order arrests. He will be convinced—nay, forced—to shoot people in the back of the head, Procter concluded.

Bradley steepled his fingers and thought for a moment. "We will need to get authorization for lethal authorities on the others," he said. "We can't be clever about this. We do this, we probably get them all killed."

"Kind of the fucking point, no?" Procter said.

He scratched a stubbly cheek. Guy apparently planned to take it easy this weekend, unshaven and on horseback alongside his wife.

"How is the laundering side of this coming?" Bradley pivoted. He had also accepted the more accurate, criminal terms for what they were up to. The highly competent and thus wildly jumpy DOJ lawyers who had signed off on the new authorities did not. The lawyers called the theft an "involuntary withdrawal" and the crypto side a series of "financial catchments"—a slippery way of describing where the CIA would stash the money after stealing it.

"The laundering," Procter said, "is peachy. Harry has been going long on Bitcoin through a broker, Polycoin Investments, that he shadow-backs. Vadim, or rather our sock puppet version, is in discussions with said broker about buying up some big blocks. And Harry is duly beginning to signal that he might want to part with his coin. We're pulling strings on both sides of this deal, the brokers in the middle none the wiser, happy to collect their fat fees."

"How much has Harry committed so far?" Bradley asked.

"About two hundred million and counting."

Bradley whistled. "That man is a patriot."

"Indeed," Procter said. "But he's gonna get it all back. Unless the crypto Ponzi scheme collapses in the next few months."

"And we feel good about keeping him out of Russian gunsights when this is done?"

"Yes," Procter said. "The nerds are building our own mixer. Russkies will never know Harry was on the other end." Mixers obscured the path of cryptocurrencies from wallet to wallet. The sock puppet version of Vadim would purchase crypto from the Hong Kong brokers, Procter explained. The techies would send the coin through the mixers and then fracture it into dozens of wallets, all disconnected from the Internet. Poof. Gone. The Russian investigation would go cold in Hong Kong.

"How is the Tomb coming?" Bradley asked. They had nicknamed the terminal "catchment" the Tomb. The final resting place for Putin's money.

Procter held up a flat black box about the size of a cell phone: it was an air-gapped cold storage crypto wallet. A smile crept across Bradley's face. "What the hell should we do with it when we finish?"

"What do the lawyers think?" Procter said.

"They are still arguing."

"My vote is that I keep it," Procter said. "I'm an underpaid civil servant."

Angela knocked on the SCIF door and said she was going out, might be back late. He said I love you, hon. No response. Bradley shook his head, muttered. Drank more coffee. Checked his watch. "What else?"

"Angela's gone, man. You've got the whole day with your old friend Artemis." She tried a grin.

He stood, stretched, told her that she should get the hell out of here.

"You know, Artemis," Bradley said as they walked upstairs, "you're starting to think like a Russian. This is easily the most conspiratorial thing I've worked in almost thirty years. Impressive."

"Thanks Ed," she said. "Means the world coming from you."

45

Moscow

ANNA WAITED FOR THE LIGHT TO CHANGE. SHE WORE A BALENCIAGA *dubylonka* lined with mink and she'd bought the lacy black lingerie thinking about him. She stood on the corner with a sturdy middle-aged woman who managed a thin smile at Anna, the Z pin on her lapel twinkling in the bright winter sun. The light changed. Anna marched across the street, leaving the woman behind. Winding off the boulevard into the warren of old twisting lanes and alleyways, toward the Street of All-Holidays, Anna neared the end of her route. She felt sure that no one followed.

She turned a corner—quite provocatively, hanging for a fluttering moment to check her tail—and entered a cozy park a few blocks from her apartment. And there it was.

She stopped. And looked up at his blue eyes.

Three stories tall, background bright blue, President Vladimir V. Putin towered in the background, saluting three soldiers in the foreground raising the Russian flag over Mariupol, shattered, of course, as all Russians were damn well told, by the neo-Nazis during their retreat from the city. She gritted her teeth. She'd heard of the Ministry of Culture's campaign, but it had been months since she had entered the neighborhood from this direction, and she did not know they'd painted one so close to her apartment. Anna looked at Putin, who looked right back. She would not come this way again. She trod through the park, cutting through the shoveled paths, listening to children playing and laughing because they didn't understand the world.

In her apartment she set the gift-wrapped chessboard on the table. She had begun to suspect that Chernov and his team had put cameras or microphones in her Ostozhenka apartment. She was more comfortable firing up this laptop from here, usually in the closet. She shut the door, flicked on the light, and sat on the floor. Entering the keyboard sequence, she pulled down a message from Sia.

1. OUR CUSTOMERS SEND THEIR REGARDS FOR THE ADDRESSES, SELECTORS, AND PERSONAL INFORMATION YOU HAVE PROVIDED. THANK YOU.
2. OUR ANALYSTS REQUEST YOUR REACTION AND COMMENTS ON THE DRAFT REF EXCHANGE AND THE DESIGNATED LOCATIONS FOR MEETINGS.
3. IN RESPONSE TO YOUR QUESTION REGARDING THE SECURITY MEASURES DEPLOYED ON YOUR HUSBAND'S LAPTOP; OUR ANALYSTS BELIEVE THAT SPYWARE—LIKELY IMPLANTED BY FSB—PROVIDES DATA ON TRANSACTIONS, ETC. ONCE OPERATION BEGINS, WE EXPECT FSB TO REPORT DISCREPANCIES, TRIGGERING ACTION.
4. WE WOULD LIKE TO PLAN FOR STEPS AFTER OPERATION CONCLUDES, INCLUDING FOR YOUR PHYSICAL SAFETY. ARE YOU ABLE TO TRAVEL AGAIN IN COMING WEEKS? IF SO PLEASE OFFER DATES AND LOCATION AND WE WILL SET IN MOTION.

The attached message included a fictional exchange between a group of coup plotters. They were, according to the context statement, arranging a meeting at a villa owned by one of Goose's childhood friends, a well-known painter who was now fabulously and inexplicably wealthy. Anna read the exchange, thought it looked pretty good. A native Russian speaker had obviously drafted it. She made a few suggested edits and then began pondering travel. The confrontation with Goose and Chernov had her on edge. If she left, might they revoke her passport, block her from returning home? Doubtful. Especially if she traveled on SVR business. But how could one know? She typed her response, noting she

312 – *David McCloskey*

would send a message soon with dates and locations. She finished her cable with a question: When will you start the operation? She shoved the computer in a closet drawer, changed, and spread herself across the bed.

In the nights since she had kicked Chernov down the stairs, since she had found that damn empty box in the RusFarm stables only to glimpse Penelope trotting through one of the snowy pastures minutes later, she would lie on the bed at night, sleep a distant memory, considering the moves and countermoves as if this were a great game of chess. She could get about five moves ahead before the scenarios dissolved to muddled speculation. How to best Goose and Chernov and still hold her dignity, her life, whatever remained of her future? How to win? Because you must win. In the games, winning was a single outcome. In life, it was whatever you decided winning might be.

But her mind's eye had mercifully granted Anna a vision of victory, and its beauty gave her confidence in the terrible risks taken to make it this far. She was in the middle game, she knew, decisions had been made that could not be taken back. But there were always choices, always alternative paths. In dark moments she would flicker between killing them herself and just getting into a car with Luka and driving out of the Rodina. Gone, leave it all behind except him. But, twisting fretfully in her bedsheets, the moves and countermoves running through her mind, those two options always led to darker places. She died quickly, badly, inside Russia. She died slowly, badly, outside Russia. Her father died in a prison camp. She always lost Luka. Sometimes he was shot, sometimes he would disappear. Those were painful thoughts. She was angry with herself for loving him. It made the games more complicated.

And then, in her lovely apartment, sprawled across her bed, an unsettling sensation ruptured her daydream. Little curls of energy were running along her spine.

She had known the feeling since the Academy. Her world narrowed to the dust dancing through slanting afternoon sunlight, her tongue polishing the skin of her teeth. In the kitchen she boiled water for tea, using the angles to scan a few of the apartment windows across the courtyard. They looked empty, but they would not be so stupid as to be caught like that. She walked into the living room, steeping the tea bag, pacing over the furry rug in front of the fireplace. The feel of it conjured thoughts of sweat and swelling pleasure and drinking beer with him in the come-down, Luka's face a little flushed from the heat of the work. Now she looked down at her toes wiggling in the rug and took a sip of tea and the hairs on her neck and arms stood soldier-straight and she let her mind consider the awful prospect that they knew of this place.

Of Luka.

Her mind swam, it could not focus or process much, but she knew that all must appear normal to them. Bad things happened when surveillance teams knew that you knew. She checked her watch, tried to visualize a route to Jean Martel that would let her check for surveillance. But there was not enough distance or time to really know. They certainly had her comms, but did they have the second phone? Did they have the laptop? Who were Sia and Lulu, she wondered, did they work for Goose? The full-tilt paranoia knocked her mind from orbit. Anna slid on her coat, collected her purse with the gift-wrapped chessboard, and left the apartment.

She was going to apologize tonight. Give him the board at Jean Martel—*I bought it at GUM, at the same counter where we met*, she planned to say—then back at the apartment she would let him unwrap her from the lingerie and sit on him by the fire until they could not be closer. When it was done, she would recline on that fur, naked and pleasantly sweaty, beer on her lips, and she would ask to visit his apartment and meet a few of his friends. He had offered many times, of course, but she'd said no, for god's sake, the rules Luka, the rules, and he would always smile kindly, but sadly, and let it go.

Now Anna was only afraid.

She walked quickly, over snowy, hardscrabble *plitki* sidewalks. The stones cracked, rose, fell in chaos, no more money in the city budget to fix them each spring. Two times she nearly tripped. Though her head faced forward her eyes spun in all directions, checking peripherals for quick movement, for the screech of brakes, for vehicles parked with their wheels angled out into the streets. The walk was not long. She saw,

314 – David McCloskey

heard nothing strange. That meant nothing, it meant everything. But that damn tingle, it stayed, zipping along her back. The biology scratching at something your mind will soon know.

At Jean Martel she looked the barman straight on and tried to smile pleasantly.

"The usual?" he asked.

"Yes," she said. "And I'm sorry. About last time."

He put up a hand, turned, and took a bottle from the shelf. From a lower cabinet he collected a plate, blew off the dust, and shuffled to the refrigerator. He put a lemon on the plate, jabbed a knife into it, and slid it across to her. He gripped the bar with two meaty hands and lowered his head.

"Thank you," Anna said, "thank you."

She arranged the cognac, lemon, and glasses on their table and tossed her coat on a chair. She spread the gift on the table, and when she sat down she was sweating and twisting a blond curl of hair in agitation. She checked her watch, slid her hand on the bottle, jerked it back. The barman brought black bread. She tried a bite, but swallowing was a challenge. She pushed it away. Checked her watch again. He was late. Not strange, she told herself, sometimes Luka is late. He was late last time.

She waited. A few drunks stumbled in and took up residence at the bar. Next time she glanced over, one had his head on the counter. The other was arguing with the barman. Had she seen them before?

She called Luka. No answer.

She could think of little other than how sweaty she had become. Sweaty and cold. She was shivering. She slipped on the coat, looked at the gift, felt suddenly enveloped by a wave of despair so deep and dark that it felt like all that remained of her.

She called Luka again. No answer. This time she left a message asking him to please call her back.

At the bar the drunks had traded places. The one who had been asleep now argued with the barman. His companion had slumped over.

Maybe a smoke to clear my head.

Outside, she sat on the bench and lit a Dunhill with shivering fingers. The courtyard was quiet. Lights flicked on as night gathered over Moscow. In one window she saw the twinkle of a New Year tree. She burned down three cigarettes in quick pleasureless agitation. Sirens bayed in the distance.

Anna returned to her table. Both drunks were now arguing with the barman. A couple at one of the corner tables picked at plates of herring and black bread. The man looked at her funny, she thought. Maybe. Running a finger over her upper lip, she noticed that it glistened with sweat. She wiped it on her coat.

She called Luka again. No answer. Checked her watch.

She slipped the gift and the cognac in her purse and pushed past the drunks to pay the barman. "If he comes by, tell him I'm at the apartment," she said.

"I will," he said. He looked her over with concern. "Are you all right?"

"I'm just fine."

"He stand you up?"

"I don't know."

Into the winter night, the sirens still wailing. Louder as she walked toward the apartment. She stumbled on a wavy rise of mangled *plitki*, breaking her fall with her hands before tumbling into a pile of black snow. The contents of her purse slipped into frozen mud. She examined the chessboard. The paper had torn. Half the bow was caked in mud. She wiped it with her sleeve but it just smeared the paper. She cursed again. More sirens. A passerby looked down at her, frowned, and kept on walking. Anna stuffed the chessboard halfway into her purse, yanked the cognac bottle from the snow, and righted it on a pavestone between her legs. Still seated, she fished her phone from the purse and called him again.

No answer.

She stood, cursing, and threw the cognac bottle into the street, but it didn't break. She went into the road and put up her hand for an oncoming car to stop, but it honked, its headlights flickered, and she jumped to the side at the last minute and screamed as it sped off. Then she picked up the cognac and smashed the bottle properly. An old woman on the sidewalk shook her head as if saying damn drunk kids. Anna's shoes crackled over broken glass and she pulled her purse tight into her body and left the woman behind.

She smelled the smoke just before she turned onto the Street of All-Holidays. Blue and red lights were dancing on a patch of ice in the road, on the windshield of a parked car, in the darkened windows of the corner building.

Around the corner she saw fire trucks, and acrid smoke invaded her nostrils. Not woodsmoke. Evil, chemical smoke. Flames escaped from the windows.

My windows.

A thick plume of smoke rose above her apartment.

She ran to the trucks.

The hoses were streaming into the neighboring apartments. She may have blacked out for a moment, because when she could again think she was arguing with one of the firemen and there were two more standing around. She had the creeping sense she'd hit one of them, because he was rubbing his jaw and muttering that she was nuts. "The fire was too big, too hot, we got here too late," he kept saying. "No one is inside. We cannot save your apartment. We must keep the flames from spreading."

They probably thought she was drunk. Cognac was splattered on her shoes and pants, she was wild-eyed, there was a battered gift tied with a muddy bow peeking from her dirty purse. They left her alone. Firefighters moved here and there, trucks came and went, thin crowds gathered and dispersed.

Her apartment burned for a long time.

When the flames were embers and the mansion was at last a blackened husk, she turned to see an old, stooped man standing beside her reviewing the dead house. He wore a black greatcoat and a ratty *ushanka* and round eyeglasses with wire frames. He looked like he had escaped from a photograph of Stalingrad. He gripped a long package under his arm.

"Was it your house?" he asked.

"Yes," she said.

His eyes sparkled behind the thick eyeglasses, tongue wetting his lips.

The package, she thought, was about the length of the box they'd left in the RusFarm stable. Maybe shorter, it was hard to tell in the dark. His energy made her want to run away. She felt like the poor horses trapped in her stables.

Something dripped from the corner of the package. Another drop plopped to the ground. *Drip, drip, drip.* Red spatter on the snow. Had this man been in her stables?

He pressed the package into her hands, blood dripping from the corner, wetting her mittens. She now noticed how short he was, shorter than even her, because he had to shove the package up to meet her arms. He was licking his lips, forcing the wet paper against her body, tongue sticking out a bit, his eyes bright with concentration. Sopping package in hand, she retreated a step.

"Chernov sent me," he said, "to tell you this: There was a sacrifice. And it went badly, Anya. It went badly because you did not listen. Sometimes the sacrifices are sweet, sometimes Russia is merciful, but not always. Not always, poor dears. And sometimes there is a message in the sacrifice, but this time there is not. The message in this one is only punishment."

Then he straightened his glasses, turned, and walked off.

———

ANNA DID NOT KNOW HOW MANY TIMES SHE FELL ON THE WALK BACK to Ostozhenka, but at some point she'd busted her lip and bruised a cheek on the ice. When she opened her apartment, she half expected to see the little old devil there. She shut the door behind her and scanned, a few blocks of light shimmering through the picture windows into the well of shadows that was her living room. At least it felt empty. Her breathing was staccato.

She slumped to the floor and began unwrapping the package. Had those animals butchered Penelope? This is probably what shock feels like, because things are just happening and I can process nothing. She was only floating, she could not think, she barely knew where she was. She pulled back the paper.

The skin on this horse is white.

This is human skin.

A human arm.

Luka's arm.

———

AFTER SHE HAD VOMITED, AFTER SHE WEPT, AFTER SHE TURNED OVER the bookshelves and smashed the coffee table to bits and ripped the sterile pictures from the wall and kicked holes in the plaster, Anna went to the bedroom and sat in a chair for the rest of the night, her chilly blue eyes shining with hate.

46

Moscow / The road to RusFarm

WHEN MORNING CAME, SHE ENTOMBED LUKA'S ARM IN PLASTIC wrap and set it on ice in the tub. She then covered the tub in plastic wrap and closed the bathroom door and stuffed nitrile gloves into the crack to hem in any smells. She was not sure what else to do. Chernov's men have this apartment wired, she thought. They will deal with it. She scrubbed the tile in the entryway where she had dropped the package the night before. She did not want to leave Luka's blood out on the floor like that.

In the guest bathroom she took a shower to clean the blood from her hands and split lip. She applied makeup, careful to cover the bruise on her cheek, and dressed in clean clothes.

From her closet safe she pulled an envelope stuffed with euros. Selecting another purse from her closet, she went out and rode the metro to Moscow State University. She walked the campus and surrounding neighborhoods for several hours, until she had convinced herself they had not bothered to put physical surveillance on her. They had her phone covered, of course, along with the apartment, and they'd probably beaconed her car. They knew where she was—why bother following her?

Skirting through crowds, Anna searched for the right profile: young, a student, not obviously wealthy, meek, intelligent, impressionable eyes. Outside a lecture hall Anna sidled up alongside a young woman in a white *dublyonka* who could not have been more than twenty. She smiled brightly, and in a firm voice said, "Hi. Are you running off to class?"

"In a few minutes," said the young woman, surprised. She stopped walking and her eyes narrowed. "Do I know you?"

Anna shook her head. "I've left my phone in my apartment. Could you help me?"

"Okay, sure." The woman began fumbling through her purse.

Anna gently, but with authority, placed her hand on the woman's arm. "Could you buy one for me?"

Now the woman was frightened. Her arm did not move; it was still stuck halfway into the purse.

Anna deftly slipped the envelope of cash from her coat pocket into the woman's opened purse. Her eyes said: *Look.*

The woman cracked open the envelope. Her eyes widened at the cash: just over two thousand euros. She looked afraid and excited, in equal measure.

"Buy me a phone?" Anna asked. "Not an iPhone. Garbage reception and all. You know how it goes. Maybe an old Nokia? Not a smartphone. One that flips open. You keep the change."

"I keep the change," the woman repeated. She was biting her lip.

"Yes. And in return for keeping the change," Anna continued, "after you buy the phone you will take it apart: SIM card, battery, all of it. Take it apart outside the shop and put all the pieces in the bag. Then you bring it back to me. Do you understand?"

"Yes."

"You know an electronics store around here?"

"There is one down near Leninsky. A short walk."

"You can still make your class?"

The girl checked the time on her phone. She nodded.

"Well," Anna said, "what do you think?"

The poor girl's teeth had almost slid through her lower lip. "Bring it back to you here?"

Anna shook her head. "No. There is a little alley behind the building across the square." She nudged her head. "Bring it there. And one more thing—make sure it's got at least a few minutes of charge before you leave the store."

For twenty minutes Anna stomped around the campus checking for physical surveillants; finding none, she met the girl in the alley and accepted the bag with the pieces of the phone.

Returning to the garage below her apartment, she collected her Range Rover and drove north out of Moscow. After an hour, deep in the endless Russian woods, she pulled the car to the side of the road. Her iPhone went into the glove box. Checking to be sure no one was around, she took the bag with the Nokia parts and tramped into the forest. After ten minutes she came to a small clearing. She assembled the phone, then dialed a number she had memorized with Sia in Switzerland. Not a permanent solution, but the laptop was gone, destroyed in the fire.

As expected, no one answered. A Russian voice said that KLP Shipping Solutions regretted that they had missed her call, but please leave a message and an associate would call back promptly. In her message, Anna explained that there had been problems with the shipments, she would be unable to travel to see customers to deal with those problems, and that she wished she had a better way to speak to the fine people at KLP Shipping Solutions but there had been an unfortunate accident. This was all she had right now. She explained that a visit from friends might be helpful to rectify the communications issue. She said she would not have this number much longer. Perhaps no more than thirty minutes. She hung up. She dusted snow off a log and sat, staring into the trees.

Fifteen minutes later a man called back and said his name was Anatoly. He asked if Anna would have this number going forward. She said no.

"Might we use your bank email?" he asked.

"I don't think so," she said. "Technical problems."

"I see," Anatoly said. A pause. "You are going to where, exactly?"

"The farm."

"I see."

"I want to see her," Anna said. "Understand? Tell me you understand, Anatoly."

"I understand."

"They should come in as soon as they can," Anna said. "They bring equipment. But most of all they bring her. I want to look her in the eyes and ask a few questions. If they land at Pulkovo I can probably arrange things. She should come with him, otherwise it will look odd. They come with good news about a horse, a sale. They can think of something."

"Maybe you travel out to see us?" he offered.

"No," she hissed. "Fuck. I told you, I cannot. Not now. Tell me you understand."

"I understand."

She hung up. She took the phone apart, put the components in the bag, and trudged back to her car.

Outside Kirishi, Anna stopped at a gas station and took the Nokia into the bathroom. She checked the stalls to be sure she was alone. She smashed the phone to bits, stopping only to flush pieces down the toilet.

When it was done, she continued onward. To RusFarm.

47

Langley

PERSEPHONE'S EMERGENCY SIGNAL WHIPPED UP A FEEDING FRENZY on the CIA's Seventh Floor: everyone wanted a bite. Procter had fought to keep crowds small, but the Director's appetite had been whetted, and when the Director got a taste, that meant meetings, the kind where gobs of useless deskhumpers would materialize so they could take notes and share those notes back with their component organizations on email distro lists so broad they probably included the green-jacketed contractors who watched over the uncleared maintenance crews working on the toilets.

That's what's happening, Ed, Procter shouted into the phone when she saw the list for the Director's Russia update, freaking toilet guys going to get this intel. We'll have PERSEPHONE's true name splashed in the papers by the time I'm done throwing up after the meeting. And it'll be in disgust, Ed. I'll be vomiting in righteous disgust. This meeting is a fleshpile, Ed, pure and simple. Gotta trim this list to me, you, maybe the Director. We gotta make this like the powwows in the spy flicks where there are three people involved in the operation, tops.

Bradley had hung up on her.

Now Procter stood in the Seventh Floor hallway outside the Director's conference room. There was a pack of about twenty people waiting for the door to open. The afternoon Counterterrorism update was running long.

It was Bradley who finally swung open the door. "Director can't make it," he said. "I'm running this one. Everyone come in."

Procter commandeered a seat beside him. The hallway crowd spilled into the windowless room, filling the oversized leather chairs at the long table and the mismatched backbench chairs ringing the walls. An analyst—at the table! the goddamn nerve—pulled talking points from a folder as if someone had asked for a lousy Russia briefing. The wall behind Bradley's seat was clotted by clocks, but unlike most at headquarters, in the Director's conference room the red block numbers were perfectly synchronized.

Before Bradley could open his mouth, Artemis Aphrodite Procter began an unsolicited address. There would be no meeting minutes, she said, no transcript. One Moscow X analyst, backbenching in the corner and out of her view, did manage to scribble a few notes, but he soon became too frightened to distribute them later. Had he done so, his teammates would have been treated to a speech promising bodily, occupational, emotional, psychological, and spiritual harm to anyone who so much as repeated a word of this discussion. When she had finished, Bradley opened the meeting and asked Procter to set the scene.

Procter started with PERSEPHONE's emergency signal through the cutout. And you know what? I buy it, she said. Girl's been producing, she's crossed plenty of lines, we've got a pretty clean poly, and, further, she's actually listening to us. An unwitting support asset, pretending to be a tourist in Rastrelli Square, snapped a photo of the horse figurine in PERSEPHONE's office at the bank. Statue does nothing, of course. It's hollow. But it's a test, and she passed. She did what I asked her to do in Switzerland. The techies have confirmed that her clancomm is not active, so the emergency signal makes sense.

Of course, it is always possible that she's been found out, Procter conceded. That paunchy, sweaty FSB troglodytes are on the other side of these comms, but then, she mused, why go through the trouble of breaking the clancomm and using the cutout? Seems unnecessary. We've also got a recording of PERSEPHONE's call for help. OMS voice

intonation specialist says she sounds more angry than fearful, which I
say is a mark against hostile control.

"Fine, Artemis," Bradley said. "Let's say we buy PERSEPHONE.
But what do we gain from sending one or both of our officers back inside
right now? We've got a lot to lose—just like the first time—but now, with
the Russian delivering, what's the rush? Dropping a computer inside
Russia is no cakewalk, but we could eventually get PERSEPHONE a
new laptop without exposing your people again."

There are, Procter said, a few problems with the wait-and-see view.
One is that PERSEPHONE is a necessary cog in this operation; in fact,
Procter said, she is the primary cog. Her intel makes it possible, and
we've got to be in real-time communications with her when we start
because we need to know how it's landing or if we need to adjust things.
The second, and larger, problem with the wait-and-see option is that it
leaves PERSEPHONE high and dry. There is a mushy emotional component here, Procter insisted. Can't be denied. We've got an asset on
the ground inside Russia who's been delivering, and she wants to know
if our moves are going to wreck her life. And we've got people who can
travel into Russia. In fact, we've got platforms designed for such travel.

We owe it to PERSEPHONE, Procter said, to give it a shot. And
with that she nodded at Bradley to signal she was done.

Bradley thought for a moment, hands clasped, head turned to the
ceiling. "I am not saying yes or no today. I want to meet the NOCs," he
said, turning to Procter. "Make that happen."

48

San Cristobal

MAX WATCHED A NERVOUS YEARLING COLT DEFECATE IN THE SAND. He was thronged by American bloodstock agents and advisers, all scattered around the ring at San Cristobal to review the horseflesh he'd opted to withhold from the Kentucky sales for this private auction. A groom led a chestnut-brown yearling into the ring. Max flipped open the sales book and his trainer started in with the pitch. Pedigree, then conformation: the legs, the muscle definition, bone structure, length of the neck in relation to the head. Max liked the symmetry in the legs. The agents scribbled furiously in their notebooks.

A bay colt trotted in. He already had a name: Mr. Octopus. Max waved one of his trainers over to speak with a few of the agents.

Max kicked the dirt, damp from a weak rain earlier that morning. The sight of his staff, these yearlings, the mist hanging over his ancestral land—it had him worried. He'd not felt peace since returning to San Cristobal. Sleep had been fitful, his chest screwed tight. Life felt more fragile, as though a great storm had been slowly gathering around his world, and he now, at last, saw with frightening clarity the black bank of thunderclouds rolling toward his farm. Another colt walked into the ring with a nice long stride. Beautiful, he thought, noble.

Since the day he'd been let in on the family secret, Max had been groomed to regard San Cristobal and CIA as mutual partners. What was good for one was good for the other. The little jolts of adrenaline from leading CIA to a scalp or jamming a spooky drive in a target's computer were rewards for service, not only to Langley, but to San Cristobal itself.

But Sia's treatment at RusFarm had given him a foretaste of what determined Russians might do when backed into a corner—and it made him ponder if this operation was no longer an adrenaline payout in service of CIA and his farm. If it was, instead, an invitation to the butcher's block. The way out, he knew, was simple: Say no, I'm done. CIA would not stop him.

At dinner, Max listened to the agents tell stories. About boats, cars, villas, guns, furs, watches, hookers, skydiving, coke, heroin. Jokes landed with the subtlety of bodies on the pavement. In the middle of a winding tale concerning the drunken hunt of an Alaskan grizzly bear, Max held up a shivering phone and apologized to his guests. Some business to deal with, he announced, I'll see you in the morning.

———

MAX DRANK MESCAL AND CHECKED FOR MESSAGES FROM PROCTER. There was just one, an urgent cable for him and Sia.

1. PERSEPHONE FLEW EMERGENCY SIGNAL ON 13 DECEMBER. IN HER CONVERSATION WITH CUTOUT, SHE REQUESTED URGENT FACE-TO-FACE MEETING AT RUSFARM, INDICATING SHE CANNOT TRAVEL OUTSIDE RUSSIA.

2. REQUEST PLANNING MEETING IN OPERATIONAL PREPARATORY FACILITY CATFISH ON AFTERNOON/EVENING OF 18 DECEMBER. CONFIRM ASAP. REGARDS.

He strolled aimlessly around the library with his drink. He leafed through the leather book with every horse and bloodline dating to San Cristobal's founding and considered what his father and grandfather would think of him. Silly, he thought, giving the ancestors a vote now. They'd lived, they'd made their choices, this was his patch of dirt. What would the old man even be able to say? He wondered about that. Then

Max extinguished the lights in the library and, slipping on his coat, made for the capilla. His father's living tomb.

For a few minutes he chatted with one of the staff, plump-faced Benito, on guard duty since his father's outburst during the Russian's visit. Benito lit a Marlboro, offering one to Max. Why not? That kind of night. They smoked in the quiet dark until a light flickered on from his father's second-floor bedroom. It was late, Max's brain swam in mescal. But he still went inside.

The old capilla's furnishings were young—he'd had it renovated for his father two years earlier—but it carried the scent of mothballs and dust and stale urine that clings to those in life's final tailspin. The past decorated the cottage: trinkets, family pictures, mementos of the old *hacendado*'s glories. Max could not bring himself to look at any of them. He bounded up the stairs. A single bar of light burst from the room onto the hallway floor. A sink was running. His father was singing.

> *De esos caballos*
> *Que vende usted*
> *Ninguno me gusta*
> *Coma el que se fue*

The words tugged at a thread sewn deep into the years, and Max was four, pretending he could shave alongside his father, the old man belting out kids' songs about horses.

> *Hágase pa'cá*
> *Hágase pa'llá*
> *Que mi caballito*
> *Te derribará*
> Come over here
> Come over there
> Because my little horse
> Will knock you down

Max stepped onto the patch of light. As a boy he had found the old man inaccessible; far-off and shuttered-in, quick to anger and slow to smile. As a man Max wished they'd had more time, more chances. Papa, he called, Papa, it's me, Maximiliano. He rapped a few times on the door and nudged it open. The old man poked a half-shaved face from the bathroom and smiled. Dollops of shaving cream plopped onto the floor.

"My son. Sit, sit."

Max eased onto the edge of the bed and watched the old man shave.

"I saw men walking the grounds with you today," his father said. "Who are they?"

It was the most in-the-flow question his father had asked in months. It was startling.

"Agents and consultants," Max said. "From Kentucky."

"Agency put you up to it?"

What was this? "No, this is part of the normal day-to-day. A private auction. I'm working something else with the Agency."

Clatter of the razor on porcelain, a rinse of the blade. "So, what's the Agency angle?" His father toweled off his face. Smacked on Aqua Velva. The faded bottle suggested the aftershave had been manufactured before Papa's mind wandered off. How long would this last? What should Max say? He didn't know; he just tried to keep it going.

"I'm targeting a guy who runs a horse operation for the Russian president. He also helps hide money. We were working him to get access to some of the money."

His father whistled. " 'Were working'?" he repeated. "Past tense."

"His wife was the better angle."

His father dried his hands and shrugged on a monogrammed robe. From his nightstand he collected his first edition of *El Complot Mongol*, a Mexico City crime noir. One of the old man's favorites. He sank into a cracked leather reading chair that had once graced Grandfather's study, slipped on his reading glasses, and opened the book to a seemingly random page. He whistled the last stanza of the old song while he read.

Come over here
Come over there
Because my little horse
Will knock you down

Was he gone? Just like that?

"Papa?"

The glaze that had been forming on his eyes seemed to thin. Glasses slid down his nose as he looked up. "Ah yes," he said, blinking and putting a finger into his ear, "the Russian. What are you going to do about him?"

"We think we've got a way to get to him."

"Good, good." A pause. "But who is the 'we'? You are not alone?"

"It's complicated."

He belly-laughed. It made Max smile; he could not remember his father laughing that way.

"I am an old man," his father said. "Where am I going? Tell me the story."

Max told him about Procter, Sia, Anna, Vadim. From the start to where he was now, which he hoped might be the end. He told his father his worries—for the farm, for his future.

"You know," his father said, "there was a time in the mid-eighties when we worried some of our ops in Saudi had blown us. Your grandfather and I had gotten access to a few royals, and CIA thought they might be on to us. We talked about what would happen. Would they approach Mexico City to investigate? Pay someone to burn the farm down? Let it all go? In the end it passed, but we had to think about the day when our little joint venture comes to light."

"What did you decide?"

The deep baritone laugh again. "Well, that was the problem. Never a good answer. Of course, the Agency would always arrange for accommodation in America, but we never wanted that. This is home. Nowhere to run. If anyone ever found this place, I decided that I would just sit on the porch with a gun and wait. Nothing else to be done, Maximiliano. We've made choices."

"Even so, I could bow out," Max said.

His father brushed the worn jacket of the novel with his fingers. "Yes, Maximiliano, I suppose you could. So why don't you?"

"I might."

"What is stopping you?"

And what, Max thought, is the answer? When it became clear he could not put words to it, his father smiled and said, "When your grandfather told me about the CIA, I realized I had been invited into a secret world I didn't even know existed. I'd been an outsider all along, then, boom, one day I'm in the inner ring, eyes wide open to the vibrant colors of the gray world. You had the same look on you when we left Langley after our first visit, so long ago. We are alike in that way, Maximiliano. You think if you say no, you'll be cast out. A faceless Mexican horseman. A civilian."

"Even if sometimes it's imagined bullshit," Max said, nodding, "I like the idea that occasionally the world moves because I'm secretly pulling the strings."

"Me, too, son." He winked at Max. "The tingle in the balls. That's what kept me coming back, taking risks, saying yes to Langley."

"I don't want to be the civilian who stepped aside to let Sia and Langley finish the job."

"There is something between you and this Sia?"

"I don't know. She is hard to read. Complicated."

"So was Alejandra Garza Sada." His father smiled with the knowledge of a man who had been fully briefed on the relationship's prior eras, but none of its recent, more depressing history. "On and off in high school. On and off in college. On and off after you came home. She loved you, she played with you, she left you, she came running back, or drew you back to her. On and on and on like that. And you remember what your mother said, eh? Find a sweet simple girl who will take care of you, Maximiliano. Instead you chased Alejandra Garza

Sada, she of the long lovely legs and wicked eyes. You seem to enjoy the complicated ones."

"You think I should find a sweet simple girl, Papa?"

"I didn't."

"You found Mama."

"And how would you describe your mother, my son?"

Max smiled, then wiped at his eye. They sat for a long and silent moment, both smiling at the other, Papa's chin quivering in rhythm with the skin around his eyes.

"You respect Sia," his father said at last. "As a partner? A professional?"

"I like playing the game with her."

His father's eyes lit up; he clapped his hands and slipped on the reading glasses again. "Then play, my son. Play."

He cast open the book to a new starting page and returned to whistling. The tune made Max think not of the spent days of a sweet childhood that had never really been his, but of the unremarkable ones before his path was set, when he had been unaware of the choices already made, the hours whiling by as the old man shaved.

When Papa stopped whistling, Max said his name, but the glazy look had settled and his father growled for Benito to leave. I'm an old man, he said, I need to rest, Benito. I need to rest.

On the way out, Max kissed his father's forehead and with each step down the stairwell hummed the old song about horses.

49

Napa Valley

THERE COULD BE NO DIGITAL DUST, NO TRAVEL ITINERARIES, NO
tail numbers connecting Max, Sia, Procter, and Bradley. Max and
Sia required cover to travel to the meeting point. Sia, for example, had
no reason to travel to D.C. If it was discovered, the Russians would wonder about a flight from Heathrow to Dulles. Then they would dig. The
CIA officers did, however, possess cover for a journey to the northern
neck of the Napa Valley, to a small farm owned by one Harry Hamilton,
and presently the home of three horses acquired during a recent visit to
San Cristobal. Bradley and Procter would take a chartered Bombardier
owned by a CIA Air Branch front that had not yet been blown. Max took
the San Cristobal jet. Sia flew commercial from Heathrow, arranging a
few meetings at Lyric to justify the trip to Benny Hynes. Her team of
associates in London would cover the rest of her exhausting workload
for a few days.

Sia arrived at the farm fighting midmorning jet lag. Max by lunch.
After a short nap on a couch in a converted office, Sia fired up her laptop
and opened her cable traffic.

And there was one. Subject line: Congratulations!

She had been promoted to GS-14.

Her 14. A big deal, and about two years ahead of schedule. Her
review board, the cable said, had been briefed on the high points of
the PERSEPHONE recruitment and decided to promote her out of
cycle, effective immediately. Scalps were what mattered; she'd taken an

important blond, Russian one. Sia had been excited about her previous promotions; not because of the money—the government pay was comically bad—but because they were rungs in a ladder she was climbing. Promotions meant she was winning, and victory brought a rush. Where was that feeling now?

She found Max outside at the firepit. "We've got a while until they get here," she said. "Let's go somewhere?"

———

THEY WENT FOR A DRINK AT A RESTAURANT NEAR CALISTOGA. STEVE'S Social Club. The main room was long, with high ceilings, leather wing chairs, and yellow-planked walls. It felt like a lodge at a summer camp. They settled into a table in a quiet corner and ordered two glasses of wine. They drank for a while in the silence of a jet-lagged couple sharing a meal.

"I got promoted," she said. "Just found out."

"Fantastic. Congratulations. Well-deserved." He held up his glass. Hers remained on the table. He set his down. "What's up? You're not happy about it?"

"Do I look happy?"

"You do not look happy. Do you know you look that way?"

"I didn't know if I looked happy or not."

"But you don't feel happy? Why? What did they say?"

"That PERSEPHONE is a big haul. I've been credited."

"So what's the problem?"

"I'm not sure."

A waitress stopped by to check on them. Max waved her off.

"I'll talk for a bit," Sia said. "You just listen, okay?"

"I've got nowhere to go."

"Yeah, you're stuck."

"We're both stuck," he said. "And what else are we going to talk about anyway?"

"Right. Exactly. The case? No, thanks. So I'll talk." Her lips spread into a reluctant smile that seemed to say, *All right, well, let's do this.* "Have you ever stolen anything?" she asked.

"I thought I was just listening."

"Is that a yes?"

He stiffened in his chair. "Well," he said, "I guess that all depends."

She said no, listen, I am not talking about stealing information. I'm talking about stuff: cars, wine, horses. Horses? he said. Horses, she said. Once. During a summer in Cape Town. No, that's wrong. Twice. Once in Cape Town and once in Texas. I was thirteen, fourteen. Anyway, weird part is, I never kept anything. Not the point. I'll tell you a story: Guy who owns the ranch neighboring ours had a big King Ranch pickup. Black. And spotless unlike most of the ranch vehicles. No cooler in there, no guns, no trash. Pristine. He washed it. Made no damn sense, but he washed it all the time. That guy, his name was Masterson, he didn't let anyone drive it. You saw that car on the county road and you knew it was Masterson behind the wheel. Everyone leaves keys in their cars because there isn't really crime out in the Big Bend. And I start thinking, it would be fun to take the truck for a little spin. But I know I've got to be smart otherwise he'll be wise to it. For a few nights I'm in bed, just thinking. How to get to the car. How to take an inventory of the interior. How to clean it after.

"Odometer?" Max asked.

She brought a finger to her nose. "Couldn't solve that without driving it on blocks in reverse like Ferris Bueller. Didn't have the time. And you know what I thought about that?"

"That you liked it."

"Exactly. I liked that there would be one little thread hanging. I could walk away pretty sure he wouldn't know. But not totally. I liked that smack in my veins. Made me feel good."

"You did it?" Max asked.

"A one-mile loop," she said. "Adjusted the seat and the mirrors, then moved them back. Cleaned off the dust with a few bottles of water and a rag I brought along. Parked it in the precise spot where I'd found it. Back in bed before dawn, even if my sister still caught me."

"You ever tell Masterson?"

She laughed. "You know how if you're playing hide-and-seek, you're sitting there in a closet and the seeker comes into the room, looking around, they're trying to find you, and you see them, but they don't see you. You're in the shadows. Well, that's what it was like. I'm out there in the darkness with the biggest secret in the world playing the only game that matters. And I'm winning. I felt like that when I ran ops. Felt like that after promotions. And now? Nothing. And I don't know why."

She finished her wine. "That's all," she said, and checked her watch. "We've still got a few hours. Another glass?"

He called for the check. Registered that through it all she'd had her left hand buried in her pocket or out of sight beneath the table.

Sia shoved her empty wineglass at him. "I'm still thirsty."

The waitress arrived with the bill. Max slapped cash into the leather flap and stood.

"You coming?" he asked, slipping on his jacket.

She did not move. "Where? Back? No. I told you. I need another."

"Come on," he said. "I have an idea."

———

THE FRIDAY DINNER RUSH AT STEVE'S SOCIAL CLUB TILTED GERIATRIC, which meant the valet stand was buried early, typically no later than five-fifteen. A line of idling cars spilled from the parking lot into the street. Occasional honks. Headshakes and frowns greeted the valet when he slipped patrons their tickets. Good business usually meant solid tips, but tonight they were slammed and understaffed. Guests didn't tip when they had to wait this long. He looked back to the line of customers waiting for their cars. First up was a tall, dark-haired woman. Behind her was a Latin guy, shouting into his phone and pacing along the patio seating. Six or so people behind him. He overheard the guy talking to the valet company, asking for more bodies. Was he one of the managers? The valet wasn't sure. Staff turnover was high at Steve's.

"Have you been helped, ma'am?" the valet asked the dark-haired woman. Her hazy gray eyes were interesting. He flicked open the door to a G Wagen. Next up was a red Bentley Flying Spur. Mr. Henderson's car. A regular. Bad tipper, but he'd park that car for free.

"Yes, I'm all good," the woman said. "Just waiting."

What was that accent? Valet hadn't heard it before. He handed the G Wagen owner a ticket, stepped in, and parked it in the neighboring lot. He sprinted back to Steve's and found the other valet scrambling into a white Porsche Panamera. The Bentley was gone.

"You get Mr. Henderson's car already?" he called to the other valet. The guy threw his hands into the air and got into the Porsche. That kind of night.

The Latin manager had gone inside. The woman with the lovely accent had left. The driver of a black McLaren 720S rolled down the window. "Hey, chief, I've been waiting fifteen minutes. You going to park the car or what?" The valet hustled around to open the driver's door. The guy snatched his ticket with a scowl. This is bad, the valet thought as he drove off. Tips were going to be lousy tonight.

———

PROCTER AND BRADLEY ROLLED UP THE DRIVEWAY IN THE BACK OF THE windowless black van that had carted them from the hangar at Napa County Airport. They hustled into the farmhouse just as the sun fired its last rays over the horizon. Max and Sia, seated at the kitchen table, looked up with what Procter thought were a pair of false smiles, vain attempts to mask their agitation at this premature intrusion. The cable dispatched from Ed's office had forecasted a much later arrival.

Something was off, she could feel it. Procter would have said they'd been fooling around, but that wasn't quite it. She'd learned to read the signs after missing them once, for a brief spell, in a long-ago Syrian life with a good case officer who made a few bad decisions. What made Procter's read in this room even stranger was that she *knew* they were screwing, at least in general terms. She just didn't think they'd been screwing today. Baffling, but she knew they were hiding something.

Bradley shook their hands and sat. "My wife Angela runs our hobby horse farm in northern Virginia," he started in. "Of all the secrets I've kept from her, CIA's partnership with San Cristobal might be the most damaging if it ever came to light. She's an admirer of yours, Max, and

I believe she would murder me if she knew I'd met with you. Or force me to buy a horse."

"Our prices are very reasonable," Max said. "She's welcome anytime."

"Vadim Kovalchuk might dispute that," Bradley responded, flashing that toothy recruiter smile, his tone starting to ring with energy, readying the pitch. Procter watched him laser in on both officers and say, "Excellent work developing this. Flawless. It'll be a case study at the Farm within a year, I've no doubt. I'm proud of you. The Director sends his thanks and appreciation. And that's a personal message—he looked me square in the eye this morning and told me to tell you. No bullshit. I've sat in fireside chats before with some senior officer blowing smoke up my ass, and believe me, this is not one of those times. The President is reading every scrap of intelligence you produce. But we're now at a crossroads. And I want your thoughts on how to play this."

They spoke for an hour about PERSEPHONE and the case. Procter mostly stayed silent. She'd said her piece on the Seventh Floor. And though she enjoyed steamrolling a subordinate as much as the next Agency manager, Procter felt it was important in this moment to grant her officer's space to speak. To let them take credit. They would have concerns with the case, she knew, and Bradley—God bless him, he didn't have to—would ask. But they wouldn't answer truthfully because he was the Deputy Director, and there were many things in this world you simply cannot tell a superior, no matter how important they might be to say. *We are screwing around*, for instance. Or, *I'd rather have my foot amputated than again place it on Russian soil.*

"We would like to approve this," Bradley said at last, "based on Procter's recommendation and my conversation with you both tonight. The White House has been briefed; they share my concerns about the risks but feel the potential payoff outweighs them. I want to know where you come down on this. Because it is conceivable that we just let PERSEPHONE sit tight."

And then Sia jumped in, without pause or hesitation. "No. We should go in. Get PERSEPHONE bucked up and ready."

Procter saw Bradley raise an eyebrow, almost imperceptibly, before he turned to Max.

"I agree," Max said. "We should do it."

Bradley glanced from one of them to the other in a sticky silence, awaiting qualifier or revision. None came.

He smacked the table. "You two and Artemis will go through the details in a few days in St. Ives, once we have the concealment and tech side worked out at Langley."

Bradley stood and shook their hands again. "You two are running a once-in-a-lifetime operation," he said. "Let me just say, again, thank you. Thank you for what you're doing. For the sacrifice. I am proud to call you both colleagues and friends." Procter hugged Sia; shook Max's hand. They shuffled out of the farmhouse.

And then Procter saw it.

Parked in the gravel drive, on the other side of the van, in her blind spot on the way in.

A red Bentley.

"Hey, Ed," Procter said, doubling back to the farmhouse, "give me a sec."

Max and Sia were still at the table.

"There is an obscenely expensive vehicle outside," Procter said. "Did you know that?"

"My rental," Max volunteered.

Her green eyes slitted suspiciously. She knew about Hortensia's little predilections, of course. Procter was her inside officer; she'd read her psychological reports. But now? Jeepers, timing was bad.

"If I go out there, will I find rental papers in the glove box?" she asked. "Maybe tossed carelessly on the floor of the passenger seat? Or jammed in the goddamned cupholder? Maybe I have a look-see?"

"Artemis, we . . ." Sia's rebuttal sputtered to a halt because Procter was actually shushing her, the Chief's head bobbing forward with each gust of air blown across the finger she'd brought to her lips.

"Ssh. Ssh. Ssh. Shut. The. Fuck. Up. Thanks. Just put the goddamn thing back pronto, Hortensia," Procter said. Okay, hon?"

Sia nodded, said okay.

Then Procter turned to Max. "You used your one freebie lie, my friend. Now, there are things I don't want to know, of course. And I get that you're a special case, Maximiliano, that unlike our friend Hortensia here, you can walk away. Hell, you can tell me no and there's not much I can do about it. But that doesn't mean you can lie to me. I ask you a question, I expect the truth. For example, I know you two are humping, but I ain't asking. You don't have to tell me. Use your judgment. We pay you for your goddamn judgment. In the end, all I've got is your judgment and honor and patriotic fervor. Nothing more. You lie to me again, and I send banditos to San Cristobal. Burn the place down. Capeesh?"

"Sí. Capeesh."

She made unsettling, intense eye contact with both officers, then said, "See you in St. Ives."

Then she was outside, sliding shut the van door. Bradley was working through an evening readbook. The driver started down the gravel path toward the county road.

"All good?" Bradley asked.

"All good," Procter said, buckling her seat belt. "Peachy."

"Why in the hell is a Bentley parked here?" he muttered, head still buried in the readbook.

"Castillo's rental," Procter said. "Rich pricks, Ed. You know how it goes."

50

Moscow / Saint Petersburg

THE BATHHOUSE AT GOOSE'S RUBLYOVKA ESTATE WAS TUCKED BEHIND a screen of trees near the kennels where he kept his Belgian Malinois. The dogs barked at Chernov as he walked alongside Goose through the frigid air. Dogs always seemed to bark at Chernov. They cut through the tearoom to a changing area. There they collected felt hats, towels, and robes from wall pegs.

They slipped into the robes and returned to the tearoom carrying the hats and towels. A butler had left a tray of mint tea. They shed robes for the sauna and sat for a few minutes in silence, clad only in the felt hats, before shuffling into an adjoining room with showers and a chilled pool. Goose winced as he dipped into the cold water. With only his head above the surface, he smacked the water and said, "I didn't want an open war. Andrei and his daughter . . . both are damn stubborn fools."

Chernov plunged deeper into the tub. He understood the water was cold, but he did not experience the sensation as others did.

Goose continued, "And the tapes from Butyrka? My god. Andrei taunts us, tells his only daughter to refuse us. Go right ahead and kill yourself, sweetheart. Feed yourself to the dogs. Papa loves you. He has always been like this." He splashed some water on his face, as though he were trying to wake up. "The daughter is the same. She is her father without a cock, but with the same balls. That look in her eyes the night we dealt with the boyfriend? Pure madness." He scratched a thumb along his neck, cursing the Agapovs.

Goose lumbered from the pool and Chernov followed him into the sauna. They sat with their heads down for a moment. "I am getting old, my friend," Goose said. "Winter is welded into my joints."

Sweat rolled like marbles down Chernov's bald head. Then they dipped back into the pool. Chernov winged his arms on the side of the tub and waited for Goose to continue. He'd grown accustomed to waiting on the boss during their years of holy war together. And Chernov was good at waiting.

Goose locked on to his eyes. "We need Anna for a clean sale of Agapov's businesses. And she will not give us one. We need the paperwork for a case to send her to Siberia with her old man. And for that we could use someone in her circle. Get us what we need clean and quick so the arrest, the trial, and the sentencing don't start a stampede among the boyars. *Neofitsialnye mery*, non-official measures, but this comes straight from the top."

Chernov nodded. "What are the rules?"

"No blood," Goose said. "At least not from Anna."

Goose made for the changing room. Chernov followed.

The boss pulled a piece of paper from the pocket of his hanging robe and stuffed it in Chernov's hand. A few lines on a single damp piece of yellow legal paper. Marginalia. No signatures. Only Goose's handwriting and the *khozyain*'s notes.

He read the message.

In the bathroom he ripped it to pieces and flushed it down the toilet.

———

FOR HIS SERVICE IN ONE OF THE VYMPEL UNITS THAT HAD FREED HUN-dreds of hostages from the clutches of Chechen terrorists at School Number One in Beslan, Chernov had been granted the Order of Courage. During the Lubyanka commendation ceremony, the President did not cite the uncomfortable statistic that 333 people, including 186 children, had been killed during the chaos of the rescue operation.

More than two decades on, and Chernov was still enjoying the award's residual benefits, allowing him to live beyond the means of most

Russian intelligence officers. He did not pay rent on his Moscow apartment. He drove a state-supplied, armored Mercedes. He could vacation at closed FSB resorts. For the FSB, like the KGB before it, is a state within a state. The nobility of the *khozyain*'s Russia.

But, though Chernov lived and worked in the Moscow glitz, even he was taken aback by Vadim Kovalchuk's apartment on the Kutuzov Embankment in Piter. From the street it appeared to stretch for most of the block, commanding sweeping views of the Neva and the Peter and Paul Fortress. This, he thought, must have been what it felt like to be a Romanov.

FSB officers do not carry badges, but Chernov's police cover ID was enough to part the crew of heavies standing guard downstairs; the team manning the security cameras extinguished them for the Prosecutor General's warrant; the door opened for the lock picker. Chernov walked inside and took a deep breath. Arkady and Daniil, two of his lieutenants, followed.

The apartment hung thick with the scents of garish female perfumes and male musk. What it smelled like, he thought, was sex. He took a quick tour. It sprawled over three stories, with balconies jutting off bedrooms on the second and third. Chernov rifled around the wet bar. He picked up a vodka bottle sporting a bulbous top inlaid with an intricate gold pattern.

"That one is famous, boss," Arkady said. "The Tsar's recipe. Filtered through diamonds and gold and probably Romanov pussy." He laughed.

"Let us find out," Chernov said. Though it was only midmorning, he filled two *stopki* with the Tsar's vodka. He placed them on the table in the sitting area.

Chernov was about to sit on one of the couches when he spotted a stain on the sofa. Probably grease, but one could never be sure. He opted for a rattan chair in a sitting area overlooking the frozen Neva. The morning was bright. Ice skaters dotted the river. Daniil's phone buzzed. "He is on his way from the bank now."

The time passed in a silence broken finally by the trill of Daniil's phone. "Downstairs," he said. Arkady opened the front door.

The banker walked in, his eyes at first hollowed by confusion, then lit with rage. They all had this look, this face, in these moments. *You are intruding,* his eyes said, *you are here illegally.* He tossed a leather bag against the wall and demanded to know who was in charge, until his eyes settled on Chernov and he mumbled, "Oh."

They looked at each other for a beat. Chernov gestured to the vodka. "Sit and have a drink with me, Vadim Yurivich."

"My own vodka. How thoughtful."

"Please, sit."

"What do you want?"

"I want you to sit and have a drink with me."

"I need to make a call," Vadim said.

"There will be no calls, Vadim Yurivich."

Vadim tugged the phone from his pocket. "Unless you have more fucking papers for an arrest, I am going to make a call."

He started pressing keys on the phone, but Arkady had him in a headlock before he could dial. Vadim squirmed, but Daniil clutched his legs. Arkady punched him in the face, evidently a bit hard, because the blow shot a spray of blood from his nose onto a zebra-striped rug. Chernov downed his vodka. He emptied Vadim's glass onto the floor. The nobles always put up a fuss, threatened to call someone, used coarse language. Damn boyars.

Daniil frog-marched a wriggling Vadim upstairs, muscling him toward a balcony on the third floor off an empty bedroom. Arkady slid open the door. Vadim's screaming picked up again at the rush of biting wind, and Chernov savored a deliciously salty ball of saliva rolling in the back of his mouth.

Arkady wiped a spot of blood from below his own nose. "Rich guys never just have the drink," he grunted. "Always give us a hard time."

Vadim was whimpering when Chernov picked him up by his ankles to dangle him off the balcony, his face turned to the river. He squirmed around for Chernov's legs but got a kick instead. Then he hung limply, muttering, again and again: Please no.

"I offered you a drink, Vadim Yurivich. And now . . ."

"Don't do it," Vadim howled. "I'll talk. I'll do what you want. Just bring me up. Don't do it."

Chernov lowered Vadim to swing him into the window below as if he were a wrecking ball. Vadim cursed, screamed, begged for mercy. Chernov beat him against the lower window once more, then raised him up so Vadim's head swung at his ankles.

"I have always found the river beautiful in winter," Chernov called down to him over the howling wind, "but do you want it to be the last thing you see? Of course not. You want to die in your bed as an old man. I will ask once more. Only once. If you give me the wrong answer, I let you slip and God sorts you out. That's that. Defiance will be quite the wager. I mean what I say and I speak for God and for Russia and you will answer me. Now, Vadim Yurivich, have a drink with me?"

———

CHERNOV FILLED TWO MORE GLASSES WITH THE TSAR'S VODKA AND brought them to an interior office. He did not want Vadim to think about leaping from a window. Some people did not want you to drop them and then after a few minutes of conversation they jumped on their own. Chernov sat enthroned behind the desk, Vadim in the supplicant's chair. His face was drained of color, save for the scales of dried blood around his nose.

Vadim shivered and stared at the untouched vodka. Chernov looked around. No medals. Not a single picture of his wife or family. A rich man with nothing.

Chernov drank his vodka and bade Vadim to do the same. The man took a weak sip and returned the *stopka* to the desk with a clatter. "My master extended an offer to your wife for the sale of the Agapov businesses and their shares in the bank," Chernov began. "She denied us. We had to punish her, in the end. She had a boyfriend. And I am afraid that she sacrificed him."

Chernov watched as Vadim's ghost-white face reddened before he looked down, taking an interest in the floor. He rubbed his head, leaned back in the chair. "You did not know about the boyfriend? I see." Chernov put down a few centimeters of his vodka. "You are holding a bad hand." He ran his fingers against the grain of the desk. Not a speck of dust. "Does it also seem that way to you?"

Vadim was running his tongue along his teeth. He bit his lip.

"Let me explain how I see things," Chernov continued. "We are making an example of Andrei Agapov. A holy sacrifice for the Russian people. His stubborn daughter—your wife, who has been cavorting with another man behind your back—is refusing to submit. Deep forces are remaking the structures supporting this government and Andrei Agapov has not bowed. He is a bad nobleman. Muscovite boyars paid the Mongols. The country estates paid the Romanov Tsars. Andrei Agapov pays the Kremlin. And Goose speaks for the Kremlin. But Andrei will not listen. And what does Andrei bring to this fight? His daughter. My God, he brings his only *daughter.* Your wife. He cannot win. Andrei is in prison. He is a dead horse. Your continued loyalty to the Agapovs, Vadim Yurivich, has been rewarded by an unfaithful wife and could very well end with you falling from your own window. An unfortunate demise for such a promising, ambitious young man."

"What do you want from me?" Vadim said. He took a slurp of vodka and stretched his jaw.

"I want your wife to say yes. Goose has given his best offer. You must convince her. Speak reason."

Vadim smiled darkly. "She will say yes to you sooner than to me. My guess is that you will need to kill my wife to break her."

"Anna Andreevna is certainly a hard woman," Chernov said. "Is that why her father brought her into this mess in the first place?"

Vadim shifted in his seat. Raised the vodka to his lips. "He wanted her to find the money Goose stole."

Chernov pounded his fist into the desk. Vadim flinched, dropped his glass. Chernov was pointing at him. "No," he bellowed. "*Theft* would be the appropriate word if it had belonged to you. Try again."

"We are, I mean she is, looking for the gold, the money taken from Bank Rossiya." Vadim was stammering down toward his knees as he righted the *stopka* on the desk and wiped the liquid away from him.

"How was your wife looking for it?"

Vadim rubbed his temple. "Anna found someone on the outside who knew where the money was hidden. And how it had been hidden."

"Who?"

"A London-based lawyer. Hortensia Fox. Works for the firm Goose's UK moneyman, Mikhail Lyadov, hired to set up the shells and the accounts. My wife is working on her."

"How has she been working her?"

Chernov heard about the bait, the trip to Mexico, the visit to Rus-Farm. The information Hortensia Fox had provided on Goose's finances. As he spoke, Vadim tenderly brushed fingers over his puffy nose.

Chernov listened intently, hands folded in his lap. "Your wife has this information now?"

"Yes."

"What was Andrei thinking in the first place?"

Vadim shut his eyes and pulled a long breath in through his nostrils. "Andrei believed that the only way to prove that Goose stole, er, took, the gold and hid it from the President was to find it. Or, specifically, the money the gold was converted into. Then he would bring that proof to the *khozyain*. Andrei is former SVR, Anna is SVR, they have contacts and influence outside the country. Andrei believed it would be easier for them to prove that the money is outside Russia than to prove it is *not* inside. That is what he wanted to do."

"Your wife has this," Chernov said, "yet she has not done anything with it?"

"Right. She is sitting on it."

"Why?"

"It was flimsier than she hoped, her father was arrested, she did not think she could even bring it to the President without Goose knowing. She did not think it would do the job."

"Which was?"

"Goose backs off."

Vadim was chewing his lip, deep in thought. He was recovering from the heavier work, sitting up to cross his legs and flick lint from his pants as if he were enduring an increasingly burdensome board-

room meeting. The caked blood on his nose and spilled vodka were
the only clues suggesting otherwise. Everything since the window
business had been rather professional. Vadim's growing comfort made
Chernov uncomfortable.

"You will give me what your wife has," Chernov said. "The information from the lawyer."

"I don't have it."

Chernov stood, lunged across the table, seized Vadim's shoulders, and smashed his head into the desk. Vadim rolled to the floor,
unconscious. Chernov drummed his fingers on the table. Whistled for
a moment. When Vadim did not stir, Chernov wandered into the living
room and selected another bottle of vodka. He poured himself a glass
and returned to the office to find Vadim curled into himself, moaning.
Chernov sat in the chair, steepling his fingers to resume the discussion.

"You don't have the information," Chernov said. "Can you get it?"

"I don't even know where it is," Vadim choked out. "She has a separate life. She is an intelligence officer. She does not live here, as you
must know."

"My master does not want a fight with you, Vadim Yurivich," Chernov said. "We are only after Agapovs. We want them blotted from history, making boots in a Siberian tannery or digging for uranium ore in
the Urals. Please, get back in your chair. I want to look at you."

Vadim struggled up, holding his head, his mind doubtless churning,
wondering if this betrayal might end with his wife's liquidation. Which,
Chernov suspected, he probably would find appealing.

When Vadim was seated, Chernov calmly continued: "Your wife is
running the London lawyer, yes?"

Vadim nodded.

"Then you will convince Anna to lure the lawyer back inside Russia. And you will be my little canary inside the cage, singing when
she comes."

51

RusFarm

I N ONE OF RUSFARM'S SEVERAL LIVING ROOMS, ANNA WAS SUNK DEEP into the velvet couch and a bottle of Armenian brandy, Queen on the record player, so drunk she couldn't be certain of the song. The week since the fire she'd been camping out and drinking at RusFarm. There was nowhere else to go. Nothing else to do. And she was waiting for Sia.

Her brandy-soaked mind swam to Luka. His arm. What had they done to him first? She buried a scream in a velvet pillow. She would not remember him this way, torn to pieces by Russia, by her enemies. By her. Anna banished the thoughts, instead channeling the last bits of her flagging energy to build one sweet image of Luka's gleeful smile, fresh off a victory in the lamplight of Jean Martel. The world began fragmenting as she tried to reconstruct him in her old apartment. The music had stopped, the turntable spun with the scratch of the needle across the dead wax. She too was spinning, faster and faster, and she worried her mind might never be able to paint his face again. She gave up, and the world spun and spun until it was gone.

———

HER EYES OPENED TO VADIM PETTING ONE OF THE ALSATIANS, HER head taut like an overfilled balloon. The Alsatian cocked its head her direction. What was the dog's name? Vadim withdrew his hand and began picking at a plate of eggs. The sight and smell of the food made her sick. She closed her eyes, rolled her face into the cushions. She had not seen him since dinner in Piter. Why had he come to the farm now? And why did he have a bruise on his head?

"Anyone else invited to this party?" he said. An uncertain chuckle, scrape of the fork on the plate. She gagged a little, pressed deeper into the cushions.

"I can't watch you eat," she said.

A sigh, clink of a plate, shuffle of paper. When she opened her eyes, a draped newspaper censored the eggs. The dog had settled near the hearth.

"I have been thinking," Vadim said, "about pursuing a partnership with San Cristobal. A broader arrangement, beyond the one-off purchase of the stallion Smokey Joe."

She tried to sit up. Her brain moved as if mired in glue—thoughts struggling mightily but traveling nowhere. "A partnership," she said. "Why?"

"For his bloodlines," Vadim said. "So we get first crack, before the Americans or Brits or anyone else. Gives us an advantage. I was thinking we might invite Max and Sia back for a few days. Discuss it. He can also collect the mare they left behind. The one you've been caring for."

He was smiling pleasantly. Something was off, and yet she could not name it. The Americans were preparing to respond to—or, at minimum, considering—her plea for Sia to return to Russia. Was it a coincidence that Vadim was now doing that work for her? She recalled the nagging sensation, in the aftermath of her father's arrest, that her husband had played some role in Goose's treachery. Whose bidding was this?

"What happened to you?" she asked.

He put a gentle hand to his forehead and smiled as if he'd forgotten all about the welt. "Bumped it on a door. Anna, I know you're hungover, but focus for a minute. What do you think about inviting them back?"

Vadim had put her in check. She'd not anticipated this. And in her addled state, she realized she could no longer see the game unfolding ahead of her. She was not certain she could plan her next move.

"I am not sure Sia would want to return," Anna demurred. "The unfortunate car accident, the blackmail. Nasty feelings and all."

"Do you want to see her?" Vadim asked.

"I suppose," Anna said carefully. "There are things she might be helpful on. She has interesting access at Lyric, the tech company."

"Do you think she told Max?" Vadim asked. "About the accident?"

"I don't know," Anna said. "I threatened that we would give the law firm proof that she compromised client documents if she told a soul. But she's back in London. And he is her boyfriend, after all."

Vadim shrugged. "Well, you must have scared the shit out of her, because I think she kept her word. Max took my call this morning about the partnership. Seemed keen to talk. Downright chummy."

"What's your point?" she asked.

"I would like Max to come here for a business discussion. Bare minimum, he might be tempted to get his horse back . . . What's the damn thing's name?"

"Penelope. And I've no intention of giving her back." Anna's tone was shrill, ringing in her ears as if the words were not hers. The mention of Penelope had conjured the box in the stable . . . and then the bloody package in her apartment. She wanted to cry, but that would give him pleasure, and nothing would disgust her more. She forced it all down. Down, down, down.

He waved a dismissive hand through the air. "Fine. No horse. Just business. Maybe we ask Sia to come along, too, since we—you—have some control over her?"

Anna shut her eyes, mind grappling for purchase. Had Sia and Lulu arranged for Max to reach out to Vadim, creating a reason for their travel? Maybe this was their clever way of arranging a visit. "How about this weekend?" Anna asked.

52

St. Ives

THEY GATHERED AGAIN AT THE ST. IVES COTTAGE. BUT IF THEIR first planning sessions had been marked by some measure of excitement, this assembly tilted funereal. The night was cloudy, the air wet and cold, and Procter's ministrations were insufficient to coax the patio Christmas lights into twinkling properly. All wore black; quite by accident, of course, but it did not help the mood. They sat around an iron table colonized by rust, huddled into their coats against the occasional slaps of marine wind. The Chief seemed unfazed by the climate; she wore an unzipped black leather jacket. Sia blew hot breath into her cold hands, then stuffed her shaky left into her coat pocket.

Their first order of business was Vadim's call to Max two days prior, an invite for the couple to return to RusFarm. His tone, Max explained, had been strange. Obsequious, even, apologetic about the mix-up with Penelope the last time, keeping the horse and all. He suggested they return to collect the mare and talk business. It had been odd, Max said, for Vadim to travel through a conversation without coming across as an asshole. "And odder still, offering to return my horse."

"Maybe Anna put him up to it and he listened?" Sia offered. "It's certainly a clean way to get us back after she flew the emergency signal."

Max arched a brow. "He's not really the listening type."

"Maybe she beat the shit out of *him*," Procter offered. "Girl's got her reasons, lord knows."

A gust of wind cut through the patio. The Chief said let's go inside to talk about the comms. And it was at this point that a troublesome thought bubbled up inside Max: Whether they might tell Procter about Anna's operation against Sia during their last visit. Namely the tossing of a cadaver onto the windshield of a moving car for the purposes of shock, blackmail, and control. But Sia believed Anna was the real deal, he mostly believed Sia, and the part of him that still had a few questions figured they had polygraphed the Russian in Switzerland anyhow, so she was probably square.

All through the preparations for another round in the Rodina, his father's words had run endlessly through his mind: *We are alike in that way, Maximiliano. You think if you say no, you'll be cast out. A faceless Mexican horseman. A civilian.*

And now they—he—had withheld information from Procter, from CIA. He'd taken a fateful step forward. Retreating would require confession, and confession would require punishment. It would be banishment, he suspected, they would sever his connection to the service.

He would be a civilian.

But a new thought now struggled with that old familiar fear: For once, civilian life seemed strangely appealing. A siren song. Maybe he would spend more time at the club in Monterrey and bring a nice girl out to see the ranch and they would ride and take in the races and eventually he would prove his old man wrong—hand San Cristobal over to a son who would work the land and learn the bloodlines, as he had. Would retreat from CIA help him honor his father and grandfather? Or would it fail them? He did not know. But of this he was certain: backing out would mean failing Sia.

That thought of retreat, of confessing, nagged, and nagging feelings were most unwelcome in the days before another trip to RusFarm.

IN THE MOVIES SPY TECH ALWAYS WORKS. BUT THE CLANCOMM-LOADED laptop Procter had schlepped from Langley did not. For a few minutes, the Chief tried to access the partition and run the checks. Motherfucking nerds, she said on the failure of the third try, Sia reading the sequence aloud for confirmation, Procter pounding keys in rising anger. An urgent cable went to Langley and the reply came quickly: Give us a few hours. "Hours?" Procter shrieked in disbelief. "The fuck? World's top intel shop, my ass. Jeepers."

Next up: concealment. Procter retrieved a saddlebag from her rental and clanked it on the living room coffee table. The gift saddle itself, she said, was presently on its way to London from Langley. The OTS Furnishings and Equipment branch had tooled the RusFarm logo into the bag's russet leather: two stallions rearing in opposite directions, three crowns above their heads. An homage to the Russian double eagle. OTS had sourced the leather from a Monterrey tannery. Procter demonstrated how to open the compartment hidden in one of the bags. A tug on one of the buckles would trigger a hidden pulley that yanked free a pin. Then fingers pressed three hidden metal snaps. A faint pop, then pull back a leather panel to reveal a compartment fitted for the replacement Asus mini laptop.

Sia practiced for a while, concerned that Anna's hands would be too small to compress the snaps, until Procter did it three times with her little mitts. But nothing could be left to chance, so Sia banged out another cable to Langley, this time requesting a precise measurement of Anna's hand based on the countersurveillance video from Switzerland. Then they would compare Anna's to Procter's.

Waiting for answers, Procter grabbed a manila folder. Let's head back on the porch, she said. Get some fresh air.

——

"EXFIL," PROCTER SAID. SHE PINNED A PIECE OF PAPER TO THE PATIO table with a loose rock from the base of the stone wall, a satellite image of the RusFarm grounds. "We've been working this for a few weeks. You two and Anna now have BEAR CRAWL escape routes seven, eight, and nine. A scrub-down was in order, given the freaky surveillance during your last visit."

Procter pointed to a blue sticker affixed to the far northern end of the farm property. "This is the best we can do without risking World War III. The place is massive, so positioning support assets nearby is tricky. But right here"—she smacked her fist onto the map—"here we can have something in place during your stay. Just in case."

"What's out there?" Sia asked, pointing at where Procter had delivered her fist. "I've ridden nearby with Anna. I didn't see any buildings or roads. Just forest."

"Electrical transmission line," Procter said, tracing her finger along the map. "Runs parallel to the northern edge of the property. That's where the support assets will be. The SCORPIONs. They've got a truck that pretty much belongs to Rosseti Lenenergo. The region's power distribution company."

"What do you mean, 'pretty much belongs' to the power company?" Max asked.

"I mean they have a truck," Procter said. "And if anyone bothers them, that truck will pass the sniff test. The SCORPIONs are Finns. From Karelia. Their Karelian homeland or whatever is split between Russia and Finland, about ten hours by car due north of RusFarm. They can move in and out of Russia and hate the fucking Russians. A beautiful thing." The Chief returned to the map. "They will have a truck parked on this service road. They don't know your names, they haven't seen your pictures, but they know that if anyone shows up at their truck and says they need a ticket north, they're to hustle them out. They can also kill the power if necessary."

They studied the maps, debating routes by car, foot, and horse. Snow could be a problem. They would pack boots and heavy parkas.

They decided on a code—the use of the word *melancholy* in any signal to Langley.

"If we get into trouble," Sia said, "we won't make it to that transmission line." Wind poured through the patio, scattering locks of black hair across her face and head, which she wiped aside.

"I know," Procter said, glances bouncing from one of them to the other. The map's brim fluttered in the wind. "So don't get into trouble."

———

STILL WAITING ON LANGLEY FOR THE KEYBOARD SEQUENCE, THEY opened a bottle of Riesling and ate cartons of chicken tikka masala. Between generous sips of wine, Sia decided to ask the question clawing at her since Switzerland. "Chief, what do you think happens to PERSEPHONE when this is done?"

Procter pushed the food aside, stuffed hands in her jacket, and watched the palm fronds twist and sway in the wind. An empty tikka masala carton tilted in the breeze. "It'll be grim," she said. "Russians shouldn't have any hard evidence on her, unlike Vadim. But they most definitely will not care about that. They'll have a lot to discuss with her, and it won't be super pleasant. She gets it, of course, somewhere in that sick head of hers she's clear on the consequences. Still, you might emphasize that again when you see her. Exfil would make damn good sense when the time comes."

They listened to the distant rumble of the surf. Procter looked to each of them for a moment. Strange, Sia thought, to see uncertainty flicker through those green eyes.

And then it was gone. "In any case," Procter continued, "the inevitable FSB investigation will focus on the two of you. Again, they won't have hard evidence, but they'll be suspicious. Hell, you struck up a relationship with Vadim and Anna in the months before it all went down. Lots of ways this could end, but I think we'll have to be careful in the afterglow. This op isn't half pregnant, it's fully knocked up. And you two are responsible."

Max was picking at the dregs of his tikka masala, hard stare boring through the bottom of the carton. To Sia his eyes seemed downcast, focused and intent, as if in that moment he had to shrink the world down to the carton or it would devour him. Sia looked up into the night sky and thought about how much she had enjoyed St. Ives before this operation, and how, if she made it to the other side, she would never come here again.

———

TWO CABLES WAITED ON SIA'S MACHINE. THE FIRST HAD ANNA'S HAND measurements. A faded ruler confirmed that Procter's hands were smaller than Anna's, a fact both operationally critical and a source of agitation for the Chief, who muttered that hers worked just fine, thank you. The second cable apologized for the gummed-up keyboard sequence and offered another, which worked. Phew, Procter said. Fucking phew. Memorization demanded an exhausting hour. A break for another glass of Riesling and then they tried again, thirty-one times, until they had it. Sia repeated the sequence aloud to Procter another six times, performing as the Chief finished a second carton of the chicken and polished off four sugar cookies.

Two a.m. Procter was satisfied, wide awake and jumpy despite the wine and a looming five-hour drive to Heathrow to make her flight stateside. The Chief clanked her suitcase down the stairs and into the kitchen, where Sia and Max were cleaning up. "This op has a life of its own now," Procter said. "Might as well be running us. We're all going to be implicated when the shit flies in Moscow. And the hard part is, it doesn't really matter what we do from here on out. If we all decided to retire and join the fucking circus, our fingerprints would still be on this thing. You two have been inside Russia, you've been with Anna and Vadim in Mexico. My name is all over the cables at Langley. We're all in now. Whether we want to be or not. We all took the little steps forward. There is no going back."

"White House could stop it," Sia said. "Pull the plug."

"Would you recommend they do that?" Procter asked.

Sia slipped a plate into the dishwasher. She started on a wineglass. Set it in the sink. Turned to face the Chief. "No," Sia said, "I wouldn't."

"Jefe?" Procter looked to Max.

He shook his head.

"Me neither," Procter said. She shook hands and gave hugs. Keep it up. Almost there. Then the Chief scudded her suitcase out the door and vanished into the night.

———

THE CHIEF'S DEPARTURE CONJURED A DRIVING RAIN. MAX STARTLED awake to the thunder and then listened to the storm, eyes glued to the ceiling, thinking about nothing and everything, brain unable to stay on task for more than a few seconds.

The sudden creak had barely reached his ears before he was up, back against the rickety headboard. A flash of lightning illuminated Sia's shape in the doorway. She wore sweats and a T-shirt. Arms folded across her chest. She cleared her throat. "You game?" she asked.

As had become true operationally, they worked well together. He was anticipating her, where she would want hands and how to move with her. He could damn well sense as soon as she slipped onto the bed that she wanted her T-shirt left on and that she was not drawn into his kiss, though she reciprocated the first and only attempt. *What do you want?* he asked, and she answered by climbing onto him. He knew that she liked when he clasped her hands and sometimes he would support her shoulders so she could rock her hips to ride the swell. It was not forced, it was not even mechanical. But it was not passionate. Even astride him, with skin shared and sticky with sweat, she was too far-off for that. As Sia's head swung back and her hips rolled and her knees bounced and the bed creaked, he entertained the curious thought that he now played the role of sunscreen applicator, back scratcher, dress-zipper-upper. Fun if you like the girl, yes, and he did, but above and before all: practical. This one had things to work through.

After, they stayed entangled on the bed listening to the storm. The air smelled sweet.

"I can't believe we are doing this," she half whispered, breaking the silence. Unclear if her meaning was carnal or operational.

"Same," he said. His answer would work for both.

And he saw in the dim light that her eyes invited him home, into the chaotic house that was her mind; the gesture made even more intimate because of its condition. Take a look, they said. He peered at the scuffed floors and peeling paint and dishes piled on the counter. He took stock of a woman in the living room, arms akimbo, and she was shrugging as if to say, *Well, this is it. You staying or leaving?* Max thought about saying things. But instead, he took her hand to trace her lines and they rolled to face the rain-battered window until, without words, they entwined together on the covers waiting for the howl of the storm to dissolve into sleep.

Part V

—=—

PREDATEL / TRAITOR

Saint Petersburg / RusFarm

AS THE PLANE FELL TOWARD THE RUNWAY AT PULKOVO, THE TREM-
ors in Sia's left hand reappeared after a brief intermission of stillness during the first few hours of the flight. They flew a Dassault Falcon
7X courtesy of Vadim, who had sent the plane to collect them in London. A peace offering. Sia glanced at the overhead compartment holding the suitcase that held the saddlebag that held the laptop that would
get them imprisoned and tortured and shot if the customs agents at
Pulkovo decided Agapov money was no longer good or, in the end,
not enough.

The flight attendant unlatched the door and winter flooded in. The
pilot warbled inaudibly over the speaker, doubtless some derivative of
welcome to Saint Petersburg! They pulled on coats, Max hauled out the
case bearing the saddlebag, flight attendants gathered the other cases
and the saddle itself, and they spilled from the plane onto the stairs
with the enthusiasm of the newly convicted delivered to a prison. An
expressionless customs officer accepted their documents on the tarmac.
Sia painted on a broad smile and tried to ignore the panicked sensation
of being buried alive. A quick glance at their papers, a long hard stare,
and the customs officer gave a curt nod, returning the passports to Max
because Sia's hands were shoved in her coat pocket.

A single black Mercedes chuffed exhaust on the windswept apron.
Vadim and Anna stood outside, no driver in sight. The personal touch.
Strange. Disconcerting, even. The flight attendants tossed their bags and

the wrapped saddle in the back. The sight of the Russians made Sia want to run, but she smiled broadly and pleasantly, a grateful and expectant houseguest. And straightaway they were all lying to each other.

Great to have you back, Vadim said to Max, giving his shoulder a rough slap.

Likewise, Vadim, likewise, Max said, shaking Vadim's bloodless hand before planting kisses on Anna's cheeks.

My god, Anna, you look terrific, Sia said, fighting the terror, just terrific. Kisses for both Russians.

But Anna's lie was the greatest of all. Welcome to Saint Petersburg, she said.

Welcome to Russia.

———

SIA CAUGHT THE THIN, MENACING WHIFF OF SMOKE AND PETROL AS THE Mercedes sped through the spiked gates and onto the darkly wooded drive that led to the main house.

As they broke from the trees and the mansion came into view, Sia was struck by an atavistic fear such as she had never experienced. There was no rush or thrill. This was not the exhilaration of the adrenaline junkie; this was the black terror of the captive bound and blindfolded and tossed into a madman's basement.

Porters hustled down the steps to collect bags. Max directed them to ferry the wrapped saddle to Penelope's stall. Sia exited the car, surprised at each step her body allowed. She sat on a massive circular couch in one of the living rooms listening to Vadim's champagne toast, making sensible chitchat, trying in vain to ignore the sickness that seemed to be slithering through her body. She lost track of time; the world seemed to rotate only around the house. She was stirred by a sharp nudge from Anna, who was checking her watch. "If we want to ride today, Sia, we should go now. The sky is clear, and we have only a few hours of light remaining."

"I have something," Sia said, perhaps too loudly, steadying herself on the chair. "It's upstairs." She wobbled up to the bedroom, where she refused to look at the dark things: the dying Mongol horseman in the painting, the gargantuan bed where they had performed for the cameras. She had brought a red bow for the saddlebag, but she slickened the adhesive with sweaty fingers and it would not stick. She abandoned it, returning to the living room with the bag unadorned. She told Anna the saddle itself was waiting for her in the stables, but she simply could not wait to give her the bag. The lump in Sia's throat felt so overgrown, it must have been visible.

"It's beautiful," Anna said, feathering fingers over the RusFarm logo. The Russian tested the pocket size with a stainless-steel water bottle fetched by a butler from the kitchen. "Perfect," she said.

In the stables Sia put the tack on her mare. They slid the new saddle on Penelope. Panic surged in Sia's chest as Anna, tight grip on a farrier's knife, sliced at the RusFarm logo embossed on the saddlebag's leather. It is not linked to the concealment device anyhow, Sia told herself, I am sure it will be fine. Dear god, please let it be fine. Anna worked the blade over the tooled leather until she could rip loose a few pieces, obscuring the logo. Flicking those onto a pile of manure, Anna stomped it into the muck and spat on the mess. Waving off an approaching groom, Anna led Penelope from the barn as Sia followed with her mare.

They swung into their saddles and trotted north, toward the birch forest and the transmission line Sia did not want to think about. The mansion and barns disappeared behind them, replaced by fields wearing wind-blown coats of snow and ice. The weak winter sun, only a few hours risen, would begin its descent in just a few more. They nudged the mares down a rolling hill, toward the mouth of the forest. In silence they rode over patches of frozen black earth, under felled birch and pine. They wound by a stream curdled into green ice. This was a different route than Sia's previous ill-fated ride through RusFarm, but it nonetheless conjured the awful memory in brilliant detail. Could she trust Anna? And were they being watched? An hour into the ride, and Sia had begun wondering about that.

———

CHERNOV WATCHED THE TWO WOMEN ON HORSEBACK FROM THE PIPED feed of a hovering FSB surveillance drone, an Orbiter UAV purchased from the Israelis a decade earlier. It was not new, but it could carry the required cameras and transmitters, the electric motor was quiet, and it could reach nearly ten thousand feet and loiter for well over three hours. More than sufficient to film this odd horseback ride.

Chernov had brought several officers to the farm—the drone operators, a small surveillance team, Daniil and Arkady for help with some of the heavy stuff, if it came to that. They'd commandeered an old administrative building at the property's edge, a cinder-block pile well clear of the main house. Chernov had considered arresting everyone upon arrival at Pulkovo. Now he wondered if he should pluck them from the horses.

But the nasty business with the boyfriend had changed Chernov's opinion of Anna Agapova. She was a hard woman. The sort that does not confess, even when her sins required it. He might lock her up, perhaps even snatch toes and fingernails, but in the end it would be fruitless. Some people will just not bend. Anna was one of those. Whisk her to Butyrka, force her to watch the dismemberment of her father, and she would coolly tell him to fuck off. Chernov had reviewed, again and again, the surveillance footage of her Ostozhenka apartment on the night she'd discovered her lover's arm. The pure hate in those eyes. He'd seen it before: Chechnya, Beslan, Syria. Hard to bend hate like that. He would see what she was working with the lawyer. Then he would make his move.

The women halted at the mouth of the birch forest. As the drone circled, Chernov reviewed the map. His finger came to rest on the road nearest the horses. It would be a stretch for the parabolic mics. He flicked on his radio and called the surveillance team with the coordinates. "Take the northern road," Chernov said. "It skirts the bottom of the hills. There will be a transmission line on top."

ANNA BROUGHT PENELOPE TO A HALT, AND SIA PULLED ALONGSIDE. Anna was fixated on a frozen pond in the clearing ahead. The mare whinnied. Dead straw near the pond flattened in the wind. "Where is the closest road?" Sia asked.

Anna nudged her jaw north, toward the hills. "Let's go deeper into the woods."

They trotted for a few minutes into the thickening birches. Then Anna brought them to a stop.

"We've got new comms for you," Sia said. She swung down from the mare, feet crunching in the snow. Anna watched curiously as Sia approached Penelope.

Sia looked up at Anna. "You should dismount." A thin smile, and Anna complied. Sia flung open one of the saddlebag pockets, removed the collapsible stainless-steel cups, adjusted the strap, and compressed the three snaps. She motioned for Anna to look inside. Sia wiggled the loose leather panel still inside the pocket, then pulled it back to reveal the laptop.

"Same machine as before," Sia said.

"How does the compartment open?" Anna asked. Sia showed her. Anna stared at the computer. She bit her lip and shut the compartment.

"The keyboard sequence is different," Sia said. "Tech problems. We need to practice."

"CAN YOU GET A BETTER VIEW?" CHERNOV ASKED THE DRONE OPERATOR.

"I will try," he said. "They are deep in the trees."

Chernov radioed the surveillance team. "The audio is shit," the lead said. "They are a ways off."

"Pipe it through anyway," Chernov said.

He clicked into the live feed beaming into the computer. Anna was speaking. "Space . . . control . . ." Then it cut out for a few seconds. "Again," he heard the lawyer say. "J. . . . enter . . ." It went on like that. Sizzling static, garbles. He scratched at his bald head. How odd.

He squinted at the video feed on the drone operator's computer. "What are they doing?"

"I can't tell. They are standing by the horses. Maybe having a drink."

"Space . . . control . . ."

How very odd.

AFTER FIFTEEN TRIES, ANNA THOUGHT SHE HAD IT. SHE OPENED AND closed the compartment one more time to be certain. She rubbed Penelope's ribs and shoulder, squinting north, toward the hills.

The hills sent those little electric curls running down her spine. She popped her jaw and mounted Penelope and looked up at the pale aluminum sun. Sia was starting north, toward the mouth of the forest and the open pasture.

"Let's go this way," Anna called, nudging Penelope south. "It's beautiful in here."

They cut deeper into the woods, slinking around the pond toward the foot of a hill piled with trees and rocks. There was a craggy overhang at the hill's base. They dismounted and Anna thought she saw Sia's hand trembling when she patted her horse. Had Sia also noticed a disturbance? Anna poured brandy into the cups. They ducked under the overhang and sat on the rocks and looked at each other for a moment. Anna felt a flash of camaraderie with this woman. Bound to her by the grim mechanics of what they had set in motion.

"Do you have someone out there?" Sia whispered.

"No," Anna said. They sat in silence. A branch cracked off in the distance. Then Anna thought she heard a low, almost imperceptible whine. Maybe in the sky. "I do not think anyone can hear us here," Anna said. "But we should not stay long."

Sia's face tightened. "If anyone saw you practicing . . ."

Anna downed the brandy in a single burning gulp. "Then we are already dead."

"WHAT DO YOU THINK, BOSS?" DANIIL SAID. THE FSB TEAM WAS STARING at the circling drone feed. The women had slipped into the rocks.

Wordless crackle piped from the parabolic mics.

"Maybe they are lovers," Daniil mused, nose wrinkled. "A tryst among the snowcapped rocks. Her husband hates her, she hates him, who knows?"

Chernov now thought he had stumbled upon something much more interesting than a crooked lawyer selling the boss's secrets to a rival. Unless they were lovers—and he did not buy that for a moment—he could see no reason for this diversion into the forest. They had the bath-house, they had the mansion, they had all of Russia. No, this ride did not make sense. This was more than Agapov and his daughter searching for their lost money. It felt evil, sinful. It felt like treason.

54

RusFarm

ANNA WAS ROLLING A SMOOTH STONE IN HER FINGERS. SHE PLUNKED it to the ground. "When will it begin?" she asked.

"Two, maybe three weeks."

"Too long. What are you waiting for?"

"More information. When you log in to the computer you will find a message waiting with a few more things that we need. Addresses, phone numbers. We have gone back and forth with our lawyers about what we can and cannot do. And to whom. We have a few new targets."

Anna nodded, but her faced was creased with agitation. "Look at me," she told Sia. "Look closely."

Sia looked into Anna's eyes.

"I am doing this because I want Goose dead or diminished," Anna said. "I want my father free, and I want Vadim gone. It is simple. Can you guarantee me that the operation will do this?"

"I can guarantee that incriminating information will be placed into the hands of senior Russian officials. But the rest? Anna, please, you know as well as I do that there are no guarantees."

Anna looked like she had questions, but they did not come. Black birds were rustling in the trees. Was something out here with them?

"I want to cover the exfil route with you," Sia whispered.

"I told you no in Switzerland," Anna snapped. "Don't fucking push me on this again, Sia."

Sia had been so in the flow that only now did she notice the damn tremor spiking in her left hand. She balled it into a fist. Petulant Russian. In that awkward silence Anna removed her hat to scratch her head. Sia had not noticed earlier, but in the light she saw that a few streaks of gray were braided into the blond. She looked hollowed out, shadows carved under her eyes.

"Anna," Sia said softly, "did something happen to you?"

The Russian's eyes ignited. For a long and heavy moment Anna did not speak. Then she said, "They took something from me."

"Tell me what it is," Sia whispered. "Who it is. Please. There is so little time."

"I had a lover," Anna said. "Goose killed him. His dog Chernov killed him. They all killed him."

The wind carried off Anna's words. Sia thought about making for the plane. Get in a car and head straight to Pulkovo.

Anna stood. "Now, I am sure you are wondering whether my information is valid. Perhaps I am in emotional distress, a damaged little girl." Anna kicked at a rock. "Tell your psychologists to screw off for me, will you? I've never been more certain about anything in my life. Our path is clear."

I go back to the house, Sia thought, and I collect Max. We say something urgent has come up. We say his father died. We say anything to get to the airport.

"Anna, I am so sorry," Sia said, choosing her words with lawyerly care. "I hope that our work together can help you find some peace."

Anna made a face. "I have known love twice in my life. From my mother, and from him. Now both are gone. Taken. There are accounts to settle. I am searching for things, Sia, but peace, well, peace is not one of them. Peace would mean they win. And I want to win."

———

THEY WOUND NORTH INTO THE PASTURE TOWARD THE STABLES. IN THE gathering dusk the hills above painted dull shadows across the fields. Something glinted in the sky, a phantom sliding through the gray linen clouds.

And then, at last, Sia knew.

She was hot and cold all at once. She could smell the sweat rolling down her ribs.

Night was falling when they hung up the tack. Horses poked heads through their yokes. Sia yanked Anna into Penelope's stall. The mare eyed them quizzically, munching her evening feed. Sia pulled Anna's ear to her mouth and whispered, "They are watching us. We need a plan, Anna. Right now."

———

THE DRONE LOITERED OVERHEAD, CAPTURING THE TWO WOMEN WALK-ing from the stables to the house. Chernov switched to the feeds inside the home. The lawyer went upstairs to her room and turned on the shower, Anna to an office on the first floor that was not covered by the cameras. *Blyad.* Fucking hell. He flipped back to the lawyer. She had her phone in hand, the other dangled in the shower, testing the temperature.

"Hey, Rhonda, it's Sia. Hey, yes, all good here. A little melancholy with the weather but the company is terrific. Just terrific. Calling for the debrief on the Acton meetings this morning. Be a love and give me the highlights?"

The lawyer listened, asked a few questions. Then she disrobed and stepped into the shower.

Chernov flipped to the cameras covering the hallway outside the office. The door was shut. Anna was inside. What was she doing?

Palo Alto

A LIGHT RAIN HAD FALLEN ON PALO ALTO BUT THE TROJANS HAD papered over the windows of the WeWork command center so no one had a clue. An emptied tub of Red Vines licorice was jammed into the trash, its replacement displayed proudly on a table alongside a gigantic cup of cherry-flavored coffee and a few bags of Twizzlers. Procter's autographed baseball bat was propped in a darkened corner. She picked it up and walked over to the glowing blue light of a monitor, where Snake sat with his hands over his mouth in a solemn triangle. He clicked play.

"*Hey, Rhonda, it's Sia. Hey, yes, all good here. A little melancholy with the weather but the company is terrific. Just terrific. Calling for the debrief on the Acton meetings this morning. Be a love and give me the highlights?*"

During the two-minute-twenty-five-second exchange that followed, Sia signaled through the clunky code words that they were under hostile surveillance and triggered the exfil. Her voice was tight as hell, Procter thought. Strung out. Procter's gnomish hands curled tightly around the ash handle.

She thought about calling Bradley, but decided against for now. She guzzled half the cherry-flavored coffee, wiped her mouth. None of this made sense.

"Have the SCORPIONs kill the lights," she told Snake. "Tell those damn Finns to be ready for three people."

RusFarm

ANNA SLAMMED SHUT THE DOOR OF RUSFARM'S FIRST-FLOOR OFFICE. The house was quiet, Max and Vadim evidently still in the bathhouse. She moved quickly, uncertain how large the team might be, or what they intended. The watchers had to be Chernov's men. They are working with Vadim, she thought. How could they not be? They have the cameras. The office had a second door that led to another corridor that wound to the gravel staff parking lot. Keys were usually left in the cars. She called Vadim. No answer, straight to voice mail. That bastard.

She flung open the cabinet with the guns. Checking to be sure the safety was on, she slapped a magazine into the MP-443 and stuffed it into the pocket of her *dublyonka*. She took an extra magazine for good measure. Finding a loose nine-millimeter round in a box, she loaded the lipstick gun and hid it in the interior breast pocket of her coat. No safety on that one. She angled it down, away from her head.

She marched out of the office, down the hall, and into the gravel lot. She found a Land Cruiser. Locked. Another. Also locked. A matte-black BMW, front doors stenciled in gold with the RusFarm logo. Open. Keys in the cupholder. Threats everywhere but they were watching, waiting. For what? Movement would answer the question.

She pumped the gas, BMW fishtailing on the icy drive. She would check for surveillance, then return for Sia and Max if she was black or could create a gap. She drove toward the northern road. No tail, no lights, no roadblock. In a few minutes she was alone on the dark road, birch and pine looming on either side like great cliffs. She called Vadim again. Voice mail. The car's headlamps painted two deer darting across the road. She checked for more, eyes bouncing between the ditch and the road.

A snow flurry kicked up. Anna set down the phone and clenched the wheel for a few kilometers. She tried to work through the problem. Nothing was clear. She could not see the endgame. The snow was falling thick and fast. She couldn't see the damn road in front of her.

Then, as she crested a rise, the headlights pooled in glowing golden eyes. She slammed the brakes and mashed the horn. Two deer darted off. The third did not. The car banged into the light-blinded deer, spilling it to the ground. Shit, Anna muttered. Shit. She reversed and backed off the empty road. No airbags. No warning lights. The engine hummed and the heater rolled. The deer tried to stand. It fell. The doe once more tried to rise, but one of its hind legs was shattered. It found no purchase and fell again. Anna looked toward the trees.

There would be no clarity, Anna knew.

From here it was only intuition, instinct.

She reached into her coat for the pistol, weighing it in her slight hands. On the day they buried Mama, her father said that death was freedom. She thought even then he was full of it because he clung so bitterly to the pain of this life. The doe's head tilted toward the car. Death is freedom, she heard her father say to a little girl she no longer knew.

Peezdetz, she whispered to the steering wheel. Fuck it all.

She swung open the door and stepped out, gun in hand. Swollen snowflakes quickly blanketed her coat. Walking toward the animal, she listened for the tick of an approaching engine but heard only the doe's ragged, labored breathing and the crunch of her footsteps through the snow.

FLOATING DOWN THROUGH THE CLOUD COVER FOR AN UNOBSTRUCTED view, the surveillance drone above caught Anna reviewing the injuries of a struggling deer. She brought a hand to rest on its head and crouched to whisper into the animal's upturned ears. Were the snow not so heavy, the drone might have caught her eyes briefly shut, as if in prayer.

———

ANNA LOOKED INTO THE DOE'S FRIGHTENED EYES, GLISTENING WET and shining under the falling snow. She gently ran her fingers from the doe's nose up its muzzle and onto its head.

Then, as if seeing the board from a new angle, as if she had walked forward in time, Anna's next moves took form in her mind, a smudge of land on a distant horizon, the endgame. Anna stroked the animal's head. "I am sorry," she said, "that I took so long to decide."

Perhaps death was freedom after all. But such mercies Anna would not enjoy. She would win. She would live.

Anna stepped back, flicked off the safety, and fired three rounds into the doe's head. Gunshots rang through the birches. The doe's chest stilled and the snow beneath its head ran red as its life emptied out.

A red haze appeared out in the snow well beyond the deer. Flickering blue. And as she turned she heard the purr of an engine come floating through the storm and soon a black car was cresting the low rise behind her. It rolled to a stop beside the deer. Two men hustled out, guns drawn. She slowly raised her own above her head. Then she set it in the snow and put up her hands.

57

RusFarm / Palo Alto

THE RUSFARM BATHHOUSE, LIKE THE FARM ITSELF, WAS NOT A PLACE where comfort was easily found. Max had asked to see Penelope, maybe pay a visit to Smokey Joe, but Vadim had insisted they start with a steam. It will be relaxing, Vadim said, the heat will settle our minds before we turn to business. But the sauna was so scorching Max could bear no more than a few minutes. The freezing plunge pool vacuumed his lungs of air and shriveled his cojones to wilted figs. Vadim had occasionally been focused, his face glued to his phone as he tapped and scrolled. But then he had also been spacey, the phone ringing and ringing without answer or acknowledgment. Since they'd entered the bathhouse, not a single word had passed between them. On their third trip through the sauna Max slashed a ladle of water across the rocks clustered atop the cast-iron stove. Peering out into the cheerless pool room, he eased onto the bench with a creak, clicked his tongue, and snapped the silence: "Where are the girls, Vadim?"

"Anya insisted I behave. For your sake, I suspect."

"She is a thoughtful woman."

"Not with me." His tone was even and cold, as if he were describing a malfunctioning kitchen appliance.

"Why did you invite me here, Vadim?"

"To talk business."

"We've not talked much."

"So talk."

msright.

"The mare, Penelope. She returns to San Cristobal. That horse is our first and only piece of business to discuss."

Through the hot air, chin snug on the heels of his hands, Vadim met Max with a gaze of miserable amusement. "Let's have the lawyers work it through. We can be sensible, can't we? Even dignified. Horse racing is a sport for kings, after all. A fight is beneath us, Max."

Max was smiling, but the humor stopped short of his eyes. "Fighting, I think, is all we have left."

That earned him a big toothy smile before a puff of steam from the rocks took Vadim behind its veil. When the cloud lifted, the Russian's head was addressing the floor. "Can I tell you something I find interesting?"

Max spat. He stared at Vadim.

"I was not raised on this farm," Vadim said. "But even I know when a storm is on its way. I feel it before the radar sees it. I didn't grow up on the land, as you did at San Cristobal, but I have a connection to this place, and it speaks to me. I know, for instance, that a snowstorm is coming. A blizzard, on its way tonight. And I swear to you I have not paid a scrap of attention to the weather reports today. The pressure is changing. The air is growing wet and it carries a faint hint of metal. Can you taste it? Smell it? Tell me, Max."

"We're in a fucking steam room, Vadim. I'm not so calibrated."

Vadim chuckled darkly toward his knees. "You want to ride Penelope today, yes, you mentioned earlier going out to the stables?"

"Maybe not with a blizzard on the way."

Vadim cinched the towel around his waist, crossed the floor, and creaked onto the bench alongside Max. "It is wise," he said, "not to ride in rough weather." He clasped Max's shoulder, then knocked a wet palm into his bare lower back. "And because you are wise, Max, I wonder why you have returned."

"You invited me."

Vadim's hand flickered in agitation. "Yes, yes, of course. But you and I both know there are things floating beneath the surface. Things deeper than a simple invitation, which of course was not such a simple thing. Unseen forces, but very real. And powerful. More powerful than us. We are pawns, Max. We are a sideshow in this whole affair. At least now. Perhaps we did not start here, but I'm afraid it is where we've traveled." Vadim stared straight ahead, his eyes sparring with the wall's knotted wood.

"Speak plainly, Vadim."

"I have a good story about Napoleon, do you want to hear it?"

"No."

"It is perhaps apocryphal, but I rather like it. He was asked once what trait he valued most in his generals. And do you know what he said?"

A metallic clank sounded in the pool room. Murmurs.

"Do you know? Have you heard it?" Vadim repeated. Footfalls. Voices.

Vadim tossed another ladle of water across the rocks. The snarl of steam drowned out the noise.

"Shit, Vadim, no. I have not."

"Napoleon said he preferred his generals to be lucky." Vadim ran his hands through his slick hair, his lips firmed into a grim smile. "I was lucky to have experienced your hospitality in Mexico before you visited us here at RusFarm. You drew first blood, as it were, during our little night in the rain. But you did so without knowing the shape of the fight, and the lengths I might journey to win. You made a mistake, though how could you have known? And now you've returned. For a horse? Not a fucking chance. You hate me for claiming your mother's mare, but you're here for those deeper reasons, the unseen things your Sia believes to be hidden from me. From us. She's a bad girl, Max, a bad, bad girl. And a crooked lawyer playing a rather dangerous double game, don't you think? Hiding money for our family's rivals and then trying to hide our own. Playing all sides. But what really is her game? I have ideas. Theories. But whatever it is, you've wandered back into my web"—Vadim began spider-walking his fingers toward Max's leg—"as I once wandered into yours at San Cristobal. These women, eh? What foul company we keep. My god, sometimes I think I never should have married, just run through whore after whore after whore. It would have been a less savage price than I paid for my wife, who is a devil with an unformed heart. The species of woman whose fights are always righteous, so she's required to kill in their cause. Kill whomever she wants. She'd murder us all if she had to. And she might, my friend, she still might." The spider-walking fingers halted, turned to fangs striking the air, then withdrew to assist in the ejection of snot from his nostrils.

Murmurs rolled against the shut door. Vadim looked at Max, who met his stare with hard, unblinking eyes. "Give me back my fucking horse."

"It's unbearably hot in here," Vadim said. He got up and opened the door. In rushed the sound of voices and the squish of boots in water and the smell of cold cement. The door slammed shut, Vadim disappeared, and all that remained was the heartbeat in his temples.

Max was still for a moment, dread crowding his throat. "*Dios mio*," he whispered. "*Dios mio.*" He put his head in his hands. Took a long pull of scorching air through his nostrils. Cinched the towel tight around his waist. Then he stood straight and walked out of the steam room and flinched. But there was no blow, no bag over the head, no gunshot, no fire of a blade stuck into his body.

There were just the two men standing beside Vadim.

They wore fur-lined parkas and boots, and their hard, dead eyes suggested they might well have been shift workers on a slaughterhouse production line. This was their work. This was another day at work.

Max stood there. Vadim knotted the towel around his own waist, tugging to check that it was tight.

"I am not accustomed to violence, Max. Only a few scrapes in school, and I've killed just one person. A pedestrian in Piter. Hit her with my car. A complete accident."

"My horse," Max said, "I want the fucking horse."

"When they are done with you I am going to butcher your mare, or my mare, I should say. If you're still alive you will watch it happen. My chefs will freeze her meat and each week, perhaps each day, I will consume more of her. I don't much care for horsemeat, but I will relish these cuts. I—"

A heavy, metallic sigh. Then the power went out.

And for a moment the world was still.

If you fly the emergency signal, Procter had said in St. Ives, we'll have the SCORPIONs kill the power. Blind the cameras.

Russian curses and footfalls.

The swish of parkas, angry grunts.

Move.

Then a click, and a flashlight was searching the room.

Max was charging toward the door when a second sinister click announced the arrival of incredible pain. Muscles stiffened and burned. He flopped onto the concrete and soon shapes hunched over him. The room was dark, his vision blurred, every tendon and muscle firing in pain, and he was watching wires sway from his own chest under the glare of the flashlight.

Vadim's voice called to him from the darkness above, then came bursts of pain in his ribs and chest and he could smell the man's sweat, sense the Russian's face hovering just above his own. The two men pulled Vadim off and he vanished into the depths of the room.

"She's steak," he heard Vadim howl into the darkness. "Penelope is steak, amigo."

The slam of a door.

Hot breath on his face. Then a snarl of angry Russian words and—

———

THEY'D TAKEN SIA NOT A MINUTE AFTER THE POWER DIED. TWO MEN. They'd kicked open the bedroom door and she'd managed to toss an end table at one of them before the click of the stun gun. Then she'd seized up, gone numb, blacked out.

Now Sia was awake and gliding and it was as black inside the hood as it had been in the house or the caverns of her unconscious mind. They were carrying her. Could she dispatch a distress signal to Anna? To Langley? To block out the fear, her mind latched on to that problem as they bumped her along hallway walls. She had no ideas. Her carriers deposited her on a hard floor. A switch flicked but no light came. More curses. Darkness. Silence. She wondered what they'd done with Max. She rolled over and waited to die.

PROCTER CRUSHED THE EMPTIED CAN OF JOLT IN HER HANDS AND threw it toward the trash can, missing terribly. Snake was dialing Bradley on the secure video teleconference, the SVTC, cursing that the connection kept dropping. Procter leaned the bat against the desk, cracked open another Jolt, smacked the table, and asked Georgie if it was ready, man, we've got to fucking move, pronto. Had anyone slapped a blood pressure cuff on the Chief at that moment, they would have been forgiven for darting down the hall for a defibrillator. And even Procter, who, like a wild animal, was in tune with the rhythms of her body without any sentient awareness of their existence, wondered if her fucking heart was going to pop like a stomped grape.

The techies were readying the phone array. She sucked down the can of Jolt. "We're ready," George mumbled. "This one will look like the restaurant trying to confirm her reservations next week. It's called . . ." He flipped through a document. "Saint Bethany."

Procter set her jaw and silently rehearsed her lines as the Saint Bethany maître d'. Satisfied, she dialed the number. Straight to voice mail. She slammed the phone into the receiver.

"Fuck. Queue another backup for Castillo," she barked at the techie. "The one that looks like his father's villa." She was absolutely dialed up, and though several reasonable explanations existed—in theory—for her officers to miss three pings demanding proof of life, she considered none of them plausible. Not after Sia's call. Procter put down a few Twizzlers as she considered the options. The baseball bat had resurrected fond memories of her more kinetic management style in the field. She missed that impounded Mossberg shotgun. Now she was stateside with a bunch of nerds while Russians goosed her officers. The curse of the Penalty Box. Her bat was slick with sweat in Palo Alto, instead of out there, wet with Russian blood. Snake was cursing at the SVTC. The connection to Langley was still static.

That was enough. Procter gently placed the Twizzler bag on the table. She scraped a piece of dried mud from Chief Wahoo's smiling face. She wandered out to the whiteboards with the bat on her shoulder.

She stared at the picture of Vladimir Putin falling on the ice during a hockey game.

She got into a nice stance, planted her feet, and swung the bat right into him. His puffy fucking face disappeared. Paper and whiteboard shards scattered about. Then she worked on one of the TV screens until it spiderwebbed and fell from the wall. She saw that picture of Putin kissing a young boy's stomach, taped right to a desk, so she went over there and beat that one to hell, too. Got some parts of the desk and the computer, but that was an accident. Techies and FINO guys were shouting and scrambling for cover. She heard nothing. Bat on her shoulder, she turned to Snake.

"Tell me when you get through to the boss man," she said. "I'll be in my office meditating."

———

SIA HEARD THE CREAK OF THE DOOR OPENING, BUT SHE COULD SEE only the darkness of the hood. She felt rough hands hauling her up, and then she was being marched from the room in darkness. No one spoke. They wended through a maze of hallways. Movement could create opportunities. To signal, fight, or bargain. They wanted *something*. After all, she was still alive. And that, she found, was worrisome.

Maybe they were Vadim's guys. Maybe they would turn her in to the FSB. Maybe they *were* FSB. That seemed like the winner. They set her in a chair and tugged off the hood. She blinked; her body clenched, waiting for the pain.

Max was bound in a chair in front of her. Their eyes exchanged confusion and terror, and then Sia tried to get her bearings. A fireplace to her right, bear head mounted above. In the shadows she saw the outlines of a piano. Thick drapes framed the moonlit windows. Her toes wiggled on cold stone.

Vadim was watching two men crumpling newspaper. He was feverishly rubbing knuckles; scratching around his eyes; smoothing his hair again and again as if he could not flatten a cowlick. Not the energy of a man in charge.

"Where is Anna?" Sia demanded.

Vadim glanced at her.

"Where is she?" Sia said. "She is your wife, Vadim."

He looked as though he might hit her, but as she steeled herself for the blow, he suddenly turned away, toward the fireplace.

The two men left. They returned with logs and a jerry can of petrol. They crisscrossed the wood and crumpled paper into the gaps. The larger one doused the logs and tossed in a match. Sia tilted away from the leaping flames. The smaller man tended the fire with a poker. The beefy one fed a few more logs into the blaze. Vadim mumbled to himself from the couch.

God, where was Anna? Sia thought. Max looked at Sia, then through her, at something behind her. The fire's glow danced across his sweat-slick face.

Then hands were on her shoulders, a genial slap on the right one.

A towering man strode past, firelight reflecting off his bald head. He dragged an armchair from beside the couch to form a ring of seats around the fireplace. He wore a trim black suit, no tie. She thought the loafers were Brunello Cucinelli. Benny Hynes had the same pair.

"Hortensia Fox," he said in English. "And Maximiliano Castillo. Welcome to Russia."

Sia recognized the face; this was one of the FSB officers Anna had suggested they frame alongside Goose. Chernov. Lieutenant Colonel Konstantin Chernov. Internal Security Directorate. In one of the cables after Switzerland, Anna said he was a freak. He is a true believer, she had written. He considers himself a priest. And Russia is his God.

58

RusFarm

ONE OF THE OFFICERS COLLECTED ANNA'S PISTOL FROM THE SNOW. "Chernov would like a word," the other said. "At the house."

They searched her: legs, arms, inside her coat. They missed the lipstick. One of the men sat with her in the backseat of the car. They drove in silence.

The sodium lights strung on the tall pines flanking the drive were dark. Not a light shone above the stables or the racetrack. Had Chernov cut the power? Agitated barks came from the Alsatian pen.

"Why are the lights off?" she asked.

The men did not answer.

They entered the circle, looping around the fountain. She glimpsed a smudge of orange firelight glowing through a living room window. The rest of the house was dark. One of the FSB officers led her out of the car by the elbow. Snow stuck to her face and melted down her cheeks into her mouth. His partner, speaking into a radio, got back in the car. The FSB officer nearly slipped on his way up the marble steps, steadying himself on Anna's elbow. As he led her through the door, Anna examined the security camera overhead, wondering if any of this would work.

————

YOU ARE A LAWYER, YES? CHERNOV HAD ASKED AT FIRST, IN HEAVILY accented English. Yes, Sia heard herself say, I am. Tell me what you gave Anna Agapova, he had said, and she did. His men went upstairs and

pulled phones and computers from cases. They brought them downstairs and made her open them. She told him how she worked with
Mickey Lyadov in London, how she hid the money. Then Chernov had
asked about Sia's ride with Anna that afternoon. The numbers, the letters, he said, I heard strange things in those woods and I want you to
explain them to me. You were out there for a long while.

"What were you talking about?" he asked.

"The information I gave her on Goose's money," she said.

"What specifically?" he asked. "Give me an example."

———

CHERNOV FERVENTLY BELIEVED IN THE POWER OF VIOLENCE, BUT HE
was no sadist. The gore brought little thrill and he did not need to
inflict pain to revel in power over others. He always felt that way. But
he had practiced violence with such zeal, killing hundreds of people
in such different times and places and fashions, that his faith was
now mature. He knew its benefits; he knew its limits. And there were
indeed limits when interrogating a trained intelligence officer. He
could torture the lawyer until she confessed, but she would doubtless
exclude bits of valuable information. She would admit to falsehoods.
Threads would be unpulled. Sinful coconspirators would be left mad-
deningly unpunished.

But violence could accelerate a confession. And now, with the espionage angle in the mix, Chernov was arriving at a drab, bureaucratic
justification to speed one along: Multiple arrests on espionage charges
would chum the waters inside Lubyanka and Yasenevo, inciting a feeding frenzy that would attract the *khozyain*. And Chernov did not want
the *khozyain* swimming toward a drawn-out espionage case involving
a pile of gold that had been smuggled out of the Rodina without his
full knowledge and participation. A quick confession here, in this firelit
room, would hack away much of the bureaucratic bramble upon Chernov's return to Moscow.

"I asked," Chernov said, "what specifically did you discuss with
Anna Andreevna on your ride earlier today?"

The lawyer started rambling. Nonsense about the accounts. He put a finger to her lips.

"I know Anna shelved this operation weeks ago," he said. "No need to talk about all that if she's dropped the op, is there? How about we start simple: You will tell me the intelligence agency that you serve. And if you do not, things will go badly for your boyfriend here." He put a hand on the Mexican's head. Mussed his hair and then gripped it tight in his fingers. He smashed a fist across his jaw, cradling the head so he would not collapse. Hit him again. Again. The lawyer was screaming now. This part always conjured screams.

———

SIA WAS SHOUTING, BUT IT DID NOTHING TO DROWN OUT THE CRACK-ing of a fist against Max's jaw, which was cursing Chernov's mother in machine-gun Spanish. Sia's shirt was sweat-drenched, her hair a damp mop swinging in front of her eyes. After a while her voice faded; she just watched, no longer able to yell.

In Sia's first courses, a lifetime ago, her trainers had explained how to manage an interrogation. It was all different for a NOC, they said. No dip passport. No immunity. You get picked up, you've got no shot at getting out. Why would they let you go? Over beers and out of earshot of the others, one trainer had planted creative ideas for suicide in captivity. You've got bedsheets and a rafter? Hang yourself. Maybe they leave you alone for a few seconds with something sharp? Slit your wrists. Sia's best idea now was to tip herself into the fire.

Chernov stopped beating Max. He sat back down to face her. Sweat was running down his head. "Tell me what you are, Hortensia."

I don't know, she thought. Not even I know the answer to that one.

Chernov scooted his chair closer to Sia's. "CIA? SIS? BND? I'd wager CIA. Come, now, Hortensia, I heard strange things in those woods. You are running Anna, yes? I am impatient to hear you say it."

"I am a lawyer," Sia said. "A lawyer who serves Russian clients. Nothing more."

He mopped sweat from his shaking head. "Hortensia, please, be smart about this. Tonight, I will arrest you, your boyfriend, and Anna. You will all go to Lefortovo. They will break you, wear you down until the truth spills out. I am doing you a favor by accelerating things with a little bit of the rough stuff. Let's get it over with quickly, what do you say?"

"I am a lawyer," she said. "I am not a spy."

"I am going to hurt him again unless you tell me the truth. Do you understand? I do not want to. I am an investigator. I take no pleasure in this. You are leaving me without options. What are you, Hortensia?"

Oh god, she thought, please forgive me, Max. Please forgive me.

"I am a lawyer," she said, in a numb voice. "Nothing more. Please. Please don't hurt him."

Chernov snapped his fingers, then spoke in Russian to one of his men, who left the room. They sat for several minutes as if around a campfire, listening to crackling wood. The man returned with a leather case and spread it open on the redwood coffee table. It was a field dressing kit. Her papa had kept one in his pickup at the ranch. Chernov fixed his eyes on the fire.

"For many years," Chernov said, "I was a soldier. I served in a special FSB unit we call Vympel. I am not sure what your American equivalent is. Perhaps Delta Force? In 2015 I deployed to Syria. Aleppo. Not two weeks in, a terrorist raiding party captured me along with three of my men. Got the best of us while we slept in a building that smelled of blood and dust and shit. They weren't, how do you say, head-choppers. No interest in snuff videos. They put us in a hole to see about a trade for a few of their comrades. I didn't emerge until my unit rescued us three months later."

Chernov poked at the fire and with his other hand wiped his sopping head. "In the darkness I often thought of my grandfather. He was raised in a village outside Stalingrad. The family fled when the Nazis arrived. They walked for days over the open steppe with other refugees. No food, little water. Constant dive-bombing from the Nazi Stukas, sirens screaming their arrival and the coming death. They found shelter with a few survivors in the marshes. My grandfather had three sisters. The youngest could not stop crying, the families feared they would be discovered and killed because of the racket, so his mother took her to the swamp, his sister begging not to be drowned, crying that she would never again ask for food. She did not come back. I was young when I first heard this story, too young, I suppose, but in that Syrian hole I finally made sense of it. God is distant. The world is senseless because the very act of its creation was sinful."

Chernov shook himself from his reverie and picked up a knife with a blunt hooked tip. He knelt by Max's feet. "After a month or so, I suppose after the negotiation stalled, our captors felt a demonstration was in order. Something to show they were hard and serious men. By the time help arrived, my men were long dead, they'd broken my back, and cut off a few of my parts." Then Chernov tapped on Max's right pinkie toe. "They started here."

He looked at Sia. "Tell me what you are, Hortensia."

"I am a lawyer," she said through chattering teeth.

He shook his head.

The two men held Max's shoulders. Chernov brought the hooked tip to the toe. Max's body shifted in the chair. *¡Para!* he murmured. *¡Para! ¡Para! ¡Para!* His leg strained against the binding. His foot squirmed on the floor. Chernov clasped it still, settling the knife back into position.

I'm here, I'm here, Sia's eyes said, but Max wasn't looking at her.

Chernov pushed the knife into the toe, tongue slung across his lip in concentration.

¡Para! ¡Pinche culero!

The delicate veins on Max's neck thickened, rising up through his skin. The curved blade rolled once, twice, three times along the toe until it slid from the foot with a wet little crunch.

Pinche ruso hijo de tu reputísima madre!

Then came a run of blood and another flurry of Spanish curses so clouded by grunts and gasps that to Sia they did not sound like words. Chernov collected and examined the toe. Then he tossed it into the fire. Max's head fell forward, unconscious. A thin trickle of his blood traced along the stone hearth.

"Max, wake up," Sia shouted. "Can you hear me? Wake up."

Chernov boxed her head like she was a bad dog. She tried to spit in his face, but her mouth was dry. There was a tinny ring in her ears. Chernov spoke Russian from what sounded like a great distance. The short security man doused Max with a cup of water. He slapped his face, grunting in broken English for him to awaken. Then she heard a woman's muffled voice.

59

RusFarm

ANNA TRIED TO MAKE SENSE OF THE SCENE. A ROARING FIRE. MAX and Sia bound in chairs. The Mexican was in bad shape—head sagged to the side, blood smeared across his face. Chernov was holding a knife. Vadim slumped on the couch. Two of Chernov's FSB men sat beside him. Her husband, too, seemed a prisoner. What *was* his role in this?

Her FSB escort stopped a few steps into the room to announce his presence to Chernov, who placed the soiled knife on the table. The escort led her deeper into the room. The two men on the couch stood and, along with Chernov, spoke to her escort, exchanging whispers and murmurs and grunts until, arriving at some understanding, the man left the room. An engine came to life down in the circle and motored off, disappearing into the distance.

Vadim, Chernov, and two of his men. Still too many of them, she thought.

"Anna Andreevna," Chernov said. He'd taken a seat to wipe stray droplets of blood from his loafers, and remained focused on the task as he addressed her. "I was just asking Hortensia about the intelligence service she serves."

Anna's gaze settled on the fire behind Chernov.

"I came for answers about Russia's money," Chernov continued, "but I have instead stumbled on a far greater conspiracy. Your strange behavior today will be enough to lock you up, of course. But I'd appreciate your confession. You of all people should know that it will go easier for you if you confess." He looked up from his loafers with a sigh. "But you are not a woman accustomed to the easy path. It is always so difficult with you."

For an almost imperceptible moment, Anna shut her eyes and caught a glimpse of Luka. She opened them. Banish all weakness. Stay in character. It would be the only way through Lefortovo.

"You are gravely mistaken," she said. "I have been running an operation against these two CIA officers for several months. And I have learned that they are collaborating with my husband and a small group of senior Russian officials to rob the state's coffers. The CIA has begun its operation, funds are poised to bleed from the accounts as we speak, and they are planning to flee Russia tonight."

Chernov tilted his head, almost in pity, as if she'd lost her mind. His eyes shimmered with the certainty of the stupid or the insane.

"What?" she heard Vadim bark. She turned to her husband. He was scowling, his face wrinkled in confusion.

"I know this because Vadim told me," Anna said. "He insisted I come with him."

One of the officers on the couch snickered.

Anna continued, "But there was a dispute about the money."

"Anna Andreevna," Chernov said, standing, "stop this. I know you are working for Hortensia. She is CIA, is she not? Did you meet her in Switzerland?"

She took a slow step toward him, ignoring the impulse to run. One meter out. I need him closer. Another step. She could now smell blood and Chernov's shoe leather, but he was still too far.

She spat into his eyes.

He blinked twice. Wiped his smiling face with his sleeve. Then he took a big step and lifted his hand to slap her, but her fingers were already in her pocket cinching around the metallic tube. His palm met her cheek with a sharp smack. He was so close, standing almost on her, but she had the tube free and jammed against his heart, palm twisting the final bit, and there was the click and a bang and her fingers were both on fire and wet with blood. His lifeless body collapsed, pinning her on the couch.

Anna groped around Chernov's belt, searching for a weapon. Finding a handgun, she smoothly withdrew it from the holster, placed it snug against the nearest FSB officer's temple, and squeezed the trigger. Blood and brain painted the lampshade. The smaller FSB officer, standing to draw his own gun, smacked the weapon from her hand, sending it over the couch, clattering across the floor into the shadows.

Anna glimpsed Sia scooting her chair toward him. Anna began wriggling out from under Chernov's body, then heard a crash as Sia flopped into the remaining FSB man's legs. He stumbled forward, back onto the couch. Free of Chernov, Anna lunged for the knife on the table. The FSB officer got off a shot that missed high and sent stone chips flying from the fireplace. Before he could steady his aim she pounced, working the hooked blade up into his chest, pushing and twisting until it was in up to the hilt. His body froze in shock. She withdrew the blade and then plunged it into his heart. Now the life drained from his eyes, blood gurgled over his lips, and she rolled off the couch, heart hammering in her chest. Vadim was sitting there, blinking and unmoved.

He is the doe, Anna thought, frozen in the lights. She stood and picked up the FSB officer's gun and yanked Vadim to the floor by his hair. She rammed the toe of her boot into his ribs. Then kicked him again. And again, harder, because it felt so good. She stopped only because it was not part of her theater.

Vadim slid away, scrunching up against the couch. He raised his hands in surrender. "Anya," he wheezed out. "What the fuck, Anya?"

She looked at him straight on. There was everything to say, half a lifetime of revenge to be had, and yet she felt peace in the silence. His guilt was her reward. She did not care if he suffered.

She looked down at him. She lowered the gun to his head.

———

VADIM SEARCHED ANNA'S EYES BEHIND THE GUN BARREL AND THEY spoke to him. "You win," he said.

———

ANNA SHOT HER HUSBAND THROUGH THE FOREHEAD.

She let the gun slip from her fingers to clank on the floor. Taking stock, she sensed that her ears were not working. Sia and Max's mouths were moving, but they were only pulsing rings. She looked at Vadim's lifeless body. There was a little bloody hole in his head. That was it. Move. What came next?

When the volume cranked back up, she heard herself repeating the lines perfectly: "Vadim, please don't do this, Vadim."

Into the fire she let loose a primal scream until her air was gone and her legs wobbled and she was on her knees. She screamed again until she finally believed that he'd left her here to burn.

"There was a fight," Anna said, delivering her lines, "and Vadim subdued me."

"Anna, what the fuck is going on?" Sia yelled.

"Vadim again tried to convince me to leave. I refused. There was a fight. Vadim beat me badly. He was angry. Drunk. You two said that we had to leave before they noticed any of the money was gone. Vadim was drinking. He drank so much. And there was a fight."

Anna picked up a knife from the field dressing kit. She snipped the cords around Sia's legs and wrists. "There was a fight," Anna repeated. Anna cut Max's restraints. He struggled to stand; Sia helped him up. Anna broke character to explain the scene.

"I will give you a head start," she said. "And a way to get the operation moving. But you will listen to me. You will do exactly as I say. Otherwise, I will kill you both. You will take the route we discussed in the stables, Sia. You will try. You will take Vadim with you. His body is the key. You will take it at all costs. You will tell your people to start funneling money out immediately. Start the operation. You will take your phones and you will signal right now. You will move as fast as you can."

"You can come with us, Anna," Sia said. "We can go together."

"No. I will not." She gestured across the bodies but could not bring herself to look at Vadim's. "You will leave with Vadim. When you return to America, you will find a way to convince Moscow that he was your agent and has been resettled. This is the only path. You get a shot at the operation."

"And what do you get?" Max asked. "They are going to kill you. Don't you see? You are going to die."

Anna allowed herself a glance at her dead husband. "I get to win. Take the body. You must take the body. I only die if you do not do your part."

Sia and Max exchanged harried, frantic glances. Sia ran upstairs for the phones.

"There are cars parked in the lot outside the office," Anna told him. "You will find one that has keys in it."

Sia returned with the phones and a suitcase holding their winter gear. They put on parkas, hats, mittens. Max vomited as he jammed his mangled foot into its boot. Anna looked away.

60

RusFarm

SIA AND MAX HAULED THE BODIES ONTO THE BLOODSTAINED COUCH. Anna fashioned a torch with the dead officer's shirt and the fireplace poker. She piled coats and pillows around the dead. She'd not noticed before how much she was sweating, but she could now taste a steady drip of salt from her lips. It slickened her fingers. It poured into her eyes. She took a gun from one of the dead FSB officers. She did not recognize the model, which was the whole point. One of Vadim's, she told herself. This gun is Vadim's. She slipped it in her coat pocket.

Anna tore down a set of the drapes and doused everything in the remaining petrol. She drenched bookshelves and the piano; she pulled every blanket from a closet and placed them on another couch in a sitting room on the far end of the first floor. From the garages they gathered additional canisters of petrol. They doused stairwells, bookshelves, drapes. Anna spilled petrol through the bedrooms built for children who'd never existed, across the library, and through the musty second-floor offices. They opened windows so air would circulate to feed the blaze. In all, they built four pyres across the house. There was no time for more.

She lit the pyre in the living room while Max and Sia lugged Vadim's corpse from the room. The flames ran across the stacked bodies. She turned away once Chernov's clothes had caught fire.

The snow glowed hauntingly in the moonlight. Beautiful, she

thought. She held the flame at the bottom of the drapes. The fire devoured the velvet and began to run across the ceiling, eating the thick paint and the molding.

———

CHERNOV WAS NOT ANSWERING HIS PHONE. THE FSB DRONE OPERATOR tried Arkady. No answer. He finally got through to the surveillance team. They were sitting in a van outside the cinder-block building. Two people just left the house, the drone operator said. Smoke is coming from the windows. Should we call the fire department?

The head surveillance man, who outranked him, said no. An emphatic no. They couldn't have idiot civilians running around here, he said. He and his team would go in. They would call for reinforcements from Kirishi. The drone operator heard the van outside the administrative building rumble to life. It sped off for the mansion, which he could now see from the feed was most certainly on fire.

———

THE FLAMES TRAVELED QUICKLY, FASTER THAN ANNA COULD HAVE imagined. Smoke filled her throat and nostrils and she felt insane for ending up on the far side of one of the living rooms, away from the door. She was light-headed, the world was airless, and she thought: I am going to die here. The heat was just incredible now, her skin and hair seemed to be smoking, and she wondered if she'd caught fire, too. She fell to the floor. Cooler down here. She could breathe and cough and hack out the strangling smoke. She crawled toward the door. It was quiet, eerily quiet. Hissing and popping and a light crackling, but no blasts, no crashes. I am going to die in silence, she thought. I am not even screaming.

Then she heard Sia shouting her name. Glass shattering. A chandelier surrendering to the inferno. A lamp popped. She was on her belly scraping along the floor for the pure clean air, but the smoke began settling and now she was in a tunnel. More glass shattered. The ceiling groaned as it buckled. She crawled faster. Air, there was no air. She could no longer slither. She pressed her face into the floor and tried to suck air through the baking hardwood. I am going to die, Luka, she said. I am going to die now.

———

SIA WATCHED ANNA STOP MOVING. "SIA, WE'VE GOT TO GO," MAX screamed from the foyer. "Come on, Sia. Come on. Move." Sia took one step toward the foyer, but as she was thinking about abandoning Anna to the flames she just flopped herself to the damn floor and started crawling. There was only smoke. Her lungs begged for air. She pawed around for Anna. She put her hand on scorching metal. Snapped it back. Patted around again. The floor. Nothing but the baking floor. Then she felt a hand. Hair. A shoulder. She grasped that hand and began scooting back, dragging Anna until they reached a hazy hallway. Still hot, but she could see. Air filled her lungs. For a minute they choked on the floor. When Anna retched, Sia laughed, but her air-starved brain did not know why. "We need time," Sia said. "Give us time."

Anna wiped a dribble of vomit onto her sleeve. She nodded.

Sia stood and extended a hand to Anna, who took it. Sia hauled her up.

"Now," Anna said. "The catastrophe."

———

ANNA'S EYES WATERED AND THE CHEMICAL SMOKE LINGERED DEEP down, almost inside her stomach. She felt a tickling urge to vomit again, but she could only hack and choke and spit, and her voice was gravel when she yelled, "Now run, Sia. Run, run. Run." From the living room a hunk of the ceiling collapsed.

God, she thought, this burning house is beautiful.

When Anna turned back, Sia was gone.

Anna watched the fire frolic and dance. Clouds of flame billowed on the ceiling's bones, the blaze glowing orange and brilliant white. The purest white she had ever seen. This fire would erase this home. It would rob her husband and Chernov of honor. It would devour her dying world. But my god, the heat. She'd never felt anything like it. And in the dead of Russian winter. She stumbled back, farther into the foyer, where the smoke was thinner. She pulled the dead officer's gun from her coat. "Vadim shot me during the fight," she recited her lines to the flames. "He left me to die in the fire."

She nuzzled the barrel into her own shoulder, careful to avoid bones and ligaments. She slammed shut her eyes. Then Anna squeezed the trigger.

61

RusFarm

THEY KNEW FSB TEAMS WOULD BE CRAWLING ALL OVER THIS CAR in less than an hour, so Max had laid Vadim in the backseat and wrapped his wrecked head in a blanket. Didn't want blood everywhere, signaling he was dead. Sia ran out the front door and down the marble steps. Her face was covered in ash. Hair stringy and burnt. For a moment Max's world funneled down to details: frost glinting on the windshield, a wad of paper crumpled in the cupholder, Sia's scuffed, red-painted nails as she slid into the passenger seat, twisting to examine Vadim's body.

The car jackknifed on the ice as they shot past the barns and the veterinary facility and the racetrack, and he thought of how he'd lost his mother's damn horse for good, these goddamn Russians. The power was still out, thank god, the only light the occasional speck of the moon and the glowing snow and the flames leaping from the roof of the mansion behind them. When he hit potholes Vadim's lifeless legs would flop in the back seat.

At the fork he tried to picture the satellite images with the thick red lines marking the BEAR CRAWL. He braked, and pain shot up his leg from his foot. Left, he was pretty sure he had to go left. Or was it? "Left," Sia said. He turned left. He brought the car to a nice clip on a straight stretch of road leading into the forest. Toward the hills north of the farm and the transmission line. Max chugged slowly up a rise to avoid fishtailing, but on the icy backside of the hill they slid into a shallow gulch. The wheels spun and spun and spun.

"We're too far to walk this," she said.

"We've got to dig," Max replied. He fell out of the car to the ground.

They clawed snow out from under the tires. Huge freezing clumps, each scoop numbing Max's hands through the mittens. He shoveled snow until the wheels kissed frozen brown earth and his fingers burned from the cold. They got back in the car. He nosed it forward, onto the road, and they slid again, but he kept it from spilling into another ditch. He clutched the wheel with his red-raw hands. The snow fell fast and thick and he could not prevent the car from sliding. He and Sia tried to piece together whether Anna's plan might work, but it was hard to talk, what with the car slithering and fishtailing and the dead guy flopping around in the back and his own chipped jaw and bloody fucking foot.

"We can't let them take us," Sia said. Her fingers were white, gripped tight around the oh-shit handle as they went over a bump.

"Does Vadim have a gun on him?" Max said.

Sia slumped into the back to fish through Vadim's pockets. "No," she said. "Shit. Shit. Shit."

"Then we'll have to make them kill us," he said.

The road dead-ended into a rickety wooden fence at the foot of a hill. He still could not make out the transmission line's silhouette above. Any minute he expected the whir of rotor blades, the bark of the Alsatians, the cries and footfalls of a chase team.

"I'll carry Vadim," Max said. He peered up the darkened ridge. "My god."

62

RusFarm

ANNA STOOD IN THE DARKNESS OF THE STABLES. THROUGH A WIN-dow she saw headlamps snake around the statue up at the house. Two cars. Vans. Eight men spilled out. She saw one speak into a radio; another made a call on his phone. They tried at least three doors, but the fire was so overgrown they could not enter the house and instead stood gawking at the blaze. There were too many of them to kill. And she could not cover it up, anyhow. She slid the door wide enough for a horse to fit through.

At Anna's approach, Penelope whinnied and stuck her head through the yoke of her stall door. She patted Penelope's muzzle and tried to put on the tack. Her left arm hung limply at her side. Anna dragged a stool next to the mare and awkwardly slipped on the saddle and bridle. Then, with her right hand, she brought her limp left to the bridle and clasped her fingers around it. Her shoulder screamed. White dots danced through her vision. She held the bridle and managed to squirm, face-down, onto Penelope's back. Nose pressed into the mare's mane, Anna heaved herself upright. She patted her coat for her phone and the gun. Still there, thank God. She trotted Penelope into the night.

The fire now rioted in the second-floor windows. A few flames had reached the roof.

She called Maximov. No answer, but she left a hasty message explaining the evening's events, warning of the gathering threat.

Then Anna brought Penelope to a trot heading north. You are dead, she called back to the expiring house. You are dead. She clamped her hand against the reassuring outline of the gun. Steeling herself for the pain in her shoulder, she urged Penelope toward the ridge, trailing the tire tracks through the fresh snow. Anna considered how she would make them believe she had tried to kill Sia. The low whine of helicopters signaled that perhaps someone else would actually do it.

———

AT FIRST SIA HEARD A FAINT BUZZ IN THE WHITEOUT, BUT IT WAS SOON drowned by their grunts and curses and the swish of boots through fresh snow. They struggled up the path, zigzagging along switchbacks toward the top of the ridge, which seemed no closer. Gusts of wind punched the side of the hill and tossed blinding mist across Sia's face. Max trudged ahead with Vadim on his back. When the wind quieted, the buzz had become the *thump-thump* of unseen rotors. Her bones were cold, her feet and fingers numb. No adrenaline left. She wanted to lie down. Max called from up ahead, outline barely visible through the flurries. Sia shuffled through the piling snow. The vast white sky was lit only by the distant coals of the house.

When she caught up, she found Max on his knees, Vadim's body beside him. They were on the edge of a precipice. Max pointed down. At first Sia could see only white. Then the flurries thinned and she saw the discarded BMW. And a horse. With a rider. Anna raised her arm toward Sia and then came a gunshot that soared into the sky. Sia fell back into the snow. She crawled alongside Max.

"Why is she shooting at us?" Sia asked. "Part of her theater? What the fuck?" Max did not reply. They had both been in that house tonight and damn well understood the futility of trying to predict what that woman would do. Should have let her die in the fire, Sia thought. Should have just run off. Slithering away from the edge, they stood, Max gathered Vadim's body onto his shoulders, and they began again to climb.

Palo Alto

Hi, Rhonda, it's Sia, just wanted to let you know we are coming back a little earlier than anticipated. We're leaving now, oh shit, Max. [Inaudible shouts, grunts] Sorry about that, Rhonda. We're walking right now and I tripped, can you believe it! We're on our way to meet the friends. Should be there in a few minutes. There are three of us and, well, I'd be quite keen on you letting them know right now so everything can be ready, I . . . [nine second string of expletives, inaudible screams, and shouts] Sorry about that, Rhon! Okay, yes, please make sure they are ready, because we're just so very adamant on leaving straightaway and with the friends. I will need to speak with Lulu promptly, important messages and all, so have her call the friends right now so I can have a little chat with her when I see them? Right now, got it? Thanks!

[S. Fox terminates call at 2:47 a.m. MSK]

Procter waved to George, who stopped the audio. Snake was lighting a cigarette inside the command center. No one complained, or even seemed to notice.

"How old is that cut?" Procter asked.

"Six minutes," George said. "Standard delay."

"They're alive," Procter said. "Sweet peaches, they are alive." Procter shook George by the shoulders until his glasses fell off. "Get me the SCORPIONs. Right. Fucking. Now."

RusFarm / Palo Alto

PEKKA JUHANI HAD NEVER HEARD HIS LITTLE BROTHER ARVO SPEAK, but words were not required to understand his agitation with the Americans. Above them roped the transmission line, a hundred meters in front lay the substation they had sabotaged earlier in the evening. PJ turned from his frustrated brother and flipped on the wipers. With each swipe he could make out the faint glow of the fire and smudges of sirens, blue and red, blinking around the blaze. Langley had told them to kill the power. They had. Then the house went up in flames.

Arvo was still signing.

"Don't complain to me," PJ said.

A message arrived in the covcom program embedded on Arvo's phone. Arvo shoved the screen in his face.

Lulu: hang tight. Three packages for you to stash. Call me when they arrive.

She gave a Helsinki phone number. "American cowboys," PJ muttered. They waited. Arvo ate three apples so quickly PJ worried he would choke. Then came the rotors. He peered through the windshield but saw nothing. Two, maybe three helos, he was not sure. They were hovering near the house. If they have infrared cameras aboard, PJ thought, we are going to die.

Arvo threw an apple core to the floor and signed to PJ. "I don't think we even have that much time," PJ said.

Arvo nodded, and he was back in the covcom program messaging the woman—that is, PJ assumed it was a woman. For some reason he pictured Lulu as a leggy, blond California surfer girl. He had never been to America, but the image meshed with the mercurial, peppy, and occasionally suggestive comms they received from her. Arvo smashed his gigantic fist into the dashboard. Lulu, PJ knew, was again insisting that they wait.

"Tell her we need a bonus if we're going to do that. A big bonus," PJ said. He jabbed a thumb toward the back of the truck. "There will be three people back there. The Russians stop us and tear this truck apart, and we're done, Arv."

Arvo tapped furiously on his phone.

———

AT THAT MOMENT THE NUBILE CALIFORNIA BLONDE OF PJ'S IMAGINA-tion was smashing her fist on a decommissioned WeWork desk, just missing the Twizzlers and Red Vines. The bright red block letters on the clock read 3:02 a.m. in Saint Petersburg. Procter stood over Snake's shoulder, absorbing the message from the SCORPIONs.

"Damn Finns squeezing us," Snake said.

"Tell them yes on the fucking money," Procter said. "And another five hundred grand when they're out of there and snug in their saunas."

———

A SINGLE GUNSHOT RANG THROUGH THE AIR.

The brothers exchanged glances. PJ stepped into the blizzard and swung open one of the truck's side compartments. He removed the old M/28-30 rifle and slung it over his shoulder. It had once belonged to his grandfather. He and Arvo used it for hunting game. His grandfather had used it for hunting Soviets during the Winter War. He stuffed two Makarovs into his pockets. Opening the cab door, he handed one to Arvo. PJ hated Russians. His grandfather had been killed by a Soviet shell at Kollaa and, more recently, one of the laundromats he and Arvo owned on the Russian side of the border had been shaken down by a group of FSB officers to the tune of half their annual profits. The prospect of killing FSB men intrigued him.

"I'm going to have a look," he said. Grandpa's rifle slung over his shoulder, PJ trudged toward the spot where the path reached the top of the ridge, taking up a position in a copse of fir trees. At the trailhead he saw nothing but white snow and, sometimes, the ghostly outlines of birches and pines. The wind howled, but between gusts he heard sirens baying near the house. After a few minutes, voices rose from below the trailhead. He steadied the rifle on a branch and scanned through his gunsight's little iron ears. A woman appeared first. The engine rumbled and the headlamps brightened. Arvo had seen her, too.

Arvo doused the woman with his headlamps, but PJ still could not get a clean look at her face. She did not appear Russian to him, much less police or FSB. She was waving. Screaming. Her words drifted into the wind.

He stuck her head between his rifle sights.

65

RusFarm

ANNA WAS WHISPERING TO PENELOPE AS THEY TROTTED UP THE hillside, winding over switchbacks, snow flocking her coat. Anna had hiked this path before and remembered that the last meters were steep, narrow, and clotted with trees. She would finish on foot. She nudged her heels into Penelope's ribs and the horse picked up speed. The snow was slowing. Good, she thought, the FSB investigators will see my tracks. They will find the bullets from my gun. Turning on a switchback, she could briefly make out the glowing house. Then another turn, and ahead she saw the end of the open trail.

Then a whiteout and for a few seconds nothing.

She trudged on, energy flagging even in her mania. Her left arm a windsock in the breeze. She could not feel the flesh; it was cold, it was not in pain, it was not a part of her anymore. With her right hand she fished her phone from her coat pocket and opened her call history. Stared at Maximov's number, blinking as flakes whipped her face.

Another whiteout.

She stopped the horse and looked down. I won't feel it if I fall on the shoulder, she thought. She tried to swing her right leg over Penelope's rear. Not quite high enough, she clipped the horse and fell into the snowpack and the wind kicked right out of her. She stayed in the snow until her lungs could inflate. Slowly she got to her feet.

She called Maximov's home number, let it ring three times, then hung up. Dropped the phone.

Then, the blizzard thinning a bit, she saw Max at the base of the steep rise. He had Vadim slung on his back. He was struggling to climb.

She pointed the gun at Max. Drifted her aim to the right. Squeezed the trigger.

———

MAX'S FEET WERE FROZEN, BUT HIS TOE BURNED WITH EACH STEP. Another bullet whizzed by. Her misses were narrow, and she was shooting in a blizzard. *Pinche rusa culera!* He dug a foot into the snow, then fell forward, and Vadim's body slumped onto him. He rolled the body off and sat there, dazed, until he heard Sia scream from the top the hill, and then a crack and the slurp of pressure past his ears. So damn close. He grabbed Vadim's arm and now just dragged him up, three big yanks until Max fell again and slid deeper into the powder.

He dug in his feet.

He tugged and yanked and pushed Vadim until he felt another set of hands beginning to pull and Vadim's body slid up and onto the ridge. Max slipped again, and there was another gunshot. Sia was shimmying down toward him. She was shouting about a ticket north. Her screams bounced between English and Afrikaans. Max hobbled to his feet and she grabbed his coat and pulled him up and he glimpsed her exhausted eyes and they collapsed onto each other at the top of the trail.

66

RusFarm

PJ WATCHED ARVO HUSTLE THE TWO CIA OFFICERS INTO THE TRUCK as another whiteout settled on the ridge. The woman was yelling in a mix of spitfire English and another language that neither Finn could recognize, much less understand. The man had passed out. The Finns hauled him into the truck first, then the dead body, which looked Russian to him. Probably the asset, poor bastard, even if he was a Russian. He wondered if the shooter down the trail had killed him. They got Lulu on the phone and passed her to the black-haired woman. He heard another gunshot from below the ridge. Handgun, he thought.

He returned to his position in the trees and looked down the barrel, right where he thought the trailhead had been. The world was white, lit only by the truck's headlamps. When the white wall broke, he could see a short woman standing on the ridge. He painted her chest in his gunsights and pushed the air from his lungs, readying to fire. She was looking at the truck. The wind died, the ridge was quiet, his hands were steady. She had a handgun at her side. Whoever she was, she was tracking CIA officers. PJ framed her head in his sights. At this range, he would not miss.

———

THE UTILITY TRUCK MADE ANNA SMILE. CLEVER. A LARGE MAN WAS dragging Max behind the vehicle. Sia was yelling, but the language was foreign to her, and the wind carried off her words.

I can smell the fire up here, Anna thought. The sweet smoke of that dead house.

There was the crack of a rifle. Was she hit?

She found herself facedown.

Warmth began to fill her body. I am too warm, she thought, to die in the snow.

67

Palo Alto / Washington

A 292-INCH SCREEN, PURCHASED AT CONSIDERABLE COST BY THE American taxpayer and yet sadly fuzzy and pixilated, flickered to life on the wall of the WeWork command center to reveal the White House Situation Room. Piper and Bradley flanked POTUS, whose vibe was edgy even through the screen. He had apparently been yanked from dinner with his family in the residence and was picking at a plate of something that looked like fried chicken. Bradley briefed the night's events. The President pushed the plate aside with a look blending disgust and agitation.

Bradley then played the recording of Sia's phone call with Procter. He was describing the exfil route when POTUS interrupted.

"How long until they're over the border?" POTUS asked.

"Weeks," Bradley said. "Too risky to try an official crossing. Especially if PERSEPHONE follows through on her threat. They'll lie low for a bit."

"This is an absolutely remarkable clusterfuck," POTUS said. "What the hell is this PERSEPHONE doing?"

No one had an answer to that, not even Procter. She kept her mouth shut.

Piper squeezed sanitizer into his hands. "So let me make sure I've got this. There is hostile FSB surveillance on our people at the farm. This Sia passes a computer to PERSEPHONE. They come back to the house. Our people get snatched up, interrogated—"

Procter interrupted. "They cut off one of our guys' toes."

POTUS made a face at the chicken.

"Okay," Piper continued, his tone clinical, "they torture our guy. Where is PERSEPHONE during all of this?"

"Upon confirming the surveillance," Procter said, losing her fucking patience, "Sia and PERSEPHONE made a game plan for the exfil. This plan . . . well, I should caveat that I am getting garbled bits from Sia because the phone call with her just now took place from a compartment in a utility truck bouncing on unpaved roads through a blizzard and she's nestled between a dead body and the toeless officer and she just witnessed a bunch of murders back in the house and the FSB is hunting them. Just for context. Anyway, this plan apparently involved PERSEPHONE heading to a room in the house they believed was not wired up with cameras, grabbing a car and trying to confirm or toss the surveillance, then using that car to hustle all three toward the exfil point. That is what PERSEPHONE was trying to do."

"Well, regardless, we should obviously not move forward," Piper said. "What the hell is PERSEPHONE smoking if she thinks we will start it now? Tonight? Madness."

The President picked at chicken skin on the drumstick. Procter had not come this far to let political diddling and tummy-gazing clobber a perfectly good op. And, worse, dump on the sacrifice made by her officers. In her mind flashed an explosion at Khost Base, a shotgun firing inside Embassy Damascus, the crack of a bottle over that goon's head in Dushanbe. Each memory popped like a bubble in her brain and then she stood and slid her neon-pink blouse up over her back and turned so the guys in the SitRoom could see the nine stars tattooed in a line across her lats. She heard the clang of POTUS dropping his fork on the table.

"Artemis, good god . . ." Bradley trailed off.

"Seven are from Khost," she began. "Two from when I was Chief in Damascus and Amman. The stars go on after I avenge our people. And if we do not set this in motion, well, gentlemen, we shit on the intelligence our officers worked so hard to collect. Their contribution goes down the toilet. Because we all know glory does not await these two.

What awaits them might be two nameless stars on the wall, then on my back. Then, done. Annihilation. And you know what, Mr. President, that doesn't fucking work for me. I care about two rules: collect the intel and protect your agent. Well, we've fucking failed on the latter. We can do the former. The only way to avenge them is to finish what they started. Take the goddamn money and kick-start our little conspiracy. See what happens in Moscow. We owe these two nothing less."

She turned to face the screen. POTUS had brought a hand to his mouth. He looked to Bradley, to Piper, his eyes landing on Procter. He nodded. "Get the team on the line. And, for god's sake, Ms. Procter, pull down your damn blouse."

NOT ALL OF THEM WERE AWAKE, SO PROCTER STOMPED THROUGH THE sleeping rooms shouting, turning on lights, shaking the pale fuckers from their sheets in the frenzied manner of a prison camp reveille. They gathered in front of the teleconference screen.

"When we start this," Procter began, "acting as Vadim Kovalchuk our little doomsday program is going to request the purchase of three hundred and forty-five million dollars of Bitcoin through an exchange in Hong Kong. This money is originating from dozens of accounts in jurisdictions all around the world. Separately, funds ranging from several hundred thousand to tens of millions of dollars will be transferred from the accounts Vadim manages into the private accounts of seven individuals inside the Russian Federation—all of which you've seen and signed off on, Mr. President. This includes Vassily Gusev, known as Goose, one of his lieutenants named Chernov, the director of the FSB, the Deputy Chief of the Rosgvardia, and three colonels who we believe would command the units the military would deploy into Moscow in the event of an uprising. Our WINKELVOSS platform, on which you've also been briefed, will scatter much of the digital dust necessary to convince investigators that a conspiracy was afoot." Procter paused. "Then we wait for them to start killing each other."

"How much money do you think will actually move?" POTUS asked.

"I don't know," Procter said. "Less than we originally thought. The FSB will be at Vadim's apartment in a matter of hours and someone is going to be inside that laptop, inside the accounts they know about, trying to unwind things."

"Start it," POTUS said.

Procter heard someone mumble oh my god, oh my god, oh my god, take a deep breath, and then the sound of typing.

———

THE CHAOS BEGAN IN WASHINGTON, BOUNCED BETWEEN PALO ALTO and Hong Kong, and eventually exploded in Moscow.

Procter sat through the night with the strung-out techies and FINO guys and by first light the workspaces reeked with the smell of burnt Pop-Tarts and the fragrance of cologne surrendering to body odor. Holds were placed on several of the transactions. None of the cash held in Bank Rossiya, for example, traveled to Hong Kong to purchase crypto. But many of the other bank transfers were duly approved. The TROJANs had burrowed so deeply into Vadim's life that the FSB was struggling mightily to uproot them.

In the late afternoon Procter flipped on the satellite television to Rossiya-1. Russian state TV.

There were four white-clad ballerinas prancing around in tutus to the rich, lyrical music of Procter's fever dreams.

The Russians were running the programming that had accompanied the deaths of Soviet leaders: Brezhnev, Andropov, Chernenko.

It was the same ballet that had run on a three-day loop during the coup attempt on Gorbachev in 1991.

Tchaikovsky's *Swan Lake*.

Procter smiled.

68

Langley

ARTEMIS APHRODITE PROCTER WOULD ALWAYS REMEMBER THOSE four glorious and chaotic December days, and she would cherish them in her heart.

On Telegram she watched amateur video of tanks and armored vehicles clumped around the FSB's Lubyanka headquarters. Iron Felix's reinstated statue stared with what Procter figured was anxiety—and some measure of grudging respect—at the layered conspiracy unrolling around him. Shaky cell cameras caught tanks parked in Red Square and black-clad operatives patrolling the Kremlin. There was a video of helicopters linked to FSB military counterintelligence units flying to air bases in the Moscow region. CIA received unconfirmed reports that several military units were arrested wholesale, packed to the east on railcars. Satellite imagery and intercepts confirmed that the chaos in Moscow had ground Russian troop movements inside Ukraine to a confused standstill.

The Kremlin was silent.

Talking heads speculated that Putin had retreated to his villa at Idokopas, or perhaps one of the presidential bunkers in the Urals. The CIA, in truth, had no idea where he was.

Antigovernment protests in Moscow and Saint Petersburg, largely absent since the opening days of the war in Ukraine, heated up as Russians sensed weakness amid the uncertainty. The protests grew—the satellite images revealed that some were ten thousand strong—until the black-bereted riot police quelled one on Bolotnaya with live ammunition. By the fourth day, the shootings and a nasty December cold snap had discouraged all but the most fervent marchers.

And still the Kremlin was silent.

The Russian ruble plummeted even lower, and the global price of Bitcoin skyrocketed over the four trading days. Only a few commentators linked the two events, and then only to speculate that investors could be piling into crypto—bizarrely—as a hedge against the clear and rising risk of global instability.

And on Christmas morning, CIA finally received SIGINT confirming what Russian opposition and civil society figures had been saying for a day or two—Vassily Platonovich Gusev, the Goose himself, longtime Putin ally, secretary of the powerful Security Council, had been arrested. Locked up in Lefortovo.

Putin delivered a speech on Christmas night.

He was pale, his face even puffier than usual. As strongmen are wont to do when staring down an uppity population, Putin appealed for calm. He blamed "foreign actors" for inciting a conspiracy against Russia and her duly elected representatives. He did not smile. Blinks were rare. He wore a Richard Mille Tourbillon watch (retail price: $583,000) with a gold skull on its face that said it was December 24, the day prior. He connected the attack on Russia to the United States, to Ukrainian nationalism (though he did not once utter the word *Ukraine*), and to Nazism, all wed together in a cabal hostile to Russia's existence and her special mission in the world. He hinted at further purifications of the nation and the unspecified glories awaiting her.

Putin was cut off in the middle of an angry monologue about the protesters (he referred to them only as "collaborators") at exactly eight p.m. Moscow time. As his watch hinted, the speech had been pre-recorded to fit Channel 1's nightly schedule, and Putin had run long. CIA later learned the original extended to seventy-two minutes, twelve too many for the designated slot. After the speech, Putin disappeared. To the warrens of the Kremlin, to his Moscow home, to his estate on the Black Sea, CIA did not know.

Procter read every scrap of intelligence emerging from the dozen or so global centers of Russia reporting. What emerged, to Procter's delight, was a portrait of general mayhem. The FSB investigation into Vadim Kovalchuk's bank transfers and phone records had triggered a wave of arrests. Lefortovo Prison had been emptied of its prior inhabitants to hold the alleged conspirators. Several died while resisting arrest, including a colonel in the military police, shot at home in front of his New Year's tree. The FSB, though, was releasing prisoners in a trickle as it became clear many had no connection to the attempted coup. A relatively new source nevertheless offered what the Chief thought was an apt read on the Russian President's state of mind: he believed that Goose, Vadim Kovalchuk, and a group of well-placed collaborators had tried to overthrow him.

Russia turning in on itself, Procter scribbled to Bradley in a note appended to the report. The bear eating its own head.

And what of Vadim Kovalchuk? The mysterious banker at the heart of the imagined putsch did not headline the news, but his name did appear in several intelligence reports arriving from a Russian source run out of Paris Station. The source claimed that Vadim had been spirited out of Russia. The FSB had scoured every inch of the country. SVR *rezidentury* worldwide had been tasked to collect on his whereabouts. No one knows, the source claimed, but everyone is asking: Where is Vadim Kovalchuk?

Procter visited Bradley in his office on a slushy January afternoon for sign-off on the CIA's answer to that question.

It was quitting time for the clock-puncher crowd. The Seventh Floor foot traffic ran around her like water on her way to meet him. She brought only a flat black box. On it was hung a small tag indicating she had Security's approval to carry the electronic device in the building. Bradley waved her in. She rubbed the Stinger and Javelin launchers for good luck and sat at the table.

She slid the cold storage wallet across to Bradley. The Tomb.

Bradley smiled. "Well, what do you want to do with it?"

"I want a speedboat. Maybe you buy Angela that San Cristobal horse before the bottom falls out of the crypto markets?"

Bradley laughed. "Anything within the bounds of what the lawyers will allow?"

"Not really."

"I'm sure you'll think of something." He slid the wallet back. Procter put it in her pocket.

"Vadim?" he said.

"Yep."

"I read your note, Artemis. I'm not sure I agree."

"Why the hell not?"

He smiled. "Well, for one, why would we formally implicate our-selves in the Moscow madness?"

"You've been reading the reports, Ed, they already think they have solid intel. Putin is blaming us publicly. You heard his speech."

"And we gain what, exactly, from giving the idea more purchase inside the Kremlin?"

"We give PERSEPHONE a shot at making it to the other side."

Bradley smoothed his tie and scratched his head. "After what hap-pened," he said, "I do not think there will be appetite for that. Anyhow, she's probably dead."

"Two things, Ed," Procter said. "Then I'll shut up. One, PERSE-PHONE's op enabled all of this. Literally none of it was possible without her. We owe her."

"Bullshit, Artemis," Bradley said. "We owe her nothing. She blew the op and maybe tried to kill our officers."

"That is possibly true," Procter conceded. " But she saved them first. If she had not intervened, they'd be dead. Buried in unmarked graves on that satanic farm. Plus, Castillo was pretty sure she was trying to miss when she shot at him during the exfil."

Bradley did not respond. "And what's the second thing?"

"Two," Procter said, "is that the clancomm we gave her is still tick-ing. PERSEPHONE didn't destroy it. She could have, easily. Hell, she rode the damn horse out over half the farm looking for Castillo and Fox. That saddlebag would have been the first thing I tossed back in the fire and she did not do it."

"She's dead," Bradley said. "Or at least the Finns seem to think so. They shot her."

"I know, I know," Procter said. "So we have nothing to lose by trying. Worst-case is we end up right here: PERSEPHONE out of the picture, Russians holding us responsible for wrecking their shit."

"No one downtown believes for a second that PERSEPHONE can get back into the game. Piper, POTUS. Maybe not even me."

"Okay." Procter gave a hell-if-I-care shrug. "But, Ed, to be fair, you said maybe. What's a girl got to do to get to yes?"

Bradley was reading the note card printed with his daily schedule, brows bunching in agitation. He sighed. "What is your proposal?"

——

IN THE DARKNESS OF HER MOSCOW X OFFICE PROCTER LEANED THE baseball bat against the desk to make room for the safe. Some of the paint and the treasured Jim Thome signature were dinged, but the shoddy WeWork particleboard had fared far worse. Two Facilities guys lugged in the new safe. They showed her how to change the combination, shooting wary glances toward the bat. She filled out a small stack of papers and they left.

Procter opened the safe and changed the six-digit combination to Vladimir Putin's birthday: 100752. On the back interior wall she taped the photo of Putin falling on the ice during a hockey game. She'd printed a fresh version after the bat work in Palo Alto. She carpeted the floor of the safe with a printout of the nudie pic that she'd shoved in Anton's pants before hustling from the Dushanbe hotel room. The one that showcased her rugged femininity. Her quiet fucking strength.

Procter pulled the wallet from her pocket and balanced it on her palm.

"Two hundred twenty-five million, three hundred and twenty-two thousand, four hundred and seventeen dollars and sixty-one cents," Procter said, like an incantation. An insignificant sum of Putin's money. But, turned back on him, it had made all the difference.

She kissed it. Then, careful not to censor her own photo, she positioned the wallet off to one side, and gently shut the safe.

69

Karelia

THE AURORA BOREALIS SHONE LIKE GREEN RIBBONS IN THE SKY. TWO snowshoers set out from the cabin hours before first light for the meadow on the far side of the lake. Karelia was a silent snow globe at the top of the world, a land of frozen water—lakes, ponds, streams. In summer, PJ said, the fields and meadows were emerald, the water bluish crystal. Now a white blanket was pulled tight over it all. It was the cleanest place she'd ever been to, the air so cold and pure that during their first days breaths were sharp, almost painful. But now, gliding over the frost in her snowshoes, Sia felt stronger than she had in weeks. Looking at Max ahead, she noted his strides were longer, stronger than even a few days before.

———

THE FIRST FEW DAYS HAD BEEN MARKED BY THE MISERY OF HELPLESS waiting that accompanies an artillery bombardment, passed in a cold basement with grubby sleeping mats and a rusted sink. The concrete walls were weepy. Two lightbulbs hung from the ceiling on slender chains. The Finnish mute brought water, black bread, sausages, and a plastic bin filled with dressings and ointment for Max's foot. PJ, they learned, was the smaller, older brother. Arvo the mute.

That first night in the basement they crawled naked under the blankets for warmth and waited for the FSB to kick in the door. Sometimes Sia craned her neck toward the ceiling and thought she could hear rotors.

Time moved only by the green block numbers of a digital clock. In those long hours, placing a pillow over her ears would not drown out the helicopters that were not there; smashing her nose into the ratty pillow would not suppress the smoke that had long since risen from RusFarm; closing her eyes would not erase the image of Chernov severing Max's toe.

———

THREE DAYS LATER, WHEN THE CLOCK SAID IT WAS LATE EVENING, ARVO had appeared downstairs with heavy clothing and adult diapers. He pointed insistently at his wrist, where the watch would have been. Sia looked at the diaper box. It was the only time she would see Arvo smile.

Only the diapers fit. So, in a baggy greatcoat, tight sweater, gigantic hat, and children's mittens, Sia ascended the stairs and entered a garage. The cold was biting. PJ was at the wheel of an SUV. The exhaust reminded her of the fire at RusFarm and her heart quickened. Arvo showed them the compartment under the trunk. Inside were bottles of water, tubes of oxygen, and packs of cookies. He put a solemn finger over his lips. They got inside.

They drove for hours. Sia's hair was matted with sweat; her toes were numb. She pissed in the diaper. The darkness squeezed until she gave in and took hits of the oxygen to even out. Max pressed his forehead into hers and she found his hand. She was hungry but worried she would retch if she ate. The pavement gave way to gravel and stone.

At last, the car stopped. The click of a latch. Sia looked up. Blinding light and freezing air rushed into the stale compartment. A few blinks. A shape stood over them. Beyond it were snow-flocked treetops and a brilliant blue sky. The shape was Arvo. The world was silent. His nose wrinkled at the smell wafting from the trunk. He turned away and thrust forward a thick hand to lift her up.

"Sorry about that," Sia said.

———

THE CABIN SAT ON A PENINSULA JUTTING INTO A FROZEN LAKE. THERE was a woodstove in the tiny kitchen and a single bedroom. The rafters were so low they had to duck to avoid head-bangs. Sia swung open the rope-strung curtains. She could not see another cabin on the lake. Nothing stirred in the trees or on the ice. Arvo and PJ lugged in boxes of supplies—food, water, matches, two first-aid kits, lighter fluid, newspapers, two rifles, ammo, books (all in Finnish or Russian). Behind the cabin PJ unrolled a tarp to reveal a pile of firewood. They lit the fire and sat on rickety stools around the woodstove warming their hands.

"Karelia," PJ said, gesturing out the window.

"Russia or Finland?" Sia asked.

Arvo grimaced.

"Russia," PJ said, scratching his stubble. "Maybe few more weeks. Lots of pressure. Lulu explain no good options on border right now. Too risky for car. No submarines. No airplanes. Lulu working on it. You wait here. Far, far north. Alone. We come back. Four, maybe five days. More deliveries."

———

DEEP SLEEP ELUDED HER UNTIL THE FOURTH NIGHT. IN SIA'S DREAM SHE rode on horseback from RusFarm as it burned. She urged the horse into a gallop to outrun the flames. Heat curled on her back. Then RusFarm was the old Fox ranch in the Big Bend and she was trampling the bunchgrass and creosote and prickly pear of the land she had once called home. Open and hard and free. A lone horse waited on a hilltop, its outline painted by the desert moon. She rode toward it.

When she woke up, Max was steeping coffee. "Up for a walk?" he said.

———

THEY SLIPPED ON THEIR WINTER GEAR AND SNOWSHOES AND CUT A path around the lake. It was dead quiet save for the crunch of their shoes packing the snow. She moved quickly, enjoying the heat in her muscles and the thirst for clean air in her lungs. After an hour they came to a spot on the other side of the lake with a view of the cabin. They dusted snow from two rocks and sat to eat the granola bars they'd brought along.

Sia dredged a mitten through the snow to make the letter *S*. Then *I. A.* She ran her boot over it. Maybe just be quiet, she thought, but soon she was talking. "If we get out of here, they will turn the screws on us for months. Polygraphs. Psych exams. Endless debriefings. A nightmare. It's going to be impossible to think. So, I'm thinking now."

"About what?" Max asked.

She coughed. "That I'm not working properly anymore. That maybe I don't know who I am." She laughed. It was insane to hear it aloud. She began rolling up a snowball.

"When we pulled into RusFarm," she continued, "I felt something I've never felt in my life. Slinking around in the shadows suddenly wasn't thrilling. It was terrifying. I wondered what else was out there. Whether something was hunting me. I can still feel it."

She watched him lean forward, mouth parting, considering words. But they did not come. He waited.

She drew the mitten off her left hand and held it up. "This is new. For instance." She watched her own fingers tremble for a moment. Then she slid them back in the glove and kept working on the snowball.

She continued, "And I'm wondering if maybe my hand is shaking because my body knows something my mind doesn't: that I don't know who I am. Am I a lawyer or a NOC? Yes to both. Am I an American or a South African or a Brit? Yes again. Was this op busted or an incredible success? Yes, yes. Did we play Anna or did she play us? Yes. Am I a phony or an honorable patriot? Yes and yes. And on and on and on. I honestly can't keep it straight anymore. I know that I'm running from something, I just don't know what it is."

She threw the snowball into a tree.

"That's it," she said. "It's not clean. It never will be."

———

MAX WATCHED HER MAKE SNOWBALLS.

It's not clean. Since the RusFarm apocalypse Max had fantasized about outlandish scenarios in which he returned triumphantly to San Cristobal as if nothing had ever happened. A foolish dream.

He'd put San Cristobal at risk. He'd spread it across the chopping block.

But had he made the choice? Maybe if I'd said no thanks to Hoyt and the CIA, he thought, then we wouldn't be here. Maybe if I'd told Procter I was done after the first visit to RusFarm. Maybe if I'd been willing to rest outside the ring, sit back, enjoy civilian life. Let Sia, let CIA, let the citizens of the secret world tilt and turn on their own. Maybe then. What wasn't a maybe was that it didn't matter. It was done. Max had hammered everything so far down that he was surprised when he began to speak.

Sia was lazily dusting another tree with a snowball.

"I've spent my whole life building San Cristobal," he said. "My family, my livelihood, it's all there. I know every horse on that farm. Every single animal. I was trying to honor the place. I . . ." His jaw tightened so hard he thought his teeth might splinter. He stared off across the lake. Sia sat on the rock and put her hand on his back. "*Que se vaya todo a la chingada,*" he said quietly, after a beat. Fuck it all.

"They are going to offer to resettle us both in the States, you know," Sia said. "In my case it won't be a question. You'll have a choice, though."

"Not really," he said. "There's only one thing I can do."

"What's that?"

"Go home."

He grabbed a fallen branch and splintered it over his knee. Then he hurled the sticks into the trees. They were watching snow slide from the firs when Max heard the snap of a branch and footfalls in the snow.

70

Karelia

SOMETHING WAS CRUNCHING THROUGH THE SNOW-COVERED UNDER-growth up the shoreline. Snowshoes? They crouched behind the rocks to watch. More branches snapping. They sank lower, almost into the snow.

Max had stopped breathing. Sia's left hand was vibrating, fingers thrumming the rock like a tuning fork. Her eyes were shut.

The footfalls grew louder.

An animal came into view, bounding on all fours. It was a large brown bear, steaming nostrils upturned to smell the air. Max braced for a charge. The bear sniffed the earth, jabbing its nose into the snow, rifling for something, then looked up at Max with its snout dusted white. They stared at each other for a heavy moment.

Then the bear walked off.

———

MAX FED MORE LOGS ONTO THE DYING WOODSTOVE FIRE. SIA BOILED water for coffee. On a cutting board she spread out a hunk of black bread, links of dried elk sausage, and a block of a Finnish cheese that smelled Swiss. The cheese was frozen, but they finished the bread and all the sausage in a companionable silence. Max refilled their coffees. Sia had not eaten this much since the fire, he was sure of it. When they'd eaten their fill, Max picked up one of the Finnish books and collapsed onto the couch. "Damn PJ and Arvo," he said, flipping aimlessly through the pages. "Not a single one in Spanish or English."

Sia laughed. She was at the bookshelf, examining the incomprehensible selection. Her cowl-neck sweater fit horribly, but her jeans were snug. She caught him looking when she spun around. And that also made her smile.

She joined him on the couch, locked her hand in his. He kissed her. He cradled her head in his hands and rubbed her temples and the nape of her neck. Without words, they knew to move slowly, to leave room for their exhausted bodies to catch up. He kissed her neck, her ears. Her hands furrowed his hair.

She stood and he undressed her; she did the same to him, but gingerly, mindful of the foot. They looked at each other in the unforgiving afternoon light. No clothes, no shadows, no masks. Max saw her moles, her cuts, her bruises, the sweet long legs. All of it. It was the long-ago cottage in St. Ives. The start of this theater, a story where they loved each other for the audience. Now they were offstage. The crowd long gone.

He watched her eyes on him, moving up and down, considering things. He did the same.

The moment felt like it might tip in any direction. She took a small step toward him, he toward her.

She took his hand, and they were on the couch kissing and running hands over each other. Sia's skin felt different than he remembered. Smoother, he thought. New to him. They sat for a moment with their foreheads scrunched together, noses touching, listening to their breathing. Was this the end or the beginning?

"What are you thinking?" Sia whispered into his ear.

His mouth opened.

She kissed it shut and pulled him into her. "Be quiet and tell me."

———

FOR SEVENTEEN DAYS THE SCHEDULE DID NOT CHANGE. IN THE MORNing they snowshoed around the lake. Lunch in the cabin. In the early afternoons they napped and sometimes made love and chopped firewood before dark. Her dream of the burning ranch house became a nightly ritual, always breaking before she reached the moonlit horse.

Only visits from the Finns broke the routine. PJ brought suitable reading material on the seventh day: English novels, magazines, newspapers. When Max asked if Lulu wanted to speak with them, Arvo wagged his finger. PJ explained: How you think they get bin Laden? Phones. No digital crumbs up here. PJ said that they would leave once Lulu felt it was safe to cross the border, and they only messaged with Lulu from farther south. He did not know how long it would be.

On the ninth day, Sia forced herself to skim a dated copy of the *New York Times*. December 27. On the front page, above the fold, was an article titled "Night of the Red Knives? New Clues Shed Light on Foiled Putsch in Moscow." She put the paper aside until the evening, when it served as kindling for the woodstove.

———

ON THE SEVENTEENTH DAY, MAX AND SIA RETURNED FROM SNOWSHOE-ing to the sound of barking and the discovery of two dogsleds parked alongside PJ's truck. Huskies lounged in the snowdrifts. The cabin blinds were drawn. Arvo emerged with big bowls of water for the dogs.

Inside, Sia saw that the cabin had been tidied up: sheets were folded, their few articles of clothing had vanished. A duffel bag sat by the door.

"Heat is down," PJ said. "We know guys on duty at border. We go today."

The CIA officers would be smuggled into Finland hidden in compartments in the sleds. Arvo handed them bags of cereal and two bottles of water. From the truck PJ collected gear: a gun, binos, blankets, a tent, a cooler. Sia took a final look at the cabin. The days here had been simple. Boring. Her days would not be boring for a long time, and that made her sad. The Finns packed them inside the compartments on the sleds, gear slung on the outside. If they chanced upon anyone, it would appear as though the Finns were dogsledding the forest on a hunt.

Ice and snow sliced underneath as the sled lurched into motion.

For hours they skidded along. Where is the border? Sia wondered. The damn Russian border.

Finally, they slowed. Russian chatter, PJ and two unknown voices. They stopped. More talk, this time harsher. She squeezed shut her eyes. Listened to her heart. Someone put a hand on the sled above her. More chatter. Tenser. Something rustling above her. She would fight them if they opened the compartment. Kill them or make them kill her. What did PJ have on the sled? Guns, knives, tent poles. If that compartment opens and I don't recognize the eyes I'm going to jam my fingers in them, she thought. And, god, my heart. More chatter.

Then a laugh. More Russian.

The sled accelerated. She put a shaky hand to her mouth.

———

AFTER ANOTHER HOUR, LIGHT FLOODED INTO THE COMPARTMENT. SIA blinked, looked around. Snow, fir trees, another cabin. This one almost identical, but with a second story.

"Finland," PJ said, beaming.

Hunched over a stove, quite agitated, Artemis Procter, clad in a neon-purple parka, was at the tail end of a disastrous coffee-making session. Grounds had spilled on the floor and coffee treacle slithered down the side of the woodstove. Procter's mug ran with streaks. Seeing Sia and Max, she smacked it onto the hearth and gave them big hugs. She held Sia tight, said she couldn't be more fucking proud.

Procter motioned for Arvo and PJ to give them a minute. The three CIA officers sat on the couch and chairs. Procter spoke of the events in Moscow, Putin's money, his bunker mentality.

They listened to the fire crackle, Sia and Max considering the reality that the Russians, nay, Putin himself, might soon place a bounty on their heads. Weirdly, it made Sia feel absolutely nothing.

Procter at last rendered judgment. The verdict Sia had expected and feared since St. Ives. The Chief's body language shifted, but to her credit she did not pull any punches. She did not equivocate. She offered no false hope.

"We've done an extensive review since the night at RusFarm," Procter began, "and there is no way we can continue supporting your platforms. They are burned up. Sia, we are going to resettle you in the States. New name, new everything. You'll call Hynes Dawson and tell Benny you're out. Nervous breakdown. Something dramatic. We'll have a team clean out your flat."

And, with that, sealed by her own wordless nod, Sia Fox's bright career as a young NOC was finished. A train of accomplishments, at once illustrious and checkered, exhilarating and terrifying, had careened off the tracks. The rupture was so sharp that she could not summon the energy to put words to it, let alone fathom its implications. Perhaps it was shock. Perhaps blind ignorance or confusion. But whatever it was, at that moment Sia Fox felt nothing. Said nothing. Did nothing.

A log collapsed in the fire.

Procter turned to Max and said, "We've put a bunch of additional security on San Cristobal. No Russkie interest in the place so far. The same package is on the table for you and your father. Resettlement. New names. Stipend. The whole shebang. I'm offering. I've got to offer. Part of our deal with you and your family."

"I'm going back to San Cristobal," he said. "I cannot live anywhere else."

"You prepared to die there?" Procter asked. "If Vladimir's evil eye finds its way?"

"What do you think, Artemis?"

Their eyes held steady until it seemed to Sia that Procter and Max understood each other.

Procter grunted. "Like I said. Had to offer."

Max's face twitched. He nodded to Procter, stood, and walked out.

Procter and Sia watched the fire burn. "You guys knew all this, right?" Procter asked, not unkindly.

"Yeah," Sia said. "We just hadn't heard it from you yet."

Sia refilled her coffee and looked out the window. Max was chatting with PJ and Arvo, who were hitching up the dogs, organizing them into two teams to pull the sleds.

Sia let go of the curtain. "Anna?" she nearly whispered.

Procter shook her head. "Don't know. We've tasked the Russia sources we trust. We're trying to get the list of prisoners at Lefortovo to see if she's on it. Or records from the morgues around RusFarm. No luck so far."

"PJ thinks he shot her," Sia said.

"Well, we don't have a single piece of intelligence that mentions her," Procter said. "Dead or alive. What do you think about that?"

"What do you mean?"

"I mean," Procter repeated, "what do you think about that, Hortensia?" Emphasis on the damn name. Procter was staring at her.

Sia had thought of Anna frequently since the night at the farm and every time she did, her mind just spun. What was Anna Andreevna Agapova? Asset? Handler? Friend? Enemy? All of them. The woman was all of them.

"I hope that Anna found her victory," Sia said. "Even if she's dead."

That seemed to be good enough for Procter, who took a sip of coffee, nodded, and said nothing.

PJ followed Arvo inside the cabin. The last light of dusk slipped into the door behind them.

Arvo was signing, fingers moving with urgency.

———

THE NEAREST TOWN, WHERE THE FINNS AND A FULL BATTERY OF Agency officers would greet them, was an hour haul from the cabin and more direct by dogsled than by car. They would again ride in the compartments, not for secrecy, but for lack of space. Procter loaded into PJ's sled. The Finn handed Procter a bag of cereal and a bottle of water. The ride was short, so they'd not brought the diapers. Well, shit, Procter said. The Chief ducked behind a tree for a minute and then hopped back in. Daylight was fast disappearing.

Arvo arranged Sia and Max into their compartment, stuffing gear around them until the light drained out. Sia snuggled her neck onto Max's. They wrapped arms and legs around each other. The sled heaved off. Soon everything became dark and still, interrupted only by the reassuring rhythms of their breathing, the swish of the sled, the occasional sigh from one of the dogs. Sia was alone with her thoughts, and in the stillness they spoke to her. As they slid through the night she had a sensation of weightlessness, of rising into the darkness above. The green ribbons of the northern lights stretched through space. She was high in the sky, looking down on herself and Max below.

They moved quickly, entwined together.

As if in a coffin at life's end, or a womb at its beginning, she did not know.

Moscow
Weeks later

T HE LEFORTOVO GUARDS CLANKED OPEN THE DOOR TO PRISONER
36's isolation cell. Hood over the head. Then they led the prisoner
into the hall. They marched quickly, the prisoner's weak legs sometimes dragging on the floor. They turned and twisted through the eerie
flat-black cellblock and into lighter corridors painted dingy blue and
beige. There was no contact permitted between inmates at Lefortovo:
no rope telegraphs to pass notes, not a glance at another's face. And
there could be no words exchanged between inmates and guards. As
they had at Lefortovo since the time of the Tsars, the guards used
metal snaps to communicate if two escort teams met in a narrow corridor. The click-clack signaled which team would stuff their prisoner
inside the wooden box at either end of the hallway, making room for
the other to pass.

This dance had become commonplace in recent weeks. Every wing
of the K-shaped prison was bursting with inmates. The rolls had 30
prisoners in Lefortovo on December 21. Now: 251. Larger cells had been
divided into multiple cramped, solitary chambers. Many of the Russian government's formerly senior officials were now confined to spaces
scarcely larger than a coffin. The prison had not been this oversub-
scribed since the salad days of the Terror, when Lefortovo had been
Stalin's favorite shooting prison.

The guards frog-marching Prisoner 36 now clicked their metal crickets at the team with Prisoner 77. They had to be quick about it. Prisoner 36 was expected in one of the basement rooms. The Prosecutor General had signed the execution orders just that morning. Contrary to popular belief, executions in Lefortovo are quite rare. Russia's decades-long moratorium on the death penalty had only recently been lifted, but it was more a patriotic nod to the country's war footing than a practical tool. Formal liquidations required far more paperwork than tossing someone from a balcony. Regardless, what was certain was that no one of this stature had been liquidated here since the time of Brezhnev or, perhaps, Stalin. The guards could not quite believe it had come to this.

The team escorting Prisoner 77 click-clacked compliance: they would tuck their charge into the box at their end of the corridor so the prisoners would neither see, smell, nor hear the other as they passed.

Click-clack, click-clack.

And so it was that two guards shepherded a hooded Anna Andreevna Agapova, Prisoner 77, into a cold wooden box.

Prisoner 36, Vassily Platonovich Gusev, the Goose himself, was skirted past to an ancient basement, where the senior FSB officer on duty read the Prosecutor General's decree and asked for a statement.

"I am innocent of all charges," Goose said. He still wore the hood and his baggy prison running suit. He did not know he faced a brick wall. He did not see the scupper drains carved into the seam at its base. He did not hear the screechy twist of the faucet handle, nor the thud of water filling the pressure hose, for cleanup.

Goose's last sight was the darkness of the hood, the last tingle in his ears the patter of footsteps approaching from behind.

His body went to the morgue. Bloody water gurgled down the drains while the guards pressure-hosed the brick and stone. Goose's baggy prison running suit was undamaged and, as state property, was laundered that evening, folded, and returned to inventory by the next morning.

As with all CIA assets executed in Russia, the cause was left blank on his death certificate.

THE DARKNESS HAD NIBBLED STEADILY AT ANNA'S SENSE OF TIME UNTIL, after some length of it, she could no longer discern minutes from hours, weeks from months. What she did know was that the blackness of her cell was broken only by visits from a nameless female doctor and a team of guards reeking of alcohol and cabbage and cologne. Each visit they slipped a hood over her head to frog-march Anna down the chlorine-wreathed corridor.

The journey to Lefortovo was a series of fragments: a gunshot on the hill above RusFarm, waking briefly in a helicopter, then again bathed in harsh light hearing the ominous beeps and gurgles of unseen equipment. There was a doctor in blue scrubs and an IV drip and she again was riding Penelope into unconsciousness. Somewhere along the way they had operated on her shoulder.

For the first few days, or maybe weeks, the guards escorted her to the second-floor interrogation rooms for visits with nameless men who would offer tea or coffee and then ask her questions. Of this time, like the surgery, she could remember little. Had she told them about Sia and Lulu? About Switzerland? The drinks, she now suspected, had been laced with SP-117. Sodium pentothal. FSB truth serum. Whatever she had said, though, she came to believe that they did not know. At some point the druggy sessions stopped. She had not confessed. Then they brought her to the same rooms but now a man called Ilya sat with her while she wrote her testimony of that night, again and again and again. Ilya asked questions, he offered alternative versions of her story that always—always—sprang from the presumption of her guilt. This was, Ilya liked to say, a matter of uncovering the details of her treason, not whether she had committed it. That had been settled, he insisted. How many versions did she write? And still, she did not confess.

After the writing, they moved on to polygraphs and electricity.

She thought it had happened three times. No more than five, she was sure of it. A rotation of guards would haul her to a clean white room with bright tile on the floors and the walls and the ceiling. The floor sloped to a drain cut into the center. A scuffed table with a computer was ringed by two chairs. A stout nurse with thinning gray hair and sparkly eyes stuck electrodes over her kidneys. The nurse would gently caress her cheek, tell her to be a good girl. Then a man with a fop of white hair and a walrus mustache would arrive. He would apply sensors to her fingers, a blood pressure cuff to her arm, and a pneumograph to her chest. He would fuss with his computer.

Then he would ask if Anna was working for the CIA.

No, she would insist. No.

Then he would push a button and the electricity would roast and seize her skin and the room would flip from day to night and back again.

He had other questions (*Were you aware of your husband's work for CIA? Did you start the fire at RusFarm? Did Hortensia Fox recruit you in Mexico? At RusFarm? In Geneva?*), each of which could be accompanied by a dose of current.

Or not. The electricity struck at random. On one visit, the polygrapher did not tap the button at all. On another, each *nyet* brought the current, and for days (weeks?) she could not stand up straight. On her last visit she wet the prison running suit at the first sound of his voice.

Still, she did not confess. It will be worse if you say yes, she told herself again and again. Then you lose, and they are all dead for nothing. Even in the fever swamp of her mind she knew that the uncertainty and anticipation, far more than the electricity, was the real torment. Did they already know? What had she told them? How long had she been here? Would she ever leave? Would the next *nyet* persuade Walrus Mustache to press the button? Simple questions. No answers.

Then the polygraphs stopped. The guards would arrive, bag her with the hood, and spirit her to another interrogation room for discussions with Ilya.

Upon arrival Ilya would sign the papers affirming her transfer from the cell block to his room. Guards dispersed, Ilya flipped a switch that illuminated a red light outside the door: *Interrogation in progress*. Anna sat at a table. In front of her would be a Styrofoam cup filled with brackish tea. No steam escaped the surface; it was probably never warm in the first place. She had never taken a sip; Ilya never made her. On the beige wall was a twist of humming pipe. Overhead hung lamps so ancient Beria might have used them to light his madness.

In the half-light she could see the yellowed skin of her hands. Her breasts had shrunk; they now swam meekly in her smelly blue running suit. Her feet were always cold. She wiggled toes in her grimy tennis shoes to be sure she could move them. The shoes were a size or so large and did not have laces—prisoners were not permitted lengths of cord, no matter how slight or small. Anna rehearsed every detail of the nightmare at RusFarm. When her mind settled on real things—shooting herself in the shoulder, for instance, or setting the fire—she would imagine wrapping the meddlesome thought in a large sack and tossing it from a tower. The heating pipe hummed and knocked while she silently practiced her lines.

Ilya shut the door and sat, smiling, across from her. He had a dark mop of hair that he wiped obsessively from his face. He would fold his hands on the table and look gravely into her eyes when he asked questions. There were no pleasantries, no preamble, never any information offered.

"The night at RusFarm," Ilya began, "why were you in the car?"

"I wanted to confirm that someone was watching me."

"Why did you think someone was watching you?"

"It was a feeling. I had been riding with Hortensia Fox that afternoon. I sensed it then. The drive was an attempt to confirm it. And I was correct."

Ilya spread his hands and began picking at a cuticle. "Why did you return to the house?"

"Chernov's men collected me."

"You know," Ilya said, still fixated on the cuticle, "several men from Chernov's team have provided a complete report on that evening. They say they were there to keep tabs on you and Hortensia Fox. They say that Chernov decided, after your horseback ride, to enter the mansion to have a conversation with Hortensia, her boyfriend Maximiliano, and Vadim. He brought two men, two FSB officers, inside with him. And here is the problem: you are the only survivor of this star-crossed meeting, which concluded in spectacular violence. So, you are back in the house. Tell me what happens next. Every detail. In order."

"The power was out across the entire property. I—"

The door heaved open. Anna stiffened in the chair. This was new. Another guard entered and unlocked her shackles. "Do you want tea?" Ilya asked. "He can bring you warm tea."

Anna shook her head.

"Nothing in it," Ilya said. "I swear."

Again, she shook her head.

Ilya rolled his eyes. "We used the sodium pentothal earlier. We will not use it again. You have my word."

That meant nothing, but she wanted warm tea more than anything in the world and so she nodded yes.

The guard fetched a steaming cup of black tea. Anna drank it in three gulps despite her tongue puckering with the heat. She'd never tasted anything more delicious.

Anna held up the empty cup. Ilya called for the guard, who brought another. This time she savored it: slow sips, face above the steam, cup clutched as if it were her child.

Ilya flicked his hand: *Continue.*

"I went inside the main house," she said. "The electricity was still out. They were talking in the living room. A fire had been lit, and they were arguing. Much of it became clear to me only later. Goose and Chernov had been after my family for months. They threatened us, they put my father in prison. What I learned that night was that there was a CIA connection, a plan to siphon off funds to finance a coup. But, as always, there was a fight over money. Vadim wanted to take a much larger sum than they had apparently negotiated. He planned to flee with Castillo, his handler, draining as much money as possible while he was at it. Chernov had probably suspected this for some time. They argued and argued, and finally Vadim and Max shot Chernov and his men. Vadim told me that I would be coming with them, and I refused. They did not like that."

"And then what did you do?"

"I stopped them."

THE GUARD BROUGHT MORE OF THE GLORIOUS BLACK TEA AND ANNA
told Ilya everything all over again. She described the nasty exchange
with Vadim. The fistfight as she tried to flee the room. Her detainment,
Max and Vadim off somewhere, probably arranging the exfil.

"I have always assumed," Anna said, "that they got out. But I know
you will not tell me."

Ilya gave his thin smile. At this point in the story, he would typically
interrupt and accuse her of lying. He would say that she shot someone,
usually Vadim, or declare that she had conspired with Sia. Or sometimes
he would falsely recap her story, adding his own details or weaving an
entirely new tale that confirmed Anna's guilt. He would then try to persuade her to agree with his version.

But this time he said, "Hortensia's role in this is strange, isn't it?"

"It is."

"Maximov tells us that you were tasked to recruit her. That SVR
harbored suspicions that her firm, Hynes Dawson, helped Vassily
Gusev—Goose, as you call him—siphon state funds from the country.
One is left wondering, after all of this, who was truly working whom?"

This was the first time Ilya had spoken Maximov's name.

"I do not know what Sia Fox is," Anna said. "But it is clear to me that
Max Castillo recruited my husband. I do not know if Sia is a true CIA
officer, or simply a witting accomplice. And I suppose it does not matter.
What I do know is that she provided information to me indicating where
those state funds traveled. A piece of the puzzle around Goose's plans,
but alas not enough to make a legal case."

"So," Ilya said, "what happened next?"

"As I refuse to leave with them, Vadim's rage becomes insanity. He
is muttering about the bodies. Talking nonsense. Max sends a message
on his phone. Sia is pleading for me to come with them. Vadim starts piling things onto the couch to start a fire. Max and Sia are helping. Vadim
works his way through the house, lighting the fires. He comes back to
where I am, in the living room, and he can't quite get to me because of

the smoke. He shoots blindly into the room, which is when he gets me in the shoulder. I'm on the chair on the floor at this point. I no longer hear their voices. They've fled the flames. I manage to get free."

"Tell me how."

"They had not planned to restrain me. They used duct tape and not enough and in the wrong places."

"Convenient for your story."

Anna sipped more tea and delivered the usual line for this part of the conversation. "It's the truth."

At this insistence, Ilya reciprocated with his customary shrug.

Anna continued: "Once free, I escaped the house and I called Maximov at SVR. You of course have the records."

"One thing I cannot quite figure," Ilya said, "is why Vadim wanted to bring you at all. I understand it was not a happy marriage."

"I was his property," Anna said. "I had to be uprooted along with him. Like a cat buried with a pharaoh. Or a slave girl set adrift on a burning pyre with a dead king. Wherever he went, so would I."

"Well," Ilya said as he smacked the table, "not this time."

———

ANNA TOOK A HOT SHOWER. HER SKIN STRETCHED OVER TENT-POLE ribs; each rinse shed more hair to twist around her fingers. She lathered in soap four times and still felt oily. A trim woman with a bun of frizzy red hair brought a cardboard box containing a makeup kit, papery underwear, a skirt, flats, and a blouse. They had misplaced the clothes she'd been wearing when she arrived, the woman said. A reimbursement from the state would arrive in two, maybe three months. In an unmarked office the woman handed Anna off to a doctor, who wordlessly shoved at her a tray of black bread and soup and another cup of tea. The doctor watched her eat and drink and then gave her a water bottle filled with a liquid the color of dark urine. Anna sniffed it—sugary sweet—and drank half the bottle. The doctor led her through a maze of hallways, and with each turn the light brightened. They came to a waiting room with velvety red sofas. On one was a black greatcoat. The doctor helped her shrug into it.

"When is New Year's?" Anna said.

The doctor frowned. "Today is February nineteenth," she said.

Anna slipped into the baggy coat and found her brain could run the numbers. Sixty-one days. Sixty-one days since the fire.

She trudged outside into bitter cold, crossing under a high metal gate. A black Mercedes with government plates idled, plumes of exhaust settling over muddy snow. She braced herself on the doctor's shoulder so she wouldn't slip on the ice. The back door clicked open.

Anna peered inside. Maximov waved to her. "Captain Agapova, get in, it's terribly cold."

Moscow

MAXIMOV DID NOT SPEAK ON THE DRIVE TO YASENEVO. THE bald spot atop his head seemed to have shrunk since Anna had seen him last. Perhaps he'd had a graft. Off the MKAD they cleared the gatehouse and rolled to a stop outside the executive entrance. Maximov caught her shooting an uncertain glance toward the door.

"This cannot wait," he said. "I am sorry."

They walked slowly to his office. He did not offer a hand, and she was glad because she would have refused. Maximov pulled out a chair for her from under the shiny pine table. An assistant brought tea.

"I will keep this brief," Maximov said, "so you can go home and rest."

Home, she thought. Where is that now?

Maximov set a folder in front of her, rapped his knuckles on it, and went to the windows. "How much do you know about what has transpired in this country?"

"I have been in Lefortovo," Anna said.

"Yes, of course," he said. "Well, you will have time to catch up. We are placing you on administrative leave for six months to recuperate."

"Okay," she said dumbly.

"When you called me that night, Captain," Maximov said, "it was the first indication we received that your husband, Goose, Chernov, and a few others were plotting a coup with CIA help. Acting on that warning, we have suppressed it. Investigations are ongoing."

Maximov was speaking to his reflection in the picture windows. "But the events of that evening were—and remain—muddled. None of it really makes sense, to be quite honest. FSB officers murdered, the flight of your husband. The forensics were damn tricky, as you can imagine. The fire ate nearly everything up. And no sign, still, of Vadim and your two mysterious visitors."

She wondered now if he'd brought her here to confess. Was this another round?

"You can see, Captain, just how tangled this whole situation became," Maximov continued. "Until yesterday the FSB boys were keen to put you against a wall and shoot you. The cousins don't deal well with ambiguity, as you know. Cleaner to be rid of you. I could see their point, but I had doubts. You called me that night to inform on the plot, for example. Why do that if you are involved? But, on the other hand, is it truly possible you were not aware of your husband's treachery? Can it be true that Maximiliano Castillo recruited Vadim without your knowledge? What was—is—this Hortensia Fox?"

She was still not altogether certain they were going to let her go, but she'd decided long ago, in Lefortovo's dim depths, that she did not care. "You have read the reports from my interrogation, yes?" She received a nod. "Well, then you've heard my answers to these questions. Would you like me to repeat them now?"

Maximov motioned to the folder on the table. "No. I would like you to flip through this."

Inside was a stapled packet. The first page bore a copy of Vadim's driver's license. There was also a CIA cable. She had seen a few passed by SVR sources. This one was marked RH—restricted handling—and in addition to the typical classification markings it bore six unique letters that Anna recognized—they signified this document's home inside a CIA covert action compartment. She started in.

SUBJ: 15 JANUARY SITREP: NROC RESETTLEMENT OF VADIM KOVALCHUK

1. DOCUMENTATION: LEGAL NAME CHANGE, SSN, DRIVER'S LICENSE, PROOF OF RESIDENCY. COORDINATING WITH FBI MINNEAPOLIS FIELD OFFICE TO SECURE PERMANENT LOCATION IN UPPER MIDWEST.

2. CIA OMS PSYCHOLOGICAL ASSESSMENT FOLLOWING SIX-HOUR VISIT WITH SUBJ IN WDC-AREA REVEALS ONGOING EMOTIONAL DISTRESS POST-DEFECTION. SUBJ CONTINUES TO HARBOR GUILT AND ANGER WITH RESPECT TO WIFE'S REFUSAL TO DEFECT. SUBJ HAS MENTIONED SUICIDAL THOUGHTS.

3. SUBJ CONTINUES TO HARBOR DELUSIONS OF RETURNING TO RUSSIA. LIKELY FLIGHT RISK LEADS OMS ASSESSOR TO CONTINUE RECOMMENDATION OF 24/7 CASE MANAGEMENT AND MONITORING UNTIL SUBJ'S CONDITION IMPROVES.

4. JOINT NROC / MOSCOW X RESETTLEMENT TEAM CONTINUES TO TASK WORLDWIDE SOURCES FOR INFORMATION ON SUBJ'S WIFE'S FATE AND WHEREABOUTS.

5. NROC HANDLING TEAM WILL PROVIDE NEXT UPDATE AT 1500 TOMORROW FOLLOWING SCHEDULED DEBRIEFING. REGARDS.

She flipped through a few more pages in the packet and set it aside. My god, she thought, who wrote this? It was either an elaborate trap, or it was freedom. Victory. Maximov appraised her with a bemused look. As if he, like her, could not make sense of it.

"We have a source in the FBI with occasional access to defector information," Maximov said. "This one came through in his last drop. What do you make of it, Captain Agapova?"

She slid the folder across the table. "What do I think? I spent two months in Lefortovo telling them what I think of this."

Maximov pointed at the chair in front of the samovar bearing a faded imperial eagle. "While you were in Lefortovo, the FSB colonel managing the investigation trucked out here for a briefing. He sat there, in that chair, and summed it all up quite nicely. He said that in truth you were either a traitor or a hero. That perhaps we would never be able to prove it—might have to liquidate you in any case—but it was one or the other." Maximov shrugged, gathered up the folder, and tossed it back to his desk.

She smoothed her sad skirt. A traitor and a hero. I am both, she thought. Like all good Russians.

Moscow / Sochi /
Cape Idokopas / Anna's farm

ANNA DID NOT KNOW WHERE TO GO. SHE CHECKED IN TO THE RITZ before they packed her off to one of the SVR's closed resorts at Sochi, a converted ski village built for the Olympics, a cluster of sunflower-yellow buildings with arcaded walkways where restaurants and shops had once been. Red pavestone trails ran along a river. The spired clock tower no longer worked. The thaw was starting. The boardwalks and paths ran with mountain water.

For a week she slept until the early afternoon, woke to a lunch of tea and dry black bread, and visited a physical therapist for her shoulder, which still moved as if sand filled the joints. Lifting anything heavier than a glass of water was taxing. On walks the weight of her left arm would eventually burst into shooting pain, as if it hung on tenterhooks.

She occasionally called Maximov to discuss her father. Drop it, Anya, he said. We have tried, but Goose set the gears in motion and the law has been difficult to stop. He remained in Butyrka. Maximov told her to stay away, in Sochi. Take some time. It's not a request.

In the quiet evenings and in her bed, she thought of Luka.

She practiced painting him in her mind so he would not be lost. She began with simple things: a smile, a laugh, the feel of a hand. By the second week she could replay matches from Jean Martel and stroll down the Street of All-Holidays and they could duck into her apartment to make love. When sleep neared, Luka's image would begin to dissolve and Anna would apologize. Sometimes she imagined Luka's portrait reassuring her, validating her choices. But these were Anna's words, not his, and conjuring them made her feel like a thief. You have already taken his future, she would tell herself, you are going to steal his words, too?

She did not think true things of Sia, nor of Max, nor of Vadim. When her thoughts wandered there, her mind, grooved in the Lefortovo hot-house, simply clicked off.

At the beginning of the seventh week, the paths flooded with melt-ing snow, a Kremlin courier arrived with a letter from the chief of the Presidential Administration. She read it three times while the courier waited outside her room.

"What should I pack?" she asked, handing back the note.

"Absolutely nothing," the courier said.

———

A GOVERNMENT MERCEDES TOOK HER TO A LEAFY BLOCK OF OFFICE buildings in Sochi. There, in a windowless room, two women conducted a thorough strip search. They X-rayed every cavity to be sure she'd not hidden a bomb inside her body. Her clothes were traded for a new black skirt, a faded white blouse, and a pair of sensible, blocky shoes that clopped obnoxiously on the concrete. Her clothes, phone, and purse were zippered in plastic bags and shuttered in a locker. A nurse swabbed her for a panel of infectious diseases. She took a PCR test and gave a stool sample.

She waited for two hours in an antiseptic room until they could confirm the results. The two women conducted one more strip search and then led her to a new room, where six members of the President's security detail lounged, reading magazines on long leather chairs. They handed her a furry *dublyonka* and hustled her outside through the rotor wash of a waiting helicopter. She sat in the middle, security men on all sides. They did not speak, they did not smile, they watched her unblink-ingly. After a few minutes this became normal. After Lefortovo, she thought, nothing again will be uncomfortable. Anna gazed into the mid-dle distance. Sometimes she rubbed at her shoulder's scar tissue. Mostly, she closed her eyes.

The helicopter set down inside the President's estate on the Black Sea, at Idokopas. The helipads bordered a bright green hill, which, her father had once claimed, concealed the President's personal ice hockey rink, buried nearly five stories into the rise. The security men rushed her from the chopper onto a wide stone path that descended toward the Italianate villa looming over the sea. It was the largest private residence in Russia. The most powerful man should have the largest house, her father had once said, with a shrug. The path coiled down-hill, by a green-roofed Orthodox chapel, through lush gardens piled with towering cypresses, trim hedges, and pines, by the clip and buzz of gardeners' tools, the coursing and bubbling of water, the crackle of radio chatter.

The security men led her into the main house through a gate topped by the golden imperial double eagle. They crossed through a shadowed courtyard with a large gurgling fountain and into a soaring hall supported by two rows of square cream-colored pillars. Next, into a hallway, past a low-hung room glowing in a purplish haze. She caught sight of a stage with a pole on it. They ended in a long room with a brown table, brown leather couches, and windows carved of dark wood facing the only thing that was not brown: the sea. They brought Anna sandwiches and tea. They watched her eat as she stared at the sandy green hills sloping into the water.

After an hour, a short, chubby man with dead eyes and lively hands took up a seat across from her. He did not shake her hand, but his moved on the table, over his head, on his shoulders.

"Do you have any questions?" he asked, rubbing his hands together.

"I do not think so."

"You understand the generosity of this meeting?"

"I do."

"You understand that you are not to approach or touch him?"

"I do."

The man motioned for her to follow. He led, she two steps behind, the security team fanned out around. He brought her to another room, this one longer, with even larger windows shoving out against the sea, parquet floors, a ceiling covered in golden friezes and plasterwork, shimmering golden curtains, and an interior wall flanked by a row of white stucco pillars inlaid with gold leaf. The gold shag carpet swallowed her shoes. This feels like RusFarm, she thought, I hate this place. There were two chairs at the table, one at either end, no less than five meters apart. The table was brilliant white. The sun's reflection hurt her eyes. The man's dancing hands guided her to one end, to a chair too short for the table, and quite obviously shorter than the other.

"He will be in soon," the man said. "Do you have to use the bathroom?"

She shook her head.

"Good. Sit in the chair, no wandering around, understand?"

"Yes."

She sat, hands in her lap like a good girl, watching the waves collect into white triangles before breaking. Seabirds flew by the window, but she could not hear their squawks and screeches in the soundless room. This is an air lock, she thought, a place where two worlds meet. She sat for what felt like thirty minutes, but, since Lefortovo, she had lost faith in her sense of time.

Then the door opened, and President Vladimir Vladimirovich Putin, the *khozyain*, President and lord of all Russia, sauntered into the room.

He wore a black suit, white shirt, and blue tie. When she had last met him, years earlier, he had been vibrant. Now his face and neck were puffy from the steroids. He did not smile. He did not approach to shake her hand. He slouched in his chair, almost hunching, and winced as though his back were tender. He gripped the table, lips pursed, and began to speak.

"Captain Agapova," the *khozyain* said, "I am still not quite sure what to make of your case. With Goose things were clearer; there was so much evidence. I almost had you shot, too. It was not an easy decision. Did I make a mistake?"

"With me, or with Goose?"

His lips quivered, almost in amusement. "With you."

"No. I am not a traitor."

The *khozyain* slouched lower. Anna caught a whiff of his smell, carried over the table by the powerful air vents. She had expected mothballs or death; instead, it was fresh laundry.

"I read the reports from Lefortovo," he said. "The investigators went back and forth on you. Couldn't make up their minds. Keep you locked up, liquidate you, let you go. Round and round. You are free because, in the end, I chose to keep you alive."

"That is logical," she said. "I am innocent."

The *khozyain* shrugged and shifted toward the windows. A gull drew lazy circles outside. His face glowed in the table's reflecting light. The sea shimmered in the bone-white afternoon. Every golden thing in that room was sparkling in the sun. He turned to face her.

And in that moment Anna was overcome by a jarring, almost God-like, sensation. You are still strong, she thought. But you, *khozyain*, are diminished. Her blue eyes shone with certainty, his with mere suspicion. I know, she thought, and you do not.

I took from a thief.

And I am going to get away with it.

———

ONE WEEK AFTER IDOKOPAS, ANNA STOOD AT BUTYRKA'S GATES CLUTCHing a bottle of his favorite Dagestani brandy. They had last drunk it conspiring at the RusFarm shooting range when the world had been young. Hinges screeched in protest as the gate cracked open.

Her father came out alone, bewildered, gate clattering shut behind. He held a plastic bag. He wore a faded blue jacket and slacks that hung well past his shoes. They embraced. He had left a dozen or more kilos and some of his hair inside the prison. He did not smell the same.

We paid so dearly for this, she thought.

"My god, Anya," he said. "My god."

He held her tight, he kissed her forehead, her hair, her cheeks. His tears dampened her face.

"We are safe, Papa," she said. "We won."

WORK BEGAN ON THE NEW DACHA IN APRIL. ANNA VISITED ON WEEK-
ends to supervise the construction and ride Penelope. Work had been
slow, the thaw had been late this year, and they were still muddling with
the foundation. She was in no hurry. Sometimes she galloped in the pasture near the woods. Others she trotted around the track. Now, with the
air warming, she was letting her hair grow out so it would whip through
the wind at full gallop.

In the stables she put the tack on Penelope. She fitted the mare with
a saddlebag that had not been used in some time. The one she did not
like to think about, that her good senses had urged her to destroy months
earlier. But Maximov had let slip something he should not have, and she
had decided she would not ignore it. She rode up the same path on which
she had hunted Max and Sia. One of the saddlebag's pockets was packed
with a rectangular canteen of water and a few pieces of black bread. The
other held a portable battery. She rode for an hour at the spine of the
ridge, checking to be certain she was alone.

The place felt peaceful, though she had nearly died here. She
liked the low hum of the power lines, the birdsong, the rustle of the
trees, the sweeping views of the pastures and stables. At the trailhead
she dismounted and slid off Penelope's saddlebag. She moved quickly,
trying the strap and snaps one, two, three times. It had been months
since Sia had shown her. At the failed fourth try she let loose a stream
of curses and looked around. You are alone, she said, you have time.
On the tenth attempt the panel popped open. She removed the laptop, plugged it into the battery, and waited for it to come to life. The
keyboard sequence required dozens of tries, and soon she was so frustrated she toyed with abandoning this altogether. But she kept at it.
When she finally got it, she typed a short message, fast as her fingers
would move.

JOINT SVR / FSB MECHANICAL TEAMS PROGRESSING ON HUNT
FOR FOX AND CASTILLO. WORKING ON LEADS INSIDE TEXAS AND
MEXICO. BE SAFE.

Anna shut the laptop. She closed her eyes. This was right. She would not regret this.

She ran a hand over the computer.

Then she set it on a large stone, picked up another rock, and set to smashing it to bits.

She wrecked the screen, the case, the circuit boards. The fragments went into the saddlebag and she mounted Penelope to descend the hill. For several hours she trotted along the stream and the ponds, halting occasionally to dismount and scatter pieces of the machine into the water.

As she rode home, her heart pounded to its normal rhythm. Her thoughts were clear. At the mouth of the pasture Anna scanned the fields and the thick woods beyond. She let down her hair and patted Penelope's shoulders.

Then she leaned forward to bring them into a gallop. The sun was bright and warm. The wind whipped Anna's hair into a blond cape. They moved gracefully over the grass, each stride closing the gap to the low rise at pasture's end. As they neared the hill, Anna leaned down to the mare's ear. Run, girl, Anna whispered, run, run.

Run.

Acknowledgments

I THOUGHT THE SECOND NOVEL WOULD BE EASIER THAN THE FIRST. How wrong I was. This book fought its own creation across numerous false starts, dead ends, misguided pathways, and the Russian invasion of Ukraine, which unrolled just as I was finishing the first draft. That the book exists at all is a testament to the many people who stepped in to help along the way; the friends and family who made the lonely work of writing the team sport that, at least for me, it must be.

I am, again, supremely grateful to my editor at Norton, Star Lawrence, who stood by this novel as it was born and, on several occasions, helped save it from certain death. Thank you for continuing to bet on me, and for hammering my writing to make it all the better.

The team at Norton, ICM/CAA, and Curtis Brown rallied around the book and made the entire process seem far less lonely. My agent, Rafe Sagalyn, walked with me through this project every step of the way. Thank you. Nneoma Amadi-obi kept it all moving; Dave Cole saved me from numerous embarrassing errors; Kyle Radler and Steve Colca knocked on doors and made sure the word got out; Emily Sacks offered wise counsel and gracious aid; Helen Manders and Peppa Mignone championed the book around the world; Alicia Gordon and Brooke Ehrlich served as trusted guides through Hollywood's byzantine mazework. The navigational guidance has made all the difference.

To Mark Richards, the indomitable Lisa Shakespeare, and Rachel Nobilo at Swift Press, for bringing my novels to the UK: thank you.

452 *Acknowledgments*

Jan Neumann, a former FSB officer, served as an invaluable consultant on the mindset, operations, and lingo of the Russian secret services. I am indebted to Jan for peeling back the curtain on this high-stakes, secretive, oft-misunderstood world. Jan, I am fortunate to be your compatriot.

Bill Witman provided a master class on all things equine, including an introduction to the world of Thoroughbred horse racing and breeding. I am immensely grateful to Bill for allowing me to accompany him—notebook in hand, armed with so very many questions—for a long day around the ranch. Thank you also for cultivating in me a greater appreciation for these noble creatures.

Several former CIA comrades graciously contributed time and insight to this novel. Glenn Chafetz, John Sipher, and Marc Polymeropoulos counseled on Moscow X's Russia operations and helped Procter, Sia, and Max avoid numerous operational snafus. Charles Finfrock offered prescient insight on CIA human and technical operations, occasionally while strolling the block smoking cigars. Steve Slick helped write the (fictional) covert action finding carried out by Procter's Moscow X outfit, giving it a shot at passing muster with the (also fictional) lawyers. Christina Hillsberg, former CIA officer and author of a forthcoming book on the contribution and experiences of women in the Agency, graciously read the manuscript and offered many useful suggestions. Don Hepburn again functioned as an adviser on all manner of CIA tradecraft, fielding dozens of questions from this unrepentant analyst on the ins and outs of ops. As always, all lapses in operational wisdom and tradecraft are my own.

My dad, an author in his own right, once again read the novel, offering helpful insight and wise counsel. Thank you, Dad, for believing in me and my writing.

Dave Michael again put the writing under terrible scrutiny, ensuring that the story emerged all the better for it. Thank you, Dave, for the ongoing, and very painful, education in how to write good.

Kent Woodyard, longtime friend (and consistently average human), again told me what was terrible and what was not-so-terrible. Thank you, Kent, for not holding back.

Michael Wasiura graciously offered expertise on Putin and modern Russia. Thank you for the candid thoughts, the insightful feedback on the manuscript, and your reporting from Ukraine.

Griffin Foster, an upstanding lawyer himself, supplied pro bono legal counsel to the crooked lawyers at the fictional Hynes Dawson. Any errors in legalese, however, are all mine.

Alex Holstein continues to be a wonderful writing consigliere, sounding board, and all-around comrade.

Jack Stewart, an exceptional thriller writer himself, offered several helpful suggestions on my aircraft selections and made sure I didn't mess up the routes. All misguided flight operations are of course my own.

The novel spans continents and countries, testing this author's memory of long-ago trips and TDYs and, in some cases, venturing beyond the borders of my mental travelogue. Michael Weiss, Kevin Rothrock, Molly McKew, and Andrei Soldatov were invaluable guides to Russia and the Russian mentality. Several former residents of Moscow and Piter graciously offered advice on restaurants, neighborhoods, food, street routes, traffic, clothing, alcohol selection, and local customs. Josie Linaker checked my recollections of Geneva and the Jungfrau and helped bring that stunning region to life on the page. Gordon Corera, distinguished author and expert on Russian intelligence operations, also reminded me that cottages in St. Ives are very unlikely to sport ceiling fans. Chantal Whiteley provided an education on South Africa and the timbre of Afrikaans. Diego Chavez read the San Cristobal scenes, saved me from more than a few slip-ups, and helped me hone Maximiliano Castillo's occasional use of gutter Spanish. For that, I am deeply grateful.

Mike Green, the book's resident doctor, advised cheerfully on all manner of horrendous calamities, including severed toes, blunt-force milk-bottle trauma, balcony-dangling, and shot-through shoulders. The author (and characters) thank him for being on call.

Thanks are also due to Jeff B., whose knowledge of fires helped Anna Agapova burn down RusFarm, quickly and efficiently.

Several other dear friends read versions of this novel and offered help along the way. Erin Yerger, Becky Friedman, Anna Connolly, Hunter Allen, John Wilson, Jenny Green: all took the time to read and offer helpful feedback and encouragement.

Terry Barrington drove me around a Texas ranch for an entire day. Then he and his wife, Angela, made me a delicious steak dinner and let me spend the night at their home, all for research that wound up on the novel's cutting room floor. I am as deeply regretful of that as I am thankful for Terry and Angela's incredible hospitality. Here's to the possibility some of it slips into another book.

Many others, nameless, lent time and insight on topics as varied as CIA commercial operations, firearms, money laundering, gold refining, Cyrillic transliterations, and the vagaries of the cryptocurrency markets. I am indebted to each of them for their time and expertise.

I also must thank my children, Miles, Leo, and Mabel, whose chorus of joyful insanity reminds me every day what the writing is ultimately all about. I love each of you more than you will ever know, and I hope that you someday enjoy this novel—ideally many, many years in the future.

And, most importantly, all love and praise must go to my wife, Abby, who again served as this novel's first reader, singular champion, and, when required, its toughest—yet loving—critic. She helped me dig the story out of the ground, piece by piece, scoop by scoop, pushing me ahead even when it was all in terrible shape and the path forward was shadowed and rocky. This book simply would not exist without her.